STRAY CAT STRUT

STRAY CAT STRUT

BOOK 6

RAVENSDAGGER

Podium

This is a work of fiction. Names, characters, places, and incidents are either products of the author's imagination or used fictitiously. Any resemblance to actual events, locales, or persons, living, dead, or undead, is entirely coincidental.

Cover design by Roger Pinheiro

ISBN: 978-1-0394-8725-3

Published in 2025 by Podium Publishing
www.podiumentertainment.com

Podium

STRAY CAT STRUT

Lucy sat on the front porch, wearing a one-piece swimsuit that was made of the bare minimum possible amount of material and sipping from a drink through a long swirly straw. She was wearing a healthy amount of sunscreen and lounging on a cushioned chair with a little umbrella set up next to her.

Cat and Lucy didn't *really* have a porch, but the large landing space at the front of their home, nestled between the two large paws of the massive cat-shaped penthouse was vaguely porch-like, she supposed.

There was no sun out, because this was New Montreal, and the best they could hope for was an evening without rain, but it was the image that mattered. Plus, this was kind of fun overall.

"Ouch, fucking, fuck," Cat said, and Lucy bit her lip in an effort not to laugh.

Catherine, in a fit of . . . Catherine-ness, had decided that she'd be the one to fix her giant warmech. The large quadrupedal vehicle was parked in the middle of the landing space, and Cat was standing on a small scaffold set up next to the front-left of the warmech. Next to her floated a "repair" drone, which she'd bought to basically do what she was already doing herself.

"Do you need help?" Lucy asked.

Cat glanced back, lips drawn together in a frustrated line. "No, I'm fine," she said.

Lucy nodded, then took another long pull from her straw. She thought she'd tire of seeing the liquid spin around in little loops before reaching her mouth, but it hadn't happened yet. Nor had she tired of watching Cat bend over to get into the guts of the mech.

Cat was wearing denim overalls, a sports bra, and about half a gallon of grease and oil. Her hair was stuck in a dirty ponytail to keep it out of her face, but that hadn't saved it from some of the liquids that occasionally squirted out from whatever she was working on.

"Hey, Myalis," Lucy said. She had a nice relationship with the AI. Myalis wouldn't help Lucy unless she thought that in doing so, it would help

Cat—the AI was very firm about that boundary—but at the same time, Myalis didn't mind chatting.

As far as Lucy could tell, it was a little strange for a samurai to talk to their AI as if it was a person, but Cat had imprinted hard on Myalis and treated the AI like an old friend, so Lucy felt like she had to reach out as well. Cat's friends were Lucy's friends, and vice versa.

Myalis's voice replied right in Lucy's ear, overriding for a moment the music that Lucy had been idly listening to.

"Yes, Lucy?" Myalis asked. Her voice was always rather neutral. Feminine, but not . . . attractively so?

That was probably for the best, Lucy figured. If Myalis had one of those really sexy accents, then she might be in trouble. "How's it going with Cat's project?"

Myalis took a moment to respond, as if she had to think on what to say. Which was silly, Lucy realized. Myalis had probably guessed what Lucy would ask before the thought had crossed Lucy's mind, and already had a million answers prepared.

"All things said, it's going quite poorly. Catherine doesn't have the 'knack' for mechanical work. She is also not very good at following the instructions from the repair drone. Nonetheless, even with several setbacks, the work is progressing, and she is making fewer mistakes than anticipated."

There was a *clink-clank* from where Cat was, then a lot of swearing.

"Fewer doesn't mean none, I should note," Myalis said.

Lucy held back an inappropriate giggle. It would have upset Cat. "So, is this a new hobby? I don't mind the butch-mechanic girl look, it's hot, but I'm pretty sure Cat's not doing this to try and . . . seduce me, or whatever."

"I suspect that this is mostly happening because Catherine is not good at taking breaks. The prospect of sitting on her laurels, even after a few very active weeks, makes her feel powerless, so she has decided to do something, even if it's somewhat counterproductive. Of all the things she chose to do, apparently fixing the damage on her warmech by hand came to mind first."

"Hmm," Lucy said noncommittally. She supposed it made some sense. Cat was under a fair bit of stress, even if she was doing nothing much at the moment. They'd only arrived back from Burlington a day and a half earlier.

That meant one night celebrating her return with the kittens, then a later celebration with Lucy in their room, then a whole day spent cuddling and fucking and then cuddling some more, and now, this morning, Cat had left and decided to become a mechanic.

Lucy sipped, and her straw made that loud slurping noise that meant she was fresh out of juice.

She sighed, then kicked her legs to the side and, with some effort, got to her feet. Her thigh and calf muscles sometimes still hurt, but she'd been assured that it was plain old muscle soreness from overuse, not anything nefarious. It was nice, being able to overuse a muscle on limbs she thought she'd lose the use of.

Walking over to Cat, she paused by the bottom of the scaffold and looked up. "Hey," she said.

Cat paused in the act of scrutinizing two . . . metal thingies. "Huh? Oh, what's up?"

"I'm getting another drink. Do you want anything?" Lucy asked.

"Uh. Grab me a can of something sugary," Cat said. "You know what I like."

"Oh, I do," Lucy purred—she'd never pass up a line like that . . .

Cat stiffened for a bit, then grinned. "Ah, uh, hey, can you do me a favor while you're in the house?"

"Sure," Lucy said.

"I printed some parts. I need them," Cat said, "for the . . . twisty bit, and the rod-shaft gizmo."

"Ah yes, the rod-shaft gizmo," Lucy said. She smiled. Cat was really getting into this new hobby of hers. It was cute. Like one of the kittens trying arts and crafts.

Cat huffed. "I just started this. You can't expect me to know what I'm doing."

"I'll go fetch your rod-shaft gizmo," Lucy said with a chuckle. "And after, maybe we can talk about lunch? It's a couple of hours to noon, but I'm peckish."

"Yeah, sure," Cat said. "Could eat too, I guess."

Lucy shook her head. Cat was starting to hyperfixate a little. She returned to her work and Lucy stepped off, heading back into the home.

It was incredible how different the air tasted just past the entranceway. There was no kerosene scent, and the air had a crisp, clean taste to it within the museum.

She sighed as she caught herself calling it the museum again. The habit just wouldn't die.

The kittens, Lucy discovered, were spread out across the main room. Half of them were zoning out, staring at nothing and probably scrolling their media feeds. The other half were running after one another and making a mess. She plucked a console out of Bargain's hands as he slipped by and gave it to Nose, who smiled thankfully and then called Bargain a dick before running off the other way.

She'd have to see about getting some sort of cleaning android, because getting the kittens to clean up after themselves was a lost cause. "You're gonna get fat," she sing-songed as she walked past Daniel.

He was on a couch, legs kicking over the edge—which was a new habit he'd gained recently, much to the annoyance of anyone passing close by—and he had a Meshgear helmet on. It wasn't so much being plugged into the Mesh that was the problem as it was the extra-large bag of chips open next to him.

He flashed her the finger, then very conspicuously grabbed a chip and ate it.

Lucy shook her head and moved into their kitchen, where she set her cup down, refilled it from a big bottle in the fridge, added more ice for good measure, and found a can of something sugary for Cat.

Then, finally, she went to the room in the back that held their printer.

It had been going nonstop lately, printing out the laser turrets they'd been selling to any buying corp or giving away in equal measure to smaller settlements.

She didn't expect to find someone in the room already. "Rac?" she asked.

The teenager jumped, and Lucy recognized the look that flashed across her face as guilt. She'd seen it on plenty of kittens before.

The girl wasn't truly one of the kittens. She was too independent and carried a different past. Yet, she was still embraced in their home, one of Cat's rescued strays.

"What are you up to?" Lucy asked.

"Uh," Rac said. "Nothing?"

She was standing next to the matter printer, and it was pretty obvious she'd just stuffed something into the bag on the floor next to her.

"Uh-huh," Lucy said. "Did that just print off some parts? Cat sent me to pick them up."

"Maybe?" Rac said.

The machine beeped, which sounded like an affirmative, so Lucy circled around Rac and opened the hood up.

There were a number of parts still steaming in the printer bed. One of them looked pretty shaft-gizmo-y, so she assumed that was what she was here to fetch, but there was also a small, neat stack of what looked like very large shotgun shells, which Lucy imagined wasn't what Cat had ordered up at all.

Lucy eyed Rac, and Rac stared at anything but Lucy.

"Well, whatever," Lucy said as she picked up Cat's part. It was still warm. "I'm on vacation, so don't start too much trouble, please," she said.

Rac seemed relieved at that.

Lucy wondered how relieved Rac would be if she knew that Lucy was *definitely* going to be keeping an eye on her now.

CHAPTER ONE

STARING

Let sleeping tigers lie.
—*Cooler Versions of Shitty Old Proverbs*, fifth edition, 2057

"Hey, bot, pass me the clickity thing," I said with a gesture toward the repair drone.

The drone was hovering there, silent and unmoving, though I knew it had some sort of propeller thing going on because there was a constant wash of warm air coming out from its bottom. I'd purchased it when I picked up my new hobby. I'd never really been able to afford hobbies before, so this was a cool change of pace.

Technically, the repair drone could get my mech up and running in a fraction of the time it took me to do it.

Also, it wouldn't mess up the repairs and break even more stuff, or lose its temper while doing it. It had the schematics for the mech in its little robot head, and could fix nearly anything wrong with it, especially with access to my matter fabricator to make parts.

But that would rob me of all my fun.

The drone passed me a tool—was it called a ratchet?—and I leaned into the mech and slotted it over a small bolt.

I hadn't jumped into this new hobby entirely unprepared. I'd bought a cheap bit of software from Myalis that gave me step-by-step instructions on how to fix this particular mech. At the moment, it was telling me what to undo and where, and which part needed replacing.

It was kind of like a big three-dimensional puzzle, but one designed by a mad scientist who'd taken a fat snort of cocaine just before they got creative.

Every part of the mech was small and intricate and linked to others, which meant that replacing one piece required me to take apart a dozen more.

I was positive that the mech had been built this way to make it as strong as possible or something. It also made it insanely fucking annoying to fix. Kind of fun, though. After spending some time thinking about what to even *do* with time off, I had kind of picked "repairing stuff" on a whim. But I wasn't regretting it. Not yet.

You know, when most people pick up a new hobby, they generally start themselves off easy, then work up to harder challenges.

"Cowards," I dismissed, mostly because I knew it would bother Myalis.

Maybe you should work on something more your speed? Like a Jenga tower? That would have mechanical properties even you could understand.

I laughed. "Low blow," I said. I chewed on my lip while flicking the ratchet around, and then the bolt I'd been working on came free and the part I wanted to replace fell . . . right in between the armored plates of the mech.

It clinked and clanked on its way down, and I just stared into the dark crack where it had gone.

"Fuck," I said.

I'm adding to the total projected time until the warmech is repaired once more.

A little counter that had been gently dropping as I worked flickered, and the 36 climbed up to 39.

"Three more hours?" I winced.

Oh. Let me correct that.

A small "DAYS" appeared after the 39.

"You really don't have any faith in me, do you?" I asked.

I do have faith in you, Catherine. I'm mostly teasing you to keep your mood up. You're unusually motivated by antagonism, even of the more friendly variety. But I do think that if you set your mind to it, you'll master this in due time.

I felt myself flushing a bit, then shook my head. "Never mind that. Hey, repair drone, fetch that part, would you?"

The drone hovered above the spot where the part had fallen, and some parts along its side unfolded. Soon a small line snaked out from the drone and into the crack, the tip lighting up faintly with what I imagined was a camera-light combo. It had little grippers too, for grabbing on to wayward parts.

The repairs so far had mostly involved taking things apart. I'd removed a few armored plates and disconnected a handful of parts, which gave me some access to the front left section of the mech where one of the Gatling guns had been.

The gun itself was . . . probably somewhere in Burlington still. It had been ripped clean off by that not-a-dinosaur, hence the repair job.

"You up for taking a break?"

I glanced back to see Lucy returning with a tray. It had a can of soda on it, next to the part I'd sent her out for.

"Just a little one," I admitted as I leapt off the scaffolding and landed in a crouch next to her. "Thanks," I said as I took the tray and set it down. I turned back to her and swept my gaze up and down. Lucy was always a pleasure to look at, but seeing her in a little one-piece swimsuit was just . . . nice. Very nice.

Myalis swatted away one of the many spy drones that had been buzzing around all afternoon. While I was pretty sure they were out here mostly to see what I was up to and to snoop on the warmech parked out front, I still felt a little jealous thrill at the thought of others seeing Lucy in her current, less-than-fully-clothed state.

"Wow, I can *feel* you staring," she said, lips quirking into an easy smile. "But two things. First, you're covered in oil and gunk. And second, I'm still sore."

I laughed. "Yeah, fair," I said as I leaned back against the scaffolds and popped the tab on the soda. "Myalis says that it'll only take me another . . . month and a week or so to finish fixing this bad boy." I gestured to the mech with a thumb.

"A month and a week," Lucy said. "Isn't that a long time?"

"Eh. If I really need it, then I'll let the drone fix it up. How long would that take, Myalis?"

Approximately three hours.

"Under a week," I said to Lucy. Look, I had *some* pride, and I wasn't above lying to Lucy to make myself look less incompetent.

She grinned like someone who knew that, and who—luckily for me— thought it was more amusing than anything else. "Hey, thought you should know, but I saw Rac in the printer room. She was making stuff for herself, I think."

"Oh?" I asked before taking a sip from the soda can. "Well, whatever. She'd been the one bringing in the most materials for the recycler. Only fair that she gets to use some of it."

"I think she was making shotgun shells," Lucy said.

"Wait, really?" I asked. I frowned, then navigated through my augs' menus to connect to the house's network—which I dared any non-samurai to try breaking into—and then to the printer itself.

The machine was exactly as smart as I'd expect from a Protector-made machine. It had logs of every item it had ever made, and who had picked each one up. There were some from me, a few from Lucy, and a heap from Rac.

Lots of turrets, which only made sense. We'd been producing and selling those on the side for a little bit. A lot of them were probably scattered around rooftops in Burlington, and while I didn't doubt that a few would get picked up and resold by someone unscrupulous, they were basically free to make.

If Rac had nabbed a few herself, then I wouldn't have batted an eye. I . . . wasn't exactly paying her. Sure, free rent and a room with however many meals a day she wanted at my place was nice, but she was a little more independent than the kittens.

Still, there were a lot of recent prints on the list that had me . . . curious about Rac's activities.

"Heavy plasma shotgun?" I read. "Myalis, how did she get the design for the printer to make that?"

You purchased a Heavy Plasma Turret Emplacement Blueprint several days ago. The gun she printed is technically meant to be mounted on a turret, so it was included in the blueprints.

"Well, well," I said.

Not only had Rac bought the gun, she'd also gotten ammo for it—a lot of fucking ammo for it—multiple times across a few days.

There were a handful of other things. Some guns, a few prosthetics, but nothing insane.

I let out a long-winded sigh. "I need to look into this, don't I?" I asked.

Lucy shifted closer to me and wrapped her arms around my waist. "Probably," she said. "I can take care of a few of your projects . . . if you promise not to add too many more to my plate."

"Projects?" I asked.

"You were helping someone become mayor, you promised to set up a free or nearly-free prosthetics clinic, you still need to do something about the Sewer Dragons . . . I think I'm forgetting a few loose ends," Lucy said. She blinked, then looked at her arm, which was covered in a layer of grease.

"You might want to avoid touching me," I said. "I'm greasy."

She shrugged. "We have very nice showers."

I considered things for a moment, then let out a groan and melted into Lucy. "Fine. I'll be moderately responsible," I said.

Lucy laughed. "How about you do things at a reasonable pace? One problem a day?"

"I think some of these things are more than a one-day issue," I said.

"You know, Myalis *can* serve as a glorified secretary if you ask nicely," Lucy said. "Myalis, make sure she has at least half a day off. Cat's technically on vacation. And how is she going to find time for her new hobby if she's running around all day?"

Duly noted.

I frowned. "Lucy, stop telling Myalis what to do. She's *my* extraordinarily overpowered bullshit AI. You're only supposed to use her to annoy me and for kinky stuff."

I'd really rather not.

Lucy gave me a peck on the cheek, the cleaner one. "If I feel like it," she said, which could have meant anything.

I glanced at the mech where the repair drone was still fussing at the section I had opened up. I could dive back into it. Actually, that's what I felt like doing, but at the same time I was already feeling the guilt that came from not doing shit tugging at me. "Right . . . where's Rac now?" I asked.

Myalis helpfully let me spy on our friend by giving me Rac's real-time location. She was a few blocks over, taking a public tram across the city.

"I should go check on her," I said. "Person-to-person, you know?"

"*After* you take a shower," Lucy said. Then she smiled. "I'll clean your back if you do mine?"

Well, I could hardly refuse that.

CHAPTER TWO

LIKE A RACCOON TO A TRASHBAG

The population distribution in modern cities means that approximately 40 percent of all inhabitants of a city live in a "megabuilding." These are not to be confused with more traditional apartment buildings or mega-condos (wherein each housing unit and the building as a whole are owned in part by its tenants).

Megabuildings are micro-cities, semi-enclosed environments with their own cultures, beliefs, companies, and sometimes even currencies. There have been recordings of massive cultural clashes, and even of megabuilding inhabitants going to war with other nearby structures.

Most of all, however, megabuildings are profitable for those who own them.

—*The Mega, An Exploration of Megabuilding Culture in New York, Detroit, California, and elsewhere in the NA Region, 2046*

I stretched my back as I walked into the bedroom, hands on my hips and spine twisted backward until something popped into place and I let out a long sigh. Showers were nice.

"Right, so where's Rac now?" I asked Myalis.

New Montreal Center. She just got off the public transportation network.

Damn, and last time I checked was nearly an hour ago. I'd almost forgotten how incredibly shit the public network was. But it was also cheap as hell and could get you nearly anywhere within the lower city.

I picked up some underwear from the floor—they were probably clean—and started getting dressed. "So, if I'm gonna go pay her a visit, think I should go in casual?"

"I wouldn't," Lucy said as she walked in after me. She was dressed already, with a big towel wrapped around her head. "But maybe you don't need to go in with power armor either."

"Yeah, that might be overkill," I agreed. So I found my skintight armored suit and slipped it on. Fortunately, it was bullshit alien tech, so the material could expand and contract as needed and I wasn't caught bouncing on the spot trying to get it to fit like too-tight jeans.

The suit was able to absorb a fair bit of damage; it would do for a little walk around town. Plus, I had my jacket lying around, which was a bit better armored.

"Where's my helmet?" I muttered as I looked around.

Lucy snorted, but she bent down and used her foot to kick my helmet out from under the bed. It didn't roll far, what with the cat ears atop it making it a bit too unshapely to roll.

"Thanks," I said as I scooped it up. I started to tie my hair up in a quick one-handed bun while I moved toward the door, helmet under my arm. The blue tint on the tips of my hair was fading. I'd have to reapply that stuff soon. "See you in a bit!" I called back.

"Love you!" Lucy sing-songed. "And remember, half days!"

Considering how it was already past noon, I imagined that meant that I could only "work" for the next few hours. But checking up on Rac would hardly, I imagined, count as work. How much trouble could one kid possibly get herself into?

I slipped my helmet on and moved through the museum, only stopping when Nose and Tim ran past me screaming at each other. Which actually reminded me, I wasn't armed!

A slight detour took me to the armory, which was . . . actually, kind of pitiful. I had like, four guns and an entire room to store them in. I picked up my handy old Trench Maker, mostly because it was a gun I was fairly comfortable with, and tucked it into a thigh-holster. Then I hesitated over whether to grab anything else.

In the end, I decided that I'd probably be okay with just the hand cannon. If anything needed a bigger gun than that to deal with, then I'd just buy one on the spot.

My bike had, at some point, parked itself in the garage below the museum, because it was just handy that way. So I headed down while checking my map to see where Rac was at now. "Any idea where she's heading to?" I asked aloud to Myalis.

She has visited a specific club three times in the last few weeks. Though I haven't broken into their security to see why, who she might be meeting, or what she's up to.

"Yeah, best not to," I said. "If she was one of the kittens, then I'd want to know, in case she was being misled or something, but she's not my responsibility."

Which is why you're currently riding on a course to intercept her?

I didn't dignify that with an answer. Rac might not have been my responsibility, and I had no right to tell her what to do or anything of the sort, but . . . well, the brat was a friend, and I did feel like I had to take care of her a little.

Fuck, maybe Lucy was right and I did need therapy or something.

But instead of doing that, I kicked on my hoverbike and took off out of the parking garage, which was surprisingly empty. I supposed that the lower floors of the building weren't quite in a state to be used yet, but still.

The aerial traffic was as bad as usual, but I skirted below it, shooting across the city in an almost straight line. New Montreal was a steel skeleton of jutting metal bones. Neon glows marked the starts and ends of buildings hidden in perpetual smog. Sure, the city had been hit by two incursions in as many weeks, but that didn't stop it from glowing.

If there was one thing that would mark the end of New Montreal, it would be the disappearance of its billion-and-one ads. But they held strong for now, filling the air with thunderous jingles and swaying gifs of seductive flesh and mouth-watering meals.

I hated the holographic ads most of all. Maybe it was because they had only started to appear in bigger numbers as I was growing up, so they hadn't been as common when I was a kid, but still, it felt unnatural to see a massive dancing woman rendered by a thousand drones using a skyscraper as a pole while text hovered around her. Was I getting old-people opinions now?

Rac wasn't on the upper levels, according to my map, so I soon had to dive, and as I did so, the ads changed. They were less . . . tantalizing? I didn't know much about the psychology of neon, but the ads meant for those living in the penthouses and traveling in hovercars were loud and yet subtle. You might see a flash of thighs or some high-end augs, but the company logos were small, the product hinted at.

Here, on the lower, ground levels, the ads were more straightforward. I parked on the same level Rac was supposed to be on, letting my bike land on the sidewalk of a multi-level highway next to a repeating gif of an animated woman giving a man head. The text "Want Fuck?" glowed bright next to me.

Parking there was probably some sort of violation. Actually, it was definitely some sort of violation, but I was pretty much certain I wasn't gonna get in trouble, so I decided not to give a shit. No one sane fucked with a samurai's ride.

Myalis updated my map, turning it into a more three-dimensional representation of the area, which was needed. Rac was currently riding an elevator up a building called HOUSE-FOUR-THREE, a massive brick of a building with the exterior painted entirely in dull grays except for the billboards covering its surface and the thousands of air conditioning vents poking out of its sides. It was the kind of place that I might have expected to live in, once.

Ten thousand miniature apartments, all jam-packed together, with a few floors in the middle connecting to the maze of buildings around it, and a handful of stores and shops tucked within so that anyone living in one of these never had to leave the complex.

I'd heard stories of people being born, raised, and dying in a single megabuilding without ever stepping foot outside.

The doorway into the building pinged my augs, asking for my age, date of birth, official name, gender(s), marital status, and credit card information, but then its rudimentary software bumped into Myalis and it shriveled up like a dick on ice and allowed the doors to open.

The interior was nothing but beige walls and graffiti. Judging by the scrawl, there were at least two gangs in this building competing for turf. Paint was caked over paint, one gang gleefully defacing the mark of the other only for the same to happen to them in turn.

My ability to read street signs was a bit rusty, but it looked like one gang was made for Karens, and the other was a younger group of native French, at least judging by all the *tabarnacs* I was passing.

What kind of shithole was Rac spending time in?

"Which floor is she heading to?" I asked.

She's heading to the fourteenth floor. But she will then need to take another elevator down to B2 in order to reach the club. That elevator leads up to the floor you're on. I can override it with ease.

I nodded. "Yeah, that seems nice," I said.

I pushed deeper into the building, past a few tweakers and some folk shuffling along until I came to an elevator bank some ways in.

I stood there, arms crossed and legs set while the tiny icon representing Rac rose and rose until, finally, the doors opened before me and I came face-to-face with the girl herself.

She was standing in the back of the elevator, eyes glazed over for a moment before she blinked her augs off and took me in.

"Heya, Rac!" I said.

A ROAMING RACCOON'S
REASONABLE RELATIONSHIPS
[PART ONE]

"Heya, Rac!" Cat said.

Rac stared at the woman in front of her with growing horror. She found her breath catching in her throat, and her mouth filled with the electric tang of adrenaline, like licking a battery, but across her entire body and all at once.

But then she hid it with a grin.

Rac was an expert at not letting anyone know what she was thinking. The barrier had to stay up, because when it went down, bad things happened. When she lived in the undercity, it was a daily requirement. Never let anyone know how sick you were, how close you were to breaking, or how many credits you had.

Maybe she'd gotten a little soft in the last week. Life had gotten better. A lot better. She wasn't even sure if it was entirely real yet, and Cat's appearance right here and now might be the dream turning to a nightmare.

But no. She'd long ago learned to operate past that kind of thing. Self-delusion wasn't a weakness of hers.

"Hey," Rac said. "What're you doing here?"

She eyed Cat up and down real quick. The older girl was . . . strange. Unique, maybe? Half the time, Rac wasn't sure what to think of Cat.

Which she supposed was normal, in its own way. Samurai were supposed to be strange, so it would be weirder if Cat *wasn't* bizarre.

Right now, Cat was in a skintight suit that reminded Rac of netrunner gear, with a heavy trench coat atop that and her neon-pink scarf around her neck. And the cat ears, of course. Hell, Cat barely looked like a samurai at the moment. Some of the better-off, more experienced punks had similar gear. Not the street punks like Rac, but the bigger players.

Cat smiled, all teeth and eyes that squinted. Cat's grins were always lop-sided, the burnt side of her face never quite moving right. "Why can't it be a coincidence that we happen to meet in some elevator in a shithole mega-apartment about a quarter ways into the city?"

Rac's grin didn't waver—she even chuckled a little—but she could feel the sweat starting to cling to her back and armpits and palms. The backpack she was wearing suddenly felt ten times as heavy. "Yeah, funny that way," Rac said.

She knew the charade would end soon, and then shit would get real, but every minute she kept playing along was one more minute she stayed alive.

Those were the *rules*, usually.

Then Cat, because she was Cat, decided to change the script and toss the rules out on their ass. Her smile grew less sharp, her ears turned forward and up a little, as if they were entirely natural ears instead of very high-end prosthetics. She stepped into the elevator, then leaned against one of the walls, boots crossing at the ankles. "Alright, look. I'm not angry. I'm not even disappointed," Cat said. "I'm mostly curious." Cat crossed one arm across her chest. The other was left limp by her side, forgotten.

Rac worked her jaw, not meeting Cat's eyes.

Cat was . . . fuck, Rac didn't know where to start with Cat.

Rac had been a nobody, of the sort whose corpse someone would stumble over some day. She was beyond just inconsequential, and the world knew it.

Then two samurai had waltzed by, broke all the rules, and decided to give Rac more than she could ever hope to have. Rac wasn't going to wax philosophical about it or anything.

When shit went bad, she worked through it. That's how she'd made it so far.

When shit got good? Like really, really good? Like working for a samurai, living in a penthouse, enjoying three fat meals a day, and having a nice gig?

Rac wasn't prepared for that.

"Did I fuck up?" Rac asked.

"Rac, I don't even know what you did," Cat said. "I was legit when I said I was worried."

Rac hesitated for a moment, but Cat wasn't corpo. Cat wasn't a bad liar, because she didn't lie.

"I found work," Rac said. "On the side."

She waited for Cat to tell her off, but it never came. "Huh. Alright. Is it safe? Safe-ish? You know, I realize that I'm not actually paying you, which is kinda fucky. Sorry, I just hadn't thought about it before just now. If you want . . ."

"No," Rac said with a shake of her head.

She had a safe place to sleep, and as much food as she could eat.

She hadn't let anyone know—except Lucy had known anyway, because that chick was scary—but in the first couple of days that Rac stayed with Cat and her kittens, she'd worried herself sick. It wasn't going to last, she knew, so she needed more.

"I don't need you to pay me. I've got . . . I've got a job, of sorts."

"Does it have anything to do with that?" Cat said with a gesture over Rac's shoulder.

She was pointing to the stock of the gun sticking out of Rac's backpack. The gun she'd printed with Cat's alien-tech machine. The rest of the backpack contained mostly ammo and a few necessities. First aid kits, some gear she thought might be handy.

She'd named the gun Heptee, because saying "Heavy Plasma Turret Emplacement" was far too wordy.

"Yeah, a bit," Rac said.

One of Cat's eyebrows rose. "Well, what's the story? I've got all day. I'm on vacation right now."

The tone she used to say "vacation" was somehow terrifying. It was the same way a hardcore punk might say they were "taking out the trash" or something. A word filled with shitloads of implication.

"Alright," Rac said, making sure she sounded more excited than she felt. She was a damned fine salesgirl, if she said so herself. "So, I was looking for work. You know, just something to make a few credits. I asked around, and I found a decent gig."

"What kind of gig?" Cat asked.

Rac shrugged. "Security work. Stand next to some low-tier suit and look tough. I made Heptee a couple of days ago." She pointed a thumb at the gun over her back. "Keeps anyone from picking on me even though I'm small. Job went well, so I got some cred, and that got me in the door. I work with a little crew now. Or I'm trying to. This'll be my second gig with them."

She was glossing over a lot. The entire truth was that Rac was now, technically, a mercenary.

She wasn't sure about all the legalese, but basically, as long as someone had a merc contract, they could sign up as a contractor-for-hire. There was a whole system in place. People needed shit done, and mercs were the answer to a lot of problems.

Crews would form and break up all the time, but mostly they were together to do a gig or two before the members would leave to join another group or do their own thing.

The system was easy enough. Rac was a step above the lowest tier, as a tier-one contractor. Nothing special, in the grand scheme of things.

"You're going to a gig now?" Cat asked. "Along with . . . Heptee the very big plasma gun?"

Rac nodded her head once. Was that it? Cat would tell her to head back, and Rac would be out of a job.

She . . . kinda liked the work. She kinda liked the idiots she was working with. But Cat's word was the *rules*.

Cat tilted her head to the side, then she smiled. "I'll come with you," she said.

"W-what?" Rac asked. That wasn't the reply she'd expected.

"Yeah, it sounds fun. Besides, I'm on vacation. What sort of gig is it? Security again? If it's actually too boring I might dip."

Rac swallowed. "You can't come," she said.

"Why not?" Cat asked.

Rac was stumped. Why not? She had about a million reasons why not, but her lips went ahead and said the stupidest one before her brain caught up. "You'll embarrass me."

Cat stared. "I'll what?"

"Uh," Rac said.

"Wait, do you think I'm not cool?" Cat's voice was low, her words clipped. She crossed her arms and stared with narrowed eyes. Rac had never seen her so offended before. It was kind of scary. She'd once seen Cat hang a guy by the neck over a bottomless pit only to drop him, and even then she'd done little more than shrug and grab the next guy. Even then Cat hadn't seemed as annoyed as she did right here.

"No, no, you're plenty cool," Rac said. She waved her arms from side to side to dispel any other thought.

Cat's mouth worked. "Holy fuck, you don't think I'm cool. What the hell, Rac? I'm plenty cool."

"Yeah, super cool." Rac nodded.

"I've got like . . . guns, and a cool trench coat. And I have a giant fucking mecha."

The mecha was kinda cool, Rac had to admit. "Yeah, you're cool," she said.

"Damnit, Rac, stop rubbing it in." Cat ran her fingers through her own hair. "Unbelievable. Myalis, do you think I'm cool?"

And there she went, talking to her AI as if the AI was just . . . there in the elevator with them. It was super unnerving.

"Well, screw you, I bet you're not cool at all," Cat said.

Rac almost started to defend herself before she realized that Cat was directing that to Myalis too.

Cat snorted, then the elevator thumped and started to move. "Right, let's go see these friends of yours. You can present them to your entirely very cool big sister Cat."

Rac felt her heart drop. There was no way Cat would be able to pass herself off as just a normal merc. The first time someone insulted her she'd blow their brains out and then . . . well, actually, that *would* be somewhat normal merc behavior.

Maybe this wouldn't be all that bad?

Rac tried to look confident as she walked.

Before, in the gutters and the undercity, she had to make herself small, inconspicuous and unimportant, like her namesake. There, but not important enough to bother with.

Up here, heading to the Barber Shop, the attitude was different. She had to look like she belonged.

"You're going to need some sort of ID to get past the bouncer," she said. "He's this big full-borg guy who doesn't fuck around."

Cat shrugged. "I could take him," she said.

She hadn't even seen Molotov and she said she could take him. Then again . . . Rac knew Cat *could* take him, and that wasn't something Rac wanted. "No. He's actually kinda nice? But he'll sound the alarm if he thinks you're corpo or a samurai."

Cat grunted. "How'd you get in? I doubt they carded you."

"I'm a merc," Rac said. "Once I had my status changed, he let me in no problem. You need someone to vouch for you to become a merc though."

"Could probably fake it," Cat said. Then she frowned. "Really? Huh. Well, that's actually kind of clever."

Rac pursed her lips and half-turned to look at Cat. "What is?"

"Apparently mercs mostly use paper. Easier to destroy, and not something Myalis can just break into. So, that idea's out."

Rac nodded along. "I think you could get in just like a normal person going to the bar, but not if you're with me. Maybe if you try to pass yourself off as a specialist? For like, a job?"

"What sort of specialist? An infiltrator? A sort of cyberninja? Oh, I can totally use Myalis to pass myself off as a Meshrunner, no problem. Or some sort of frontline alien-killing badass. I'm pretty decent with bombs too. And stealth."

"Uh-huh," Rac agreed. Cat probably could get away with all of that, but it wasn't the kind of shit that an actual merc did. Well, maybe some of them, but the work of an average merc like Rac was a lot less complicated. Her last couple of jobs had been standing around looking tough, or helping load up some crap into the back of a van in a hurry, or escorting someone through a rough part of the city.

Cat, being a samurai, did the kind of crap that legends did all the time, but most of the people in New Montreal were as far from legends as they could be.

Rac heard the Barber Shop before she could see it. A low, distant thrum of bass-boosted swing music from last century. She could smell it, too, a faint stink to the air that was unique to this one level of the megabuilding. It was piss—which wasn't unique—but also booze-filled vomit and sweat and cigarette smoke.

They came around a corner, and the front of the Barber Shop was right there. A big rotating door, painted in blue and white and red, with Molotov the bouncer standing next to it, massive arms crossed over his chest.

"Hey, Molotov," Rac said as she came closer. The music was louder now, so she had to raise her voice. She had a feeling Molotov could still hear her. The entire upper half of his head was prosthetic. Borg eyes in a chrome skull. It stopped around the upper lip, where he had a long, rather awesome beard and mustache that he tucked into his three-piece suit.

His eyes twitched down, scanning her, then shifted back up toward Cat. "Hey, Rac. Who's your friend?"

"She's a specialist," Rac said. "Lookout specialist. Thought we could use the extra hand today, and I wanted to introduce her to Millennium Animal."

Molotov eyed Cat for a long, long time, then he gestured them in. "Behave, little Raccoon," he said. "And your friend too. The Barbers don't like trouble."

"Yes sir," Rac said hurriedly. If he wasn't going to question things, she wasn't going to linger.

They slipped through the rotating door, and the music hit her like a slap to the face. Loud swing music accompanied a woman on a far stage swaying her hips and multiple fox tails while she crooned through a song.

The bar was split into three distinct areas. There was the big central dance floor, with the stage and its musicians and a few holograms of men, women, and anthropomorphic animals in suits and nice dresses from over a century ago dancing along the edges, and to the left was the bar itself, with a bunch of round tables and a counter that ran the length of the room.

The place wasn't as busy as she'd seen it before, probably owing to it still being early in the day. Still, there were some three dozen or so people around the bar and the floor, some in nice anachronistic suits, others with varying amounts of animal parts worn either as clothes or elaborate pros-thetics, and a few just . . . normal street people, like she could have seen anywhere.

The right side of the bar was where she dragged Cat. There was a divid-ing wall, the bottom half fake wood, the upper bulletproof glass. Behind that were the booths, which was where business happened.

"Who's Mister Millennium Animal?" Cat asked.

"He's the one who hands out jobs," Rac said. "He's a troubleshooter. Peo-ple give him jobs and he gives them to the crews that hang out here."

"And what's with his name? Sounds samurai-ish."

"It's because he's old," Rac said. "Apparently he was born in like, 2000. And the 'Animal' part is, uh."

They entered the booths section, and Millennium Animal was right there. He was a fox today. A well-dressed, dapper fox, with a little fedora on and everything.

"You didn't tell me he was a *furry*," Cat hissed.

"Aren't you?" Rac asked. She glanced at Cat's ears, then the tail hidden under her coat.

Cat's mouth worked, and Rac noticed her cheeks warming up before she glared. "I'm not," she said.

Rac shrugged. "Okay. Whatever suits you."

Millennium caught sight of her and waved even as the mask he wore twisted to give the impression of a smile. "Little Raccoon, you're right on time. And you brought a friend too. Nice ears, ma'am."

"Thanks," Cat bit out. "I'm Rac's . . . big sister, of sorts." She walked right up to Millennium and stared him down, ignoring Rac's quick attempt to gesture for her not to do that.

Millennium was *big* in the Barber Shop. He'd been here since forever ago, and while he was definitely . . . weird . . . he had one of the best reputations for troubleshooting in New Montreal. A lot of people didn't pick him for jobs, mostly because he kept things on a smaller scale, but he also refused a lot of clients. He also almost exclusively *picked* which mercs he was going to work with.

It was practically a fluke that she'd gotten in with his current crew of low-tier mercs, and that was only because of her name.

And right now, Cat was glaring at him as if he was some double-digit alien threatening to eat a baby.

Millennium took it in stride. "I'm afraid I didn't catch your name, Miss Big Sister of Sorts? I'm Millennium Animal. It's a pleasure to meet you, especially seeing as how you seem to care so much for our dear Raccoon here."

Cat's anger subsided a little, and she glanced at his outstretched hand for a moment before shaking it.

Rac sighed. She wasn't about to shoot her boss.

"Call me Cat," Cat said. "And I'm not a furry."

"As you wish," he said with a shrug. "A lot of us would rather identify as the animal within rather than be identified by the community without, and that's perfectly acceptable as well. In any case, how can I help you?"

Cat seemed to be caught flat-footed for a moment before she shook her head. "Look, I just discovered Rac was doing . . . something with you, and I was worried. I wanna see what you're all about. Make sure it's on the up-and-up."

Rac's prediction had been right. This was embarrassing. She wanted to curl in on herself and die a little, but that wouldn't have been good for her image, so she kept her face neutral and her back straight.

Millennium laughed. "It's anything but that. And it's not entirely safe, either. I run a good crew, and I pick my jobs. The price isn't the best, but the work is as safe as it can be." He shrugged again, and somehow his ears and tail moved in such a way that he looked way more innocent than Rac knew he was. "As we used to say when I was young, it is what it is. Now come, sit. Today's job is nothing complicated, and if you're as comfortable with that handgun as you look, then maybe you'll want to sit in on it?"

"I wouldn't mind that," Cat said.

Rac held in a groan. Not only did she have to introduce Cat to her friends, but now Cat would be *babysitting her* on a job.

"Can't see why you'd want me on a job, though. You don't know me at all," Cat pointed out.

"Free labor is free labor," Millennium pointed out with a fox-like bark. "I don't look gift horses, or cats, in the mouth. Now come, I'll show you to Raccoon's friends, and you can determine on your own that she isn't so unsafe."

"Hey! What makes you think I'd work for free?" Cat asked before she set out to follow him.

Rac considered maybe just silently running away, but no, she couldn't do that.

CHAPTER THREE

STRANGE ANIMALS

No one wants a career! Do you think you want to work for the same boss-punk for thirty years of your life?

Gigs are the way to go! Work for more credits, work when you want, if you want! And the day your boss steps on your toes? You're off to the next gig!

—Gigs-R-Us ad, 2031

I wasn't sure if I liked the Barber Shop. The music was weird as hell, and while the chick with the fox tails had a killer voice, I could still pick out the synth notes when she started to croon. I suppose that was one of the downsides of having really good cybernetic ears.

Plus, the place had too many people wearing too much faux-fur for me to be comfortable.

She spent time around people dressed like that, yet thought *I* wasn't cool? What the hell?

I'm sensing that you dislike the aesthetic.

"Mm-hmm," I muttered. Rac glanced up at me, and I waved her concern off. "Show me to your friends, Rac. I'll try not to be too *uncool* around them."

It probably shouldn't have bothered me so much, but it did anyway. Maybe my ego was a little more fragile than I'd like to admit. But . . . well, fuck it. It wasn't cool to be so worried about what others thought about you anyway, so I made an effort to let it go.

It's just that I thought, for some reason, that at least in Rac's eyes I was the badass older sister she never had who could solve all of her problems by blowing them up. I guess I wasn't quite there, though.

Sucked, but that's what it was . . . at least for now. There was still time to impress the brat, even if it really, really didn't matter.

"Don't be weird around them," Rac said.

"I won't be weird," I growled. "Have *some* faith in me."

That would be misplacing her faith.

"Oh, shut up, you," I muttered. Rac gave me another look, but I ignored it. Myalis was being extra sassy right now, probably because she knew that this was embarrassing for me, and she knew that I knew that it was silly to be embarrassed about it to begin with. She loved this kind of circular thing.

Rac led me to a booth some ways into the bar-slash-club, where the music from the dance floor wasn't quite as loud. There was a wall cutting off some of the noise, and a row of fake plants along the other walls partially hiding some of those foam sound-buffer things that cut off vibrations.

The booth Rac led me to had two people sitting at it already. One was a massive woman with a plastic half-mask on her face that made her look like a gorilla. The look was only made more gorilla-like by her arms and upper back. It looked like she'd had some pretty extensive cybernetic work done. Her shoulders were huge to compensate for the size of her arms, which were also massive. They ended in hands that looked like they could crush melons with no effort. Or a person's head.

Those are interesting. A human design, but based on a Vanguard's discarded prosthetics. They're about ten years behind the current technological trend, mostly used for carrying heavy weapons.

So, she'd gotten her hands on military surplus? Or, rather, her hands *were* military surplus.

The guy next to her was a lot less daunting to look at. A skinny runt of a guy, maybe a year or two older than Rac and a bit younger than me. He had a skintight suit on with a leather jacket thrown over that. He was wearing a full-face mask, with little mandibles and some hints at more eyes on it.

Not cybernetics, just a customized piece of high-tech gear that gave him a spidery look. He gave me a peace sign with a freakish hand—too many joints, fingers that were too long—then scooted over so that Rac and I had room to sit.

"Guys, this is Cat, she's . . . sort of like my big sister, I guess," Rac said. I smiled at the lot of them and nodded. They were listening, but not really passing judgement just yet. "Cat, this is Coco, and that's Jerusalem." She gestured first to the gorilla woman, who shifted to the side to raise an arm up and over the table so she could wave, revealing a banana peel decal on her inner arm, and then to the spider-looking guy, who gave me a thumbs-up.

"Yo," I said. "So, is this the whole crew?"

"Nah, Garter's not here yet," Coco said. "Where is he, anyway?" That last was directed to Jerusalem, who tilted his head to the side, then he made a trio of quick gestures, ending with a "three."

"Does he not talk?" I asked with a gesture to the guy.

"He's mute," Coco said.

Jerusalem shrugged, which I guessed was his usual response to the question. Then he continued to stare at me for a while before he recoiled. He looked like he'd just been shocked.

"What is it?" Coco asked.

Jerusalem made a few more complicated gestures in the air that I couldn't understand.

But apparently Myalis could.

He's telling Coco about his recent encounter with your automated cybersecurity systems.

I didn't want to give away the game, and I was kinda shit at subvocalization, so I ended up opening a text app in my augs. *My what?*

Me. He tried to slip into your augmentations, and he bumped into me. Don't worry, I didn't do anything more than what a decently good cybersecurity system might do. I didn't even chase him, just gave him the digital equivalent of sticking his fingers in a mouse trap.

Jerusalem shook his head as he finished telling Coco what happened, and the big woman just laughed. "Well, maybe you should know your place then, huh?" she asked. "Raccoon, what's your big sister do?"

"She, uh," Rac said. She looked at me, then back to her friends, and the silence started to stretch just a pinch too much.

"I'm stealth and infiltration," I said before she could demote me to lookout.

"Same as Jerusalem, then," Coco said. "You coming with us on today's gig?"

"Maybe," I said. "Probably, even."

"That case, you might want to let Jerusalem connect you to our network. We use it for comms. And he uses it to send text messages to the lot of us. I'm assuming you're literate?" she asked.

"I can manage," I said.

I glanced over as a guy walked over to our table. I didn't lean that way, but even I could tell he was an objectively handsome man. He had that model chin and wavy blond hair, curled up at the front in a messy-but-not sorta way.

He was otherwise pretty nondescript, especially for a place like this. The only animal feature was maybe his jacket, which was all snakeskin.

He was carrying a metal tray which he set down on the table before us. "Banana smoothie for the walking stereotype, bourbon on the rocks for the spider, root beers for the Raccoon and her gorgeous friend, and a little something for me," he said as he placed down drinks in front of each of us. Mine looked like a lump of soft serve on top of some soda. Root beer, I supposed.

"You're almost late," Coco said as she accepted hers.

"Almost isn't," he replied. I took it that this was Garter, the last member of the crew they'd mentioned. "So, Raccoon, who's the friend?"

"This is Cat," Raccoon said. She smiled, and I noticed a hint of red spreading across her cheeks as she accepted the float.

I glanced between her and Garter, who sat down across from us on the other end of the booth, one leg folded up casually while he swirled something dark in a small tumbler cup. "Well, any friend of Raccoon's a friend of mine," he said with a wink.

Ah.

Right, I was putting two and two together here and reaching four. Was Raccoon afraid I'd make her look bad in front of this guy specifically? I was glad I kept that app open. *M, how old is this guy?*

Garter, AKA Garfield Lebeau, twenty-seven years old, currently marked as unemployed, but clearly works as a freelance mercenary. I can dig deeper, if you want?

Way too old for Rac to have any sort of interest in. Then again . . . he was about the right age to be in a boy band, and plenty of girls had crushes on those.

If this even was a crush. It could be nothing, or maybe I'd need to have a very serious shotgun talk with the guy. Hopefully he'd listen and I wouldn't need to paint the walls with his brains and figure out a way to console Rac for the loss.

"Wow, that's a look," Garter said as he looked at me. I couldn't decide if he was checking out my gear or me. "So, Millennium Animal said that you might be coming with us on our next gig?"

"Yeah," I said. Was this the third time I'd been asked that? "If you don't mind me coming along. I just want to see if Rac's kept safe."

Rac pressed her hands over her face next to me and I grinned. Poor girl didn't want me around while she made eyes at her crush, huh?

"That's fair," he said with a nod as he took a sip from his glass. "Well, in that case, maybe I could go over the gig?" That had all the others sitting up straighter. "It's a three-hour job. Some kids from a sub–level two gang discovered a corpo warehouse and want to empty it out. Problem is, they figure they can't do it themselves. So we're going in to do the hard part for them. We go in, break down the security on the place, then let the kids grab anything they can. Maybe we help them load up."

Jerusalem made some gestures that Garter seemed to get.

"Nah, we're paid a fixed rate. Ten-k credits each. Flat." That wasn't all that bad of a payday for a three-hour-long job, I figured. More than anyone would make working a register. To my surprise, the others didn't seem to agree. "I know, it's low, but it's also low-risk and easy work. It's that or we burn credits sitting here instead. So . . . we in?"

CHAPTER FOUR

BACK TO CAT

- This quarter's going to be the first where our profits aren't increasing.
- You mean we're losing money?
- No, I meant that our profit margin isn't going to be bigger this quarter than it was in the last one. We're still in the black.
- That's unacceptable. How am I going to explain to the shareholders that we're making less profit?
- We're still making billions.
- Yes, but we're making fewer billions than we were before, and that's not going to fly. Figure something out.

—Private anonymized discussion on the Nimbletainment C-Suite Chat, 2057

"Is this how it usually goes down?" I asked Rac as the two of us followed her . . . work friends.

I wasn't sure where we were going, exactly, but the others seemed to know. We pushed through a door at the back of the Barber Shop and into a service corridor lined with cubicles and stacks of boxes. It was a lot less glamorous than the main section of the bar, but the music still carried in here.

"Yeah," Rac replied. "Most of the time the jobs are pretty cut-and-dry. Go somewhere, scare someone. Steal something from a corp. Stand around and look scary. Sometimes we escort stuff." She shrugged. "It's alright work. Mostly it's good because it's fast. Half a day, a few hours."

That made some sense, I supposed. Rac was often back home, so whatever work she was doing here had to be quick.

"Raccoon hasn't come on any of the actually dangerous jobs," Coco said as she glanced back at me. When we'd first met, Coco had been sitting down, but now that we were both standing I was again taken aback at how big she was. The woman was a good half-foot taller than I was, and a whole lot broader at the shoulders. "But we don't usually take on jobs that are that bad."

"Mostly because no one wants to take the risk," Garter complained. "Even if that's where all the good money's at."

Jerusalem's hand twitched, then he looked my way and tilted his head to the side.

Jerusalem has sent you a link to a limited party chat. It seems like it's what the team uses to communicate. Specifically with Jerusalem himself.

So he'd text into the team chat? Yeah, that made some sense. "Gimme a sec," I told him. "If this chat's safe, I'll join it."

Nothing will get past me.

I opened the chat, shifted it to the corner of my vision so that it wouldn't be too annoying, then adjusted its opacity until it was only barely visible. "Got it," I said.

Jerusalem gave me a thumbs-up, then a line of text appeared in the chat.

Spider: The good money is in the bigger jobs.

Spider: The bigger jobs take a long time. Or they're dangerous.

Spider: I like danger. But not right now.

"What's wrong with danger right now?" I asked.

That earned me a look from Garter that practically shouted *Are you a dimwit?* "Didn't you notice the incursion?" he asked. "The big walls they're building on the edge of the city? The conscription? The club was half empty. A month ago the place would have been booming at this time of day."

"Lots of good folk got themselves zeroed," Coco said. "You didn't notice."

"Oh," I said. "I noticed, yeah, just . . . guess I didn't think about how that would impact the . . . whatever you'd call this kind of job."

"Merc work is fantastic right now," Garter said. "That is, if you're willing to sit on the front line for an hourly rate and pop aliens. There's a lot of low-risk work too . . . so a ton of us have signed on with different merc companies and PMCs to go stand on the walls and blow up aliens and immigrants."

"Immigrants?" I asked.

"People from outside the city," Coco said. "Every damned shelter's packed to overcap, and there are more hobos on the streets than ever. The undercity's crawling with them. Every hotel, motel, flophouse, and shithole apartment's taken. It's all those damned rural people trying to squeeze into our city and take our shit. Some samurai blew up parts of the city too. To kill aliens, but still."

I decided not to comment on her opinion there. Although, on the surface it made sense. New Montreal was surrounded by smaller cities and hundreds of little towns. All those people had to go *somewhere*. They couldn't stay out in the country when there was such a massive incursion going on, so they came here, to the big city, where the walls would keep them safe and where the locals were oh-so welcoming.

I kinda got where Coco was coming from, too. New Montreal was a crowded shithole at the best of times. Packing it full with a few million extra souls wasn't going to improve anything.

Jerusalem nodded, then a few more lines appeared in the group text.

Spider: Water's down across most of the city.

Spider: Lots of corps are laying people off too.

Spider: Things aren't good right now.

Spider: Things are only going to get worse.

"Alright, enough whining," Garter said, cutting into the doom-and-gloom talk. It was a little forced, but it was at least an honest attempt to get things back on track. "We've got a job, people. It'll put credit in our accounts and food in our bellies. We can't complain too hard, can we?"

Garter pushed through a door at the end of the corridor we'd been traveling down, and I was hit with a wonderful bouquet of rotten eggs and unrefrigerated meat. I placed a hand over my nose and blinked a few times as my eyes watered.

The looks I got from the others, the sly little smiles and the motion of Jerusalem's shoulders, suggested that they'd known exactly what we were walking into. And that was . . . some enclosed back alley. We were closer to the center of the megabuilding, and there was a large shaft running from the top to the bottom of the entire structure. A vertical tunnel, filled with hundreds of AC units and a massive platform on every level where that floor's trash was dumped into large containers.

A truck hovered in the air above us, currently grabbing onto one of those containers with a pair of heavy-looking forks. A few chunks of trash fell off the dumpster's edge, and I followed them with my gaze as they dropped down and down and down into the abyss below the building. There weren't enough lights down there for me to guess at where it all went.

Probably just under the city. I imagined there had to be a pile of lost trash down there tall enough to be a mountain by now.

Maybe someone tossed something flammable down every so often, to burn some of it down.

"There's my baby," Coco said as she moved over to an old minivan parked halfway off the edge of the platform. It looked like it was just barely hanging on there. Coco's eyes flashed and the hovercar rumbled to life, the sliding door on its side screeching open even as she popped the driver's-side door open and climbed into an extra-wide seat.

"Get in," Garter said as he hopped in himself. The back of the van had a couch along one side, and a couple of fold-out seats near the back. There were also some suspicious-looking crates, and the back of the passenger side seat had a gun rack welded to it.

Jerusalem slipped to the front, sitting next to Coco with his knees folded up to his chest, and I found a place on the couch next to Rac while Garter latched one of the folding seats down and then slammed the door closed.

"Right, job's on sub-two, under Nimbletainment Six," Garter said.

"Is that the corp we're hitting?" I asked.

"Nah, NB's big. This is just some numbers company. Not that I'd look too deeply into it," he said.

I, however, have looked into it. The job was given to Millennium Animal from a self-proclaimed gangster. The warehouse in question is being rented by a corporation whose name is a series of numbers. It's owned by another numbers corporation, which is in turn owned by a conglomerate. But digging deeper, the line of ownership ends at a Nimbletainment subsidiary. It seems like it's mostly a corporation set up to provide deniable resources to undisclosed projects.

"So, what are we going after?" I asked. I was aiming that at both Garter and Myalis. Hitting a corp's deniable resources seemed a little higher-risk than I'd want to see for Rac.

"We don't want to know," Garter said.

Experimental smart ammunition.

Coco lifted us off, and instead of climbing upward like I expected, we dropped. The van had some lights on the front, which flicked on and illuminated the interior of the tunnel as we descended.

"Job's about as simple as it gets," Garter said. "We rock up to the warehouse, Jerusalem disables their security, Coco breaks the door, and then we let our local pals rob the place blind."

"What about corpo security?" I asked.

"Barely any out and about right now," Garter said. "Most of them were moved to keep corpo assets safe from the aliens. It's the only advantage we have right now in all of this incursion shit."

"Good thing, too," Coco said. "Cost of ammo's tripled, and fuel costs have skyrocketed. It's getting hard to be an indie merc right now."

Garter shrugged in an easy *what can you do* kind of way. "At least with so many mercs working for corps right now, it's easier than ever to get your rep up. Once everything cools down, we'll be the top of the top, you know?"

"Uh-huh," I said.

This wasn't what I expected to be up to when I followed Rac, but it was interesting all the same, and I was already along for the ride.

CHAPTER FIVE

FUNNY BUSINESS

Security, especially good security, is all about obscurity. If the enemy doesn't know, then whatever you want to keep secured is at its most secure. After lack of knowledge comes obfuscation, then misinformation, then, after all that, comes physical security.

—*A Guard's Guide to CorpoSec*, 2031

We dropped out under the city and right into that dark, cavernous world beneath the megabuildings, where massive pillars held the city in place and where the only light came from flashing red warning lights or as small glows from the holes above.

Coco leaned forward, and Jerusalem reached up, flicking off the cabin light, as if that little bit less light would make us that much less noticeable.

Fortunately, we didn't go far. Coco turned the van around and we started to rise. "Sub-two," she said as we crossed up past a large wall painted with "S3" and into another section with "S2" stenciled on it. "Going to find a place to park, Garter, or do you want us right at the door?" she asked.

Garter licked his lips. "Right up to the door. The street kids will be waiting nearby already. Should be clear."

Coco nodded, and the van came to a hovering stop before a grated metal door.

Jerusalem leaned back in his seat, pulled out a wire from around his neck, then plugged it into a small device with a couple of blinking lights. The lights flickered, and the grate started to rise, opening up into a long corridor wide enough for a pair of trucks to slip past each other, if only barely. Rac picked up Heptee and checked its magazine before shouldering the gun.

Coco's van touched down, and we continued to roll forward, the hover engine humming to a stop. "I hate these places," she said as we rode down a tunnel lit only every twenty meters or so by some recessed lights above.

"No one likes these," Rac said. "They're dangerous."

"Why's that?" I asked.

"Corpo routes," she said. "They're used for carrying corpo cargo. The transportation corps sweep through these tunnels every so often. If you're caught in them, you're either gunned down, or worse, cleaned up."

"Cleaned up?" I asked.

"Trucks that spray acid on everything, to sanitize things," Rac explained. "It'll melt your clothes. Then it'll melt your skin."

"It'll just burn you. Polyesters and plastics and hair," Garter said. "Real materials, leathers and the like, are fine. Metals too. They'll burn your eyes right out, though. And the water's hot. Very hot. But don't worry. Street kids wouldn't be here if they knew a cleaning truck was coming by. And besides, we're in a van, so we're fine."

"Uh-huh," I said.

Myalis helpfully added the tunnel to my map, then highlighted the entire network while zooming out. The underground route traveled across the entirety of New Montreal, a spiderweb of passages just under the city's skyscrapers. Or . . . no, it was in the spaces *between* the buildings. Were the tunnels built into the seams between the plates of the city? Weird.

The van turned a corner, and Garter jumped up and grabbed on to the seat behind Coco. "That's them," he said.

I looked over his shoulder as well, a hand pressing to the ceiling to stay up. There were several small hoverbikes parked ahead, a few of them with trailers, and a single van not too dissimilar to Coco's, if a bit rustier.

Accompanying those were about a dozen punks.

The oldest in the bunch looked like he was only a year or two older than me. The rest all ranged from about Rac's age to mine. They were teenagers in ratty clothes, almost like a uniform but only because they all wore an uncomfortably large number of spikes.

The leader's face was a mess of spikes. On his lower lip, his chin, across the bridge of his nose and eyebrows, and strangest of all, on his eyelids, so that when he closed his eyes there were two little needle spikes that covered his eyes.

Spider: These guys hired us?

Spider: Who the fuck even are they?

Garter glanced toward Jerusalem, clearly having received the same message. "They're nobodies. But they're nobodies who paid. Come on, let's look like the pros we are. New girl . . ." He paused and looked me up and down. "Just keep to yourself, don't ask questions, and try to just fade into the background."

"Alright," I said while resisting a smile.

Garter nodded, then opened the side door of the van.

We loaded out. Rac carried Heptee so that the gun was slung low by her side. Coco was only armed with her . . . well, her very large arms, and

Jerusalem stepped out of the van while loading a magazine into a compact SMG. Then he loaded a second into another identical gun.

Spike-face walked over to us and eyed Garter before doing that guy-nod that men do when they're greeting each other. "You the people Millennium sent?" he asked.

"We are," Garter said. "Just here to go in and out. No funny business."

"We transferred the credits already," Spike-face said. "You'll get your pay once the job's done." He reached into his mouth and fiddled with one of his piercings.

"Right," Garter said. "Where's the warehouse?"

Spike-face nodded his head to the side, toward a closed garage door with a bubbled camera above it. Someone clever had sprayed the camera down already.

"Got it," Garter said. "Jeru, get the door. Coco, Raccoon, new girl, stand by for trouble."

"And here I thought we weren't expecting any," I said. I checked my Trench Maker, making sure it was nice and loose in its holster. I knew it was loaded and otherwise ready to go. I never stored my guns unloaded.

Garter shot me a look, but didn't say anything until we were close to the door. "Some jobs are easy, so you make them look hard. Some jobs are hard. Those you make look easy."

"He read Sun Tzu once," Coco said over her shoulder.

Garter rolled his eyes, then tugged out his own gun. A little handgun, without anything real fancy about it.

Jerusalem walked over to the side of the door and started to fiddle with a panel there. He paused, then turned toward Coco.

Spider: Rip it.

Coco chuckled, walked over, then grabbed one edge of the plastic panel. She grunted, and the entire thing tore out until it only held on by a few bent hinges.

Jerusalem bobbed his head in a nod, then tossed the cover aside, revealing a hole filled with wires and electrical doohickies. He pulled out a small wire from his pocket, used it to connect two parts together, then pressed on a small button labeled "reset." The door started to rumble open.

Then Garter sniffed at the air. "Fuck. Masks," he said immediately.

Coco tugged out a small rebreather from her pocket and shoved it on while Garter slid on his own, just a simple two-filter mask, slim enough to tuck away in his snakeskin jacket.

Rac set her gun down and tugged a much bigger mask from her backpack, a proper full-face thing that looked very Cold War-ish.

I sent a quick text to Myalis. *Mask?*

One moment, I'll get you something cheap but functional. It's in your right-side pocket, and you're down fifteen points.

I reached into my pocket and felt something rubbery and hard in there. Pulling it out revealed . . . a mask. Though the front of it was molded to look like a cat's nose, and it had teeny-tiny whiskers.

I rolled my eyes as I pressed it in place. The mask sucked onto my face, then held. It was clearly designed to fit perfectly onto my face, even as I wiggled my nose and jaw. This wasn't going to help the furry allegations . . . or make me look cool.

"Hey!" Garter called back to the street kids. "Got deterrent gas. Mask up or back off."

That sent Spike-face and his less-spikey friends scurrying for masks of their own. "Is this normal?" I asked.

Garter glanced at me, then stared at my mask for a moment. "So-so. Just typical corpo shit," he said.

The door was fully open by then, and I couldn't see any signs of any sort of gas, just a decently sized room with another garage door at the other end, and a loading bay at about the right height for a truck to back into.

"Anything?" Garter asked Jerusalem.

The man shook his head, then stepped into the room. We followed.

"Myalis," I muttered real low. "What's the gas?"

I'm detecting nothing. The air is slightly stale, and there are trace particulates, but fewer than what you'd find at street-level.

Then what the hell was all of that about? Then I glanced over to the street kids, cowering away while we walked in like big damned heroes and I caught on. Garter was putting on a show. Making the easy job look tough. The clever little bastard, he was making sure that the client felt like his crew earned their cost.

Jerusalem was the first to the next garage door, checking it up and down and obviously looking for something that he didn't find.

Spider: Can't find anything.

Spider: Looks like a new door. Can't hotwire this one.

Spider: No exterior way to open it.

"Going to need to do things the old-fashioned way, then," Coco said.

Everyone ran to the side, and Coco rammed her fingers into and through the sheet metal of the door. Then she grunted, and the entire thing crumpled in toward the middle, opening a small space between the bottom of the door and the ground.

"Raccoon, get in there," Garter said.

I tensed up and started to protest, but Raccoon tossed me her rifle and I caught it out of the air, which distracted me long enough for her to drop to all fours and scurry under the door before I could protest.

CHAPTER SIX

FINE LITTLE FIGHTER

Robotics and automation go hand in hand with the growth of artificial intelligence. If a company can replace most of its white-collar workers with a few AI and AI services, then why shouldn't it do the same with its blue-collar force?

So the entire field of robotics, once lagging behind, suddenly gained the attention and budget it needed to supplant humanity.

—*The Electronic Workforce*, a report on digital and mechanical automation, 2032

Rac was a big girl who could take care of herself. She didn't need me. She'd lived most of her life without me, and in some pretty awful conditions at that.

So it was stupid of me to worry. She wasn't one of the kittens, she wasn't one of the kids that Lucy and I had inadvertently become responsible for. But I worried anyway, because . . . fuck, I don't know, maybe I just wasn't a heartless bitch? I was tense, Trench Maker in hand, primed to run and gun at a moment's notice. Which was probably why I jumped when Coco tapped my shoulder.

"She'll be fine," the big woman said. "Raccoon might be new to all of this, but she's a damned fine little fighter."

"Good merc," Garter agreed.

I gave him a look and Garter glanced around, as if searching for the reason I was staring him down. This was what they considered safe work?

"Yeah, she's a good kid," I said. "Emphasis on kid, though. I don't know what kind of stuff you guys do most of the time, but if this is an *easy* job for you, then your normal can't be all that safe. Rac's . . . Rac's her own woman, even if she isn't one yet. I'm not gonna tell her what to do, or who to hang out with, but I will break fingers and blow out kneecaps if things go wrong."

Spider: Scary.

Spider: So, what's your story?

Spider: You don't smell corpo.

I snorted. "I'm not corpo," I said.

"That's what corpo says," Coco replied with a laugh.

"Focus, boy and girls," Garter muttered just as Rac slid back out from under the dented gate. "What did you see?"

Rac sat on the ground, a little flushed after crawling around. I looked her over, but she seemed fine, if a little dusty. She adjusted her full-face mask before she spoke. "It's a loading room. Not much there. Some crates and stuff. But it looks like there're a few storage rooms. Big metal doors with electronic locks."

"Nothing too bad," Garter said. "Did you see how to open the door, or will we have to crawl through?"

"Yeah, there's a button," Rac said. "But there's also a bot."

Garter swore under his breath, and I saw his stance shift, getting ready to fight. "What kind?"

Rac shrugged. "Not sure, but I took pics," she said before glancing at Jerusalem.

The team's hacker paused for a long moment, head tilting to the side as if in thought, then he nodded and I got a ping from him: an image. An image taken with a shitty, lower-res camera. Rac's eye augs? I'd never checked on her specs, but I imagined they weren't top quality. Probably something after-aftermarket.

Still, the image was pretty comprehensive. It was a wide shot of several all-metal double doors, maybe made of stainless or something, then in the shadowy corner, a big shape, like a trash can turned upside down.

"That's the bot, in the corner?" I asked.

"It's not an android," Coco said.

"They wouldn't have an android on security, especially not in a hidden spot where it isn't meant to be seen," Garter said. "Jerusalem?"

Spider: Just checking.

Spider: Got it. Model PBY5788.

Spider: 1.25m tall, 0.7m wide, cylindrical chassis, four articulated wheels. Lithium-ion cell batteries. Low center of gravity. Can climb standard stairs. Armed with a 12.5mm compact machine gun. Forty-round drum magazine. Tear gas dispensers are built into the chassis and provide an organic-disabling smokescreen that doesn't interfere with the PBY5788's thermal vision system. The PBY5788 is also armed with your choice of a self-reloading 75,000 volt Taser, or a sub-compact machine gun that fires standard 9mm NATO rounds!

"Did you copy-paste that from the manufacturer's website?" I asked. The text was too clean for Jerusalem.

Jerusalem shrugged.

Fair enough. I wouldn't want to have to write all that down either. "So, is the job a bust?" I asked. A bot like that was something you might see hanging out around a jeweler's or a weapons shop, the kind of machine that'd scare off anyone with sticky fingers.

Garter considered it, then shook his head. "No. Jerusalem, you detecting anything else? Turrets, more bots?"

Jerusalem shook his head.

Garter clapped his hands. "Alright. In that case, here's how we'll do it. Rac, I need you right over here with your big gun. Jerusalem, get out of the way, monitor what you can, and let me know if more security goes off. Coco, I need you to the side. Get ready to move." Garter glanced my way, then pointed to the ground nearby. "Stand there, aim at the door."

"What's the plan, Garter?" Coco asked.

"We know where the bot is, right? I'm gonna stick my head out on the other side, my augs are pretty alright. Jerusalem, remember that fancy bit of trig you did on the casino job? Same idea. Raccoon will shoot the bot through the wall, and Coco, you'll pull me back out before the shooting starts."

I stepped back and watched them get to work. It was all . . . kind of boring. Which was probably for the best. Garter got onto the ground, stuck his head into the other side through the same hole Rac had slipped through, then inched forward until he could presumably see the bot.

Jerusalem did some fancy math, then showed us a nice sketch of a bunch of angles. Garter's head and eyes gave him an idea of the distance of the bot, which he used to pinpoint where on the wall Rac would need to shoot to hit it.

He made an X with a bit of gravel on the wall, and Rac shouldered her gun, aiming at it.

"Pull me back," Garter asked, and Coco tugged him out. "Thanks. Raccoon, give me a second to plug my ears, then fire away."

Everyone tensed up, then Rac fired. The recoil had her taking a step back. The wall didn't stand much of a chance as the shot blew a fist-sized hole in it. Then she adjusted her stance and fired three more times into the hole.

Rac ran to the side, and Jerusalem tossed something through the hole while we waited. He nodded.

Spider: One bot: dead.

Rac grinned, and Garter patted her on the shoulder. "Good work. If that's the only security . . . you see anything else, Spider? No? Alright, get in, and get the door open for us, Raccoon."

Rac slipped under the door again, and a moment later the entire thing rumbled upward, only to stop three-quarters of the way up as the bent section met the top and it couldn't fold away. Still, it was more than enough to just step in through.

No more security? I typed to Myalis.

Not that I can detect. The bot was also offline to begin with.

I sighed, but kept my thoughts to myself. Would Myalis have warned me if it wasn't the case? Should I have asked . . . I should definitely have asked. Fuck.

"Jerusalem, keep an eye out for more sec," Garter said. "Let's check the rooms, one at a time. Watch out for more bots, and ceiling-mounted guns."

We checked the rooms. Or rather, the team did. They had a method for it, opening the door, then scanning everything within before moving in. It was slow, but it was careful.

It took a good ten minutes to scan everything, and by the end, the piercing enthusiasts were chomping at the bit outside to get in. They'd found some paper masks to cover themselves up, which really ruined the whole *lots of spikes* vibe.

"Is it clear?" Spike-face asked.

"It's clear," Garter replied, stowing his handgun away, which seemed to be the signal for the others to do the same. "Come and get your stuff. Our part's done. Jerusalem, think you can pull anything valuable off that bot?" He gestured to the corner where the bot was.

It had four holes large enough that I could fit a hand through on one side, and the other side was an exploded mess of tangled metal and melted plastics. The interior had caught fire at some point, or maybe that was from the plasma rounds doing their thing. In any case, the machine was properly fucked.

Jerusalem glanced at the bot, then shook his head.

Spider: Battery might be worth something. But it's heavy and I don't have the tools to extract it.

"Yeah, never mind," Garter said. "I don't wanna waste half an hour down here for a few thousand credits that we'll wind up having to split. Let's get going everyone."

The street kids started moving in and out of the warehouse, carrying crates with them in teams. But we just left. Back to Coco's van, which she started up right away, and then we did a three-point turn and started heading out.

"That was it?" I asked. I was a little surprised. This had only taken an hour or so, and the only fun bit was seconds long, at most.

"Like I said, easy job," Garter said. "You know, you didn't carry yourself that badly. Not a pro, but not bad. Might be some hope to get you as a merc. If you're looking for that kind of work, that is."

"Ah, no thanks," I said. "My kind of work is usually . . . different from all of this. Well, not that different, but different." Rac gave me the side-eye and I stifled a grin.

"Mysterious," Coco said.

I snorted. "I'm usually shooting a lot more things and more stuff is trying to eat me."

"Ah, you're a cleaner," Garter said. "You work for a PMC?"

"Something like that," I said with a dismissive wave.

This whole thing was weirdly anticlimactic. And . . . yeah, these guys weren't so bad. Clean and efficient and probably better at their job than I was at mine. Maybe Rac wasn't doing so poorly.

I'd still worry about her, though.

CHAPTER SEVEN

THE KIND OF WORK
THAT MAKES YOU HAPPY

You should be happy working, because work IS happiness!
—Sunshine Outlook: Global HR, 2035 slogan

Coco landed her van in the same dank and stinking spot where we'd found it earlier, then the bunch of us leapt out. I decided to keep the mask on, at least until we were back inside the Barber Shop and I felt like it was too annoying to keep on.

I noticed Rac doing the same, ripping off the full-face mask and shoving it into her pack as a tangled mess of straps.

"That was a pretty clean job, guy and girls," Garter said. "Uh, Cat, was it? I'd usually be all for paying you for the help, but it'll have to be something of a group decision, you know?"

"Huh? Oh, I don't mind skipping the credits," I said.

"Are you sure?" Coco asked.

Spider: She didn't do anything.

"He's right, I didn't do anything," I said. "Besides, it's not like you expected me to ride along. I really don't mind. If things had gone pear-shaped and I had to save your asses, then I'd gladly make you pay, but . . . yeah, that was a clean gig."

"I don't mind taking her share," Rac said.

Garter snorted, then ruffled her head. "Cute, but no luck, kid," he said.

Rac pouted and glared at the ground, and I was pretty sure I was the only one that picked up her whiny, whispered, "I'm not a kid, dammit."

We filed into the main floor of the bar, and I noticed that the dance floor had gained a few more patrons since we left. The music was still the same, ancient jazz and swing with some heavy synths and electronics overlaid atop them. There was a new lady singing, a big chick with a big voice war-bling in French about her big problems.

Garter led us back to the same booth we'd started in, and when he sat down it was with a big, weary sigh. "Alright, let me get everyone's pay sorted out, then the first round's on me."

We all slipped into the booth as well, with Rac and I sitting on the edges. I didn't figure I'd be staying here for very long. Garter did as he promised, and the mood improved noticeably as Coco and Jerusalem and Rac got their pay. Then the conversation turned to guns, and Garter and Jerusalem started to argue with the same kind of tone I'd expect from an argument that had been had before.

"So," I said to Rac as I leaned back. "Is this how it usually goes?"

She shrugged. "Only been at it for a few days," she said. "But . . . yeah, usually. I like to stay and eat after, but then I always get back home and back to work. The credits are good, though."

"Yeah, I can see that," I said. She was probably making more than any line worker. "Riskier than the work you do at home."

"Just a little. Garter picks good jobs. Millennium Animal doesn't have bad clients," she defended.

I nodded along. "Alright. Well . . . yeah, I guess I've seen what I had to see. Would you mind walking me to the door? I might get lost on the way out."

She glanced at me, then at the exit, which we could see from our seats. "Uh, okay?"

I said goodbye to Coco and Jerusalem, shaking their hands and going through the usual pleasantries. Garter kept a hold of me when I shook his hand. "Hey. If you're ever looking for work. . . . Well, Raccoon hasn't said too much, but she might have mentioned that you saved her from a lot of trouble, and it looks like you came here today because you were worried." He smiled, warm and honest. "We can use that kind of person on our team."

"I'll think about it," I said. "But I've got my own sort of work, you know?"

"That's fair," he said. "Stay warm."

"You too," I replied before giving him a shake, then ducking back.

Rac followed me, but not without pointedly leaving her stuff at the table. She didn't say anything, not until we were out of the bar and had moved to the side, where a passerby would have to go out of their way to get within hearing range. "Are you going to have me stop working with them?" she asked.

"No," I said.

"Does that mean you . . . don't want me to work for you anymore?" she asked next.

I shook my head, then smiled. "Rac, don't worry so much. I really did come out here because I was worried for you. If I was worried for you, then obviously I'm not going to kick you to the curb."

"Then . . . what was all this about?" she asked.

I shrugged. "I'm on vacation. It's not much more complicated than that. If you want to keep being a merc, then yeah, go ahead. Just be careful, alright? And maybe pick your jobs? We might be having words if your next job is less about robbing a corp and more . . . I don't know, blowing up an orphanage or something."

"I wouldn't take a job like that," she said, arms crossing.

I grinned, then rubbed her head, because it looked like fun. At least for the one doing the rubbing. Rac twisted out of the way and looked hilariously offended.

"If you need more ammo for that big gun of yours, don't hesitate. And maybe try to get some armor? I can look into it. Oh, and . . . I'll have Myalis give me a catalog with some basic cybernetics. You should get your augs replaced. Yours are kinda shit. Your team, and you, will appreciate having better gear, trust me."

Rac hesitated for a bit, then nodded. "Alright," she said.

I patted her on the shoulder. "Go back, get that free drink from Garter before the offer expires, yeah?"

"Okay," Rac said. She paused. "Cat?"

"Yeah?"

"Thanks," she said.

"No problem!" I grinned and started to walk away, only to pause. "Oh, and Rac? He's *way* too old for you."

Rac flushed, glared, and darted off without saying anything. I laughed, then spun on my heel and headed out. I figured that counted as my good deed for the day.

Are you serious about that cybernetics catalog?

"Can't cost that much, can it?"

That's true. I'd suggest getting something in the two to three hundred point range. It will give you several options for augmentations and consumer cybernetics on par with the best commercially available options. Also, if you want to prioritize Rac's safety, then perhaps an under armor blueprint catalog? You have gone through a few sets of armor yourself. It would only take a half dozen more for you to start saving money with the blueprint.

I sighed. Myalis was probably right, though, and we did have some resources to spare. If any of the other kittens decided to start running around the city causing trouble, then I'd want them to have the bare minimum gear with them too.

"You know what, that sounds really fair, Myalis."

Thank you! We can discuss budgets if you want. Though that depends, what are you planning to do with the rest of your day?

"What do you mean? I'm on vacation, aren't I? I'm done for the day. Though . . . maybe it wouldn't hurt to plan for tomorrow's disaster on the walk back." My bike was a good two minutes away by foot.

Certainly! Which issue did you want to tackle tomorrow, then?

"Right so . . . far as I'm aware, there's the mayor that needs to do some explaining for me. The fucker got re-elected somehow, and I have a hard time believing it was in any way honest. Then there're the sewers. Shit, might have to take care of those sooner rather than later. The more we leave them alone, the worse they'll get. Oh, and the prosthetics thing. I started to set that up, then got distracted."

I see. Let me draw up a schedule for you. But first, a few more minor details. Did you want the mayor's visit to be done on official terms?

"Hmm . . . yeah, send him a nice warning that I'll be visiting him. Make it like, right after he's supposed to be done for the day, and tell him that it'll be 'wherever he is at that time.'" I laughed to myself. Making politicians sweat was just fun and proper.

Very well, then! Tomorrow, the sewers. The day after, you'll have an appointment with the mayor. And then the day after that an appointment with the people setting up your prosthetics charity?

"Eh, we can do the mayor thing and the charity thing on the same day. Telling the mayor off can't take more than a couple of hours, right?"

Yes, I'm certain you'll be able to navigate through complex politics without any issues.

I rolled my eyes. "Come on, have a little faith in me. It's hardly complex politics. It's me threatening someone. I can do that in my sleep!"

CHAPTER EIGHT

CHECKING OUT THE STINK

Rosetta Stone 2041 presents: North American Mid-level English!
With our expertly-crafted, AI-enabled teaching software, you can become fluent in middle-management in only 720 hours!
—Ad for a corpo-English language module, 2041

After coming back home and whining to Lucy at length about my little adventure with Rac and the mercs over some warm coffee, I spent the rest of the day . . . doing very little of import.

I felt a bit bad about not spending time with the kittens, so I bullied Nose for a while, put Bargain in a headlock when he tried to sell me a cola from my own fridge, and basically annoyed Junior and Katallina as much as I could without pissing them off too much.

We played aug games, with Daniel kicking everyone's ass until I let Myalis join in and the AI found herself incapable of doing anything but playing perfectly. Unleashing an AI on a cart-racing game was just unfair for everyone involved.

Before I knew it, it was deep into the night and the sugar and caffeine was wearing off. I took a languid, wasteful shower, then bought some PJs from Myalis, then I bought a second pair for Lucy when I discovered something important. When the Protectors decided to make something soft, it was *disgustingly* soft.

We just cuddled, warm and soft and tangled up together in a way that was comforting and familiar, until at some point I drifted off while Lucy was murmuring a story about some puppies she'd seen online.

I awoke sometime in the late morning when Lucy crawled out of my arms. "Need to pee," she mumbled sleepily, and I'm sure whatever I said in reply was articulate and sensible before I rolled over and tried to sleep some more.

Lucy came back and passed out right away while I snuggled into her, but I couldn't sleep, especially not after checking the time on my augs, then checking my messages, then checking on some news. I had a tab open with updates from Burlington, and it seemed like things weren't entirely dire over there yet.

I was now fully awake but still just scrolling through the news, and memes, and memes of the news. Eventually I had to piss too, so I rolled out of bed and started to take care of my morning . . . actually, almost-afternoon, ablutions.

"So, we're checking on the sewers today, right?" I muttered. The whole Sewer Dragon situation had been handled . . . well enough, I figured. Gomorrah and I hadn't done that bad a job of it for two newbies. The overall sewer situation was more dire. There were memes about toilets in the lower city exploding, and apparently even the rats didn't want to stay down there.

That was the plan, yes. I've done some cursory research, and I think there are two points of interest that you should visit.

"Two?" I asked.

Indeed. First, the City of New Montreal Sewage and Maintenance Head-quarters. The main bureau. While they are more of an administrative branch, they do have connections to the entire sewer network.

That seemed perfectly reasonable and logical. "What's the second?" I asked. I discovered some toothbrushes in the bathroom in a little mug, then shrugged and picked the less-used one to brush my teeth with. Teeth care was not much of a priority at the orphanage. I wondered if my nano treatments had taken care of my cavities.

The second location is the Family's New Montreal Headquarters. The organization has become the center of the local Antithesis-combat infrastructure, at least as far as logistics and administration goes. They have expressed concerns over the water and sewage issues in the city and might be able to assist you.

Right, we both wanted to take care of the same issue, so it made sense to pair up with them and get things done. "Is there a samurai on the case?"

All of the local Vanguard are either working on the city's defenses and clearing the surrounding area of remaining pockets of resistance, or they have been relocated to areas in more dire need of Vanguard support. With the exception of yourself, there are only five unoccupied Vanguard in New Montreal. Gomorrah is one of these. You're also familiar with Crackshot Cowboy and Emoscythe Mordeath Noir.

Shit, things were a little more dire than I'd expected, then. The unoccupied samurai might not even be active ones. Some of them just . . . retired or whatever. Laid low and minded their own business.

So it was more or less all on me. "What's Gomorrah up to?"

Social media feeds suggest she's assisting in light cleanup duty along the walls.

"That sounds like work," I said. Work wasn't gonna happen if I was on vacation. Well, not that kind of work.

She's testing new firebombs on suspected nest sites from a relatively safe distance.

"Ah," I said. Never mind, then. That wasn't work, it was pleasure.

I stretched my back out, then started getting dressed. I found Lucy yawning awake and trying in vain to get her hair into some semblance of order. "Morning," she said.

"Heya," I replied. "Sleep well?"

"Mm-hmm. I'm never removing these PJs, Cat. Never." She hugged herself, hands trailing over the fluffy material. "You're going to have to learn to live with celibacy."

"I'm sure I can think of a way to work around that," I said with a grin. "But later? I need to get going. Need to see some people about some pipes."

Lucy frowned in thought, looking rather confused for a moment before she shrugged. "Okay? Well, be careful, and don't come back home too late. Or if you do, let me know? I don't want to worry."

"Yeah, of course," I said. I gave her a quick kiss before I started searching for my boots. It only took a minute to find the first one, but the second was hiding well enough that it was a while before I found it.

Since I didn't know what to expect when heading out, I decided that more was better than less. I tossed on my coat over my skin-tight armor and grabbed both my Trench Maker and a compact Laser Pointer . . . was it a submachine gun or an auto shotgun? I wasn't sure what the gun was, but it was relatively small and easy to carry on a sling.

I grabbed a chocolate bar from the pantry on the way out, noted that it was probably the healthiest thing there and that we should do something about that, and promptly left without doing anything about it.

My bike was sitting out front, next to my mech. I promised myself that I'd get back to fixing the mech later on, whenever it was that I came back.

But first . . . I was burning daylight.

The skies over New Montreal were uncharacteristically clear, with large holes in the cloud cover above bathing parts of the city in bright sunlight. The rest of the cloudy ceiling was, of course, pouring a deluge of water onto the city.

I tugged up the lapels of my coat and slid on my helmet, making sure that my ears were properly tucked into their slots so that the helmet wouldn't pull them. Then I was off.

"Maintenance HQ first?" I asked as I circled our building.

Certainly. I think it might be best to get a good look at the condition of things before requesting assistance.

"Requesting? I don't feel like begging," I said.

Purchase a larger gun and demand it, then.

I snorted. "Ah, yeah, demanding assistance. 'Help me or I'll shoot you' is always super convincing, I'll bet."

It has been demonstrated to work before. It's almost a universal rule among intelligent beings evolved from predators that "might makes right."

I nodded along. My augs had the destination locked in, and fortunately, while the headquarters were basically on ground level, they weren't in the undercity. "Do you know a lot of species that are . . . uh, is it sapient or sentient?" I asked. "Well, whatever. I mean smart and also non-predator-based."

There are several thousand on record. Many of them still live and thrive within the greater sphere of the Protectorate. Most find the idea of violence abhorrent. Often this is a great detriment when the Antithesis inevitably appear at their metaphorical doorstep.

"Damn, yeah, I can imagine," I said.

It's not always bad. Some species, especially those well-versed in agriculture and who have a solid technological and industrial base are able to hold out on their own for prolonged periods. I can get you a few documentaries on the subject.

"Heh, file that for later. Maybe if we want to do a movie night or something." I wasn't super interested in the goings-on of some unknown species halfway across the galaxy from me, but not being super interested didn't mean I wasn't a little curious.

I refocused on my flying. I didn't need to crash into some car speeding by while distracted. I suspected that the training whatsit that I'd taken to allow me to pilot my mech was also helping me with my bike, because even without turning on autopilot I had a much better . . . *feel* for how to maneuver through the city.

Which was why I punched the throttle to the limit and pressed myself against the seat, breaking every law in the books as I headed out on a quest to find some trouble and fix it to death.

CHAPTER NINE

USELESS CRAP

People are impossibly fond of useless crap. Slap a number on it, call it collectible, and make it even moderately interesting, appealing, sexy, or cute, and you'll trigger something real deep in that person's mind.
—Clown "Red Nose" McFace, CEO of GimmeUrCred
Non-Fungible Physical and Digital Collectible Crap Publishing, Inc.

The City of New Montreal Sewage and Maintenance Headquarters wasn't a standalone building. It was relatively rare for a corp to have an entire building all on its own. Even though the really big corps owned megabuildings downtown, they still rented out sections for profit.

What I was getting at is that the NMSM Headquarters was located at the base of one of the older buildings in the center of the city. It was a big, boxy thing, brutalist nouveau, with a few balconies sticking out of the side for old school AA emplacements. Basically, one of those first megabuilding projects that had gone up way back in the late '20s or so and which was probably showing its age in a million ways within.

The seventh floor had been converted into a parking garage for hovercars at some point, so I drove my bike in and felt myself naturally trying to make myself smaller. The ceiling was way lower than it should have been, and the space was a disorganized mess.

I parked on the curb next to an elevator and my augs flagged an incoming fine from the building's automatic parking system for the violation.

I hopped into the elevator, then sighed. It had one of those shitty old touch-screen button panels, with the looping advertisements. I'd have to time it so that I pressed the right floor between ads. "Can you punch in the right floor?" I asked Myalis.

I actually can't. The elevator isn't networked at all. It's floor 1, in any case.

I shook my head, then stabbed a thumb against the screen after an ad for Molly's Miracle Mugs, which were just a collection of mugs with some dog's face on them, but they were collectible and had little cards that came with them, and I was sure this was exactly the kind of shit that Lucy would be into.

The elevator rumbled down, bumping along a bit more than it should have, and I was already having some pretty serious doubts about the "Maintenance" part of the New Montreal Sewage and Maintenance group.

The doors opened up onto a plain corridor. A guy in a button-up was cursing at a vending machine. I slipped past him, following ceiling-mounted signs that led toward reception.

There, I found a room filled to capacity with random people. Old men, old women, some small families speaking in something other than English, lots of random folk. Too many to fit the seats in the relatively small reception area up ahead.

Button-up guy came up behind me, muttering while holding a can of soda to his head. "Hey," I said. "You work here?"

"Not for long," he said. He almost brushed past me, but I grabbed onto his shoulder, giving him pause. "I'm sorry, please take a ticket and wait. We're doing what we can here."

"Yeah, I see that. Look, I'm here to talk to whoever's in charge."

He shook his head. "That won't work. Half the Karens in the room tried that one already."

He tried to move again, but I held him back, a bit harder, this time. "Give me a sec," I said. "Myalis, can you send a nice message to everyone here's augs, the people waiting? Tell them that I'm on the scene and that I'll have the sewage thing fixed as soon as I can, and if I can't, those responsible will be thrown off the roof by this evening."

Certainly. Message sent.

My new pal blinked dumbly and lowered his soda as people gasped, then there was a small flood as first one, then more of them started to leave the reception area. Unfortunately, my entirely unplanned actions had entirely predictable consequences as every granny saw me and put two and two together. The swarm descended.

"Yup, yeah, I'm sure, that's nice. Sorry, coming through. No, I don't do handshakes, or autographs. I don't need to know about your nephew. I'm gay. No, not the niece either. Excuse me." I went through a small litany of excuses and gestured for people to keep moving. Fortunately, there was some momentum as those behind were pushing those ahead, and soon enough I'd slipped into the reception room itself.

"Greetings," an android said. It was one of those torso-only models, fixed into place behind a plexiglass wall to give people something to look at when they came in. "Please take a number and wait. A representative of the New Montreal Sewage and Maintenance organization will be with you shortly."

"Uh-huh," I said as I walked past it and to a side door. It had one of those biometric lock things. I barely glanced at it before Myalis had it open. The guy in the button-up followed me in.

"Wait, wait," Button-up said. "You're a samurai?"

"Yeah," I said as I started through a carpeted corridor lined on both sides by offices. The place had an internal map, which I downloaded and opened in my augs. It was just a basic floorplan with the location of different members' offices. And then I realized that I had no idea how to deal with all of this. "Hey, didn't I have an appointment here?" I asked.

"You did?" Button-up asked. He was keeping up.

You did.

"Can you tell the big bosses that I'm here?" I asked him.

He blinked dumbly. "They're not here."

"Well, where are they?" I asked. "Which floor?"

"No, I mean . . . they left."

"Before I arrived?"

He shook his head. "Last night. Just . . . up and fucked right off. Left middle-management to take care of everything. Which isn't so bad, since we usually don't need the C-suite for much."

One moment, let me look into this some more. Ah. It seems as if the organization's entire C-suite has left New Montreal. Or nearly all of them. Two have spoofed some systems to make it seem as if they've gone, but they're still within the city.

"Damnit," I muttered. This didn't bode well for my quick save-the-day plan. "Button-up, what's your job and what do you do?"

Button-up blinked, then stuttered out a quick reply. At least he wasn't too slow on the uptake. "I'm an accountant. I do accounting," he said.

"Been here long?"

"Seven years," he said.

"Good enough. Round up everyone in this organization with a lick of common sense and anyone who's good at getting shit done. Is there a meeting room? Oh, I see a control room there on the map, what's that?"

He shrugged. "The control room? It lets us see the state of the stuff we maintain. I'm in accounting, I don't take care of that part."

"Fine, tell everyone to meet me there in . . . call it fifteen minutes." I spun on a heel and started down the corridor, only for Button-up to run past me. He was sweating, and it didn't look like he was enjoying this all that much.

Then again, more and more of the city was without water and without plumbing. People being a little sweaty wasn't a big loss.

I walked through the corridor, then started following the map, only slowing down to let some office drones move past. Most were human, but the office did employ a few literal drones that zipped around delivering papers and office . . . stuff. This place felt like it was on the edge of falling into chaos, and I could understand that. The leadership had jumped ship already, which usually meant that the ship was sinking. And now I had to fix it.

I ran into security halfway to the command room. Two overweight guys, looking particularly nervous, blocked my path before a sort of checkpoint station. It was one of those booths where you'd need to present a card or something to be let in deeper.

"Uh, halt?" one of them said.

The other smacked him in the side. "Can we help you, samurai, sir?"

"Yeah," I said. "People aren't allowed on the other side?"

Smarter-guard shook his head. "No ma'am, samurai, ma'am. Command has sensitive information and systems, and not just anyone can be let in close to those."

"Right," I said. "Well, *I'm* going in. And so are a bunch of others. Special circumstances and all that. The city's falling apart, and this place is supposed to prevent that and it's not, so . . . yeah, are you two going to help or will we be having problems?" I casually rested my hand atop my laser pointer.

"We'll help!" Smarter said.

"How?" Dumber asked.

"Just be real nice to folk," I said. "Maybe stand at the back of the room and carry anyone too annoying out when I tell you to. Are you all there is for security?"

"There's one more guy in the camera room," Smarter said. "We're all that's here."

Three people for three floors with some rather sensitive shit in them. Well, moderately sensitive. It was just the sewer controls. The worst that could happen was . . . probably already happening.

"Alright, fine," I said as I continued. An alarm went off, probably detecting that I wasn't authorized personnel and that I was packing, but I kept on moving through. There was a city's worth of unshowered people to save!

CHAPTER TEN

THE STINK

Sewage as a system was a mistake.
—Former Mayor Bennico of New Montreal, 2038

"Can someone explain why all of this is the way it is?" I asked.

I was standing in the command room, which was an old-school sort of place, with several dozen workstations all facing one wall with massive screens and holographic readouts on it. The workstations were a mess of knobs and buttons and touch-screens, with little keyboards at the bottom and enough stuff going on to put the average nuclear submarine to shame.

Right now, the wall-to-wall main screen was displaying what looked very much like a readout of the state of the city's sewer system. Green, I imagined, was good. Orange was probably a little fucky. And red was bad.

Everything was red.

That wasn't *quite* true. There were a few sections still tenaciously clinging to their greenness, but the orange was encroaching in, and there were a few splotches of orange in the sea of red.

But it was mostly red.

"Um, are you supposed to be here?" a timid office-looking lady asked. She was behind one of the workstations near the middle of the room. I noticed that most of them were unoccupied, which was probably not ideal considering the number of warnings I was seeing on their screens. But what did I know? I was just a girl with a gun.

"Who's going to stop me?" I asked her. "Besides, I'm here to fix this shit. And it definitely looks like a lot of shit's going on."

The door into the command room opened, and Button-up stepped in, accompanied by five more clearly-reluctant employees. One of the guards who had accosted me earlier—Smart—followed him in.

"Miss Samurai," Button-up said. "I've gathered some of the people you asked for. This is Aaron Mitchell, head of cybersecurity; Brenda Rodriguez, the highest ranking member of our mesh-interface division; Charles

Whitaker, an on-site engineer; his assistant engineer, and this is Diana Nguyen, from HR; and Ethan Brown, the senior member of maintenance."

I nodded and looked over the group. They were all mostly office-worker sorts, though some of their work habits showed in their manner of dress. Lots of sloppy untucked shirts and crooked ties. There was a lot of anxiety. Shifting feet, wandering hands. These folk weren't the kind of people that should ever have to meet a samurai in person. I, of course, instantly forgot all of their names and waved off the two who came to shake my hand and do proper intros. "Alright, so shit's fucked, but I need to know what flavor of fucked we're dealing with."

Button-up glanced at his comrades, who had formed more or less a semicircle around me. They glanced at each other, then one of them—HR chick, Nguyen or whatever—stepped up to the plate. "Things aren't looking good on the employment front. We have the highest turnover rate we've ever had."

"How bad?" I asked.

"One hundred and thirty-seven percent."

I frowned. I wasn't great at math, but that sounded . . . wrong. "How?" I asked.

"Nearly half of all the employees are gig workers, and some are double-booked for several quarter-time jobs," she explained. "If they don't show up, and they haven't been, then things go . . . sideways. Usually we'd just hire more, but the market for employment isn't optimal at the moment."

"What she means to say," the security head said, "is that with the incursion, everyone has either fled, or is working for a PMC. The hiring is better, the pay is better, and a lot of people want to help on the front because otherwise it might mean that we'll all be eaten by the week's end."

"Right," I said. "And the C-suite?"

"Gone," Nguyen confirmed.

"Okay," I replied. "Other problems?"

The engineering guys looked at each other, and I could almost see the discussion passing between them over a private network. Finally, one of them spoke up. "Like Diana said, a lot of the maintenance personnel were gig workers, so they're gone. But even before that, we've been lagging behind on maintenance for years. We're lacking tools, materials, people with training, access to the places we need to maintain, and the backup we'd need to reach those places. Some sectors have been red for over a year and we can't do anything about them. Do . . . do you know who the Sewer Dragons are?"

"I'm intimately familiar," I said.

"Right. They did a lot of the deeper work. We'd slip them materials, they'd patch things up. We'd get to mark it down as done without stepping into their territory. They gave up, broke apart, or something. Not answering calls, not in the sewers anywhere. Basically, if we want the work done, we need to do it ourselves now, and that's a problem since there are only maybe a hundred certified people left to do decades' worth of work."

"Fantastic," I said. "So everything's all sorts of screwed, then?"

He shrugged in a sort of *what can you do* way, and I couldn't even be mad at him. Clearly people had been skimming from the top . . . and the middle . . . and the bottom, and now it was time to pay the piper.

"Anyone else have problems to add to the pile?" I asked.

"Things have passed the event horizon of bad," the other engineer said. "It's going to get a lot worse, very rapidly. By tomorrow we'll have bursts on multiple levels, brown water will flood some levels, and with the automatic shut-offs, we're going to have pipes backing up in literally every megabuilding in the city all at the same time."

I closed my eyes for a moment, then glanced at the wall again. I didn't think it was just my imagination, but it looked like there was just a little bit more red on there than there had been several moments before. "Okay, cool, I need solutions."

"The . . . the sewage system for the city was built piece-by-piece, often before the buildings connected to it were built at all," the same engineer said. "It cost billions then, and a lot of the parts had to be custom made. There's no . . . just replacing those. Which is what we'd need to do if everything fails."

I glared at him, not that he could see my expression through my helmet. "I'm not asking for an even worse assessment, I'm looking for solutions. Can the system be fixed?"

There was more discussion, with a lot of engineering terminology that was beyond me. But the consensus they came to was simple enough. Sorta.

"The worst of the damage can be mitigated, but we'll need a lot more hands working on fixing things. Then we can reopen the system, one part at a time."

I nodded along, then stepped back, turning so that I was facing the screen of red fully. I felt better without making eye contact with . . . the people whose names I'd all already forgotten.

"Myalis," I muttered. "What can we do here?"

That would depend entirely on how much you're willing to invest into the problem. If you allocate the necessary resources, you'll end up quite broke, but New Montreal will have a functional sewer system by the end of the month.

I checked the date. We weren't near the end of the month. "Shit," I said. The implication there was rather obvious. I wasn't about to sink all of my resources into sewage. "Alright, so intermediary steps," I said.

Again, that depends on the resources you want to sink into the project. Do you want to give the maintenance people better equipment like you did for the Kittens in Burlington? That could be relatively inexpensive and will make them more productive, but with the current situation, it's unlikely to prevent a collapse, only delay it from happening for a little longer. If you want, you could invest in drones and automated repair systems that would slowly fix the sewers. The more drones, the faster they'll be able to fix things, but they would still need raw resources to work with.

"I'm not going to be able to fix all of this on my own," I said, both because I reached the obvious conclusion, and because I wanted the others here to know.

A few shoulders slumped, but it seemed as if that was expected already.

"Which means . . . we're going to have to bully others for help. HR girl, I want you and everyone you can to cut the pay from the C-suite, split it between the rest of the employees evenly. My AI will send you instructions on how to empty their accounts too."

On it.

I pointed to the engineers next. "I'm going to be threatening the others until they come around to help. We'll still need you to do some work. Lots of it, even."

"Yes, ma'am," the head engineer said with a quick salute. He did have that ex-military bearing to him.

"Security guy . . . just, do your job, I guess."

"Uh, okay," Smart said.

I nodded, proud of a job well done so far. If I couldn't fix the problem, then I'd take a page from the Karen playbook and just bully the shit out of someone else to fix the problem.

Which meant that my next stop was the Family's New Montreal headquarters.

CHAPTER ELEVEN

SMILING FACES

Corporate culture generally differs from company to company. If you're a job-hopper, you might suddenly discover that what was acceptable on one jobsite is no longer so on another. This can be confusing or even distressing to discover.

Nonetheless, there are some things that are universal, such as how to treat a higher-up, or how to handle HR!

—"Job-Hopping and You!" article, 2046

I moved with a slight sense of urgency. Back out of the maintenance place, up the elevator, and straight to my waiting bike.

Once on it, I shot out of the side of the building, then up and into the sky, letting the autopilot do much of the work while I thought about the situation.

Shit was fucked in a big way, and this was only the sewers. If something as relatively important as the waste and water systems were in this bad of shape, then how badly off was all the rest? Was the city's electrical grid about to go down? Its internet and Mesh connections? Would public transport just . . . shit the bed?

Actually, the last had done that from the moment it was built, but I could always count on it getting worse, somehow.

What I couldn't count on was the Family being gung-ho about fixing it right away. They were the biggest samurai organization in North America, but that didn't mean it was all sunshine and rainbows. They were supposed to help and support samurai, to give them—us—a logistical hub to work with. They mostly did just that, but I didn't believe it was all altruism and happy feelings all the way down.

The Family's HQ wasn't far. They'd stationed themselves close to the newer downtown area, somewhere more or less between the NMSM Headquarters and my place, and when the Family installed themselves, they did so at the top of one of the bigger skyscrapers.

There was a particular and not very specific distinction between a sky-scraper and a megabuilding. Skyscrapers were tall, thin buildings, some-times fancied up with spiraling architecture and lots of glass. They were showpieces as well as living and working spaces.

My new home was in a skyscraper.

A megabuilding was a fuck-huge block of concrete and despair. They were so fat and large that from afar they didn't look all that tall. It wasn't until you compared them to the skyscrapers next to them that you realized that they were about the same height.

The highways and skylanes passed through the megabuildings, because going around would add an hour to anyone's commute. That was less about the distance and more about shitty traffic, but whatever.

I zipped through a couple of big blocky buildings, then back up toward the top of a skyscraper whose entire upper floor section was narrowed to a shiny point, like the end of a fat teardrop. The side of the swooping sec-tion was open to the elements, revealing several floors of parking space for hovercars.

Nice hovercars, I noted as I came in for a landing. There wasn't a mom van or old beater in sight. The cheapest car in the lot was a German import and it was only a couple of years old at most. The rest were all luxury sedans, mini-limos, and Italian supercars.

I parked my bike by the side of an elevator entrance and then swung my leg over the side of it to dismount. By the time I was standing, a man was walking out of the elevator at a bit of a rush and moving toward me.

"Stray Cat," he said with a bobbing nod of his head. "Welcome to the Family New Montreal Headquarters. I'm Eric. I was assigned as your guide." Eric the guide paused and quickly tugged his jacket on straighter, then adjusted his tie before giving me a winning smile.

"Hey," I said. "Is this normal? Having a guide?" I gestured between the two of us.

"Of course," he said. "The Family exists to assist samurai, and so we're always ready to expect the arrival of one or the other. Is there anything in particular we can help you with?"

I raised a finger at him in a "one second" gesture. "Myalis, did you tell them that I'd be coming?" I asked. Eric here was out and ready to greet me in under a minute, and unless he was waiting in the elevator all the time, that was just suspicious.

I did notice that you were tracked on the way over. The headquarters has a number of radar installations around the roof that keep tabs on incoming and outgoing traffic. Your bike was flagged from a distance.

So, this could be innocent. And I didn't really have a reason to be suspi-cious right out of the gate. Except I was anyway. I hadn't lived this long by trusting corps to have my best interest at heart. "Alright, thanks, Eric," I said. "Maybe you can help me."

"Of course. What do you need assistance with?"

"The sewers," I said.

Eric blinked, but he pretty much instantly started to follow me as I headed toward the elevator. "The sewers? Um, one moment . . . ah, there are a few outstanding reports about wastewater management issues?"

I glanced his way and noticed that his eyes had a particular glimmer to them. Was he connected to some local Family network? Actually, scratch that, it would have been weird for him not to be. We got into the elevator, and I noticed that I'd gotten several pings to my augs since landing on the roof.

I idly checked them out. An invitation to the local wifi network, a link to some page with local rules, a few feel-good ads about the Family. Surprisingly, no pop-ups and redirection ads, or any outright scummy malware shit.

"So, the sewer system for the city's fucked," I said.

"Do you want the Family to intercede with the local authorities about it?" Eric asked.

"No, I did that already. They're fucked too, and those responsible fucked off. I might have emptied their accounts for them, though, so they probably won't go as far as they'd wished. What we need right now is manpower, and a lot of people who know what they're doing. *If* we get on top of things, then maybe we can stop things from getting significantly worse. Hell, maybe we can turn it around and start actually fixing things."

"And just to be clear," Eric said. "This is a priority for you, Stray Cat?"

"I'm on vacation," I explained.

He nodded, as if my vague response made perfect sense.

I was getting the feeling that if I told Eric the moon was made of cheese, he would nod and agree without an ounce of hesitation.

The elevator door opened again, and I realized that we were on another floor. I hadn't even felt it moving. Eric stepped out, and then paused, waiting for me by the threshold with a smile that showed off how much he'd spent on dental. "I'm sure we can help you," he said.

"Right," I said. I was more than a little doubtful about that, but I decided to keep my opinion to myself.

The elevator opened to a lobby area, with comfortable leather seats to one side and a faux fireplace against the other wall with a big-screen TV above it. It was properly fancy, and something about it set me on edge.

"Please, sit down," Eric said with a bow, obsequiousness turned to the max. "Do you want anything to drink? We have water, all the sodas, any sort of liquor or alcohol."

"No," I said.

"Are you certain? There might be a small wait," Eric replied. He had his hands together and bowed a bit as he spoke.

"A wait?" I asked, perking up a little. I wasn't going to lose half of my day off sitting in a waiting room, was I?

"Until the people who will address your issue have time to gather," he replied.

"Right," I said slowly. I looked around the room, then back at Eric, who stood there, just smiling. Weird fucker. This place was giving me more and more bad vibes. I started walking off deeper into the building. Eric followed, his footsteps echoing out ahead of me.

"Myalis," I muttered, keeping my voice down so Eric wouldn't overhear. "I've got a bad feeling."

Interesting. I can't see anything wrong at the moment. Then again, there is suspiciously little to find in terms of electronic signatures. There are entire floors of this building that don't have cameras, and where phones and cybernetic augmentations are shut down.

Extra creepy. What was this place, a black site in the middle of the city? "I . . . don't think I give a shit," I said. "Are they reacting to me being here?" I asked.

Yes. I can see a few executives preparing for a meeting with you.

So, Eric wasn't yanking my chain. I sighed. This was growing increasingly frustrating. I didn't want a meeting, I wanted to tell some idiots what needed doing so that they could jump and *do it.*

"Miss Stray Cat," Eric said. "The meeting room is this way, if you would follow me?"

I bit my tongue. For now, it was probably worth it to just play along. The Family struck me as somewhat corpo, so it made sense that they'd do things their own way. But if they tried to string me along and waste my time, then I'd have to see about expediting things.

Also, I just really enjoyed a good excuse to make some CEO shit themselves. They were infringing on my vacation time, after all.

CHAPTER TWELVE

THE TASTE OF BOOT

Unlike any aesthetic of the past, transhumanism is a permanent one. You might outgrow your goth phase, you might decide one day that you don't want to only wear pastels anymore, and maybe work will force you into an officecore look, but replacing your arms with tentacles is a far, far more permanent statement of aesthetic value, far more so than even something as semi-permanent as a tattoo.

—Excerpt from *Vagrant's Future Fashion Blog*

I hated this very much.

The moment Eric the bootlicker led me into the room, I knew I'd hate it, but I didn't spin around and leave just yet. I still needed the Family's help.

The organization had been useful in the past. They'd bankrolled PMCs to pitch in, they had their own troops, and they were in contact with a multitude of samurai. A few of the samurai that I'd consider friends, or at least acquaintances, were part of the group. Longbow, Deus Ex, a few others.

So I didn't want to ruin the Family's day by throwing a fit. They did good work.

But leading me into a boardroom, with one of those massive all-wood tables surrounded by expensive office chairs and screens on the walls rotating through promotional crap? That was pushing it. I wasn't some exec or C-suite that was here to negotiate, and I sure as shit wasn't going to be impressed by fancy corpo shit.

The room was filled with half a dozen people wearing properly nice suits and nicer smiles. They asked me to sit down, buttered me up with compliments, and asked me if I wanted anything to drink.

When I cut through and started talking about my problem of the day, the sewers, they were all terribly attentive. I got a panoply of "uh-huhs" and "go ons" that rankled me. It was like getting constantly splashed in the face with lukewarm water. Annoying, but not something that'd kill me. It just felt like I was wasting my time in a big way.

"So," I said several minutes later, once I'd explained everything.

The yes-men and yes-women looked at each other, still smiling their empty smiles. The next one whose turn it was to talk nodded. "Of course. The Family exists to help the samurai. If you deem this issue to be of vital importance in safeguarding humanity, then we'll do everything we can to ensure that things get done in a timely manner."

"Right," I said. That's what I wanted to hear. Which was why it bothered me so damned much. "So what's the plan here?"

"Well, first, we should have some people check out the situation below," Yes-Woman One said.

"And then reconvene with their findings. It's only reasonable to know what kind of work needs to be done before we delegate it to the right people," Yes-Man Four said.

"We should hire some professionals. Perhaps set up a council to direct the efforts," Yes-Woman Two added. "Can't have people not know what to do and where our attention will be best spent. You suggested that you might be able to deploy some samurai-grade equipment to help?"

"Yeah, a little," I said. I looked over the group, eyeing them one at a time. "How long do you think this will take?"

They looked between each other again, then as if it had been rehearsed, collectively shrugged . . . "It's impossible to tell," Yes-Man One said. "From your report, it seems like the infrastructure had been left unmaintained for a long time. It might take months to bring everything back to standard. As for patching things up more temporarily, it's impossible to tell with so little data to work from. We'll be sure to put every effort into repairing things, however."

"Right," I said. That part wasn't what I'd wanted to hear, exactly, but a perfectly reasonable and realistic answer.

So why was it rubbing me the wrong way?

The meeting ended with a flurry of handshakes and thank-yous and lots of back patting. I was left with a long list of items that the Family would "enjoy" in order to help them accomplish what I'd asked them to.

Was that the catch? But the list was literally what I was willing to offer to begin with. A few hundred suits capable of functioning in the sewers, some tools from plumbing, a number of repair drones and their blueprints. Myalis tallied it up, and it added up to nearly ten thousand points, but that felt . . . low?

"Myalis," I muttered as I left the boardroom. Eric was, of course, waiting for me just outside, but at that point I'd stopped caring much.

Yes, Catherine?

"What was all that?"

From what I can tell, they are being, for the most part, honest.

"Most part?"

I suspect that any equipment you give them will be carefully observed and cataloged, and the moment it is no longer in use, it will be deconstructed and new patents will be drawn up. In light of that, it's possible that in the long term, the Family might make more money from your involvement than their assistance here would cost them.

"Make money off of sewer maintenance tools?" I asked.

I'm aware you have no way of knowing this, but most Vanguard who purchase items either buy things to improve their quality of life, or items that allow them to better kill the Antithesis. Tools meant to be used by ordinary people are an uncommon purchase. It stands to reason that they'd be more valuable than a new weapons platform.

"Huh." I said. That actually made some sense. And it made me feel better. Was that the only way they planned to screw me over? Probably not, but at least I knew of one of them, and it didn't bother me too much. That was reassuring.

A corp was always going to fuck you over. There were only two ways to deal with that: you either had to know what they were planning early enough to avoid it, or be prepared to mess them up first.

Being a samurai didn't change that reality. It just gave me better tools, so I was more often than not the one doing the messing.

"Can you keep an eye on them?" I asked.

Certainly. Although some members of the organization have already reached out to several plumbing companies within the region, it seems as if they're attempting to hire independent gig workers as well.

So, they *were* getting to work, and without all the jerking around I'd been expecting. "Okay . . . okay, cool," I said.

Maybe I wouldn't have to throw a fit or toss someone off a building after all. That was nice.

As I left the building—Eric still in tow—I couldn't help but feel a slight sense of disappointment. The meeting was professional, and their answers were technically correct, yet despite all that, there was still just something . . . off. Maybe it was the dissonance between their fancy office and the grimy, failing infrastructure I had just seen. Or maybe it was the overly polite, corporate way they wanted to handle the issue.

I paused outside of the building. The exit wasn't so far from the edge, and on a whim I walked over to it. Eric didn't follow. I imagined that he was sane enough not to want to stand on the very edge of a very long fall, especially not when there was little protecting us from the wind.

Looking down, I could see all of New Montreal, or maybe just this one half of it on this side of the building. I was up high enough here that few buildings pushed higher.

The city being this massive from this height put things into a weird perspective. The individual problems of the people below were minuscule, but at the same time, this was a massive place, and anything that I didn't fix, like the sewers, would hurt millions.

Maybe that was it? The upper echelon of the Family was detached from the rest of the city, living so high above it all. They didn't see the grime and shit. To them, the issues of the world below were purely intellectual.

That was my world, though. They were in their clean suits, surrounded by glass and steel, talking about the city's problems like they were numbers on a screen, while I was the one who would have to go down there, get my hands dirty, and deal with the issues head-on.

"Time to get back to the grind," I muttered to myself, looking one last time over the cityscape. My vacation was on hold until this got sorted out. I was eager to get back to work on my mech, eager to spend time with Lucy, but not so much that I'd just let things fall to the side and let the world go to shit for so many people.

You still have an appointment with the mayor tomorrow afternoon.

"I'll be there. He needs to answer for why this wasn't taken care of already," I said. "In fact, I think I can trace a lot of the blame here back to his office." People followed examples, and the mayor should have been setting the trend. It wasn't a good sign that anyone in a position of power in the municipality was running away.

Let me look things over. The local government does have oversight over this sort of thing. Infrastructure maintenance is one of their primary duties.

"You do that," I said. "I'm looking forward to my chat tomorrow. Bet there's a whole lot to learn. And a lot to answer for."

CHAPTER THIRTEEN

LONG DAY

Keep in mind that different vegetables need to be cooked differently. Organic vegetables are somewhat more fragile, and yet preferred by many. They need to be boiled, sauteed, baked, or otherwise cooked before being cut and prepared for serving. Synthetic vegetables usually come pre-cooked at the right consistency and are pre-cut and ready to serve or mix into a larger recipe.

—Footnote in Home Cooking, 2044

I walked into our bedroom, shuffled over to the bed while shucking off my coat, then did a half-spin and fell back-first onto the bed.

"Long day?" Lucy asked.

"Yeah," I said to the ceiling. "I had to deal with *people*."

"Aww, poor kitty cat," Lucy crooned. She moved over the surface of the bed, and soon I found her sitting just above me, soft pajama-clad thighs on either side of my head. Her face hovered over mine, upside-down from my skewed perspective as she started to press her fingers into and through my hair. "Wanna talk about it?" she asked.

I let out a sigh, part frustration, part relaxation as she pressed into my scalp in just the right way. "I headed out to see about the sewers," I started.

"Mm-hmm, you'd mentioned it."

"Yeah. I figured they were kinda fucky, but didn't know *how* fucky they were, you know?" I said. "There's this corp called the . . . New Montreal Sewage Maintenance . . . something or other. I can't remember their name."

"That's a terrible name for a corp," Lucy said. "You'd think they'd go with Sewageco, or something banal like Green Solutions."

I chuckled. "Yeah. I think it was city-operated for a while, then it went private. At least, that's the impression I was getting. They're the ones who are actually supposed to be taking care of the sewage and water and all that."

"Oh, so Brown Solutions is a better name, then?" she asked.

I laughed. "Yeah, maybe. Got there and all the C-suite suits had run off. Myalis nabbed their bank accounts, but they're still gone. I don't have the time or energy to chase after them. I swear, people are such . . . urgh."

"They probably had a good thing going. Skim off the taxes people pay for maintenance, maybe keep some corps properly connected to the water lines for a little extra on the side."

I nodded. "Yeah, the usual shit. It's not even imaginative. It's almost insulting how predictable it all is. I mean, come on, are we in a capitalist hellscape or a kleptocracy? Someone should teach these people to stick to their lanes."

Lucy leaned way forward and pressed a kiss on my forehead. "It's okay. Did you find a way to fix things?"

"Not really, no. Got the employees back on task, promised them some support, then ran to the Family. The non-samurai part of the Family's *weird*, by the way. Too many smiles, too much . . . enthusiasm. It creeped me right out."

"Bad vibes?"

"Weird vibes," I clarified. "I think they'll actually try though, which is nice. If they don't, then I'll have to be disappointed at them."

"Disappointed *at* them?" Lucy repeated.

"Mm-hmm, I've got all this stealth crap and rarely use it. Bet I can scare the smiles right off their faces if I apply myself a little. But I'm on *vacation*, and you keep telling me I'm not supposed to be working this hard."

"Did you just want to sleep it off?" Lucy asked.

I groaned, then with a monumental show of effort, sat myself up. "I'm going to go play outside," I said.

Lucy snorted. "You mean work on your mech? I'll cook you something to eat."

"You'll cook?" I asked. Lucy had never *cook*-cooked anything before. Not unless it went in the microwave or came in a box. Making mac and cheese counted as cooking, I supposed, but that almost felt like a cop-out. She'd arranged different ordered foods together into a proper meal once or twice, but that was about the extent of it.

Her cheeks flushed, almost unnoticeably. "I want to learn. You're just going to have to suffer through my culinary experimentation."

"Whatever you say, Chef Lucy," I replied as I finally got to my feet. I decided to leave my coat on the floor. It was a bit heavy for mechanical work. Though . . . maybe it was raining outside? I wasn't so sure. In any case, I now had a good reason to build up an appetite. "So what's on the menu today?"

"I'm not going to start with anything complicated," Lucy said. "I ordered some fish, and I have broccoli, and brown rice. Can't really mess that up, I think."

That did sound nice, I supposed. It wasn't a burger, but I'd probably eaten enough junk food my entire life that I'd ruined my own taste for proper, real food. It wouldn't hurt to step back and eat something mildly healthy for once. I was sure Lucy wouldn't be a five-star chef from the get-go, but I'd eat it all regardless.

"Have you seen Rac?"

Lucy nodded. "She popped by for a few hours. Dumped some things in the printer room, then grabbed some food and ran off again. I think she's back to gathering stuff for the fabricator."

"Did she tell you that?" I asked.

"No, but she changed from her going-out clothes to her picking-up-trash clothes," Lucy said. "I think she's trying to keep her work clothes clean. Or at least, clean*er*."

I hadn't noticed that myself. It made sense, of course. Rac seemed like she wanted her merc friends to think highly of her, and that meant not being dressed in rags. Especially if she really did have a thing for that Garter guy.

"Let me know if she comes back. I just want to check up on her," I said, then a thought crossed my mind. "Have any of the other kittens been getting up to anything?"

"Not really," Lucy said. "Some of them are cheating on their lessons, the ones Miss Grasshopper signed them up for, but I figure learning how to cheat's a good skill too. But otherwise, they're mostly just chilling. Daniel's probably the only one who might move out. He's been finding odd jobs to do on the Mesh, and he left a couple of times to meet some online friends, and to walk around. I don't know where he thinks he's going to live, though. Junior and Katallina are talking about finding work and living the high life, but I think they also like mooching off you, so don't expect them to just disappear."

That was nice to hear. I worried about them being on their own sometimes. Just a little bit, though. Daniel was . . . about my age? A legal adult, or else he was going to be one soon, and he'd probably be fine. But the girls were a bit younger, and I'd be more concerned if they moved out.

"I'll be tinkering," I said. These all felt like long-term things to worry about, not anything pressing.

"Have fun!"

I couldn't find a jacket to wear out into the New Montreal drizzle covering the balcony out front, but a shitty raincoat was only a couple of points from Myalis. I still worried when I bought it though, especially since I had a set of big expenses in my near future. I was determined to fix the sewers at some point, and I was willing to sink about ten thousand points into it.

I'd started my vacation with just shy of forty thousand points. I'd splurged here and there, spending some on stuff at home, tools and drones and more security and some upgrades for the kittens.

Current Points: 33,451

That was a good nest egg. And I was seriously considering burning a third of it away to fix what corpos had ruined . . .

Fortunately, I was still gaining points, about a dozen or so a day. Myalis said that it was mostly people in Burlington scoring some kills using gear I'd given them. So as long as the cleanup continued around Burlington, I'd earn a tidy little amount. Emphasis on little.

Stepping out into the rain, I walked across to my mech, then stretched out my back. "Right, where was I?" I wondered aloud. Myalis's only reply was to bring up some schematics on my HUD, a list of things left to take apart.

The repair drone woke up and floated over, ready to assist.

There was a lot to do still, but for the most part the work wasn't so complicated that I couldn't let my mind wander. It was nice to get lost in it, trying to undo a puzzle that was impossibly complex and which I had no hope of understanding in full, but where I could figure out little pieces of it, where I could tell what was broken and what needed replacing.

It sounded like an ass-pull metaphor for what was going on with New Montreal as a whole. The city was broken. Not so much so that it wasn't functional still, but the break would spread and the problems would only get worse. The wall was holding, but wasn't stopping things from being strained. The corps would be looking to recoup losses, which meant lots of cut corners, people being thrown out of jobs . . . shit, it was getting bleak.

I tackled the things on the repair list one at a time, and for the moment, I was mostly just ripping parts out and tossing them aside or handing them to the repair drone who floated them over to a bin.

Maybe I could squeeze that into my metaphor too?

"Cat!" Lucy called from the entrance. "Supper's ready! Come eat while it's still hot!"

Now . . . how would *that* part fit in? Was Lucy and her supper the samurai, or was she . . . wait, no, I was overthinking this. "Right, I'm coming!" I called back.

CHAPTER FOURTEEN

MAYORAL IMAGE

Protesting as a form of protest—that is to say, the gathering of large crowds rallying for change—is dangerous to the economy, to the health of the individuals, and to the health of a government.

That is why taking immediate, violent action against protestors is often recommended. It puts a complete stop to the protesting action early with a minimal loss of potential revenue and a heavy reduction in the amount of property damage suffered, all for the cost of a few lives.

—Copcore promotional material, 2029

I woke up an hour shy of noon the next day, and the first thing I did, while still half-covered on the bed with a softly breathing Lucy next to me, was check my messages. I'd slept . . . kinda poorly. My stomach was real grumbly all night long. I didn't want to blame Lucy's cooking but, well, she was no better a cook than I was a mechanic at the moment.

There were a lot of messages. Most of them I dismissed while skimming through. The Family had sent a long form with requisitions and updates on the whole sewage situation, and there was a reminder from the mayor's office about our meeting in . . . forty minutes.

I rubbed at my one fleshy eye as I moved on to a kindly worded message from Peter Silverbloom about that prosthetics clinic. "Right. Forgot about that," I muttered. I'd promised him that we'd set something up to help the people we saved from the Sewer Dragons. Free printed prosthetics. "Myalis, can we set up a meeting with him tomorrow?"

Certainly. And good morning, Catherine. I was contemplating waking you up soon. You still have time to shower and dress for your meeting with the mayor.

Did I want to shower and dress for a meeting with the mayor? No, no I did not.

But I had to. Not only did I not want to come off as the sort of person that couldn't be held to her word, I also . . . actually, that was really the only reason. Well, that and I'd just end up having to reschedule the meeting. I yawned and sat up.

Besides, the mayor had some explaining to do. The buck was supposed to stop at his corrupt office, not at my doorstep.

I slithered out from under Lucy, giving her head a peck when she grumbled sleepily, then trudged over to the shower and stood under scalding hot water for a while. The building had some sort of water recuperation and filtration thing going on, separate from the rest of the city's water grid. This was a luxury few people would be able to afford soon if I didn't get moving.

With time ticking onward, I rooted around the bedroom for something to wear, then decided to head out fully kitted. That meant a clean undersuit, good samurai boots, and a long coat, all with enough stealth tech to make me a nightmare to corner.

"Make another note," I said to Myalis. "We need to go clothes shopping at some point."

I couldn't just wear samurai gear all the time. I needed threads for more casual stuff. Lucy was having fun printing T-shirts, but I sure as shit wasn't going to wear a shirt that said "Wired Wrong" or "My Girlfriend Has Vibrating Fingers" on it.

The shirt with "I Know Where Cat's Reset Button Is" on it was just too lewd to be seen in public. Although . . . it might embarrass the mayor.

Oh well, next time. I was already dressed, and I had only twenty minutes to get to the meeting nearly halfway across the city.

I snuck out the front of our place, noting that some of the kittens were already up and some hadn't gone to sleep yet. I waved them goodbye before heading out.

It was, of course, raining, so I slipped on my helmet (which I'd definitely need to drive around anyway) then walked over to my bike, which I'd parked near the mech. Myalis was kind enough to have already punched in the location data, so the bike knew where I was going before I even took off.

The flight was what I'd expect from a trip across New Montreal. Long and tedious, even if I was cutting across traffic and zipping through no-fly zones the entire time. Myalis kept a running tally of the automated tickets I was getting, which were just as automatically dismissing themselves.

The mayor's office was in the city council building, which I noticed had a bit of a crowd forming at the front. Dozens of people, some with cheap signs, others with holographic projectors sending out banner messages over their heads. Then there were the police and the news crews, all crowding closer to the front.

Had word gotten out about the sewage? It was rare to see crowds gathering like this. Protesting was super illegal, and the cops weren't shy about opening up on a crowd. Then again, the city was in a deep shithole at the moment, and the cops lining up behind the fence looked a little . . . anemic from up in the air. No big groups of fully armored SWAT troopers, no combat androids, just a few dozen guys in light riot gear.

They'd get seriously fucked if the crowd turned on them.

I hesitated. I could park nearby, somewhere discreet and out of the way, then slip into the building nice and subtle-like. Hell, I could park on the roof and kick my way in, then just walk over to the mayor and say hi.

But those people were there protesting because no one was doing anything. At least, that's what I figured most protests were about.

So I swept down and revved the engine on my bike before lowering it down right onto the steps by the front of the city hall building. Dust kicked up around me as I swept off the bike. The crowd was shouting, the cops were confused, but no one seemed willing to stop me. So I left the bike there, still running so that it wouldn't just tip off the side and roll down the steps.

I felt a little under-armed at the moment as I looked over the crowd. All I had was my Trench Maker.

I really needed to get into the habit of carrying a bit more with me.

A few calls of "Stray Cat!" proved that at least a few people in the crowd knew who I was. Hopefully that'd be enough to let them know that something was being done.

I walked up the rest of the steps and checked the time. I was right on the dot as I crossed through the entrance. There were some more cops inside, hands on their short-barreled auto shotguns, but none of them moved to do anything as I crossed the lobby toward the receptionist. "Meeting with the mayor," I said.

The young lady behind the counter, an actual human instead of a droid, jumped and nodded. "Yes ma'am, we were expecting you. The mayor said he'd meet you down here."

"Alright," I said.

A pair of double doors to my left swung open and out waddled Mayor Dupont. He was somehow imposing for a man that looked part rat, part politician. His suit was impeccable and he looked freshly shaven and cleaned up. His gaze locked onto mine, beady, intelligent eyes curling up in the corners with a charismatic smile that I didn't trust for a second. "Stray Cat!" he greeted as he came closer. "I'm glad to see you here, and just on time too, very punctual."

I crossed my arms and pretended not to notice the hand extending to shake. "Only because you've got some explaining to do, Dupont," I said.

"Ah, yes, I know, I know," he said with a shake of his head. "This city, I swear. So many problems and so little time. The sewers, the emergency election, the aliens chomping at the gate. It's quite exciting."

"Uh-huh," I said. He was being more . . . agreeable than the last time I'd talked to him. That felt like it had been a long time ago, as opposed to just a week or two back. "And what do you intend to *do* about it? I warned you that this would happen, and now you have protestors outside with no water and shit flowing out of the drains."

The mayor nodded. "I know. We should have acted sooner. But I do intend to do something, and right now. If you would, please follow me."

Curious despite myself, I followed Dupont. He didn't head deeper into the building, but toward the exit I'd just come in from.

Dupont stepped right outside, and one of his aides kept the door open for me to follow after him. The noise of the crowd grew considerably as they saw him, and I imagined he was currently the image of a lot of hate.

Then Dupont moved to the side, grabbed the lapels of his coat, and gestured to the crowd with a big winning smile. Another aide rushed over and soon a small drone-mounted microphone was hovering before him. "My dear citizens!" he began.

The crowd actually quieted down.

"I can see that you are upset, and rightly so!" he continued.

Catherine, this is being broadcast across a number of channels.

And I was right there, in the background, arms crossed but with the framing it probably looked like I was tacitly supporting him.

The absolute fucker.

"Our city is facing a myriad of issues, and I assure you, they are not being ignored! It pains and yet gladdens me to see so many gathered here in protest. You are right to be upset, but we will overcome this challenge together. We are too resilient, too tough to allow some adversity to put us down."

Dupont stepped to the side slightly and gestured back toward me. Suddenly I could feel thousands of eyes on me.

How long had he been planning this for? Since I made that appointment? Did he know I'd park out front? Fucker.

"Ladies and gentlemen and others, meet Stray Cat, one of New Montreal's own, a hero and symbol of the city's strength, and of course a valiant friend of the Dupont management and proof that we *will* solve your, and our, problems!"

"No," I said. No one heard me though, one voice against Dupont's, which was being blasted out from speakers the aide had set up. "Dupont, you sack of shit."

"With the help of New Montreal's own samurai we will . . ." and on and on he went, political nothing, but people were *listening* because I was here.

If I had been in that crowd, what would I have thought?

Samurai were fucking mythical to some people who didn't know better. I'd been one of them, one of those to think that we could fix anything. And now Dupont was rubbing himself all over that image.

I was only aware that I'd pulled my Trench Maker out of its hip-sheath when Dupont's voice cracked.

Probably because the barrel was pointing unwaveringly at his head. "No," I repeated. "Myalis, patch me in."

Done.

"You don't get to use me as a fucking prop to cover up more empty promises. You were given a chance to fix things. I warned you once already. Today was meant to be your second and last."

Dupont's own mic cut off. An aug? An aide pulling the switch? In any case, when he next spoke, it was just between the two of us. "You're going to threaten me in front of this entire crowd? You can only get away with so much. I'm the rightfully elected mayor!"

"You had power. *Had.* You wasted it, didn't even try to make things better." My voice rang out over the square.

"Stray Cat, this isn't a nice image."

"Fuck your image," I said. Then, before he could talk me out of it, I pulled the trigger.

Dupont flopped to the ground, the upper half of his head sprayed out behind him. The crowd, predictably, screamed. The cops were clearly undecided on what to do next.

I turned to the crowd while tucking my gun away. "Go home," I suggested. "Or don't. One way or another I'll fix this."

Waking up before noon was a mistake. It always left me so damned grumpy.

CHAPTER FIFTEEN

EMPIRICAL

Though empirical evidence may have demonstrated that there's no such thing as karma, we still find ourselves attracted to the idea. It is so simple and elegant a system that it's hard not to begin to think that the world works on such karmic scales when we know it does not!

—On the Philosophy of Guilt, 2045

I rode my bike up and to the top of a skyscraper some dozen blocks away, then slowed down and parked on the roof.

Leaning forward, I let my head *thunk* against the bar and closed my eyes. "Fuck," I muttered. The adrenaline was washing off. The image of what I'd just done replayed itself in my head. Of all the times I had to not miss.

"Fuck," I repeated.

Are you okay, Catherine?

I nodded, took a deep breath, then just stewed in the moment. This was going to have consequences. If I was a smarter girl, then I'd be able to guess at those, but right now, I had no fucking clue.

Samurai were above the law. At least, that was how they acted. I'd acted that way too. It was useful, it let me do shit without having to worry, it had let me save lives.

I knew there were stories about samurai shooting politicians, mobsters, CEOs, but those had always sounded like legends. A cynical part of me, a big part, always suspected that those stories existed because it gave stupid rebellious morons like me a reason to believe that there was still some karmic justice out there.

I'd never seen a samurai blow up a politician's head on live TV.

"Wait. Myalis, was that being broadcast live?"

Mayor Dupont's speech? Yes. It was on television as well as several live feed sites. Do you want viewership details?

"Was anyone watching?" I asked. I sure as shit wouldn't watch anything like that. Cartoons would be a better waste of my time than listening to the mayor complain.

Initial viewership was low, but news that the mayor was working with a samurai spiked viewership. Initial views started at around thirty thousand and increased to 2.2 million at the time of your shot.

"Shit," I muttered. I didn't mind being known, but I wasn't sure I wanted to be known for *this.*

The clips have gone viral. It would be a considerable amount of work to track down the total viewership of those, but it's safe to assume that it's in the tens of millions already.

It had only been a few minutes! I groaned. There was no hiding this.

I imagine it will spread a lot more as the afternoon goes on. If it helps, initial views suggest a generally positive response.

Yeah, no shit. Pre-samurai me would have been gobbling this shit up. The ugly mayor getting his skull vented after being a douchebag would have been like poetry. Okay, so I was still kinda proud, but this was going to have consequences.

I flicked a few buttons on my augs and made a call.

Lucy picked up on the third ring. "Huh?" she asked. She was very clearly still asleep.

"Hey, Lucy," I said, voice low and reassuring. "I had the meeting with the mayor."

"Oh, yeah, okay," she said. I heard her yawn, then shift around. She was definitely still in bed. "So?"

"Lucy, how would you like to be the new mayor?" I asked.

Lucy was quiet for a while. "I'm going back to bed. Night."

I blinked. "She hung up on me," I said.

You did disturb her sleep. You'd have had the same reaction.

Well, I wasn't going to call her a second time. That would just annoy her. Taking a deep breath, I shifted on the seat of my bike, then gave it a bit of gas and rode off the edge of the roof. "Let's head back to Family HQ," I said as I entered the address into the bike's autopilot. "The meeting with the mayor was supposed to convince the city to clear up some shit, get the ball rolling. Maybe they needed to expedite permissions or do some bullshit paperwork or whatever."

You suspect that won't be a problem any longer?

"Do you think whoever's gonna take his place is going to stonewall us?" I asked.

It's highly unlikely.

Yeah, I figured as much. Whichever poor intern or career politician had to fill in for Dupont would probably be pretty aware that they were even more expendable than he was. If I was in their shoes, I'd be walking real carefully and jumping at shadows.

I approached the Family's headquarters and glided to a stop in the rooftop parking lot, leaving my bike near the entrance. I took my time slipping off the bike, giving the Family some time to figure out that I was here. "Should I expect any trouble here?" I asked.

Hmm . . . this is interesting.

I froze up. "What is?" Were they planning to off me? It wouldn't have surprised me all that much. I started to check my gear.

It seems as if the Family was planning on assisting you with your sewer repair and reconstruction project.

"Good! That's exactly what we—wait . . . *was* planning?"

They had yet to truly begin other than to appoint some interns to start communicating with outside groups. One moment . . . I'm in their communication suites. It seems like the work they did overnight was perhaps less than what they could have done if they put all of their efforts into the project.

"I was getting sidelined?" I asked. The fuckers. Then again, the Family was a big deal. They probably had a lot of work going on across a lot of the city, and beyond New Montreal as well.

"Was" is the operative term. It seems that news of your interaction with the mayor has reached the Family and that, in turn, has encouraged them to increase the priority of your mission.

I had been expecting the consequences of my actions to be negative for me. This sounded like it was pretty much the opposite. I started heading toward the elevator doors, only for them to open up and for Eric to stumble out of the elevator. "Miss Stray Cat," he greeted. Eric was sweatier than I remembered him being, and his guileless smile had taken on a new look. "We weren't expecting you."

"I came to see how things were progressing," I said.

"Ah . . . yes, of course. That's your prerogative. Yes, of course. Please follow me? The, ah, group in charge of your project is hard at work, but I'm sure they'll make some time for you."

Cat, you might want to see this.

I slipped into the elevator while Myalis brought up a small screen in my augs. It was a camera view from somewhere in the building. I recognized some of the people as the smiling weirdos I'd seen last time I was here. Yet this time, instead of smiling and nodding, they were panicking.

The audio popped into my ear. "She's coming! She's coming and we don't have *shit* to show her?" one of them was saying.

"Calm the fuck down. It's not that bad. It's been barely a day, she can't expect us to be that far along already," another said.

"She can expect us to have done *something*!" Shouty replied. "I barely put an hour in last night."

"We did do something," one of the women shot back. She was a good deal calmer, though she lacked that blank corporate composure they all had yesterday. "Let's present what we have and hope that it's enough."

I cut away from the camera feed and laughed. Eric spun around to look at me, but I waved him off. "I saw a funny meme," I explained.

"Ah, of course," he replied.

The elevator stopped at the same floor as the last time, and Eric went through the same spiel, asking if I wanted something to drink, and politely asking that I sit down and wait.

It was a lot easier to wait when I knew that the people making me wait were the ones dreading the meeting. Based on what I had just seen, I had a few minutes of sitting around to do, so I split my attention between watching Myalis's spy-feed and checking out some local media sites. The video of the mayor getting shot was out already. The official livestream had cut off nearly as soon as my Trench Maker fired. Fortunately, there were some hundred-odd people in the crowd filming everything, so there were dozens of angles of the mayor getting hit.

It was still weird seeing myself in third person. I couldn't help but notice how strangely I stood there. It looked like I didn't give a shit that a crowd was watching. I should have been a little more self-conscious or something, because this didn't look natural.

Some people had a gift for being charismatic while just standing there. I wasn't one of those people.

"Miss Stray Cat, they're ready to see you now," Eric said as I was going through a third video of the shooting, this time with VTuber commentary.

I followed him into a boardroom. The smiling faces were all at their places, grins fixed, but I noticed the sweat. I could almost smell it on them. "So," I said as I grabbed the seat at the head of the table and pulled it away so that I could stand there. "Tell me about your progress."

CHAPTER SIXTEEN

BOARD MEETING

Not all of the new technology we have came from the Protectors. In fact, most of it is human-made. Human ingenuity counts for the majority of new creative technologies, and I won't waste my time listening to people who think that everything we've worked hard to invent is merely deconstructions of alien technology.

—Bob Manperson, defending his company's patents in a congressional hearing, 2029

Corporate board meetings were a lot more enjoyable when everyone else at the table was aware that you might shoot them. That was a nice discovery, but I didn't get to revel in it for all that long.

We were only half an hour into the meeting when my phone app went off. "One sec," I said as I stepped back from the table. After the first ten minutes or so, I had started to regret shoving the chair away at the start. Sure, it made me more intimidating, but my feet were starting to ache from standing for so long. "Got a call, I'll be back."

I stepped out of the room and into the corridor just outside while answering the call. It was from Lucy.

"You shot the mayor," she said as an introduction.

"Hi Lucy," I replied. "Love you too."

She sighed. "Cat, why are you on TV?"

"Because I . . . shot him?" I said. "I can fancy it up, if you want?"

"Fancy it up?" she asked.

I grinned. "I ensured that his chances of re-election were diminished," I said while trying to sound as snooty as possible.

It worked. Lucy snorted on the other end of the line. "You're such an idiot," she said fondly. "Also, no, I don't want the job."

"You sure?" I asked. "You'd get a swanky office. And get to wear girlboss suits. You'd look really hot."

"I generally don't think someone should get into politics just so they can wear cool suits and have a nice office," Lucy said. "Also, if you wanted to see me in a suit, you just had to ask. I'm sure something could be arranged."

I laughed. "I might take you up on that. We haven't done any shopping, have we? I was just thinking I needed some new streetwear. Maybe we can hit up some shops in a couple of days. Tomorrow will be busy, and today's a bust, but the day after?"

"Sure," Lucy said. "I wouldn't mind that at all. What are you up to now? Hiding from the cops?"

"Nah, cops wouldn't know what to do with me. I'm at the Family's HQ, scaring them shitless. I think they were planning on being lazy about the whole sewer thing, even after I came here, hat in hand, asking for their help. Now they've clearly reconsidered. It's nice."

"Reputation's important. You just reconfigured the mayor's brainpan in front of a million people. That'll make people think twice about messing with you. That'll be good and bad."

"Yeah," I agreed. "I'll have to see how it shakes out in the long run. But, uh, there's no undoing that one. Even if Myalis went nuts and deleted all the footage, it would still circulate."

"Can't put the bullet back in the barrel?" Lucy asked.

I shook my head. "That was awful."

"I try," Lucy chuckled. "Think the Family will be able to handle everything now?"

"No. I'll still need to help them so that they can help me, but at least they're taking the sewer situation seriously now. I . . . should probably go."

"That's okay," she said. "You'll be back soon? I'm making submarines. I've got chicken and bacon and turkey and tofu and six kinds of cheese."

"Are you going to put any vegetables in the subs?" I asked.

"Where would I fit them?"

"I can't wait to try it out. Keep some for me, I should be back home in . . . urgh, three, maybe four hours?"

"Alright," Lucy said. "Love ya."

"Love ya too," I replied as I carefully hung up.

I stood in the corridor for a moment, eyes closed as I let the stress settle. The back of my mind had been going for a while, worrying about everything all at once, but Lucy was okay with what I had done, and besides, she was probably right. This might be a good thing. Dupont deserved it, in any case. The ass was putting the entire city at risk with his bullshit.

Maybe I could talk to some friends about it? Gomorrah had a level head for this kind of stuff. Though I wasn't sure about her stance when it came to shooting people as opposed to burning aliens.

Oh well.

Turning around, I stepped back into the conference room, grabbed the chair I'd shoved aside earlier, and sat myself down at the head of the table. "Alright, sorry about that. Where are we now?"

What followed was a fairly productive hour. The suits might have come here to appease me, but once they caught on that I wanted to *work*, not just have my ass kissed, they started to actually put in the time to get things done.

The meeting turned into a more spread-out . . . thing, with the different suits making calls, checking over AI-drafted emails and riding the backs of some poor interns and underlings to push things along. I mostly asked questions and tried not to look stupid. There was a method to all of this that these suits knew. The right person had to be called in the right way, bribes had to go out, people needed to be talked to, companies outside of the Family needed cool tech dangled in front of their noses to catch their attention.

"Huh," I said after being quiet for nearly half an hour. I'd decided not to intrude as much after a while. They didn't need me riding them too hard to do their jobs now, so I was mostly poking at things that Myalis was highlighting for me. That "huh" got some heads to rise, so I pointed to one of the office chicks. "That company you hired, uh . . . Green Impact Ecological Sewage? They just took your cash and funneled it away. They're not doing shit."

"Um," she said. "Thank you. I'll start the charge-back proceedings and send the contract to legal."

I nodded, then continued to skim through Myalis's reports. She was able to more or less verify every company, subsidiary, and independent contractor, which was impressive because with every hour that passed another couple hundred people were mobilized toward fixing the sewers.

This was quickly growing into a *project*. I didn't like the idea of multiple levels of management, but with so many companies working together all at once, it was going to be impossible to keep tabs on anyone without that kind of net.

Maybe the Family's slow moves at the start were justified after all. A little bit. They were still slow-rolling me, but some of these things could only move so fast. Committees to arrange committees.

"Ah, Miss Stray Cat," Eric said as he came over. If he had a hat, he'd be holding it in his little hands looking pitiful with it. "We've arranged a space for you to summon up the equipment you, um, agreed to provide, ma'am."

"Right," I said. "You guys in here keep up the good work."

The work *was* starting to move forward. Slowly. The first people being sent on site were inspectors. Independently hired ones, with at least a few years of experience and a low corruption index score. Some were scouring the sewers right now, checking on the state of things and sending their findings back.

It was bleak, for the most part. There were some areas that were better than I'd hoped, mostly close to some corps that had decided to maintain things on their own dime for a while. Other parts were outright fucked. There was a section of a main sewer line that had apparently collapsed months ago, the entire pipe breaking open as the earth shifted around it. Black water was seeping out into the dirt around the pipe and probably into the water table.

Since that pipe was large enough for two city buses to drive past each other inside it, that meant this was a *problem*.

But it could, in theory, be fixed. It would just cost a fortune. And that fortune had to come from somewhere.

That somewhere was me.

By all rights, it should have come from the city and its taxes, but the Family said that for whatever reason, the city bureaucratic engine was currently sputtering.

I followed Eric through the headquarters until we reached a room whose door was only labeled as "Warehouse 17." The corridors up until there were all the pretty faux-marble ones, with nice paintings every few meters and carefully placed sofas for guests to sit on, so it was a little strange when Eric opened a door into a room that really fit its name.

Warehouse 17 was . . . a warehouse. It was all cement and shelves, and the space was large enough to fit a dozen semi-trailers' worth of stuff. There was even a forklift parked in the corner, and some garage doors presumably leading deeper into the building's less-pretty sections.

Eric handed me a computer pad before I could say anything. It had a list of the shit the Family wanted.

Half of it was gear and equipment for the reconstruction. Multi-tools, small handheld scanning devices, stuff that I could scrounge up that would be better than anything commercially available. That accounted for three-quarters of the budget.

The rest were odds and ends. Different sorts of grenades, guns, ammunition, some gear, and then a lot of household stuff that I happened to have access to from my catalogs.

I sighed. The exchange here was simple. I'd give them fodder to deconstruct, tech that was decades ahead that they could try to figure out, and they'd bankroll this project off of the future profits. I'd be getting my share of royalties from it, of course.

Didn't stop me from feeling like a bit of a sellout.

CHAPTER SEVENTEEN

A HOME VISIT

French was, until the fall of Canada and the dissolution of the province of Quebec, the official language of the Quebec region. It's still a language widely spoken today, with well over 50 percent of the population in the region being at least conversationally fluent in French.

However, the language of the modern world is English, and without governmental oversight, educational reforms, and most importantly a powerful cultural background, most people in the region will continue to learn English as their primary language.

—*On the French of Canada*, 2043

I arrived at home entirely exhausted. The sun had set behind the wall of skyscrapers along the city's edge, so I'd flown through the dark with nothing to beat back the neon glare of the city.

It wasn't *that* bad. After all, my current entirely-reasonable sleep schedule had me waking up a bit before noon, so it really only felt like lunchtime. Still, coming home after dark made it feel like I'd been working all damn day long.

Plus it had been a bit of an eventful day. Productive, sure, but eventful.

I was a little surprised to notice a car parked out front right next to my mecha. The house had defenses, and I'd told Myalis that using them on media, police, or anyone who seemed annoying was totally fine.

Once I got a little closer, I could see why the car hadn't been blasted off the roof. It was a muscle car, all sleek, aggressive lines and painted a black so deep that it swallowed the light around it.

I'd recognize *God's Righteous Fury* anywhere. Which meant that Gomorrah was here.

Or maybe Franny had taken the car out for a ride. That depended on whether Gomorrah would allow her favorite person to drive her favorite car. I wasn't sure which of the two sat higher on Gomorrah's list of priorities.

I parked my significantly-less-cool-than-the-*Fury* bike a couple of meters away, then leapt off of it.

"I'm home!" I called out as I opened the front door. I removed my helmet and tossed it onto the nearest couch as I made my way in deeper. The kittens were spread out and around, doing their own things, and I got a few hellos from the older ones.

Then Nose ran up to me and stopped right in my way with shining eyes. "You blew up the mayor!" he said.

"Just his head."

"That was awesome! Can I have a gun?"

I considered it. The responsible thing to say was no. "Sure," I said. "But not right now. Maybe ask Grasshopper. She can give you like, safety lessons first. Stop you from blowing your own head up."

I wasn't going to teach someone how to aim when I could barely figure out depth perception myself.

I patted Nose on the head until he squirmed away, then made my way deeper in. There was noise coming from the kitchen, someone laughing, music playing at a fairly low volume. I paused by the entrance and looked in to find the kitchen more occupied than ever before.

Gomorrah was sitting on the little island thing to one side, dressed in casual clothes. Or as casual as Gomorrah ever was, which meant a blouse and button-up sweater over a skirt that stopped below the knee. It was all very 1950s housewife chic.

Lucy and Franny were by the stove, Franny cutting up some carrots with swift *clack-clacks* of a knife while Lucy stirred something in a large pot. Lucy had tossed an apron over her PJs, and Franny looked like her style was more street punk than anything, but it was pretty toned down at the moment.

"Hey," I said. I felt a little overdressed in my coat and skinsuit armor.

"Catherine, you're here," Gomorrah said at the same time as Lucy shouted, "Cat!"

Lucy abandoned her post to run up and give me a quick hug, a peck on the cheek, and a pinch to the ass before she grinned and ran back. "I'm cooking!" she said. "Operation subs . . . didn't work out. This is plan B!"

"I see that," I replied before going over to the island. "What are you two doing here?"

"Just visiting," Gomorrah said. "Thought you could use some company."

"Aren't you on vacation too?" I asked as I sat next to her. "I figured you'd have better things to do than spend time with the likes of me."

Gomorrah shook her head. "You're not terrible company," she said. "Not great, not terrible."

Franny snorted at that, and I had the impression I'd just missed out on an in-joke between the two of them. "Well, I'm glad to have you over! You'll be putting Lucy's grub to the test? She made this fish thing yesterday that was pretty good."

"Pretty good?" Lucy asked. "If you want to taste fish again, you might want to try a bit more flattery than that!"

"It was excellent," I said. "Best fish I ever had. Finger-licking good." Gomorrah looked at me strangely, but I dismissed her concern with a shrug. "So, enjoying your time off? I heard you were burning some stuff."

"Testing some new equipment," Gomorrah said. "What about you, Catherine?"

Should I continue to call her Gomorrah? She was in casuals, without a flamethrower or nun outfit in sight. It felt a little strange to call her Gomorrah when she was in the guise of a hot blonde from every teacher kink video ever.

"Urgh, I'm doing half-days. Afternoon, once I wake up, I work. Evening, I play. It's not working out so well though, as you can guess by the time."

"Yeah, I saw you on the news," she said. Her voice dropped a bit, keeping things between us under the cover of the noise Lucy and Franny were making across the room. "Did you want to talk about it?"

"The mayor thing?" I asked.

She nodded.

"Not really. Look, it's our job to fix shit. Kill aliens, keep people alive. He was making that last bit hard. I gave him a chance. He decided to fuck around. So . . . I did what had to be done."

"Is that Stray Cat talking, or Catherine?"

"What's that mean?" I asked, a little confused. Did she think I was two people? One barely fit in my head as it was. "It was just Cat. There was a rat in my city and I dropped it at the city's doorstep, that's all there is to it."

Delilah nodded along. "Okay."

"Hey, if you two want, you don't have to stay in the kitchen," Lucy said. "I want to tease Franny and that'll be hard to do with the both of you here. Besides, it'll be another half hour before this is done." She gestured to the big pot still on the stove. There was some steam coming from it that smelled like . . . beef? I wasn't actually sure what she was making. A stew, maybe?

"Sure," I said, then turned back to Delilah. "Have you seen my mecha up close? It got damaged and I've been trying to fix it up."

"You know how to fix things?" Delilah asked.

I shrugged. "Come, I'll show ya."

We stepped out and started across the living room when we ran into Daniel. The oldest kitten of the bunch paused in front of us, then eyed Delilah up and down. "Wow, you are *hot*," he said.

"Dammit, Daniel," I said. "She could literally light you on fire."

"I know, I'm warming up already. What's your name, hotstuff?" he asked.

"Wait, you know she's a samurai, right?" I asked. Delilah seemed content not to have to interact with Daniel at all.

"Yeah. That only makes it better, no?" he asked. "Hi, I'm Daniel. Big fan."

"Hi," she said. Somehow Delilah managed to communicate "I will skin you alive slowly" with a single syllable and a narrowing of her eyes.

Daniel went pale and raised his hands in surrender. "Okay! Cool. Nice to meet you, I'm gonna . . . not be here."

"Fantastic idea," I said as he stumbled off. "Sorry. He's a . . . hmm . . . fucking moron?"

"You keep him around because . . . ?" she asked.

"He's a kitten. Well, he's a little old for one, but it doesn't matter. Him mooching off of me doesn't really cost anything." I held the front door open for her and we stepped out. It was a bit chilly out, and the wind was pretty strong, but it wasn't bad enough to need to head back in just yet.

The mech and my deactivated repair drone were sitting where I'd left them. Delilah seemed actually interested as I started to explain what I'd been fixing on it. Unfortunately, I wasn't so smart or deep into the work yet, so I wasn't going to be able to hold up the tech talk forever.

"You're actually moving things along nicely," she said. "Especially considering how much stuff you're doing all at once."

"It's not that bad," I said. "I . . . I wanna keep busy. It'd feel wrong not to."

"But we're on vacation?" she asked.

"Yeah, I guess. Doesn't change that I have to do something."

The wind hummed between us, and eventually Delilah nodded. "I understand. Cat," Delilah said after a brief but awkward silence. She brushed some of her hair away from her face. "I think I need to ask you for a favor."

CHAPTER EIGHTEEN

HOME

You want to buy a house? In this market? Are you delusional?

—Everyone, 2023

"A favor," I repeated. "What is it? You need dating help?"

"Dating help?" Delilah shook her head. "No, why would I ask you for dating advice?"

Well, that was rude. "Hey, why *wouldn't* you ask me for dating advice? Lucy and I have been steady for years. You think it was easy to convince her to date me?"

Delilah blinked, then looked away across the city. "Okay, I hadn't thought of that. I guess I just figured you two somehow skipped the dating phase entirely."

"I mean, fair, we are both very horny," I admitted.

Delilah sighed. "I don't want to hear it, please. I just know Lucy's putting ideas in Franny's head right this moment."

I laughed, then swept some hair out of my face. I needed a haircut one of these days. Also, my hair was getting thick enough that it was humid as fuck. It wasn't even raining, yet the city managed to make it feel like it was. "So, what's this favor?" I asked.

"It's a little awkward," she said.

"I was already down to helping you with dating stuff, so I think we're past the 'a little awkward' phase."

Delilah poked me in the short ribs with a knuckle. "Don't be an ass," she said. "I've got . . . domestic problems."

"With Franny?"

"No, not with Franny, she's . . . never mind my relationship. It's complicated, but not in a bad way. It's the rest that's a problem."

"You mean with where you're living?" I walked over to one of the legs of the mech, then sat down on it. The cat-like mech was sitting like a sphinx at the moment, so there was plenty of room to use it as a bench. A rather uncomfortable one, but still.

Delilah looked around for a place to sit, then hopped backward onto the head of my repair drone. The poor thing just sat there, frozen. "It's the nuns," she said.

"The . . . oh, right, you live in a nunhouse."

"It's not called a nunhouse," Delilah said. "It's a convent. And an orphanage and school and a few other things all rolled into one. I didn't mind staying in the dorms a few months ago, before . . . all of this." She gestured vaguely at the mecha and the house and the two of us.

I took it to mean she was talking about all the samurai stuff. She became one a few weeks before me.

"But now it's getting to be a bit much. The head of the convent is insisting that I take their personal rooms, the others are either fawning over me or tiptoeing around and . . . and Franny and I can't get a private moment anywhere. I don't mind the attention, and it's nice to be treated well, but I grew up with these women."

"You're not an orphan though, right?"

"Me? No, my parents are . . . I don't really want to talk about them, to be honest. They'd send me to the convent for nine months out of the year, so I feel better there than at home."

"So, you want me to put the fear of Lucifer in the nuns so that they leave you alone?"

Delilah snorted. "No. God no. They'd *like* you. As weird as that is to say. You're like the embodiment of the ideal samurai, and they practically worship that idea."

I blinked. I was the *what*? There was no way that I was the ideal anything. Hell, Gomorrah was better at this job than I was. When I thought of calm and collected, she definitely came to mind. Or maybe someone like Deus Ex or Longbow or . . . well, not Grasshopper. She was cool but also clearly insane.

I really didn't feel like opening that can of worms before dinner.

"So, how can I help? You need a place to stay?" I asked.

"Exactly," she said. "I was planning on asking you what you were doing with the rest of the space in your building."

"Huh? Wait, you mean this building?" I tapped the ground with a foot.

"Yes, obviously," she said.

I thought about it for a second. The building was pretty large, with plenty of room for another samurai in it, and it was mostly empty at the moment. I was only taking up the top floor. "You know, I only own the top two floors, right? I mean, we added to it, obviously, but that's all I own. If you want to live below, then . . . I guess, buy a floor."

"You don't own the entire building?" Gomorrah asked. "Really? Aren't you worried that someone might move in below and cause trouble?"

"They'd have to be *really* loud to bother me. And any . . . violent trouble can be handled with violence in turn."

Delilah shook her head. "I wouldn't want to live with neighbors I don't trust, not if I invested this much into a home. But I suppose no one will try anything. You *did* just shoot the mayor on TV. It sends a message."

"Damn right," I said. "So if you want to move in, go ahead. I don't know who owns which floors, but I'm sure they'd sell to you. You can be scary that way."

"Why not buy the entire building?"

"What's the point? I live here, not down there. I guess if I wanted more space or something, I might do the floor right under this level. It'd be nice to have some storage space, and I'm pretty sure it's not being used at all. Also, you buying a floor here isn't asking for help. You can do that without my permission."

Delilah smiled. "Atyacus has a list of owners and has sent a few feelers out," she said. "Thanks, Catherine. You really don't mind us being neighbors?"

"There's no window in my bedroom, so it's not like you'll hear anything kinky, and I'd rather have you nearby than someone I don't know," I said. "Well . . . there's the fire risk."

"I'm very careful about fire," Delilah replied.

"When will you be moving over?" I asked.

She shrugged. "As soon as I secure ownership. It might take a day or two. It's late, so I imagine anyone receiving my request might take a while to process it."

"If they try to cheat you on the price, let me know. Apparently I'm scary. Also, let me know when you're actually moving so I can give you a hand."

"I don't have that much to move," she said.

"Good, less work for me, but I still expect free pizza out of it." I grinned, then glanced at the front door. "Speaking of, think supper's ready?"

We chatted for a little bit more, mostly whining about the problems in the city. Soon enough I got a text from Lucy letting me know that things were almost ready. We stood and made our way back inside while chatting about homes and such. Delilah didn't have any house-related catalogs, but she did have a lot more points on hand than I did. She suggested pooling our resources a little to sabotage-proof the rest of the tower, which wasn't a terrible idea. I'd placed a few turrets out and around the top floors already, to keep things safe, but with two samurai in the same building I expected that our security would need to climb a bit.

Lucy was leaving the kitchen just as we got closer. "Come on, food's ready!"

"Are the kittens eating with us?" Franny asked as she set the table with bowls and utensils.

"And making a mess?" Lucy asked. "Nah, I made enough for them, but they can eat out of paper bowls. Also, Cat, we need a cleaning bot."

"A cleaning bot?" I asked.

"Yeah, like that repair drone you have. There're stains on the stove that I can't get off, and I'll bet every last credit I have that the kittens will be turning this place into a dump before the month's out."

That . . . was actually a fair point. "I'll look into it," I said. In the meantime, we'd just need to clean things like they did way back in the day: by hiring someone poorer than us to do it.

Lucy brought the pot over to the table, then started to ladle food into our bowls. It was a brown gooey substance with chunks of meat and . . . beans? "Is this chili?" I asked.

"Oh, hey, I didn't mess it up so bad that it's unrecognizable," Lucy said.

"It smells nice," I said.

"It's real meat!" Lucy cheered. "Or as real as I could make with the printer, in any case."

"So . . . real meat that didn't come from an animal?" I asked.

Lucy shrugged. In her defense, it was probably better than the vat-grown shit we could order online.

With everyone served, Lucy returned the pot to the kitchen, then called the kittens to get their food. She very quickly handed over the job to Daniel, though, and returned to us.

"I'm assuming you don't do prayer before eating," Delilah said.

"I don't do prayer in general," I said.

She shrugged, then took a spoonful. "Hmm, this is good," she said.

I took a spoonful, shoved it in my mouth, and chewed for a bit before my eyes started to water and my mouth started to burn. "Lucy, why is this so hot?" I asked.

Lucy frowned. "I'm not sure. I did exactly what the recipe said, a cup of pepper . . . or wait, was it a tablespoon?" she muttered.

CHAPTER NINETEEN

HARDWARE

In the '80s and '90s people kind of assumed that the future would be full of cyborgs. We have early sci-fi and movies like Robocop to thank for that, I think. There's something romantic about a person combining their weak flesh with powerful technology.

Unfortunately, romantic and realistic aren't the same.

—*Techtransitionalism*, a video essay, 2040

I sat on my bike, adjusted my helmet, then finally decided to look at where I'd be heading to.

I had a noontime appointment with one Peter Silverbloom, a man that I'd met in person all of once and yet who I still kind of just . . . trusted.

Peter was a bit of a weirdo, but he wasn't a bad sort. In fact, it was the opposite. He struck me as very nice. Not a saint or anything, but maybe the closest thing to that in a shithole like New Montreal. His service record was basically nothing but volunteer and nonprofit work, and not the hyper-corporatized sort that was flashy and self-serving, but actual get-your-hands-dirty work.

And I had an appointment with him in about half an hour.

"So, where are you, Mister Silverbloom," I muttered.

I'm assuming that was rhetorical?

"More or less," I said. "Did he send his location for this meeting?"

Via email three days ago, then he sent three corrections since.

"Wow, he really can't decide where to meet? Should I be worried about traps or something?" I asked. My map app opened up and pins appeared in the locations that I assumed he wanted to meet in. They were all lower city spots, mostly close to the more urban parts of the city, but that was the only common thread that I could see at a glance.

Every location is a different nonprofit. I dug into it out of curiosity, and it mostly seems as though Peter is just a busy man. His attention is constantly being diverted to issues with different groups across the city. He is quite good at putting out metaphorical fires.

"Huh. I guess that makes sense. This guy's not gonna live long if he's spending this much time chasing after problems. He won't be able to fix every problem in New Montreal." I turned my bike on and then gently rolled it off the side of the building. My flight drooped for a bit before I started to fly properly and then did a long, slow circle of our home.

His success rate at solving those problems is quite impressive, and his record suggests someone who is genuinely selfless. I'm happy to see you helping him, as it might help a lot of others.

"You know, he sounds like a pretty good candidate for being a samurai," I said. I'd never done any charity work before, and I was a bit of a bitch. I also couldn't picture Peter blowing up the mayor. He'd probably convince even that old asshole to be a better man. Or he'd try, at any rate.

He has a lot of the traits that we search for. He lacks some others.

I locked the last location Peter had sent me into the bike's autopiloting system, then let it lead me around and out across the city. "I don't know. He sounds like a nicer guy than me."

Niceness is desirable. Peter Silverbloom is too *nice. His desire to be diplomatic at all times would be a hindrance. There are other factors as well, though they might be difficult to explain because of your cultural background.*

"My cultural background?" I repeated.

You are human. You value human qualities.

That was needlessly cryptic and a bit creepy. In any case, I decided to cut that line of discussion off. Discussing what made a good samurai wasn't going to go anywhere except to make me feel bad about myself. Besides, comparing yourself to others was a great way to fuck up an otherwise nice day.

Still, the thought worried at me. Was Myalis ever disappointed that she was stuck with my dumb ass if there were others out there who were so much better?

As I neared my destination, I swooped down to the lower levels, then slipped into a parking garage on the ground floor.

I could tell already that this place was a bit of a hole. The building, an older residential complex, was streaked with rust and grime, and the interior of the parking garage was filled with old beaters. Cars twice as old as me were crammed into the corners, and it looked like a number of them were parts cars.

There was a camp at the back of the garage, a handful of containers set in a semicircle that enclosed a few tents and lean-to shanties. Several ripped-apart neon signs were stacked in the middle with a fire-hazard nest of wires leading to them. It provided a surprisingly bright light for that corner, which let me see the folk hanging around there.

There were a lot of homeless people. Although . . . I supposed that they did have a home of sorts.

I got off my bike and started toward the back where there was an elevator. Peter was on the fifth floor, according to what I'd gotten from him.

One of the locals called out to me, asking me if I wanted some "puff" for cheap. I wasn't even sure what that drug was, but he raised a cheap inhaler my way, then took a hit from it himself and let out a giggle. I politely declined and kept going.

"Nice place," I said as I slipped into the elevator and stabbed at the button for the fifth floor. I rubbed my finger off on my pants. The button was sticky.

The elevator's stereo tried to play some ads, but someone had ripped the panel off and stabbed a screwdriver into it, so the noise was more of a gargling hiss that accompanied me until I made it to the floor I was heading to.

The place was . . . old. Old and not terribly maintained. Sure, the paint was peeling and the stainless half-wall panels were marred by thousands of scuff marks, but someone had swept the place and mopped the floors, so even if the flooring was cracked and worn down, it was still clean . . . ish.

I checked the address Peter had sent and compared it to the imprint some numbers had left next to a doorway nearby. "Weird place," I said.

As far as I can tell, it's mostly safe.

"Mostly?"

There's a drug production facility two floors down that doesn't meet even the loosest of safety standards. There are also several dozen armed people on this floor, and hundreds more across the rest of the building, including addicts and gang-affiliated people spread around you, but for the most part, the local threats are unlikely to be able or willing to harm you.

"Right, so mostly safe," I said.

The place Peter wanted to meet me at was in the center of the building. There was an open space where a bunch of corridors came and met in what might have been supposed to be a sort of "town square" area. There were two automated fast food places, a couple of boarded-up stores, a pawn shop, and a place called Death Bread, which was apparently where we were supposed to meet.

I slipped into the entrance and took a look around. It was a bakery, of sorts. The food looked . . . actually, kind of decent. Next to all the prices— which were all in the low hundreds of credits, some even in the double-digits—were little plaques with expiration dates. Most of those were a few days ago.

The young woman that came up to me had a smile and no human eyes. Her hand reached out to shake, and I realized that it was a skeletal prosthetic, one of those older cyborg arms. "You must be Catherine," she said. The upper half of her face was a cavity with plastic skin and a trio of cybernetic eyes.

"Yeah, that's me," I said. "You don't look like Peter, unless he had a serious makeover?"

She snorted. "Nah, Peter's in the back dealing with something. I can tell him to drop it, if you want. It's probably not that important?"

"No, it's fine," I said. "So, you're his . . . assistant?"

She shook her head a little. Her shirt's neckline was just loose enough to reveal that her neck was reinforced. "No, I'm Laura. Friends call me See-Three. Peter called me over for a consult, of sorts, if you wanna borrow the corpo term. Nice arm, by the way."

I glanced down at my mechanical right arm. "Thanks. A consult, huh?"

Laura nodded. "He said you were donating a bunch of prosthetics. Don't know where you're getting them, or what sort they are, but I know my metal bits better than anyone else."

"How'd Peter find you?"

"I work for a charity that fixes folks' cyberware for cheap. Poorly installed gear is a nightmare. Cheap gear is awful. Combine the two and you can make someone's life not worth living real fast. Been there myself, so I try to help where I can."

"That sounds like exactly what we need," I said.

A door farther into the bakery opened, and Peter came out. He saw me, smiled, and beckoned me inside.

CHAPTER TWENTY

UNSUB

Everything today is based on a subscription system, why not air?
—AirCo, Premium Air Services, 2038

Peter was, at the moment, in a dress shirt and slacks, a corpo outfit by any measure, except that it was clearly about half a decade out of fashion, his topmost button was undone, and it looked like his shirt had been pressed by someone unfamiliar with an iron.

Somehow it all came together to make him look like someone who was professional but not corporate, trustworthy but not infallible.

If he was doing it on purpose, then Peter was way ahead of everyone else. If he wasn't, then he either had a damned good secretary or whatever dressing him, or his instincts were on point.

"Sorry for the delay," he said as he raked his fingers through his hair. "Just had to take care of a few things." He smiled at me, then glanced at the cyborg next to him. "Ah, I take it Laura's introduced herself?"

"As See-Three," I said. "What's up with that name anyway?"

Laura shrugged, then gestured to her face. "Three eye-sensors. The name just kind of stuck. It's gotten to the point that I'm a little worried about switching out to something different."

Her eyes *were* pretty weird. Three short tubes poking out of a plate buried into her face. Instead of a nose, Laura had a small filter tab off to one side of her face with a tube running back to where her nose should have been. I couldn't help but be a little distracted. It was a bit of a fucky look.

"I guess the name makes sense," I said. I didn't have rocks to throw from my glass house. "Stray Cat" was a lot harder to explain as far as names went. Hell, I had a *house*. I wasn't a stray. I'd even go so far as to say that I was properly house-trained. I shook my head and refocused. "Anyway. I'm here for the thing we talked about a while ago."

"You had prosthetics to donate," Peter said. "It's why I had See-Three come over. She's the best when it comes to this kind of thing."

"I'm hardly the best," See-Three said.

"You're certainly better than I am," Peter shot back. "The only thing I've got going for me are my augs and some body sculpting. Oh, and a pancreas."

"Your pancreas?" I asked. That had come out of nowhere.

I think my confusion came through, because he chuckled at that, then waved dismissively. "Family history of diabetes," he said. "I got some bio-mods for my pancreas . . . about ten years ago? Trust me, I couldn't stand being in this place if I couldn't handle some sugar."

I nodded and glanced around the bakery. Some of the food being sold here was probably not great when it came to that kind of stuff. Or something. I'd never really been keen on looking at nutritional labels. "Okay. Yeah, that makes sense."

"So, what kind of stuff are we dealing with?" See-Three asked.

"I've got a catalog of basic prosthetics," I said. "Arms, legs, the usual bits."

"Knees?" she asked.

"I . . . think those would be included in legs?"

She shook her head. "No, they wouldn't. Knees, hips, shoulders, they're tricky as hell. It's easier to get a femur-down replacement than it is to get a new knee. Knees are complicated. Making an entire leg is less complicated."

"That seems counterintuitive," I said.

She shrugged. "That's just how it is. We've had good knees for a while, but they're still disproportionately more expensive."

I didn't quite get it, but it didn't sound entirely implausible. "I think I can manage knees and the like too."

"Where are you getting these?" See-Three asked. She looked between me and Peter. "Or is this one of those things where I'm better off not knowing?"

Did she not know that I was a samurai? "I have a machine that can print them," I said. "We've got some other things in the queue as well, but as long as we have raw materials, we should be able to pump out about a dozen limbs a day—or a few knees, since apparently those are tougher."

"Like with a 3D printer?" See-Three asked.

"Something like that," I said. "Did you have a place in mind for the clinic, Peter?"

He nodded. "In this building, actually. It's why I wanted to meet here. I don't know if this is too far from your place to be convenient?"

"It's a ten-minute drive, then another five to get to this floor," I said. I could have the prosthetics printed in the morning and here by the afternoon, no problem. "Not too bad, all in all. Probably significantly longer for someone that has to follow road laws. But yeah, I guess it isn't too bad. What about safety?"

Peter nodded, then gestured to the door. "Follow me, please?" he asked before leading us out. "This bakery is something we set up about nine months back. We buy surplus, nearly-expired goods from a couple of places, then resell them here and at two other locations for as low as we can. It keeps people fed. When we were picking out locations, this one felt pretty natural. This isn't one of the best or worst residential buildings, it's well connected to a few others, and the gangs that run this floor are pretty . . . amenable."

"You had to negotiate with them?" I asked.

"Did it myself. I won't say that they're good people, they push drugs and prostitution and have a record that's longer than my arm, but most of them also live here. Cheaper food means a lot to them too."

I nodded along, then glanced around the open space. There was a decent amount of foot traffic here. A few families, some people on their own, a couple of people pushing carts, and even a bit of mobility scooter traffic. It was a passing spot. I noticed the gangsters too. Just younger guys and girls, hanging out together on the street corners, watching people go by.

A lot of them were watching me. I figured they could keep watching as long as that was all they did.

"When we took the lease, the corporation that owns these shops insisted that we take two lots," Peter said. "They wouldn't even negotiate otherwise. So we ended up with the bakery and this shop location over here."

Peter moved across the square to a second shop with boarded-up windows. He stared at the door for a while, then there was a hard clunk as it unlocked.

Tugging the door open, he gestured us in.

It was dark, but I had enough sensors and shit in my helmet to make it seem as bright as if the entire place was lit up. I imagined it was the same for See-Three because she stepped in without a worry.

"Ah, let me . . . right, the lights breaker is down," Peter said. He slipped past and toward the back, pulling out an old smartphone for light as he went.

The shop might have been used for something else before, but it was hard to tell what. There were three workstations to one side, without any chairs or anything, but with mirrors on the walls in front of them, and a counter at the back. The only other furniture were some plastic chairs to the left. It was clear that at some point there had been dozens of ads or signs of some sort on the walls, but they'd been removed, leaving discolored squares behind.

"What was this place?" I asked.

"A Stop and Chop hair salon," Peter said from the back. It looked like there was a small maintenance room back there, maybe with some storage or something. He was rummaging around in a breaker box. "Found the lights!"

The lights came on with a click and a hum, bathing the space in bright neon white. It had looked nicer when it was dark. In the full light, the stains on the ceiling became more obvious, and the broken linoleum seemed far worse.

"It's . . . not the worst place," I said.

"I'm hoping that we can turn it around," Peter said with a winsome smile and his hands on his hips. "We haven't negotiated a price for the prosthetics, but . . . well, I felt like you were trying to be charitable, so I imagine that we'll be getting a fair price. I think that the cost of the prosthetic accounts for most of the cost with this kind of thing, right?"

"About two thirds," See-Three said. "Maybe less, actually. When you get a new mod, a good chunk of the cost is the mod itself, then the rest is the installation and whatever initial fee there is for your software subscriptions."

"Subscriptions?" I asked.

She nodded, then wiggled her hands. "For software updates for your limbs and bits. Cheaper models cost more per month, higher-end gear is cheaper. Depending on how long you have something for, going better can save you a lot in the long run."

"Well, we won't have subscriptions," I said. "And the prosthetics will be free. If you can make the price reflect all of that, then I think we might have a good thing going."

CHAPTER TWENTY-ONE

ETERNAL OPTIMISM AND PETTY SPITE

As climate change continues to grow in scale and scope, the world will continue to become less hospitable to humankind. We should have addressed this fifty years ago, and it's too damned late to do anything about it now, but that doesn't mean that we will just keel over and die without putting up a fight.

It's why we seeded clouds across the entire planet. It's why we live in more and more cities with enclosed environments. The world might kill us, but that doesn't mean that we'll go out so easily. No, our death will be a slow, dragged-out affair.

—Professor U. Shuda Listened, Climate I-Told-You-So Expert, 2025

"A lot of my plans hinge on the fabricator," I said as I slowly flew up and through New Montreal's skyline.

That's understandable. It's one of your largest purchases, and one that's primarily designed to allow a Vanguard to outfit themselves and produce an abundance of resources. It would be strange not to place it at the center of your plans.

"Does every samurai get something like that?" I asked.

One in eight Vanguard will branch out into some sort of production system. Most of these focus on making tools and consumables that they commonly use. As they progress, most Vanguard will also turn these production systems toward larger goals.

"So, like what I'm doing?"

Your actions have precedents. It's only logical that a Vanguard capable of producing goods should produce goods, and seeing as how Vanguard are chosen from among people who wish to help the world, it again only makes sense that they would use their abilities to provide goods and equipment to the wider world.

I continued to think as I flew toward home. As I rose over the top of the majority of the towers around me, I was able to make out my place out in the distance. The weather was nice out, for once, a bit of sun coming out from between gray clouds. "So, if there're a bunch of samurai who are able to make shit, why's the world still a shithole?" I asked.

Think about the things you're planning on crafting, in regard to that question. Are the things you're planning to make enough to improve the world as a whole, or are they just enough to help those you want to help right now? As a Vanguard grows in abilities, points, and power, the scope of the help they can provide grows as well, though this growth is more linear than you might expect. Though the world is a better place because of them, it's likely that you just take a lot of the growth they provided for granted.

Was that it? It made some sense, I supposed. Different samurai would care about different stuff. If I gave Gomorrah unlimited creation abilities, I bet she'd invest in giving everyone a flamethrower, or she might invest in helping the nuns or whatever that she was used to working with. That probably would help the world in a small way.

Someone like Grasshopper would probably invest a lot of time and effort into making educational stuff better, which would also help, in its own way. Hell, I was pretty sure she was already investing into doing that. I think she had a whole set of interactive children's books being made.

"Well, whatever," I decided. I'd use mine to make the shit I cared about better. For now, especially since I just had the one fabricator, it wasn't like I could change the entire damned world. I'd start with what I could do on a scale I was used to working on, and if things didn't go to shit, then I'd see about expanding.

The printer at home probably had one hell of a backlog already, so we'd have to see about improving it, or getting a second one.

Could I use the first one to make more of them, or was that cheating?

I flew around the museum, then came to a nice, gentle landing out front. It was gentle mostly because I let the autopilot do all of the work; I was a damn good driver, but landing was hard.

Stepping off the bike, I stretched my back out until it popped, then removed my helmet and shook my hair out. The air was damp and humid, but it wasn't raining for once. The parking space was still wet though, and I couldn't imagine the rain not picking up again before the evening was up.

I barely made it to the front door before it opened and Lucy came strolling out. She collided with me in a hug. "Hi!"

"Hi!" I said as I returned the hug. "You're in a good mood."

"When am I not? My eternal optimism is my third best feature."

"Third best?" I asked. "What are the other two?"

"My hair comes second, obviously," she said.

Her hair *was* nice, a big poofy ball of tightly knit curls that was fantastically bouncy. At least when the humidity didn't get to it. "And the first best feature?" I asked.

"Boobs," she said.

I thought about it, then nodded. "Boobs."

"So, did you shoot any other politicians today, or was it a normal day at the office?"

I snorted, then leaned down, chin resting on her head. "It was a normal day at the office," I said. "Peter's still too good to be true. Met this cool chick with three cyborg eyes and no nose who does prosthetics stuff, and Peter set up a shop to get things done in. We'll start getting orders tomorrow. Ah, we'll have to convince one of the kittens to help, or hire someone, but I'd rather have one of the kittens do it. Peter said they could take care of transportation, have a van fly over once a day or something."

"That sounds good," Lucy said. "And what will you do now? More tinkering?"

The mech was just sitting there. "Ah, maybe later," I said. "Hey, what are you wearing?"

"PJs?" Lucy said. She was in flannel pants and a big T-shirt with . . . I leaned back to see what was printed on it, because I'd been distracted by the boobs underneath earlier. There was a picture of a chibified kitten on the front, with a sword in its mouth. "Katana kitten?" I asked.

"It's alliterative," Lucy said.

I shook my head. At least she had a nice, mostly harmless creative outlet other than her cooking. "Want to go shopping for a bit?" I asked. "I think I've been complaining to myself about not having enough clothes for a while, and it looks like you could use some stuff too."

"Oh, is this a shopping date, or just normal boring shopping?" Lucy asked.

I grinned. "It's whatever you want to make of it," I said.

Lucy bounced up to the tips of her feet and gave my cheek a peck. "I'll get changed," she said before running back inside.

I walked back over to the bike, then leaned up against it. "I'm gonna need a helmet for Lucy," I said to Myalis.

Perhaps I should have encouraged you to purchase a fully enclosed vehicle. In any case, an inexpensive enclosed helmet should only come to a few points.

When Lucy walked out—now wearing a skirt, an old blouse, and my old jacket—I tossed her a brand-new helmet. It was just a plain dark thing with a glass front . . . and a pair of protrusions on the top that looked suspiciously ear-like.

"Thanks!" Lucy said before fitting the helmet on. "So, where are we going?"

"I don't know, where do you want to go?" I asked.

"Nowhere fancy," she said. "Maybe one of those cool markets where people make their own shit?"

I nodded along, then slid a leg over the seat of my bike. Scooting forward, I gave Lucy some space to squeeze in before me while I locked in our destination. There were a lot of malls and shopping centers in the city, but Myalis quietly helped me narrow the choices down. It wasn't exactly close by, but being able to fly over the city made the commute easy. Plus I got to enjoy Lucy pressing herself into my back the entire time.

We kicked off and took to the air, then I received a call from Lucy. "You know, you could just shout," I said as I answered it.

"And ruin my voice so early in the day?" she asked. "I want to save all the screaming for later."

I grinned and shook my head. Lucy was being very . . . Lucy today. She started chatting while we continued to move across the city, talking about the progress some of the kittens had been making and the long-distance work she'd taken on.

It mostly had to do with the Kittens association we'd left in Burlington. They were still reaching out to Lucy for help, and she was spending an hour or so a day just organizing things and writing nasty emails to people she found incompetent.

I enjoyed just listening to her rant about whatever came to mind. Lucy's eternal optimism was balanced by a deep and powerful level of spite and pettiness that she was always willing to use on the things that annoyed her.

Listening to her was a nice way to cool down.

CHAPTER TWENTY-TWO

DRESS FOR STRESS

I'm not saying that counterfeiting should be punishable by death . . . but I'm not not saying that.
—Bert McWeathers, Deputy Head of the Treasury Dept., Former United States of America, 2036

Pop-up stalls were a pretty common feature in New Montreal. A corpo would rent out some walking space in a busy part of the city, and overnight a stall would appear selling whatever. Those sorts were usually manned by some kind of android and would have overpriced stuff for sale.

It was pretty normal to see one appear in front of a competitor's shop, just as a sort of insult, or as a way to drag customers away. It made for good artificial drama, and I used to love reading about two luxury brands being pissed at each other on social media.

That was before I grew old enough to realize that both brands were owned by the same megacorp.

In any case, pop-up stalls were kind of a neat way to switch things up in an area, but they had their limits. Lucy and I were heading to a corner of New Montreal that was known for its stalls. I'd never been there before, because it was the sort of place that was a bit too exclusive to let the likes of me in.

At least, it had been that way before.

We circled a large building a few blocks over from the center of the city. "Finding parking here's gonna be tough," Lucy said.

"Eh, I could park in the middle of the road," I said.

Lucy laughed. "No, don't! That's just abusing your privilege."

I didn't comment on how I'd done it a few times this week already. Instead I circled around another time while connecting my augs to the nearest building's parking system. It wanted me to download some parking app thing that'd let me check on availability and reserve a place in exchange for a monthly subscription.

Myalis seemed to take umbrage to that, and the system folded as she poked at it. My autopilot found a spot in the VIP section and I turned the bike in that direction.

Slipping into a parking garage and past its security, we drove up a ramp and into the reserved section, then right into a nice open spot. "Alright," I said.

Lucy pressed herself closer to me as she swung her leg off the back, then she hopped off properly and wiggled her helmet off while I stood. Her hair came out in a big poof, and I couldn't help but laugh.

"That's racist," she said.

"What? How?"

"You're mocking my hair, just because it can't handle hats," she said before placing the helmet on the bike's bench. She ran her hands into her hair and tried to fix it, but the helmet had done a number on it.

"I think your hair's fabulous," I said.

Lucy sniffed haughtily, but I knew that look in her eyes. Lucy was a lot of things, and vain was certainly one of them. Not too much so, but she did enjoy a solid compliment. "So, what is this place?"

"I imagine you mean beyond the parking garage?" I asked, then ducked her swat. "It's a clothes place. Myalis helped me find it. It's basically an entire floor with nothing but pop-up stands and merchant stalls and stuff. It's a bit exclusive."

"Oh, sounds fancy," Lucy said. "But you know, I'm not all about that fancy stuff, right? I do need new threads, but it doesn't need to be something too chic. Those credits could be spent on something else."

I reached out and pulled Lucy in for a hug. "I want to spend a lot of money to make you feel pretty," I said. "I can go back to eating nothing but ramen noodles if that's what it takes."

Lucy returned the hug. "You're an idiot," she said. "And besides, feel pretty? What if I want to *be* pretty, hmm?"

"You're already the prettiest," I said.

Lucy laughed, light and chiming and very much pretty. Even after all this time, it made my insides squirm. "You're so cheesy, Cat."

"Just a little," I admitted. "Let's go!"

It wasn't too far from the parking garage to the rest of the building. We stayed close as we rode an elevator down, then made our way through a few corridors. The deeper we went, the more people were around. Eventually we rode a travelator along with some dozen other people to a sort of toll booth.

The booth was manned by a pair of androids checking people's ID and charging a small fee for entrance. It was just a thousand credits, about what someone would pay for a half-dozen cans of soda from a vending machine.

It was probably just enough to keep vagrants out and to pay for the security itself. Lucy and I passed without any issues, which was nice. Myalis spoofed the ID thing to keep things private, and I transferred over the entrance cost since . . . well, money wasn't as much of a concern, and while I could probably get in without paying, that seemed needlessly dickish. "Welcome to the Arcade," the android said in a smooth, feminine voice.

The area beyond the toll was a wide open space, but first there was a wall just ahead of us, which forced people coming in to pick a side and move. The wall did have a large screen on it with a map that would switch out to ads every few seconds.

"Okay," I said as I looked at the map, then I frowned as it switched out to another ad. "Fuck's sake." Lucy giggled next to me. "Right, uh, looks like the middle part is all corpo stalls. Fancy clothes and shit. The outer ring is smaller shops and, uh, it looks like single-worker shops. Bespoke stuff."

"Bespoke?" Lucy asked.

"Yeah, that's the gimmick here. A lot of the smaller stalls on the outer ring are basically run and owned by the same people. So they sell stuff that they make. Some of them even make things custom on the spot."

"Oh, that sounds kind of awesome," Lucy said.

"Expensive, I bet, but yeah. There's supposed to be quick printers for harder parts and they have machines to put the clothes together on the spot. Some of them do things by hand too. You can get custom designs and gear."

"That's pretty cool," Lucy said. "Where do we start?"

"I think that'd be up to you," I said. "You're the one that needs clothes more than I do."

"You think you don't need new clothes?" Lucy asked.

I worked my jaw. I did need new clothes. I'd been complaining about it to myself for a while, but now that I was here, I remembered how much I hated shopping for myself. "I mean, I can go out in samurai chic any day. It's kind of a universal fit that way, you know?" My gear probably wasn't appropriate for every place, but it was also samurai gear, which meant that I didn't need to fit in.

Lucy reached down and grabbed my meat hand, then pulled me after her. I jogged to keep up, then ran a little faster as Lucy lost her footing on a slight incline in the floor. She was still just a little bit clumsy.

"Right, okay," she said. "So obviously we need to work on your design."

"My what?"

"Your look, your style."

I frowned. "What's wrong with my style?" I asked. "Is it the cat ears?"

"No, those are fine. The tail is too, when you have it. It's more . . . Hmm, actually, your overall design isn't bad, but it's not all there. You've got the long-coat and all-black gear going. The pink highlights are a nice touch—they break up the darker shades and give some things room to pop. The cat theme is pretty subtle overall, too."

"Alright," I said.

"But I think it could be better!" Lucy nodded. "You don't really give off a strong image except for like, the impression that you're cool and dark and mysterious. At least to people who don't know you."

"And that's bad?"

"Obviously! You could pivot around and be cute and cuddly . . ."

"I absolutely refuse," I said.

Lucy turned my way and batted her eyes. "But it would be *cute*," she said.

I poked her cheek. "No," I said.

Grinning, Lucy continued to walk ahead. "Alright, fine. Right now your look doesn't say much about you, though, at least not to anyone looking. You don't have a lot of visible utility stuff, so you don't come off as militaristic. You don't look sloppy enough to be casually cool. Dark and mysterious fits with the stealth stuff, but you don't have that . . . femme fatale assassin look."

"Should I?" I asked.

"Well, you'd need to ditch the long coat and wear much tighter gear." Lucy licked her lips. "That's not a bad idea, actually. A literal *Cat*suit."

"I . . . don't know about that," I said. I wasn't uncomfortable in my skin, but the idea of wearing nothing but something entirely skintight was pushing it. I didn't mind being exposed at home, between just me and Lucy, but going out in public that way would make me way too self-conscious. I wasn't shy, but I wasn't averse to modesty either.

"Hmm, that's fine too. Still, we have to work on your image! Right now you're the unapproachable girl who shot the mayor. That might work for some samurai, but I think you're the sort that wants people to work with her. So . . . wardrobe change!"

CHAPTER TWENTY-THREE

FREE AND COMPULSORY

With the modern love for quick fashion comes a modern movement opposing quick fashion that centers around a dislike of trashed clothing. Fashion changes so quickly that by the time something is designed according to a new fashion, made, then shipped to its market, the fashion it was designed for might have moved on and become démodé.

Which, naturally, leads to entire shipping containers being dumped. You can't unmake clothes and remake them, and shelf space is limited. It's cheaper to throw it all away and start over.

It's unforgivably wasteful. If you're going to waste so much effort, then why not save yourself the trouble, apply some skill, and make fashion that will never fade?

—Audrey Alice Darnell-Forsythe, president of Cutting Edge Fashion, 2051

"What about something like that?" Lucy asked, pointing to a massive floor-to-ceiling banner ad in front of one of the shops in the inner circle of the Arcade. The shops and stalls here were all corpo clothing places.

Not that the clothing they sold was necessarily corpo fashion. There was plenty of designer casual wear. Hoodies and T-shirts and jackets with looping gifs on the back or tracksuits with RGB stripes. The kind of shit you'd never be caught wearing in a board meeting. Still, the brands were corporate, even if what they sold didn't fit that aesthetic.

It looked more like . . . well, samurai gear, but cheaper.

My jacket was a pretty good example of classic samurai gear. It was cut and tailored to fit me: the flaps or whatever they were called stopped exactly at the knee, the back part was fit precisely to the length of my shoulders, and the front bit bunched out just enough for my breasts.

I'd paid a hundred or so points for this coat, and what I got was something very precisely tailored for me. That wasn't even the selling point. When Myalis made gear, it worked for me, and I didn't need to specify or pay more for that.

I'd mostly worn hand-me-downs of hand-me-downs my entire life, and it was kind of miraculous to just get clothes that fit right. The last coat I had was way too tight at the front, and I couldn't zip the damned thing up, and the sleeves were too long.

Anyway, I looked at the sign, then squinted a little. "That's *very* corpo," I said.

The model on the banner was a tall, skinny woman in a pantsuit. She was strutting toward the viewer, but the camera was backing away at the same rate so she remained in focus the entire time.

"Yeah, but it's hot," Lucy countered. "She's got that . . . 'I'm going to top you' energy going on."

"You find that hot?" I asked.

"Oh yeah," she said with a nod. "Well . . . I guess you're right, it would be silly on *you*."

"I didn't say that," I said.

She grinned. "Of course not." I glared at Lucy, but she just smiled smugly at me and pulled me forward. "It's not right for you anyway. You're too casually dangerous for that kind of thing. Plus it kinda goes counter to your cat theme."

"Cats can be serious," I said with a gesture to the ad. "Glamorous and graceful or whatever. Cats are notably like that."

"Yeah, of course, but that's not the kind of cat you are."

"What?" I asked. "Then what kind of cat am I?"

"Alley?"

I sniffed. "That's just mean."

"Alright, so maybe something more casual? But we don't want to be too casual, because casual and violent combined comes off as sloppy," Lucy said. I nodded along, because it was nice to see Lucy so enthused about something, even if that something risked ending with me dressed in a stupid costume by the day's end.

"How do you figure that?"

She slowed down, then leaned into me as we walked. It was something she'd always done, at least until she needed more help to walk than just someone to lean on. "Okay, so, you're walking down an alley."

"Is this an alley cat thing?" I asked.

"Yes, it's a joke," she confirmed with a grin. "Now stop interrupting, I'm painting a picture with my words."

"That's called hallucinating, and it's not good for your health."

She jabbed an elbow into my side, and I laughed. "You're walking down an alley. It's night, so it's poorly lit. You're not in the safe parts of the city. Then someone steps out ahead of you and tells you to stop. What's the first thing you do?"

"Shoot?"

"*Cat*," she whined.

I shook my head. "Ah, okay, so, dark alley, it's probably a mugger, or someone like that. Your word-pictures are a bit stereotypical."

"Okay, maybe, but what's *actually* the first thing you do?"

I frowned. There was a hint of seriousness there. She was trying to make a point, and she wouldn't be able to if I didn't pay attention, so I did. I imagined the scenario, then shrugged again. "I guess I'll look at the person, see if they're armed, then either bolt or fight."

"Exactly!" Lucy said. "So, humans are wired weird, right?"

Tell me about it.

I decided to ignore Myalis as Lucy went on. "When we see a threat or whatever, we kind of instantly lock onto it and go through a mental checklist. Is it a person? Is it an animal? Is it an alien, which I guess folds into animal for hindbrain purposes? Is it something else? And if it *is* a person, then do we know them? If you worked for a corp and the person telling you to stop was in the corp security uniform, then you might be scared for a second but you'd calm down. They're not a threat. If you're in a gang, and the person in the alley's in the same colors, then you're safe."

"Right, okay," I said. "That makes sense. People are good at sussing people out at a glance."

Lucy nodded and was clearly quite proud of her . . . whatever that had been. "Exactly. So, a normie might see a cop and feel safe, or see someone dressed in rags and get scared. What if they see someone dressed like that?" She pointed to the banner ad. The woman was gone, replaced by a chisel-jawed Chad-type guy in corpo-wear.

"That'd be a real high-class mugger," I said.

"So they wouldn't be as scared, right?"

"Right," I agreed.

"So that's why you want to pay attention to what you wear. Casual is good for telling people that you're not serious, but it also doesn't disarm people. Casual is too . . . variable? Anyone could be wearing casual stuff."

"You know, your girlfriend is pretty smart," a strangely familiar voice said from behind me. "Which is surprising, all things considered."

I turned around and locked eyes with . . . someone I didn't know. A woman, maybe in her late twenties or early thirties, half a head shorter than me. Very little makeup, but what was there made her high cheekbones stand out and darkened her eyes. She had that noble look going. And she was dressed in very nice corpo-chic. A glossy skirt and suit jacket, with a few tasteful accessories in silver. I didn't know enough to recognize brands or anything, but it looked at once very expensive and understated.

It reminded me a little of those stupidly unaffordable luxury hovercars that just looked like a nice car, without any bells and whistles, and which cost a CEO's annual salary.

"Who are you?" I asked.

She blinked once, then one eyebrow perked up very slightly. "I suppose you don't know me in this form, but I've hardly switched faces since we last met. Should I be insulted, Miss Catherine Leblanc?"

"Cat, who's this?" Lucy asked.

She didn't strike me as a weirdo. Well, okay she did, but not the dangerous type. She didn't have the feel of a rabid fan or something like that either. More . . . like she was a businessperson here to do business.

I looked her up and down again, but nothing came to mind. "Sorry," I said. "Who are you?"

She sighed. "I'm Audrey Alice Darnell-Forsythe. And from what I hear, you're doing the intelligent thing and are looking at improving your image."

"We're just buying clothes," I said.

"I'll help," she said.

"I . . . no?"

Audrey shook her head. "Didn't I once tell you, consultations are free and compulsory."

It clicked then. The all-black outfit, the face, the voice, and then that particular line. "Emoscythe?"

"Emoscythe Mordeath Noir," she corrected before frowning. "Though at the moment, I'm Audrey."

So, out of uniform she wasn't a samurai anymore? "No one knows who you are here?" I asked. "Uh, I mean, when you're out samurai-ing?"

She shook her head. "Plenty know. Those who should, in any case. There are a number of employees who work for me here. Some know about my extracurricular activities. Others only know me as the president of whatever company they work for."

"Wow, that sounds like a lot of work," Lucy said. "I'm Lucy, by the way."

Emoscythe-slash-Audrey glanced at her and nodded. "A pleasure, Lucy. And in regards to it being a lot of work, I enjoy it . . . Otherwise I wouldn't bother. In any case, I overheard you two talking about image, so I decided to drop by and assist."

"Drop by?" I asked. "You weren't here already?"

"Why would I be here? This market is interesting, certainly, but it's one of a half-dozen in New Montreal currently running. I had no reason to be here now."

"So you came here from home or whatever after overhearing us?" I asked, just to be sure.

She rolled her eyes. "Don't say that as if you're unfamiliar with the idea of proper surveillance. I have assets here. I keep an eye on things. My AI informs me if a samurai is shopping at one of my establishments. Most of the time I leave them be. Everyone needs clothes, and it's none of my business what sort of underthings someone prefers. But if it sounds like they need help, then I help. And you need help. Once again, consultations are free and compulsory."

CHAPTER TWENTY-FOUR

RUDE, CRASS, COMMON

You either fashion, or you fashoff, right boss?
—Emoscythe Mordeath Noir's former personal assistant, first (and last) day
on the job, 2053

"So, what do you think of Cat's image problem?" Lucy asked.

Audrey frowned and looked me up and down. We weren't the only people on the shopping floor. Far from it, even, so the crowds walking around had to part to make space for our slow asses.

"It's clear that so far her AI has been making most of the stylistic choices for her, and the rest has been more or less instinctive," Audrey said.

"Hey now," I said. The way she said it felt like how someone might say "Her mom picked it out for her," and that hurt a little. Even if it was mostly or entirely true. "I'm not that bad," I said.

"No, you're really not," Audrey said. "You could be dressing substantially worse than you are. I've worked with plenty of samurai who have no idea how to manage their own image, and while you don't seem to be invested in the process, your looks fit with that kind of casual dismissal. You genuinely have a good instinct for this, Catherine."

"Yeah, you're hot," Lucy agreed.

I pushed back the flush that was trying to overtake me. Compliments weren't my forte. "Alright, so we're good, then?"

"Oh no. An instinctual understanding isn't the same as an educated understanding. You still have a long way to go before I'd say that you're capable of handling your image."

I sighed. "Fine. Just, point out some clothes from here and I'll wear that."

Audrey blinked. "Oh. No, I think we've run into a fundamental misunderstanding. I don't care what you wear."

"You don't?" I asked.

She relented, shaking her head a little and pursing her lips. "I supposed I care a little. How you dress is obviously an important part of your image, but it would be foolish to assume that it starts and ends there. And I don't just mean posture and physical appearance. Image is more than just that. It's about how the world at large perceives you." She glanced past my shoulder, and I had the impression she was looking at something I couldn't see. "Follow me," she said.

Audrey didn't wait before stepping by and walking off, which meant that Lucy and I had to move quickly to catch up. "She's weird, right?" I asked as I glanced at Lucy. Sudden samurai intervention was more common in my life than most, but this was beyond the norm even for me.

"She's a little intense," Lucy said. "Bit too . . . top for me? Still kinda hot, though."

"I mean, yeah, but I was talking more, you know, personality-wise?" Emoscythe was pretty attractive, but that was part and parcel of being young, fit, and having the ability to murder things with ease.

"Oh yeah, totally unhinged, but in a super-focused way. She reminds me a bit of Grasshopper, but less intense?"

"You two know that I can hear you?" Audrey asked.

"We do!" Lucy chirped. "We didn't say anything too bad, did we?"

"No, I suppose not. Being compared to Grasshopper is actually quite nice. She's a good woman." Audrey brought us to an area on the outer ring of the market where the stalls weren't quite as corporatized. They were more often simple plastic tables with a few banners, some basic dividers, and racks full of clothes for sale. Farther away, closer to the outer edge, were some stalls where the merchants were making clothes live, some of them with a small audience. "This is what I wanted you to see."

I looked away from the bespoke stalls and refocused on the shop Audrey had stopped before. It was a semicircle of tables with a few walls behind them from which T-shirts hung on bars. That was all they sold here, shirts and more shirts. A machine was printing something on a shirt while the stall keeper and someone that was presumably a client waited.

"What am I looking for . . . oh," I said. There was a row of shirts that were me-themed. Or Stray Cat themed? I hadn't noticed, but nearly all of the shirts here were samurai merch.

I chose to ignore the ones of me for the moment and instead looked at the others. There were a few samurai I didn't recognize, and plenty more that I did. Pouty-faced Deus Ex, some chibi art of Grasshopper, some very bright shirts with Neon Girl Happy-chan. Some locals that had passed away a while ago too, or that had probably left Earth. Emeraude was there, and I knew they had been a New Montreal local once. It was strange thinking that I'd actually met some of the people on those shirts.

The row with my own image was the weirdest of all.

There was an anime-style illustration of me in a cool pose shooting someone that was probably the mayor with "Shut up!" written above it in big bubbly letters. Damn, that had only been two days ago. The rest of the art tended toward darker and grittier. Lots of "Get fucked" and art of my cat-logo with bleeding mice in its mouth.

Also, some of the art had my gear stripped down to little more than my helmet and a bikini bottom, with a strategically placed Void Terminus to cover the chest. "I'm buying these," Lucy said.

"No," I shot her down as I reached over and plucked the lewd shirt from her hands.

"Aw, but Cat! It's sexy! Look at how *big* they made your boobs!"

"No," I said. I got up on the tips of my toes and hooked the shirts on the next rack up, just out of reach of Lucy's grasping fingers. "Is this what you wanted me to see?" I asked Audrey.

"Yes," she said. "Look at how artists have decided to portray you. *That's* your image. This is, in part, what people think when they think of Stray Cat. These items are what people who support what you do will wear."

That put a new spin on things. The art—big-tiddied versions of me aside—was almost all gory and violent and gritty. It wasn't *necessarily* bad. But it didn't feel right either. I wasn't exactly a bastion of hope and fuzzy feelings, but I didn't think I was leaning this hard into the heavy-metal band aesthetic.

"Once an image becomes rooted in people's minds, it can take a lot of effort to change it. You're still early in your career as a samurai. You still have time to change and shape what you do."

"That's going to take more than just dressing in brighter colors, isn't it?" I asked.

"A lot more, yes. Though it is a start, *if* that's the direction you want to go in. Clothes maketh the man, but gear maketh the samurai. The equipment you use and how you appear will change your image to some degree. Deus Ex is still considered disarmingly cute, even though she could easily level a city. On the opposite side of that same coin, some samurai are considered threatening even though they're not nearly as powerful. You're starting to inch your way in that direction. Your image is of someone dangerous. Not necessarily in a bad way, but still dangerous."

I chewed on my lip. "And that means people will treat me a certain way."

"Yes. The same way that you might approach others based on what you think of them, they will approach you based on what they think of you. It's how humans function," she said.

I nodded along. It was all common sense shit, wasn't it? But it was also common sense shit that I hadn't spent any time actually thinking about until now. "This image shit is going to make some of my projects harder, isn't it?"

"Projects?" Audrey asked.

"Yeah. I've got this whole thing I'm setting up, getting cheaply printed prosthetics out to people that need them. Mostly the people I've rescued here and there, but also anyone else that needs it."

"That's kind of you," she said.

"Cat's good at being nice," Lucy said. "She's less good at *looking* nice."

Audrey crossed her arms and scowled at the floor for a moment. "That puts a certain spin on things. You were readily willing to kill a politician, at least as far as the public is concerned, but you're also doing charity work. You did some work in a position of leadership in Burlington as well. Huh, that's an interesting angle to work with."

"Angle? I'm a little bit lost," I said.

"She wants you to go full Robin Hood," Lucy said. "I think you'd look great in tights and with a cloak."

I snorted. "I'm not exactly . . . well, I have stolen from the rich, but I mostly just use that to fix the shit they should have been fixing themselves."

"That'll still count," Audrey said. "Yes, I can see that working. A rude, crass, common sort of girl who's righting wrongs where she sees them, taking from those in power and using what she takes to correct some of the problems they've caused. It's a nice narrative."

A narrative? I wasn't here telling a story, I was trying to get things done. Besides, the idea of a narrative made me jump to things being less-than-true. "Hey now," I said. "That sounds a bit too fictional, no?"

"All images are fictional. It's about *image*, not about truth. But don't worry. Truth tends to shine through, to some degree or another. You'll manage. Now . . . how do we make your image and style reflect your actions?"

CHAPTER TWENTY-FIVE

COTTAGECORE SAMURAI POWER-COUPLE

Victorian is always in fashion.
—Emoscythe Mordeath Noir, to the crowd of a fashion show she held at gunpoint, 2051

The thing that I was afraid would happen, of course, happened.

Lucy and Audrey started to get along.

Mostly I blamed Lucy's charisma. While it was fine when she was trying to butter me up, or trying to accomplish something we both wanted, it could be a tiny bit annoying to see her turn the charm on others. Not that I was the jealous sort.

Actually, no, I was definitely the jealous sort. It was probably not my finest quality, but I wanted to keep Lucy all to myself sometimes. She wouldn't want that, though. There was no keeping my bird in a cage, even if it was nice and gilded. So I stood on the sidelines as Lucy and Audrey talked.

"What about your own image?" Lucy asked. We were walking around the outer ring, taking our time and mostly just chatting. "You're obviously the expert here, so I imagine that you spent some time on your own PR stuff."

"I have, although . . . I think I might be something of a poorly shod cobbler. I haven't had to put great effort into my own image in some time, and I think it's due for an upgrade. Did you want to see my current costume?"

"Costume?" I asked. I'd noticed that some people in security uniforms had cordoned off an area some ways away, redirecting traffic into the inner ring. Since most of the traffic all came from the same direction, it meant that the area we were in was a small pocket of quiet.

The VIP treatment felt a little whatever, but I couldn't say it was bad. I didn't need people clamoring over to take pics or bother us.

"Different samurai use different terms for it, but I always found 'costume' to be the most accurate," Audrey said. "It's not just the gear you take with you into the field, but the look that you choose for yourself. It's a costume because it's a way of dress that reflects the work that you do, but unlike a uniform it places some importance on style and flare."

Audrey opened her hand to the side and a small beam of light was projected onto her palm from the strap of her watch. It swirled for just a moment before turning into a gently spinning image of Emoscythe, or at least a rendering of her, in her full samurai getup.

It was the same style I'd seen her in already. A dark, gothic dress, with lots of lace and fancy trimmings. "This is my usual costume," she said.

"Oh, pretty!" Lucy said. "Very, uh, is it a Victorian-doll look? Kind of goth at the same time. The makeup is what gives that impression though."

She nodded. "This kind of fashion is . . . perhaps not a look that I would choose today."

"It isn't?" I asked. "After everything you said about image, I thought you'd be pretty keen on keeping up your own."

"As I said, I'm a poorly shod cobbler. Not that I'm not fond of my costume. I can't see myself changing it now because I have history with it. It's become part of how people recognize me. But when I first stepped out into the world as Emoscythe Mordeath Noir, I was much younger, less informed, less experienced, and I wanted very badly to project something. I think I succeeded at that, despite my shortcomings. But I have grown, so perhaps I'm due for some slight upgrades, delivered over a long period of time to soften the transition."

"You were trying to look innocent but dangerous?" Lucy asked.

Audrey nodded. "Exactly so," she said. "A young woman in an outdated dress should, by all means, seem innocent, but that same image of innocence had been co-opted by so many tropes that it is now a threat display. It's one of those strange, somewhat counterintuitive cultural things. I caught on to that early, and decided to center my image around it."

"And if you were to start over?" Lucy asked.

Audrey glanced at Lucy, but I had the impression she was looking past her. "I think, were I to start over, my image as a samurai would better reflect what I am now. Though . . . I suppose that's foolish. Your initial image can hardly reflect who you *will* be, it can only be a reflection of who you *are*. But that's not quite what you asked. If I were to choose now, I think my costume would look a lot more like this ensemble I have on."

I raised an eyebrow at that and looked her up and down real quick. "You're dressed like a corpo," I said.

"I'm dressed like a businesswoman," she corrected, though I wasn't sure I was wrong. "This image is more suitable to convince people in business that I'm willing and able to understand them. It's not as intimidating as your own outfit, and it's less likely to be dismissed as my own samurai costume might be. The way you appear will inform others how to treat you." She met my eyes and I felt myself rooted to the spot.

Audrey was intense.

"Which is why you should decide how you want to appear. We've been talking about it for some time, but I've yet to get anything on the most important factor in determining your image."

"What's that?" I asked.

She sniffed. "What *you* want, Miss Stray Cat."

"Oh," I said. I suppose I hadn't *really* put that much thought into it, and it probably showed. Audrey looked at me expectantly for a long moment, and I could feel a kernel of stress building up in the pit of my stomach.

"Give her a minute to cook," Lucy said, her voice pitched low. "In the meantime . . . we're looking for, like, casual wear too. You know, things to wear around the house? Our place doesn't really fit the aesthetic, but I'm really tempted to go all cottagecore myself. Get those housewife vibes going."

Now that Audrey was successfully distracted, I took a moment to actually think. It was harder than I'd expected.

Do you need help?

I considered it, but then shook my head. Myalis would produce stuff for me with an eye for style no matter what, but if I asked for something more specific, she'd probably still twist things her way.

So, what did I want?

I liked looking badass and cool, and I wasn't sure I wanted that to change. Then again, how badass was I really? People didn't take me as seriously as I wanted, sometimes. It led to me having to make examples.

If I'd rocked up to the mayor the first time covered in skulls and dripping blood, maybe he wouldn't have fucked around enough to find out.

At the same time, I didn't *want* to be scary, did I? Maybe by reputation, because that was fine, but I didn't want someone who'd never seen me before to be scared shitless upon meeting me for the first time.

What did that even lead to? Was there a set of sliding scales of badassery and scariness that I needed to dial in?

"Alright," I said. That caught both girls' attention. "Look, I don't have an exact thing in mind, but I kinda know what I want. More or less."

"Go on," Audrey said. Then she glanced around. "Or maybe hold onto that thought? Let's go talk in my office upstairs. It's a little more private. Lucy, if you wish to join us, you may, though you're also free to remain here to shop."

Lucy grinned. "I'll come with! I might have to put my foot down if you insist on Cat wearing nothing but a neon leotard or something."

"That's fair," Audrey said.

I thought it was very much *not* fair. Did that mean she'd been considering the neon leotard idea? Because I was definitely not okay with that. If Audrey tried to put me in some sort of magical girl outfit, I was gonna go full gunslinger on her ass.

Audrey didn't hear my mental rant, so she happily led us through the market and to a side exit that unlocked when we approached. We went up a couple of floors, then through a rather long corridor that culminated into an office with a glass floor.

I stared down, somewhat worried about walking on glass, but Lucy seemed to think that it was fantastic and started to jump on the spot, as if testing the glass for cracks. "This is cool!" she said.

We had a pretty great view of the entire marketplace below from two stories up. "Can they see us?" I asked. I hadn't looked up when I was down there, so I had no idea.

"No, it's one-way glass," Audrey said. "I like wearing skirts," she added, as if that explained everything, which I suppose it did.

There was a large, imposing desk to one side of the room, as well as some plush seats, but she led us to the side, where a couple of loveseats were positioned around a coffee table.

"Now, you've had a few minutes, so let's hear what you came up with," Audrey said as she sat and crossed her legs.

CHAPTER TWENTY-SIX

STRAY CAT'S CUT

You gotta at least try to look good. Otherwise you'll be made the fool.
        —Mayor Dupont, to an administrative aid, 2057

"Uh," I said.

There was a hovering projection of me standing in the middle of us, the hologram's feet brushing just over the coffee table's surface as it gently spun.

"That's just me," I said.

It was. I'd been talking to Audrey and Lucy for what felt like several hours up in the office, but was actually closer to just the one. We'd gone over what I wanted for my image. It wasn't too complicated. Or that's what I thought, at least.

I wanted to be scary to those that needed scaring, and I wanted people that needed help, people in the shitty sorts of situations that I'd been in, to trust that I'd help them.

"Yes. Did you expect me to show you someone else?" Audrey asked.

"No, I mean." I gestured at the hovering me. "That's literally just me, in my normal gear."

The hologram was me, in my long coat, scarf around my neck and cat-eared helmet on. The image wasn't armed, but I could imagine myself carrying one of my usual guns.

"This is you as you are, yes," Audrey said. "Now, I have had a few ideas for how you could lean into the image and style you described, and I've compiled them as we talked. I don't think these fit exactly, but I'll still show you them so you can see different options."

She waved her arm and the hologram split into three. One was still me, but my coat was sharper, the helmet sleeker. Everything under the coat was synthetic and clean. Basically, it was me as a corpo stooge.

The image next to it was a hard contrast. The hologram was standing a bit to one side, hip canted out. I still had a coat on, but it was ratty around the edges, and the entire back of it was one large glowing cat face. My pants were covered in straps with logos and there were pins all across the coat. The shoulders were covered in little spikes and the helmet had a generic sticker slapped onto the side. So, a corpo me, and an all-out punk me.

The third image was a bit strange. No coat, instead the outfit was . . . superheroic. There was a cape, and the rest of the gear was sleek and accentuated my stomach and chest.

"Oh," Lucy said. "I like the superhero look!"

"It's nice," Audrey agreed. "But it's not Stray Cat. You do embody a lot of traditional values the public might associate with superheroes, so you could lean into those tropes, but it doesn't quite fit. Superheroes are supposed to be clean and fight for what they think is just, with a minimal amount of disruption and death. You don't fit the antihero role either. I don't think it's the right way to go."

"Okay, so none of these," I said. The grungy one did kind of call out to me, but I could see why it might not be right. I was . . . well, I *was* street trash, but I wasn't a street punk. There was a difference. Probably not one someone up top would notice, but it'd be obvious to any real punks.

"Agreed. My final idea, though, I think you'll like. Here's what I'd suggest," Audrey said. She made another gesture and the three images winked out. They were replaced by another me.

"Oh," I said.

It was kind of obvious. Right, in a way that was just . . . right? It was like finding the square peg for the square hole after slipping in every other shape because they just happened to fit.

The coat was there, but different. It cut off at the knees and had a much more pronounced collar. And a hood. A really cool hood that had space for cat ears. The coat was black, with armored pads over the shoulders and elbows.

It was covering a tight shirt with several clasps running across it. A little bit corpo, but also a little military. That look was broken up by the belts. There were a few of them, actually. One around the waist, another at the hip. Belts with a few small pouches that looked to be about the right size for one of my grenades, and there was room in the belts for both Void Terminus, my sword, and my Trench Maker.

The boots were big, clunky things, and as Audrey spun the hologram around, I saw a small, tight backpack fixed to the middle of the coat. It had nozzles, and I recognized a jump-jet.

My helmet was almost unchanged, though it had been adjusted a little to appear more like the face of a cat.

"Fuck, that looks good," I said. "But it also looks like, uh—"

"A bounty hunter," Audrey finished. "That's purposeful. You're not a bounty hunter, but you fit into a similar role. Someone who works within the bounds of the law, but only just, who kills those who are hard to kill, but who doesn't necessarily work against the society they're part of. There's a bit of ninja in there too: the hood, the mask, the utility belts. That part just fits well with your tendency to use stealth when you feel like it."

I stood up, then slowly walked around the image. It was pretty cool. "What do you think?" I asked Lucy.

"It has your scarf," she said.

I looked back at the hologram. It did. Wrapped around "my" neck was a familiar hot-pink scarf, the same one that Lucy had picked out for me a while ago. It clashed with the rest of the gear a little, though . . . well, the armor did have some pink glowy bits, otherwise how would people know to take me seriously?

"I like it," I said. And I was being entirely honest. It looked right, like something that someone called Stray Cat would wear. It was a cyber-ninja-hunter-badass outfit. It almost felt *too* much like what I wanted to be.

Audrey smiled. It was slight and yet incredibly smug. "Why thank you. I'll send you the design files. You don't need to change into this all at once. In fact, I'd discourage it unless you want to go out and make a big splash. Small, subtle changes over time are often more appreciated than you might expect."

"Are you sure this is all free?" I asked.

"Of course I'm sure," Audrey said. "Even a samurai needs a hobby, and this happens to be mine. Actually, samurai especially need hobbies."

"Cat's been trying to get into repairing stuff," Lucy said. "It's . . . well, she's spending a lot of time on it."

I gave Lucy a flat look. "Thanks," I said. "I appreciate the vote of confidence." Lucy just giggled. "Anyway, this was a lot more than I expected to get out of all this," I said.

"You're welcome," Audrey said. She sighed, then slowly got up. She smoothed down her skirt and glanced at the doorway. "Unfortunately, I carved out some time from another project to help you. I'm certain the world will fall apart if I don't get back to work."

"The world?" I asked.

"Of fashion, of course."

"Right," I said, a little dubious. "We still need to buy stuff anyway. It's kind of why we came here in the first place."

"Oh, right. I thought we'd be back home by now," Lucy said. "How long is the market open for?"

"Another couple of hours," Audrey said. "I'll let you have the friends discount, which should help you grab more clothes. Though . . . do *wear* the stuff you buy. I always find it insulting when someone buys something only for it to rot in a closet."

"Don't worry, we're not the sort to stay in any closets," Lucy said, earning a smile from me.

We said our goodbyes. Audrey stayed back in her office, and as Lucy and I were leaving one wall lit up with a multitude of smaller screens, each with graphs and images and camera feeds and enough information to probably make the average person dizzy. The door shut behind us and all the noise was masked away.

"That was something," I said.

"That was. Are all the samurai so intense?"

"You've met some," I said.

"Delilah's a little intense, but she's polite. Grasshopper is very intense, but also nice . . . She's aggressively nice, actually. I barely met Deus Ex. And now I've met Audrey, who is, ah, the way she is."

"That seems like a decent sampling."

"That's five, counting you. I guess I ran into some in Burlington, but never long enough to form a good opinion. I thought that Grasshopper was, like, an outlier. But maybe you're the weird one."

"I'm not weird," I defended.

Lucy leaned into me. "Mm-hmm," she said.

"What's that mean?"

"It means mm-hmm."

I rolled my eyes at Lucy being Lucy. "Well, she's pretty normal for a samurai, I guess. I haven't met *that* many, but I think they—we—tend more toward the very focused and intense side of things, as a general rule."

"That's alright, then," Lucy said. "I do like it when you're being intense. It's kinda hot."

"Ah, well, I'll try to be intensely in love with you."

"Dork."

CHAPTER TWENTY-SEVEN

NUN TOO SOON

H-hi everyone!

My name is Giga Shimmer Aurora Dove Love Magnet Cosmic Dreamer, and I'm the magical girl that's going to save your sorry asses! Can . . . can I get an uwu?

Please?

—Beatrice "Quantum Lovely Bubble Pop Honey Bliss Laser Ranger" Smith, during her first livestream, 2040

I stared at the part in my right hand, then the one in my left. They had grooves designed to interlock together. I knew this, because I had seven more nearly identical parts, all of them now slotted together, sitting on a table in front of me.

I pushed the two parts together.

They didn't fit.

"What the fuck?" I muttered as I tried shoving the two parts together with more force. Unfortunately, extra enthusiasm didn't do anything.

These doohickeys all fit along a line that ran from the mech's leg up into a sort of little actuator in the shoulder. The actuator needed replacing, which meant that I had to take apart all of the little clamps that kept the line in place.

It had taken a few hours, and was rather tedious, but I'd figured it out and became pretty decent at it by the end. There was some skin missing from my knuckles, but it wasn't that bad.

Now I just had to put it all back together. The new actuator had fit into place like it belonged there, and these fiddly bits I was working with were the old ones—they should have fit in well, because I'd literally taken them out an hour ago.

That was only if I could get them to click together. I tried again, but the part didn't fit into its opposite. Squinting, I looked at the two, then noticed that they were slightly different. "Myalis, what's going on?"

That's part 256B that you're trying to fit into 257G. They aren't meant to be together.

"They're all different?" I asked.

Yes. 257B is on the table to your left. 256G is currently linked to 257C. 256G and 257C happen to click into place, though the tolerance is off.

"I did that like, ten minutes ago," I said. "You knew!"

I did.

"Then why didn't you tell me?" I asked. I was past frustrated by that point, but I figured I owed Myalis at least the chance to explain herself.

I am very good at running predictions. If I corrected you, you wouldn't have made the mistake. You also wouldn't have learned a lesson. I predict an extremely high likelihood that, moving forward, you will be significantly more attentive about labeling and marking out your parts.

I sighed. She was probably right. "Okay, so how do I fix this?"

The parts on the table started to glow as my augs highlighted them. They were each painted in two colors, and it didn't take a genius to figure out that the colors went with those they matched to.

"Oh, hey, this one's not fucked," I said as I picked one up.

A legitimate coincidence. You were going to fit it into the wrong place, but then you dropped the incorrect part and fitted it into the right one instead. That part has rolled under the mech, by the way. There should be ten parts in total.

I grumbled to myself as I went to look for the part. The mecha was looking . . . disassembled. Which was actually an improvement. The busted, bent, or otherwise fucked bits were all gone. Now all that was left were missing pieces. For the most part, I was done removing the bad, and was now working to shove in the good.

It was just taking a lot more work to replace parts than to remove them.

I was on all fours under the mech when I noticed a large van moving toward our place. It slowed down, then flew toward the lower floors and out of sight.

I shimmied backward out from under the mech (with the part I'd gone down to get), then returned to the workbench. "Hey, we got eyes on that van?" I asked Myalis. There was basically a bubble around our place that was more or less free of aerial traffic except for high-flying cars and the occasional racers that didn't mind dipping in and out of the area.

The ground traffic was the same as always, and with the buildings all around us getting refurbished, there were plenty of construction crews moving through the area. I figured people would be moving back in soon. It didn't make sense to keep a large section of the city empty, especially with so much of the incursion damage being repaired.

I supposed that building the wall around the city might have temporarily slowed down construction, but the need for housing was probably high enough that the distraction didn't last.

The van is a transport owned by the same church that Gomorrah lives within. It was piloted by Franny.

"Oh," I said. Well, that made some sense. I looked over the stuff I had laid out on the table, then at the repair drone hovering nearby. "How about you fix these up and then go on and place them into the mech?" I asked the drone.

It bobbed up and down, which I took to mean yes.

You're not going to do the work yourself?

"Hey, I do want to finish all of this sometime in the next year. This part's easy anyway." At least, when I didn't mess up.

You might be missing out on an important lesson.

"What am I supposed to learn from replacing all of those fiddly bits one at a time?" I asked, genuinely curious.

How to deal with tedium?

"That's what I thought," I muttered. I picked up a rag and started to wipe my hands free of grease and oil. I walked back into the house and found the kittens mostly lounging around lazily, though Junior currently had Nose in a headlock and was frozen staring at me, her knuckles buried in his hair.

"What'd he do?" I asked.

"Spat in my cereal," she said before shrugging. "It was the last of it."

I nodded and walked on past, ignoring Nose's cries for mercy and help.

I found Lucy in the bedroom, lying on her back with her legs up against the wall. She was staring at the ceiling with the kind of dull-eyed focus that people had when looking at their augs. She shifted her focus to me as I came in. "Hey. Done with the work?"

"Just taking a little break. Gonna head downstairs. I think Gomorrah's stuff has arrived. Figured I'd talk to her, see if she needs help moving in."

"Oh," Lucy said. She flopped to the side, then climbed to the edge of the bed.

"You're coming?" I asked.

"Nah, you go. I don't want to get roped into helping move boxes. But I will make a cake! That's what all the old-timey housewives do in the vids when they have new neighbors."

"Well, as long as you dress like one of those old-timey housewives," I said.

Lucy grinned. "If that's what you want, I can certainly try." She curtsied, which mostly meant pulling up the edges of her oversized T-shirt until the lower part of her belly was exposed.

"Mm-hmm," I said distractedly. ". . . Right, anyway. I'll be back in not too long, I think."

I got changed into some new casual wear we'd ended up buying from that market yesterday—cargo pants and a graphic tee with a pouty Deus Ex on it—then splashed some water on my face to clean it off before heading to the elevators. They were the only way down, unless I wanted to drive to the parking garage a few floors below, but that just seemed silly.

I only realized that I wasn't armed when I was three floors down. I felt a small shock of unease at the realization, but I took a deep breath and calmed myself down. I was home, so I was probably safe.

If I wasn't, then it would only be a few seconds' work to arm myself right back up.

The door dinged a few floors down, and I narrowed my eyes against a blast of stale, warm air. I hadn't been down to the parking garage in . . . a while. I was vaguely aware that the mecha cats we had at home for protection tended to patrol the entire public space in the building, usually while stealthed, but that was the most interaction I'd had with this place.

It was strangely empty of cars or any other signs of life. Then again, maybe that wasn't so strange. I took up two floors, and a number of others were vacant. I was pretty sure that no one had really started to fix up the lower areas with the shops and such.

I found the van parked not too far from the entrance, with the *Fury* resting next to it. Franny was in the back, along with two others who looked . . . nun-like, even if they were dressed casually. Something about the straight backs and proper postures gave me those vibes.

"Heya girls, welcome to the cat house. You need any help with those boxes?"

CHAPTER TWENTY-EIGHT

MASTER OF NUN

God has not forsaken us, though the hour is dark and the days grow long! We have new, shining beacons of hope, raised from the best, the sinless, those who are redeemed! Bow your heads in prayer, sheep of God, and allow the shepherds to guide you to a better tomorrow!

This sermon comes with a 15 percent discount for the devoted members of our enlightened church!

—Pope Roboticus the First, New Christian Order, 2037

One of the nuns stopped to stare at me. She was a few years older than me, maybe in her mid-twenties, and she didn't look impressed with my choice of clothes. "Pardon me, miss, but this area should be off-limits," she said. I don't think someone could sound more prudish if they tried.

"Is it?" I asked. "I don't recall there being anything like that."

"This is the residence of a *samurai*," she said. "You don't want to be caught spying on a saint, do you?"

"Sister Datamaria, is something wrong?" the other nun said. She came to stand next to . . . Datamaria? That was a new one.

"Just an interloper, Sister Ethergrace," Datamaria said.

I glanced between the two. They weren't dressed like on-duty nuns, so no habits or whatever, but there was no mistaking the style. Long skirts, long-sleeved blouses that covered everything, hair done up in severe buns. Datamaria was the taller of the two, with light-brown hair and eyes too blue to be real.

Ethergrace was much shorter, and it looked like maybe she had spent more time snacking on the alms than handing them out. She looked my way and smiled though, and I got the impression that she was far nicer than her companion. "Hello dearie," she said. "I'm sorry, but Sister Datamaria is probably right. We're here to move things to the floor below. I don't think we need any help, however."

"Ah, that's alright," I said. The floor below *and* this one? Had Gomorrah gotten two floors? Actually, that kind of made sense. She'd want space in the parking garage for her car. "I genuinely don't mind helping. I was just taking a break from work. If you want, I can have a drone help you carry stuff." I pointed past her to the van. It looked like someone had been playing Tetris with furniture in there because it was packed to the brim.

Sister Datamaria sniffed. "I said we don't need the help."

I was about to pull away. I didn't feel like getting into an argument, let alone with someone that was probably the friend of a friend. Starting something on the back foot like this would take a lot of work to fix, and I really didn't feel like it.

Then Franny came around the van, a small stack of boxes held in her hands. Her chin was resting on the topmost box, keeping it pinned in place. She saw me and the two nuns, then brightened. "Cat! I didn't think you'd show up," she said.

"Well, I told Delilah I'd help, but we didn't exchange exact times or anything, so it's fair," I said.

She chuckled, raspy and dark. "I thought you'd be out shooting more politicians or something."

"I really hope that's not the only thing I'm remembered for," I said. "That's the kind of rep that'll be hard to work my way back from."

"Do you know this girl, Sister Pureheart?" Sister Datamaria asked.

I blinked. "Wait, Franny, your name is—"

"*Don't,*" Franny snapped. "It's . . . a nun thing. We get names given to us. We don't pick them."

"That much is obvious," I said. "You'd have picked Sister Hellion, or Sister Inthecloset or something."

Franny's look was flat and unamused, but the gasp from Sister Ethergrace was worth it. "Honestly, yeah, I probably would have picked something rude and gotten the switch for it. Pureheart is just so . . . tacky though. Before you ask, Delilah is Sister Holy Firewall."

"Huh." Yeah, that tracked.

Sister Datamaria shook her head. "Is this one of your street friends, Franny?" she asked, dropping the title.

Franny sighed. "Sisters, this is Catherine . . . I can't remember her family name. Something French?"

"Leblanc," I offered. It was a name that was too fancy-sounding for me, but I didn't pick it. I guess I could see where Franny was coming from.

"Right," Franny said. "You probably know her better as Stray Cat. She's the owner of the giant cheesy cat-shaped floor above us."

"Hey," I said. "It's not cheesy. Tacky, kitsch, gaudy maybe, but not cheesy."

The sisters both gasped, and Ethergrace almost dropped what she was carrying as she slapped a hand over her mouth. "You're a saintess," she said. "Sister Datamaria, apologize, quick!"

Sister Datamaria did just that, bowing twice before she spoke. "Forgive me, saintess. I allowed my poor judgement to overcome my good sense. I will accept any punishment you see fit to hand out for my conduct."

"Uh," I said.

Franny rolled her eyes, and I got a text message from her a moment later. I supposed she didn't want to say what she was thinking aloud.

Franny: This is why Delilah's moving.

I could imagine. "It's all good," I said. "And my offer to help was legit. Is Gomorrah here too?"

"She's back home, dealing with some stuff," Franny said. "Uh, the church home, not here, I mean."

"She let you take the *Fury*?" I asked. There was no doubt about it, Delilah was in capital-L Love with Franny if she was letting the redhead take her car out.

"She was worried that someone might try to rob the van while we were moving," Franny said.

I blinked. The van looked like it was twice my age. Not too much rust or anything, so it had been decently maintained, but still, not exactly a prize worth stealing, and the contents looked like boxes of random stuff. "Why would anyone take that old thing?"

"It's filled with the possessions of a saintess," Sister Ethergrace said. Her eyes were practically shining.

"It's Delilah's crap," Franny added.

"Franny," Sister Ethergrace hissed. "Some decorum, please?"

"Some of it's alien tech. In a rickety old van, that's a juicy target," Franny continued, pointedly ignoring the sister.

That was probably fair. I supposed that I'd kind of grown used to having Protectorate stuff at my fingertips, so it didn't feel so special anymore, but some of the gear I tossed aside was probably worth enough to change someone's life if they got ahold of it.

A van full of samurai tech? Yeah, that'd be worth a fortune. The sisters were carrying the equivalent of a few gold bricks around, it made sense to want to defend it.

Also, I'd be annoyed if someone stole my shit. I'd have to track it down and kill people, which would cut into my vacation time. Having the *Fury* flying around would discourage anyone from trying anything.

"Well, it should be safe here," I said. "Or around the building. We've got turrets mounted on the outside, and there're some cats roaming around."

"Cats?" Franny asked.

I nodded, then turned back toward the parking garage. I was pretty sure there was one in here. It took me a moment to find the right app in my augs to call it over. There was a muffled *click-click*, then the air warped as the invisibility dropped around one of my cat mechs. It was just one of those I'd bought to guard the house, a mechanical cat drone with a few guns.

It was scarier more because of its ability to go unnoticed than anything else. "One of these," I said. "I'll probably buy or fabricate a few more, if Gom doesn't mind. If we're gonna have this whole building be a samurai place, then it makes sense to keep up the security."

"Cool," Franny said.

"So, need help?"

Franny shrugged, then shifted her hold on the boxes. "Yeah, sure. We're taking up the two floors below this one."

That'd leave a floor between the museum and the parking garage. Actually, that was decent. It gave me some room to expand downward if I needed it. "Nice," I said. "Is Gom planning on taking over some of the garage too?"

"I think so. Just a corner of it. She wants a lift to park the *Fury* in the house. Which I think is a bit silly, but whatever."

Yeah, she *would* park her car in the living room. I went to the back of the van, aware of the two nuns staring at me, and reached for one of the boxes. I don't think Sister Datamaria meant for me to hear her whispering to Franny, but I picked it up anyway.

"Sister Pureheart, you can't ask a *saintess* to do menial labor for you!"

"She offered," Franny said.

"Out of the grace and kindness of her heart, but you should have refused."

"Oh, don't get your panties in a knot, it's Cat. She's alright."

I had to hold back the urge to puff out in pride. Damn right I was alright. I picked up a box, then almost dropped it when Myalis spoke up and surprised me. She could go hours without saying anything sometimes.

Lift with your knees.

"Really?" I asked.

It'll save you points later. Unless you want to replace your spine now? If you don't, then proper posture will save you from future pain and point expenditure.

I rolled my eyes as I shifted my grip on the box. "Yeah, yeah," I muttered. "Alright, Franny, where are we dumping all of this?"

"Follow me," Franny said. "I'll show you the place while we're at it."

CHAPTER TWENTY-NINE

UN-CONVENT-IONAL INTERIOR DESIGN

Eye-linked augmentations, or augs, are a necessary part of life in the 2050s. Almost everything uses touchless interfaces now, most of which require some sort of aug in order to link with it.

When it works, it means that someone can interact with the world around them without ever doing any more than glancing at it!

—*Augworld*, digital magazine, 2051

Franny turned to the side so that she could stare at the elevator panel without a stack of boxes blocking her vision. Some augmented reality stuff was useful, and some of it was downright stupidly designed. The elevator's button panel was probably one of the latter.

"Okay, so, Delilah's planning on breaking down a lot of the floors between the two, uh, floors that we're building on."

"That makes sense, I guess," I said. "I can't remember what the two levels were before."

"Offices, mostly," Franny said. "There was one small factory space in the northern end that already covers both levels, and there's a salon too. The rest is all offices, call centers, server rooms. That kind of stuff."

I nodded along. The elevator arrived soon enough, and we stepped in. The ride down didn't take much longer. A floor hummed past, then we stopped at the next one down and Franny led the way into . . . not much of anything, really.

The space had at one point been a few separate offices, but now the walls between the different parts of the floor were torn down and piled to one side, four-by-eight panels that had been bolted onto the girders that supported the building. At glance, it looked like the walls were maybe fifteen centimeters thick, with room for cabling and such between them.

The flooring was even the same across the different offices. Basically, it was like each office was a macro-cubicle for whichever company owned it, with smaller cubicles inside for the poor fucks working for them.

Now everything was stacked up to one side, a heap of walls and cubicles and desks. "What are you going to do with all of that?" I asked.

"Sell it," Franny said with a shrug. She carried her boxes over to a small pile, away from the disassembled walls and cubicles. "The church is helping with that. Only took a day to find someone interested, but they'll only be around to pick it all up tomorrow."

"I guess there's a market for this kind of stuff?"

"Right now? Yeah. Lots of damaged buildings, and I think those wall panels are like some sort of universal fit. The desks and cubicles are just desks and cubicles. Someone will want them."

I set down the box I was carrying next to the pile. "Makes sense," I said. "So, want to show me around? I'm kinda curious, though I guess there's not much to show for it yet."

"Yeah, sure," Franny said. "Plus it'll get me away from Datamaria for a bit. She's . . . a lot. Ethergrace is nice, though. She didn't sleep through the 'don't be a judgmental bitch' lessons the way Datamaria did."

I snorted. I wasn't involved enough with anything religious to be able to comment on it, but I had the impression that there was a lot of drama behind closed doors. "She was a bit much. Weird to see her immediately turn nice when she found out I was a samurai."

"They're all like that," Franny said. "We're taught that samurai are saints, one step down from the damned pope. Plus, you know, samurai are celebrities already. You're getting pretty popular too."

"Am I?" I asked. The nuns hadn't recognized me, at least not dressed in casuals. "I don't pay too much attention to it."

"Yeah. You were behind Delilah for a while, until, you know, you shot the mayor in a livestream. Now you're two thousand ranks ahead." Franny shook her head. "I was sure Delilah would break the top ten-k before you."

I blinked, then made a note to look at my popularity rankings. I didn't have the time or inclination to obsess over that kind of shit, but I was also pretty curious.

"Anyway! This is the lower floor, where we'll have most of the 'outward facing' stuff. That's what Delilah calls it," Franny said. She pointed to one end of the room. "That'll be where the chapel is. Just a little one, mostly so the old bats back home don't get their dusty old panties in a knot."

"Alright," I said. I wouldn't want a chapel in my place, but Delilah would do as she pleased.

"That part over there, without the windows? That's the factory part. It was one of those 3D printer places. You'd order shit up online and they'd make and ship it."

"Oh, nice," I said. "Is the stuff still there?"

Franny shook her head. "Nah, all gone. The company that owns it picked it up a bit ago. I guess the machines are worth enough to move them around to a new place. Anyway, it's a big, empty room with reinforced parts. Delilah wants to install the lift for her car there. Like a mini interior garage."

"That's cool," I said.

"So, chapel there, garage there. I guess we can have like, a lobby space or something here. And I guess offices or something there? There's a lot more room than we need, honestly." Franny walked over to one of the staircases, and I followed her. "I think we'll block these off. I don't really like the idea of someone being able to walk right through. The elevators can continue, I guess, but we might want better security on those."

"I'll talk to Gomorrah about it," I said. "But yeah, it makes sense. Better cameras, and a scanner maybe? Something dangerous in case someone we don't like comes in. I can definitely shove some bombs in there."

Franny gave me a very flat look. "I'm alright with living in the same building as you, Cat, but not if you're going to bomb the place."

"I didn't say I'd set them off. Besides, I have some bombs that wouldn't take the building down. And you're one to talk, your girlfriend lights shit on fire on the regular."

Franny's cheeks warmed up, which was blatantly obvious under the smattering of freckles across her nose. "Whatever," she said as she continued to stomp her way up the stairs. "So, this is the living floor."

I followed her up and into the next floor. This one was only half-cleared, but there was something at work on the rest of it. I stopped to stare. It was a robot of some sort, set on a wide wheel base with six small rubbery wheels. It had a large, boxy frame with several articulated arms coming out of it with tools on their ends.

The robot was taking apart one of those wall panels with one of its arms, which had a drill on the end, but the thing was moving at a snail's pace. The arm with the drill slowly, slowly moved up to a corner piece, then carefully slotted the drill in place before spinning a screw out of its hole. Then it moved down, and dropped the screw into a small receptacle before moving onto the next, all at the same pace.

"What's that thing?" I asked.

"It's some sort of car maintenance drone," Franny said. "I don't think we named it. It does oil changes and stuff on the *Fury*. Not that I think it's ever really been used for that much? Mostly, we used it to change lightbulbs and do maintenance at the church. We brought it over earlier, and it's been disassembling things."

"Huh," I said. Well, that made some sense. Gomorrah probably had a few catalogs that she could have ordered it from. Judging by the unfanciness of it, and the lack of speed, it was probably even relatively cheap. A couple hundred points or something. "I guess I could use my repair drone for the same kind of thing. Maybe when I'm not using it."

"Delilah wants to reinforce the entire building. But that'll take a while. And maybe also permission?"

I nodded and looked around. Most of the floor was cleared out, and it felt surprisingly cavernous and empty. There was a lot of room in here for stuff. "What are you going to be putting in here?"

Franny turned and started pointing. "Kitchen, living room, then guest bedrooms. There should be two bathrooms. One near the dining room there, and another in the master bedroom. Plus there're two more bathrooms downstairs. It's actually kind of a lot. This place has half as many square feet as we have back home, but back home houses something like a hundred nuns."

"It's a lot of room," I agreed. "So . . . do you have your own bedroom, or are you going to be . . . sharing?"

Franny swallowed, then looked away. "So, that's the garage part. I think we'll have access to it from this floor. And the outer walls will be changed out. That'll be a big job, I think. Delilah might just have them all stripped out, then order in new ones that fit into place already. They need to be tough, and also fireproof. In fact, the whole place will be, especially around the armory."

"You didn't answer my question," I said.

"A-anyway, this is where the kitchen will be."

"You said that already, Franny!"

CHAPTER THIRTY

CAT NAP MISHAP

I heard that she did it because the mayor said something about her girlfriend.

—Sam-I-Yam, gossip forums, 2057

I woke up because of a buzz in my head. A call over my augs.

Groaning, I turned in bed and tried to ignore it, but the call kept ringing, and I finally snapped my eyes open. I was in my room, covered by thick blankets. The room itself was cold, a fan sweeping cool air over anything not bundled up. Lucy was next to me, breathing slowly and evenly.

I blinked a few times, then took in the time. Two fifty-six, in the a.m.

I shifted to the edge of the bed, then sat there for a moment as I processed things. "Why?" I asked. I wasn't coherent enough to make that any more specific.

The origin of the call suggests that it's important enough to be let through. I'm sorry for waking you up.

I groaned, then stood up, turned, and fixed the blankets around Lucy. I'd left a gap open, and I didn't want her to get cold. She grabbed the blankets in her sleep and curled up tighter around them.

"Hello?" I muttered low enough not to wake Lucy up.

"Cat?" The voice was familiar, but it took me a moment to place it. See-Three, the cyborg chick in charge of the prosthetics place. We'd sent over the first shipment just yesterday. Or Lucy had, in any case. She was taking care of all that stuff for me.

"Yeah, that's me," I said as I padded across the room toward the washroom. If I was gonna be up anyway, I might as well take a piss.

"Someone broke into our place," See-Three said.

I paused by the entrance to the washroom. "Are they still alive?" I asked.

"Yes? We didn't have anyone staying there overnight. That was probably a mistake. I got a turret thing from . . . I think she's your girlfriend? Wife? But we hadn't had a chance to install it yet . . . "

"Okay," I said. "Do we know who it is?"

"I'm talking to someone right now. I think it's just some local punks. Not the gang that runs the floor we're on, but the one two floors down. I don't know anyone well enough to ask, and the clinic doesn't exactly have a lot of loyal customers yet," See-Three said. She sounded pissed, and tired.

I sighed. "I'll call you back in ten minutes," I said. "Are you at the clinic?"

"I am."

"Alright, stick around there. Stay safe. I'll come over. Try to get, like, an inventory of what was taken."

"Okay, thanks, Catherine."

We hung up, and I went and did what I needed to do, which now included splashing cold water against my face to wake up properly.

"I'm going to need a few things," I said.

Certainly. I imagine one of them is something to wake up?

"Yeah. Hit me with that alien caffeine. Or . . . what do we have that's stronger than caffeine?"

I have several options ranging from methamphetamine to cocaine, but for what you're looking for, I'd suggest a cheaper, less harmful alternative. For a point, I can get you a cup of a hot, coffee-like substance laced with a well-measured cocktail of neurostimulants. It's not chemically addictive, and it's a tier-zero item.

"Fuck it, sure," I said. Made sense that something like that would be available to any samurai without a catalog. It seemed like a basic necessity.

My toilet paper was also tier-zero, after Lucy had forgotten to restock, and I wasn't sure I'd ever be able to go back to the normal stuff.

A cup appeared by the edge of the sink, just a little styrofoam container with a plastic lid . . . that had a pair of cat ears and whose mouth was shaped vaguely like a cat's.

I rolled my eyes as I took a long pull from it, then almost spat it all out. It was rank. Like coffee that had been left to boil for way too long, and it was grainy too. "This is awful!" I hissed.

The disgust you are currently feeling is the best way to counter any habit forming. It's not chemically addictive, and now it's too distasteful for someone to voluntarily want to drink any in excess. I think it's quite clever, actually. Like spritzing a cat in the face with water.

"Don't you fucking dare," I warned as I forced myself to take another sip. The effects were pretty obvious already. A tingle raced up my spine, and the hazy cloud of sleepiness I had been feeling just melted away. "What's my point total sitting at?"

Current Points: 33,571

A bit higher than yesterday, and at a decent number.

"Okay . . . you remember that outfit from Audrey, uh, Emoscythe? I think I want to give it a go. We might need to intimidate people in a few minutes, and I might be caught on camera doing samurai shit. It's as good a time as any for an image change."

I was expecting this to come up. You already have a decent undersuit. To bring the look together, you're mostly just missing a jacket and some utility equipment, notably the belts and pouches.

"Yeah," I said. "But I want something better than what I had before. I mean, weather- and fire-proof, better invisibility. If I'm going to upgrade my looks I might as well go all the way, you know?"

Understood. Give me a fraction of a millionth of a second to work that out.

"It took you longer to say that than it did to do the work, didn't it?" I asked.

Yes. How does nine hundred points for a suit sound? It would contain all the equipment and gear you usually carry, with a small jump pack mounted to the back and ankles for added mobility and kinetic absorption plates in strategic locations. The material is a pierce-resistant, full-spectrum camouflage weave, with the usual environmental protections, of course. It isn't a full exoskeleton, but it's about as close as you can come, and it's still compact enough to fit within your armor and mech.

"Got room for some of those shoulder guns? I like those. There should be plenty of pockets and such for grenades, and room to holster my sword and sidearm."

That can be arranged, of course. Call it twelve hundred for a full set?

I glanced at myself in the mirror, just in one of Lucy's oversized T-shirts. "Yeah, sure," I said.

A box appeared on the counter with a thump, close enough to our toothbrush cup to make it rattle. I started getting dressed.

It was actually tricky. The outfit didn't just go on like a coat; instead, it had its own pants kinda built into it that I had to squeeze into first, and then I had to contract my arms a little to fit the top part on. I shrugged it on in the end, then looked in the mirror again while zipping up the front.

It felt . . . pretty awesome, actually. The suit was fitted so exactly to my body that I didn't think anyone else would be able to comfortably wear it. It was built more like a jumpsuit than normal clothes, but without the usual puffy formlessness of a normal jumpsuit.

I looked like a ninja bounty-hunter.

Alright. I suppose that's the kind of look I was aiming for. It was badass, but it was also pretty much exactly as Emoscythe had designed it.

"Alright," I said.

You'll want to retrieve your weapons before you leave. There's a sleeve for your Void Terminus, and a holster for your Trench Maker.

"Mm-hmm," I mumbled as I left the washroom while checking my remaining points.

Current Points: 32,371

More than enough to cause some mischief.

"Cat?" Lucy mumbled from the bed.

"I'll be back in a bit," I said. "Just gotta take care of something."

Lucy's head fell back down, and I suspected that she was too out of it to make any sort of sensible reply.

I went and found my boots in the corner. While stumbling into them, I grabbed my favorite handgun, checked to make sure it was full, frowned as I noticed it was missing one round, then realized I didn't care that much about one round before I tucked it in place.

The coat had a flap at the back and a magnetized harness that let me wear my smaller, bullpup-style Laser Pointer at the small of my back, where the coat would cover it entirely. Then the sword went into a long, flaccid sheath hanging from my other side. It was a snug fit, and I tried to be mature about the way it hung there.

I was ready for war. A small war, but war all the same.

The last thing I did was grab my helmet on the way out through the main part of the house. I fitted it on as I walked outside and started for my bike.

It was just past three in the morning, and someone, somewhere, was going to regret waking me up.

CHAPTER THIRTY-ONE

THE SKINNY LOWDOWN

Oh, Stray Cat!
Bang bang bang, bang bang bang!

—NPC Streamer #31,501, TikTok Two, 2057

I landed my bike in the same parking garage as last time, then got off and started for the elevator. Halfway there I tested my suit's invisibility. The surface of my coat wavered for a fraction of a second, then there was nothing. I could see straight through my arm to the floor below.

Waving my arm around revealed only a very slight blurriness. It refreshed so quickly that it was almost impossible to tell that anything was wrong. If I wasn't looking for it, I would have dismissed it outright. It looked too much like a heat haze. Or . . . no, a heat haze was more visible. Maybe like those little floater things that moved around in my eye when I was looking at something really dark? They were easy to dismiss when I wasn't looking for them.

"This stealth shit's a bit better than what I'm used to," I said.

It's a slight improvement over your last set of similar equipment. Don't worry, you paid for the difference in quality.

"Yeah, I bet," I said. My chat with Audrey-slash-Emoscythe the other day had me thinking a little about fighting styles. Well, mostly she'd put a lot of ideas about *fashion* style in my head, but that kind of led from one thing to another.

I needed to work a little on refining my fighting style as well as my image. They kind of went hand in hand. So far I'd been a bit wishy-washy about what I used. Bombs, sure, and some more silent weapons. But once in a while I'd pick up an SMG, or a crossbow, and I still carried my Trench Maker around.

I wasn't focused on a single weapon type or platform, which was . . . probably okay? It gave me a bit of flexibility, at least, but there was a lot of value in hyperfocusing. Gomorrah's fire shit was probably leagues ahead of what I could manage by now.

The only advantage I had was the versatility of bombs as a weapon. They let me punch up enough to keep things interesting.

Eventually I'd fall behind someone like Gomorrah or Grasshopper who specialized, though.

My stealth stuff was . . . rough. Back before I was a samurai, I'd gotten some experience sneaking into and out of trouble, but it wasn't a mindset that I slipped into all that easily. Stealth was a great trick to have up my sleeve, but I wasn't sure if I wanted it to be my *thing*.

I was still in the honeymoon phase of being a samurai, however. I still had time to experiment and try shit, and it wasn't as if there was a lack of things to experiment on at the moment.

"I'm gonna need something to knock people out, I think," I said.

I'm sure I can find something that can do that. Flashbangs? Gas-based grenades?

"How about, uh . . ." I ran my hand against my front, checking for empty pouches on my suit. "Two of each?"

Myalis summoned the grenades for me, and I stuffed them away by feel alone. It was nice to have a small contingency for when shit inevitably went south.

By the time I'd tucked everything away, I was back on the same floor as the clinic. It was a little strange being indoors so late at night, mostly because there was no way to tell what time it was. The LED lighting was the same off-white as during the day, and there were plenty of people wandering around, doing their own things.

Stores that were automated didn't have much of a reason to close at night either, so while a few places were shut down, plenty were still operating. I walked into the central open space where the clinic was located and glanced around. There were more gangsters than I had noticed last time. The bakery was closed at the moment, which made sense, as it was operated by actual people.

See-Three was pacing in front of the clinic, arms crossed while two more cyborged-up people lingered in the clinic. I moved past her silently, carefully avoiding a few heaps of broken glass on the floor.

The clinic had been spruced up a little since I'd last been here a couple of days ago. We had chairs now, and a dividing wall between the front and rear areas. The back had two operating rooms set up. They weren't exactly super clean, more like dentist offices than real operating rooms, but that would do for replacing prosthetics.

The rest of the space in the back seemed to be a small workshop of sorts, combined with a small office space and break room, all squeezed into a tight little place that probably wouldn't be all that comfortable.

"So, what kind of theft are we dealing with here?" I muttered, too softly for See-Three to hear.

One of the cyborgs turned my way, but dismissed the noise after a moment.

She didn't lie about the lack of cameras in here. I noticed some linked to other stores in this area. Their recorded footage is kept offsite, however. It'll require some finesse to grab it from their servers. Or permission. Do you want me to contact the owners?

I nodded. Getting a recording of whichever dumbass robbed the place would help. Not that I thought we'd really need it.

There was a massive painting of a rat sticking out of a green pipe painted across one of the walls of the clinic, right over our new waiting-room chairs. It was actually pretty well done for some quick graffiti.

I took a picture of it with my augs, then stepped out of the clinic. My invisibility shut down as I came to stand behind See-Three. I hesitated. How could I show up and not scare her now that I was here? Could I walk out and then back in? That was way too much trouble, so I just winged it. "Does that giant rat image mean anything?" I asked.

See-Three gasped and spun around, her hand—made flat like a blade—rushing toward my neck.

I stepped back and out of reach of the wild swing. "Hey there," I said. "Sorry, didn't mean to spook you that bad."

See-Three paused in the act of ripping a handgun from a holster. "Who the fuck are you?" she asked. "You're not a Vent Rat."

"I'm Cat? New outfit. You literally called me out of bed about . . . twenty minutes ago."

See-Three scanned me up and down, then she slid her gun back in place. "I didn't see you come in," she said. "Nice outfit."

"Nor did I," one of her cyborg buddies said. His voice sounded entirely text-to-speech, without anything fancy to make it more properly human.

"I didn't want to be seen," I said simply. "And I wanted to get a lay of things before anything else. I got my look though. What can you tell me about what happened?"

"See-Three, you didn't tell us you were dealing with a samurai," the borg said.

"I . . . wasn't sure," See-Three said. "And it didn't seem prudent to bother her with it."

Well, that was nice, but it didn't answer my other questions. "Was this caused by those Vent Rats you mentioned?"

See-Three pulled herself together surprisingly quickly. "We think so. Not too much was stolen, actually. They broke through the front door. We had electronic locks and a metal bar lock in place, but they were able to get past that. Then they were in."

"A smash and grab," the borg guy said.

I turned toward him and his other pal and took the two in properly. The more talkative of the pair had a squared-off head like something ripped from a drone, linked to a robotic upper body. His legs looked mechanical too, and I had to wonder how much human was left in him. The other looked a lot less extreme. Two human eyes, a few mods tacked onto his skull, one robotic hand that looked like it was designed to carry a rotating set of tools.

"Right. Well, this is unacceptable," I said. "Do we know what they grabbed?"

"The prosthetics we received were all in a big container at the back," See-Three said. "There must be a million credits worth of tech in that box. We had a lot of tools, too, and some are missing."

So, the Vent Rats come over, break in, then leave with everything valuable. "That wasn't very smart of them. Witnesses?"

"Locals, yeah. They didn't move to help," See-Three said. It clearly frustrated her. "The gang on this floor let me know where the Vent Rats ran off to. So that's something, but no one will do anything about it."

"What do you mean?"

"This building isn't linked to city police," Borg-guy said. "It's got its own security offices, and they're unlikely to help."

"Of course not," I sighed. Then I pulled out my Laser Pointer with a shrug. "Welp, time to make an example. Can you three stay here, maybe clean things up? I'm going to see if I can't get our shit back."

"Alone?" See-Three asked.

"See-Three, she's a samurai," Borg-guy said.

I pointed to him with my free hand and nodded. "I can probably handle a little crew of common street thugs. Like, I don't want to sound overconfident, but I'm maybe a little *over*qualified for this. But we can talk about that later. I'm gonna get our things back, and then we can chat, alright?"

See-Three didn't seem entirely pleased with that, but she didn't press the issue. "Alright," she said.

"Cool. See you in like, half an hour, tops." It wouldn't take much more than that to figure this out, right? Then I could be back in bed, snuggling up with Lucy, and get the rest of my beauty sleep. Easy.

CHAPTER THIRTY-TWO

RAT HUNT

No one wants to live in a megabuilding.

Not like we have any damned choice, so might as well make the best of it, right, you fucking rats?

—Jeffery "Whiskers" Tablespoon, 2055

"So, where can I find these"—I paused to yawn—"assholes?" I was already walking deeper into the building, toward the far end of the square that held our little clinic. I wasn't sure where I'd be going, but there were several corridors leading off into the distance, so it was a good bet that it'd be in this general direction.

I'm tracking them now. Unfortunately, there are surprisingly few working cameras outside of the market areas and obtaining access to some of these systems is difficult.

Myalis opened a little box in the corner of my vision and started playing a video within it. It was the front of the clinic, seen from the corner of a camera.

I turned, matching the angles of what I was seeing until I spotted where the camera had to be. It was hidden behind the signage for a little automated doughnut shop across the square from the clinic.

The video continued to fast-forward until it paused on a group of five people standing in front of the clinic. One of them had a crowbar that he was using with expertise to rip the door open.

"Why is this kind of footage always a blurry mess?" I asked. "It's like . . . can you even buy cameras with such shitty quality anymore?"

The camera is able to capture much higher fidelity. It's the data-transfer rates for off-site storage that encourage the owners of the security to reduce the quality of their footage.

I shook my head. It made sense, I supposed, but it was still annoying. I watched the five rip into the clinic, then come rushing out with a crate held between them. A sixth member rushed over pushing a wheeled trash bin, and they dumped the container with all of our prosthetics into it.

Then the lot of them took off running while pushing their trash bin filled with the prosthetics and tools they'd nabbed. Myalis switched cameras, and I was able to see which passage they took.

"You lost them after this?" I asked.

I tracked them down two floors, which brings them close to the floor operated by the so-called Vent Rats. There isn't any clear evidence of who committed the crime, however.

The screen split into six, each showing a still image of one of the assholes. Myalis added some metrics next to the photos, heights as compared to the doorway and approximate weights and presented genders. "Right," I said as I took them in. There weren't any faces. All six of them were wearing full-face masks. Just black ovals with holes for eyes with some sort of cloth covering, and most of them had hoodies on over that. We had some skin color from the two members not wearing gloves, and one who'd reached up and exposed their waistline, but that was it.

They were surprisingly clever about this.

I followed the direction they'd gone. Myalis continued to point toward their last known location, and soon enough I found myself in a stairwell, climbing over sleeping forms on the steps and passing graffiti murals that had been there so long they were peeling.

I made it to the right floor, then shoved my way past a pair of guys standing guard at the door. They cursed and looked around, but I wasn't visible, so their search turned up nothing.

This was a residential floor, which meant a square grid of corridors lined with doors that had numbers on them. The Vent Rats, as it turned out, weren't making much of an effort to hide where they were hanging out.

I found a group of some dozen or so younger people hanging out in one of the dead-ends to one side of the floor, all dressed in black and most wearing plastic rat masks. The walls behind them were covered in images of rats, all done in a sort of cell-shaded style, often with large green pipes.

It was a miracle that a Nintendo hit-squad hadn't wiped them out already.

I slipped between a few of the Vent Rats by the entrance of the dead-end, then stepped over a few more deeper in who looked like they were knocked out by whatever shit they were plugging into their own veins.

I wasn't surprised by the drugs. I was surprised by the amount. The Vent Rats were doing well for themselves. Interestingly, I didn't notice much by way of cybernetics. Maybe one or two eyes, or some cosmetic mods, but no borgs or even an upgraded arm or leg in sight.

My gaze kept sweeping over the group. These people looked either sleepy, or just tired. That fit with the hour, I supposed.

Moving deeper into their little corner, I found that the apartments at the end of the hall had the walls between them ripped out to create a much bigger floor space. That was probably their main hangout. The interior had a few fridges, some couches, and a very expensive entertainment system pressed up against one wall.

A shirtless man with whiskers tattooed on his face was sitting on a big-ass couch, one leg over the arm, a hand resting on a fuck-huge revolver. He was dozing peacefully.

"That the boss?" I asked Myalis under my breath.

According to his NMPD criminal record, this is Jeffery "Whiskers" Tablespoon, the leader of the Vent Rats.

I blinked. "Fucking *Tablespoon?*" I said as I uninvisibled myself.

I didn't pick his name.

I couldn't imagine that Whiskers here had picked out his family name either. With a name like that, I might also have considered a life of crime. I kicked his shin, and Whiskers jumped, blinking fast as he looked around himself.

Reaching down, I plucked his gun away and tossed it to the far end of the room, then pulled out my Laser Pointer and aimed it at him. He stared at the floating gun, mouth agape, and didn't seem to know what to do about it.

"Hey," I said.

"Who the fuck are you?" he asked. He was awake now.

"Just the friendly neighborhood Stray Cat. Where's my shit, Whiskers?"

Whiskers looked around, but his buddies weren't as quick to move as he was. He looked around for his gun, then started to reach for another one left on a side table nearby. I poked him in the chest with the end of my rifle. "Who are you?" he asked as he fell back.

"Someone that was woken up at a stupid hour of the morning to deal with you morons. Where's my shit?"

Whiskers fell back into his seat and looked at me. *Really* looked at me. "Did the seventh-floor fucks send you?" he asked.

He's actually looking you up now.

I squinted. Yeah, his eyes were twitching very slightly in that telltale sign he was using his augs. It was pretty subtle, though. "Ah, shit, you're a samurai," he said.

"An annoyed one," I said.

"It wasn't us," he said.

"What wasn't you?" I asked.

He swallowed. "I don't know, but whatever it was it wasn't us," he said.

This guy . . .

"Look, some punks stole from a clinic a few floors up, one that's under my protection. Give me back all the shit you stole, maybe grovel a bit, and this won't end in bloodshed. I really don't want to have to take a shower before getting back to bed, you know?"

He nodded, started to say something, then paused. "We really didn't take your shit, though," he said.

"Myalis, send him the videos, and that pic I took of the tag they left in the clinic."

Sending.

It took a moment for Whiskers to look over everything, but he was shaking his head halfway through. "That's not us," he said. "I know my rats, and that's not any of them. We don't wear that kind of mask. And the tag's all wrong. The rat only has one tail, and the pipe's the wrong green."

I turned, looked at the nearest wall. There were a few gang tags on it, rats poking out of pipes and tunnels, some rather graphic images of rats doing all sorts of weird shit. And Whiskers was right: they all had two tails. The pipes were all a cartoonish green too. I compared it to the picture I'd taken while in the clinic. It didn't quite match, either stylistically, or with the number of tails. "Huh," I said.

"It's a setup," he said.

"The people that took my shit brought it to this floor," I said leadingly. Whiskers was being pretty helpful so far.

"We only run the east side. There's a service elevator on the west end. They could have gone right through. Wait, here, I'm linked into the cameras there. We use them to see who comes in."

Whiskers sent me a quick link, which would have been exceptionally stupid to open, so I let Myalis play with it.

Interesting.

I pulled back, lowering my gun away from Whiskers's chest. "Interesting?"

"What's interesting?" Whiskers asked, but I ignored him.

Another little box with some footage, this time of the gate in front of an elevator. The same six people rushed to it and pulled the gate open, then loaded themselves and that trash bin in. "Oh, for fuck's sake," I muttered before going invisible again.

This was going to take all damned night, wasn't it?

CHAPTER THIRTY-THREE

CLEANING UP

Gangs start when people have a reason to stick together. If the world was all nice and good, if it wasn't split because of class and race and violence, then you wouldn't have anyone deciding that the best way to earn some peace and respect is to stick together and mess up anyone that gets in their way.

—Laserjack, 2051

I rode up the elevator with my arms crossed, glaring through my visor at the doors until the entire thing came to a grinding halt and the doors shuddered open.

I didn't wind up doing anything to the Vent Rats. They weren't to blame, so their leader got a stern warning to keep on minding his business before I left. It wasn't fun, this chasing after thieves in the night while Lucy was waiting for me back home.

The elevator had a small computer in it that tracked which floors it had stopped on previously, with timestamps and all. It was easy once I was there to hook Myalis into the elevator's little control panel and let her do her thing.

It meant that we were now on the correct floor, about three floors away from ground level, deep into the pits of the megabuilding. That didn't seem ideal.

The door finished opening and I stepped out invisibly into a dank corridor. I paused.

The corridor was clean.

I had come here with a clear and obvious preconception, expecting more graffitied walls and floors with years of grime stuck to them, but that wasn't the case. The linoleum was worn in the center where people walked more, but it was otherwise spotless. The walls were free of mold or grime. Even the ceiling was clear of spiderwebs or smoke stains.

For some reason, the sheer cleanliness set me more on edge than if I'd walked out to discover an army waiting for me. "Who lives on this floor?" I asked.

There is a database of residents, but it doesn't exactly include their gang affiliations, nor would I consider it overly accurate. One thing does stand out, however.

"Yeah?" I asked.

Over four fifths of this building's cleaning staff live on this floor, and law enforcement reports suggest that one of the gangs inhabiting the building is called the Janitors.

"Janitors? So they're what, a gang of cleaners? Or is it a euphemism? They 'take out the trash' or something stupid like that?"

There is little information available on them on the net. Far less than I'm finding about the other groups in this building. A cursory search suggests that someone is making an effort to delete and suppress any discussion of the group. It's all archived and retrievable.

"So, they hid information about themselves, but you can still get to it?"

Yes. But the mere act of suppression and deleting that information has dampened any discussion. Oftentimes, the information I can learn about someone is circumstantial, or pieced together from several sources that each only give me a few small pieces of the puzzle. With discussions kept to a minimum, I have little to work with and less information that's trustworthy or corroborated from multiple sources.

"Right," I said. I more or less understood that. It was like listening to gossip to learn about someone. Only probably more complicated than I cared to dive into.

"So, the Janitor gang. Any idea where they hang out? On this floor, I mean?"

A few members have active social media accounts tracking their movements. They seem to concentrate in a small, unlicensed bar called the Broom Closet. I'll direct you to it.

Of course they called their bar that. Myalis helpfully tossed the directions up onto my augs and I started making my silent way across the floor. It took a few turns before I met anyone in the corridors. I slid to one side to let a trio of middle-aged guys in jumpsuits move past. They weren't wearing gear that matched, color-wise, but it was clear that they had a theme going.

Or maybe jumpsuits had become stylish for forty-something guys when I wasn't paying attention. They had a whole host of drab colors to pick from, and it looked like at least one of them had decorated his with some patches and a utility belt.

I didn't miss the gun tucked into the belt either. Last I checked, handguns weren't cleaning implements.

"Takes all sorts," I muttered before stifling a yawn.

Fuck, I wanted to be back in bed already.

It didn't take too long to find the Broom Closet. I just had to follow the noise through too-clean corridors. All of the clubs I'd been to had a thing for loud noises, and this one wasn't an exception, though they weren't play-ing modern music but some oldies. Maroon 5 and Adele and the kind of stuff older people liked.

The entrance to the Broom Closet was, unsurprisingly, a broom closet. Just another small doorway with a mop and bucket logo on the front of it. The only hint that it was something more, other than the music, was the way the linoleum was worn out.

I paused next to the door. "Any cameras?" I whispered.

None pointing to the doorway.

I nodded, then carefully turned the handle enough to undo the latch. A little pull after that, and I let go, the door slowly opening on its own momentum. Hopefully it just looked like it wasn't latched properly to any-one looking.

I waited, expecting someone to come over and pull the door shut, but when no one did, I slipped into the closet. Then I chuckled, because I knew Lucy would love this bit in the retelling.

The Broom Closet really did start off as a large utility closet. One of those rideable floor-cleaning machines with the pads on the bottom had been left to charge, and a few mops and buckets stood in a corner. There was a second door at the back, which opened up and led into an entirely misplaced bar.

I snuck past the cleaning supplies, then paused by the threshold of the bar. It was surprisingly festive in here. A long counter ran along one wall, with an automated bartending machine behind it. The rest of the room had a few round tables and tall chairs, though a number of them were pushed to the side.

A half dozen men were moving around, laughing, clinking drinks, and bobbing their heads in time with the music. I blinked, then noticed that some of the men were women. Jumpsuits turned everyone into a genderless blob that was more janitor than person, I supposed.

"Ah, there they are, the fucks," I muttered.

At the back of the room, sitting in a corner booth, were four guys in all-black outfits. Two were wearing familiar masks on their heads, and there were more of the masks on the tabletop next to half-empty mugs of beer.

Four of the six assholes that had broken into my clinic, just sitting back and patting themselves on the shoulder for a job well done. Probably proud that the Vent Rats would be taking the blame for their shit.

The fucks.

I don't know if it was the lack of sleep, the untimely interruption, or just the way the group looked so damned pleased with themselves, but I was getting to be pretty pissed off.

I crossed the room in a straight line, only slowing down to rip one of the chairs out from behind a guy in the middle of the room. I dragged the seat after me, its feet scraping across the floor and drawing a few eyes its way. Chairs didn't usually scrape across a room all on their own.

I spun the chair around in front of the corner table, pulled out my Trench Maker, then sat down and flicked off my invisibility.

The idiots in the booth reeled back for a moment. "Alright," I said. I was liking their expressions a lot more now. "Where the fuck are my limbs?"

A couple of guys bolted out of the Broom Closet, making me realize I probably should have closed the door. A few others pulled out guns, mostly little handguns, but one guy had an old-school pump-action. No one was pointing anything yet, but the tension in the room had reached a dangerous high.

If all of them unloaded on me, what were the chances that I'd come out alright?

"Put your guns away," I snapped. "And someone turn off that noise."

The music cut off with a snap, pitching the entire bar into a sudden silence that only made everything so much more tense.

"You're Stray Cat," one of the Janitors said. He was one of those with a mask.

"Yeah," I said. It was nice, being recognized when I was trying to scare the shit out of someone. "Where are my limbs?" The last was directed at the idiots sitting across from me.

One of them, who looked particularly stupid wearing his mask on top of his head, sat up straighter. "Don't know what you're on about," he said.

I blinked. "Let me put it this way. Either you chucklefucks"—I assumed that was a term these old guys would understand—"give me back the arms and legs you stole from my clinic. Or I start grabbing replacements."

CHAPTER THIRTY-FOUR

SOMETHING'S DIRTY DOWN IN CLEANTOWN

Laundering materials and equipment have, strangely, become exponentially more complex, even as crime has mounted and become far more common. That's because of technology like this. A simple RFID tag, no bigger than a grain of sand, can be hidden in nearly any piece of equipment and will allow you to track it across a city.

—Securatek Demonstration, 2031

"No one wants to talk?" I asked the silent room. I looked around, but all I found were grown men and women in baggy uniforms who didn't want to meet my gaze. They were still fondling their guns, though. The four I was confronting were clearly part of the crew, otherwise the rest would have abandoned them by now.

Honestly, this whole thing could go pretty damned poorly. I was probably mostly bulletproof, but there were two dozen of them to one of me, and if they piled on, it would get messy.

"Okay," I said.

I stood up from the chair, then flung it aside. It crashed to the ground with a bang, and I saw half the room jump at the noise.

Reaching down, I plucked a grenade from one of my pockets and placed it on the booth's table right in front of the four masked morons. "Who came up with your plan?" I asked.

None of them answered, but their eyes gave them away. Two of them glanced to the side and I turned, following their gaze to the end of the room where a man was standing next to the sound system. He was a middle-aged guy, balding, a bit sweaty, and holding onto a large beer with white-knuckled fingers.

I touched the grenade I'd placed on the table. "If any of you four move, this goes off," I said.

Then I carefully put my Trench Maker away.

The tension in the room relaxed a hair, at least until I drew my sword.

The Void Terminus didn't look like much when it wasn't active. There wasn't a blade on it. Instead, the entire shaft was a long rod with a sort of cap on the end. It almost looked like a tool rather than a weapon.

I walked slowly across the room, hoping that no one would try anything funny, then stopped before the balding guy. "You the boss?" I asked.

That's Robert Brigadeiro. He's the manager of this building's janitorial unit. He's the suspected leader of the Janitors gang.

Robert swallowed, but he was quick to get his shit together. "I'm the manager, yes," he said. "I don't know what you're doing here, Miss Samurai. We have nothing to do with you. We're just the cleaning staff."

"Well it looks like you, or at least some of your buddies here, cleaned out my clinic upstairs. I'm a little annoyed about it, to be honest. And I want to know where my limbs ended up. Those were meant to help people, you know."

"I'm sure I have no idea what you're talking about," he said before he basically repeated himself. "We're just cleaning staff, that's all."

"Uh-huh. You won't mind if I have my AI check your augs then? Just to be sure?" There had to be spyware in his and his pal's augs that'd show Myalis everywhere he'd been.

Robert was sweating bullets and blinking fast. He wiped the back of his hand across his face. "I . . . I don't know. I mean. No. I don't want that."

"Then tell me where my shit is, and you can . . . well, no, I'm not just going to allow you to go back to partying after robbing from armless and legless people."

Robert shook his head. "It's too late," he said.

"What do you mean, it's too late?"

"Let my people go, please," he said. "Most of them have nothing to do with this."

"Most of them are here partying too, aren't they?" I asked. "Spill."

Robert licked his lips, scanned the room for support that he didn't find much of, then he spilled. "We sold them. Everything we grabbed. You have to understand, we're the cleaning people, no one cares about us, we're practically third-class citizens and it was a lot of credits. We're invisible to most people, so it was—"

I poked him in the chest with the end of my sword's rod and he fell back against the wall, arms rising in surrender by his sides. "Who did you sell them to?" I asked.

"I don't know."

"Where did they take them?"

"I don't know."

"Can you get them back?"

Robert shook his head. His jumpsuit was stained with sweat, and it looked like he was shaking. "I don't know!"

"Fuck you!" I barked.

The Void Terminus snapped, then it filled the room with a powerful hiss. A black, empty crack appeared between one end of the sword and its hilt, a space dark as night with only the faint glimmer of distant stars within.

Immediately, a powerful gust roared across the entirety of the Broom Closet. The pressure in the room mounted as air was sucked into the crack in reality.

A loose piece of paper fluttered through the air and into the cut, disappearing in a blink while Robert pissed himself and cried, trying hard to push himself through the wall holding him in place.

"All of you, listen to me," I said over the sword's hiss. It was a damned good thing the door wasn't closed, otherwise the room might be running out of air soon. "Right now, you're going to find my stuff. You're going to look *real* hard for it. Then you're going to come back here. You have five minutes, and I'll let your imagination fill you in on what'll happen if you don't produce results . . . Go!"

I turned, tossed the sword up and caught it with my other hand, then pointed to the four in the booth, who had just started to get up. "Not you four," I said. "You four call the other two that helped you on your little heist and tell them to come here before I have to go get them."

The janitors took off running out of the room. I was pretty sure I wouldn't be seeing most of them again, warnings be damned. The four in the booth, though, were looking particularly petrified, and Robert was trembling and breathing hard while staring at the void that hovered a little too close to his neck for comfort.

I sighed and flicked the sword off, then quickly spun it around and slid it back into its sheath. "So, why'd you do it?" I asked. I had been angry . . . and I was still a little pissed, but a lot of that anger was fading now.

Robert swallowed and pushed himself away from the wall. He really had been trying to melt through it. "There was an offer," he said. "It was worth a lot. A quarter of what we all make in a year. I couldn't pass that up, not for such an easy job. It was our first time on a job like this. We . . . we don't do this kind of thing."

"Really? So you went from no crime at all to breaking and entering while disguised as a rival gang in one jump?"

Robert looked a little fidgety. "The most we've done is carry things around, maybe dispose of bodies for the other groups above."

I couldn't decide what to do about Robert and his pals, so I just kept an eye on the lot of them and hoped that me standing there would spook them into behaving while I dumped the problem on someone else. "Myalis, what do I do?" I subvocalized, basically speaking without really "breathing" the words out. Kind of annoying to do, but Myalis heard it.

In an ideal world, you could contact the authorities about this. You may not be legally beholden to any laws, but the Janitors are. Do you want me to call the police? They're bound to answer.

I shrugged. "Screw it. Sure, call them in. I can't imagine they'll be happy about this either, but maybe it'll send out the right kind of warning." It would also save me from having to figure out what to do with criminals, which was far from my area of expertise. I didn't want to become a mobile executioner. Murder couldn't be my default solution to everything.

Understood. Message sent. Their response time for this area is thirty-seven minutes.

"How far away are they?" I asked. That amount of time didn't make sense.

The police force I contacted is the nearest. They're stationed on the topmost floors of this building.

"That's literally just a three-minute elevator ride away," I said.

They only respond to calls like this in force. It may take time for them to armor up and prepare. I'm not excusing them. This level of inefficiency is impressive only in its scope.

"Tell them to send a token force down first, dammit. I've got these idiots cowed, I think." I glanced at the Broom Closet's entrance as two more Janitors in Vent Rat costumes came in and moved toward the booth in the corner, shooting nervous glances my way.

I moved toward the booth, then crossed my arms for a moment.

"Care to tell me where my stuff is now?" I asked.

One of the two newcomers, some younger guy with a bit of hair on his chin, actually spoke up. "We-we sent it off," he said nervously.

"Sent it off where? To who?"

Whom.

I rolled my eyes which the idiots in front of me couldn't see, but which Myalis would no doubt notice.

"The service dock for trucks on the bottom floor. We loaded it into a self-driving truck and it took off," the guy said.

"Fucking hell," I muttered.

How hard would it be for someone to have the stuff switch trucks? I'd be able to track things eventually—once the prosthetics got used, they'd probably be easy to track, or be recognizable—but until then?

"I'm going to need to ask for help," I muttered.

I had someone in mind, someone who I'd been meaning to use on a few small jobs and who'd probably enjoy it if I owed them a small favor. It was worth a try.

CHAPTER THIRTY-FIVE

OUTFOXED

Samurai and law enforcement go together like matches and open containers of gasoline. It's generally a terrible idea to mix the two, unless your intent is to light a bonfire.
—Chief Jeffrey Waters, Winner of "Most Corrupt Cop" Public Voting Award, 2046

It took another half an hour for all of the local police to show up, but when they did, they came in force. Twenty-odd guys and girls in full body armor with taser guns, pepper spray, and LMGs came barreling onto the floor. Within moments, anyone wearing a janitor jumpsuit was pressed to the floor, hands tied behind their back.

The cops weren't being gentle about their arrests, and I found it hard to care.

I spoke for a minute with some sergeant sort who was accompanied by a lawyer in full SWAT gear. They assured me that everyone would be punished to the full extent of the law, and then some.

I told them to chill the fuck out, then let Myalis handle the charges. The thieves were in for a rather terrible rest-of-their-lives, but most of them would come out of it alright, which was probably for the best. I didn't need this many people having a heap of resentment against me.

Once everyone was cuffed up, I walked into the nearest elevator and pressed the "up" button. Myalis had done what she could to follow the truck that had left with my shit, but that trail went cold far sooner than I would have liked.

If I was going to track down my stolen crap, then I'd need to spend time going after it. Time and maybe some resources.

I decided to do something entirely different instead.

The first step was calling See-Three. "Hey," I said as soon as the line clicked.

"Hello? Stray Cat? Are you okay?" See-Three asked in a concerned rush. "Any luck?"

"I'm fine. Sorry for taking longer than expected. And as for luck, some," I said. "Tracked the goods down to some group called the Janitors a few floors down. They sold everything to some third party already and my leads are all cold. I'm not sure I can get the prosthetics back right now, but I think the clinic should be safe for the moment. We might want to take a serious look at upping our security. Or . . . yeah, let's talk about this later."

"Alright," See-Three said. "One of my friends agreed to stay here. I'll be returning home to get some shut-eye, but I'll be back before we're meant to open. Someone needs to explain to our first clients that we don't have their limbs."

I ground my teeth. "It didn't take long to make the first batch, right? Try to delay things like, six hours? I'm sure we can at least get half of that stock made again."

"That would be nice," See-Three said. "The last clients we were supposed to meet tomorrow—or today, I guess—were all warned that the first operations might go long anyway."

"Cool. Cool," I said. I sounded tired, even to myself. But things weren't entirely a disaster.

"Thank you, Stray Cat. I don't know about anyone else, but I, at least, appreciate what you're doing."

Well, didn't that just warm me up? "Yeah," I said. "See you around. I need to talk to someone about something."

We said our goodbyes just as I was arriving in the parking garage where my bike was waiting for me. I hopped on, flicked on the engine, then roared out of the building in a rush. I had someone to get in touch with right then.

My first step was to send the next person I'd be chatting to a quick text, asking them if they were even available and awake. I got a reply within seconds. It was wordy, but it made it clear that they were willing to at least discuss things.

So I turned my bike toward a megabuilding in the distance. House Four Three. This time I parked where it would be easiest to get to where I wanted to go, got off my bike, and strode through the building looking like I didn't have a care.

Within a couple of minutes I was standing before the muscular frame of the Barber Shop's bouncer. The same full-borg that I'd passed with Rac a while ago. "I've got business with Millennium Animal," I said.

He looked me up and down. "You were with Rac," he said.

"Yeah."

"Huh. Didn't recognize what you were, last time," he said as he stepped aside. "Go on in, Miss Samurai."

I nodded, then slipped past him and into the Barber Shop proper. The place was a little less lively than the last time I'd been here, probably owing to it being . . . almost six in the morning. The sun was going to come up soon. The sort of person that liked to party late was gone by now, and even the early partiers hadn't gotten out of bed yet. It was that magical time of day where everything was at its calmest, and it showed in the choice of music.

Some softer jazz was playing, the lights were slightly dimmed, and the only people in the main dance area were a pair doing a little swing routine, with frequent stops as one showed the other how to do some specific moves.

I found Millennium Animal in the act of standing up at the bar. "Hey, Myalis, what's the sitch with this guy?" I asked as I started to make my way over. I had a lot of bar to cross, so there was a bit of time to poke around about Millennium.

How deep do you want me to dig?

"Surface-level shit," I muttered.

Millennium Animal, born in 2001, has been a Fixer in New Montreal for twelve years. Before that, he has a record of mercenary work extending back another ten years, mostly specializing in information gathering, corporate spywork, and private detective work. He has a few black marks on his file, but nothing egregious or which I think you'd have a moral issue with. He does seem fairly reliable.

"Let's see about that," I said as I walked over to Millennium. He extended a hand to shake, his left, and I reached out and shook. "Hey," I said.

"A pleasure to see you once more, Stray Cat," Millennium said. So, he knew I was a samurai. Had he known last time? He smiled, and with his face looking like a fox's, it came off as exceptionally sly. "I like the new look. Intimidating without being terrifying. It's a fine line to walk." He let go of my hand and grabbed onto the lapels of his suit.

"Thanks," I said. "So, how does a tired samurai go about getting you to help her with a problem?"

Millennium chuckled. "First, a drink? Or at least a seat?"

I nodded and followed him to the bar. We grabbed stools at the far end of the bar, where we weren't under any lights and where it was a little quieter. The bartender glanced our way, then kept on minding their own business. If I wanted something, I could order it via a local aug-app. I didn't.

"So, how can I help you?" he asked. "I would usually keep on with the pleasantries, but I have the impression that you're in something of a hurry."

"Not exactly a hurry. It's just . . . I have better things to do than look after this, and you seem like someone that I can maybe trust with my little problem."

"Certainly," he said with a nod.

"Right, right. So, some fuckwits stole from a clinic I opened up. A place to hand out essentially-free prosthetics to people that need them. Nothing too good, but still basic samurai tech, even if it's the mass-produced printed sort."

"I imagine they stole something valuable?"

I shook my head. "Just some of those prosthetics I mentioned. Like I said, 3D-printed. I can make more. But it's the thought that counts. Those were meant to help people, not be yoinked away the night before they were gonna be installed. It's a bad look for my clinic, and it kind of just pisses me off."

Millennium Animal nodded along, seeming entirely sympathetic to my problem. "Do you need help making an example of someone?"

"Nah, I already did that part. What I need is help tracking the goods. Myalis, can you package up what we have and send it over?"

Certainly.

Millennium Animal blinked a few times, his fox eyes lighting up as he checked out something I couldn't see. "I received the information," he said. "But it will take some time to review."

"Look, all I need is someone who can track things down, figure out where they ended up. And maybe someone that can get my shit back, too."

"That's two jobs," he pointed out.

That was fair. Two jobs, and I wanted to do neither. "Okay. So what would that cost?"

"Hard to say without verifying everything. Retrieval will, of course, depend on who has your items, so that's even harder to predict the cost of."

I worked my jaw. "I'll give you ten points to find the prosthetics. Ten more to retrieve them, negotiable if it was actually hard."

Millennium Animal froze up for a moment. "That's generous."

"Twenty is what I'd make over two days, which I've got the impression is what it would take me if I did it all myself," I said.

"Ah, buying time. That makes sense. Twenty points of anything? Or from pre-existing catalogs?"

"Pre-existing," I said. "And I'm holding veto rights. If someone wants a plague bomb from my Esoteric Explosives catalog, I'm saying no."

"That's eminently fair," he said. "I can think of a number of people who might be interested. It's not as worthwhile monetarily, but mercenaries tend to crave getting their paws on samurai tech."

"Uh-huh. One last thing: If it's possible, keep my involvement on the down-low?"

"That'll be complicated, but I think I can manage it," he replied.

CHAPTER THIRTY-SIX

SLEEPY

Long-held international conflicts, as well as conflicts that have arisen between racial and religious groups, will not fade away just because of an existential threat to all of humanity.

While it is optimistic to hope that such groups will set aside their differences in the face of a threat the likes of which the Antithesis pose, such wishful thinking has little basis in established fact.

Some of these groups are already facing existential threats, perceived or real. The addition of another alien threat isn't a cause for them to cease their attempts to fight through long-held grudges.

There is a non-zero chance that the last bullet fired by the last human won't be aimed at an alien, but at their fellow man.

—US Intelligence Services Report, June 2025

I stumbled into my place feeling like I weighed fifty kilos more and like all of my limbs had been replaced by sludge. My jaw was aching from all the yawning I was doing, and I was pretty sure anyone could convince me of anything at the moment.

Which is probably why it took me a second to register that Lucy was standing in front of me wearing nothing but short-shorts, a tank top, and a large apron that read "Kiss the Me."

"Hi," Lucy said.

"Oh, hey," I said before stifling another yawn.

Lucy nodded, then reached over and started taking my jacket off. She tossed it on the couch, then pushed me forward. I didn't have the energy to protest, and just let her press on until we were in our room. "Come on, let's get you out of these clothes," Lucy said.

She pressed herself against my back, warm and soft. Her hands trailed along my side, then worried at the button of my pants. "Lucy," I said.

"Mm-hmm?"

"I love you."

"Yup."

"But I don't know if I'm in the mood," I complained.

Lucy snorted. "You stink too much for that," she said. "Come on, let's get you in the shower. The warmth will help."

I didn't have it in me to protest. Instead I left a trail of dirty clothes in my wake as I made it to the washroom and then into the shower. Soon, warm, pre-soaped water was pouring down onto my head, and I just stood there for a moment. It was nice.

I came out of the shower some indeterminate amount of time later. Lucy was waiting for me with a large, fluffy towel. She wrapped it around me, then wrapped herself around me too. It was warm, both the towel and Lucy.

"Come on," she said before she started moving the towel around and drying me off.

"I can handle it," I said. "I'm tired, not infirm."

"Don't care," Lucy said simply. "Also, we need to do something about your hair. The highlights are almost all gone."

I blinked, then glanced into the mirror. My hair was still wet and matted down. My usual ponytail had come apart and my hair was down around my shoulders, longer than was fashionable at the moment. She was right, the pink highlights I'd had at the front were barely there anymore. "Yeah, I guess I could redo those," I said.

"I bet Myalis has beauty stuff for cheap," Lucy said. "Or, you know, we could buy normal stuff. No harm in that."

"Mm-hmm," I agreed.

Lucy stopped toweling me, then grabbed some clothes from next to the sink. They were pajamas, big, thick, fluffy ones. The kind of extremely girly shit that I didn't usually jive with, but which I was totally going to give in to right then and there.

Shit was soft.

"There you go," Lucy murmured. She guided me out of the washroom, and I blinked as I noticed the bed was all done up, which was extremely unusual. Most of the time, the most "done" our bed got was when all the pillows and blankets were heaped onto it and there weren't too many dirty clothes on the edge.

"You made the bed?" I asked.

"I'm trying the whole stay-at-home-wife routine," Lucy said.

"Oh."

"Don't get used to it. Cleaning sucks and I refuse to do it full-time. I'm going to try the stay-at-home-businesswoman-who-hires-a-maid routine next. It seems way more fun."

"Okay," I agreed.

Lucy ushered me into bed, tucked me in the way I'd seen her do for dozens of younger kids at the orphanage, then she pressed a kiss onto my forehead.

I felt a little babied at the moment. It was kinda nice though.

"Sleep tight," Lucy said. "Myalis, can you let me know when she's up? I'll make sure there's something warm and hot ready."

"Hmm, are you sure you don't wanna keep up the domestic routine?" I asked. My eyes had closed already. I didn't have the strength to open them, nor did I want to.

"Positive," Lucy said.

If she said anything else, I lost it as I fell asleep.

I wasn't sure if I dreamed at all. I just woke up with no clue what time it was. There weren't any windows in our bedroom, not that there was much point in looking at the sky most of the time. So I glanced at the clock in my HUD and groaned. "How long did I sleep for?"

Five hours and thirty-two minutes?

I stretched. "Feels longer," I said.

You did get a few hours of sleep before you left. Your total sleep time adds up to just over eight hours, which is about what I'd recommend you receive.

"Mmm," I murmured as I stretched my legs out from under the blankets. I rolled onto my side, then got up. It was three something in the afternoon, and I decided then and there that I wouldn't be doing anything productive for the rest of the day.

Well, maybe a few little productive things, I amended for myself as Lucy walked into the room with a tray. She paused by the entrance, smiling. She was wearing a lot less under the apron this time.

About an hour, an entire can of whipped cream, and a second shower later, I found myself wandering through my place feeling a happy little buzz. "Any news from that fox guy?" I asked aloud. Lucy blinked, but didn't ask.

Millennium Animal hasn't yet sent any concrete updates. He has posted the job, and there is some interest on the more public bounty boards. A lot of the interest is in the form of whether or not the price for the contract is worth it. There is a lot of speculation about the catalogs and items people could pur- chase. Some seem to think it's not worth as much as a pure-credit translation, though others are speculating otherwise.

Yeah, that tracked. Generous, huh? Twenty points seemed like . . . not much. "Well, keep me posted if he sends anything, please?"

I can do that.

I found some rags to wear, then headed out. It was surprisingly chilly outside.

The mech's repairs were . . . well, they were progressing. "I think," I said after I spent the first twenty minutes of work not doing any work, "that we're almost to the point where the mech could be used. Like, that bit's connected to that part, and we just need to close that doohickey there and slap the armor back on, right?"

That would make it usable, yes. Though you'd be missing one of your primary guns, and the other wouldn't have its full aiming radius. Also, there would be a noticeable weakness on that side.

"Meh, it's good enough to know that I can get the mech out and moving again with just a few hours of work. I don't want to close everything up yet, though."

Doing that would mean that I'd have to remove things again once I decided to fix the rest of the mech up, which would be a pain in the ass. Still, the fact that I had that much basic knowledge now was nice. I was improving. It felt like I was getting better pretty quickly, too.

Then again, that might have just been a symptom of picking up a new skill. Those tended to improve quickly at first, from what I could tell, then things would slow down drastically once the basics were down.

Oh well, I could live with that. Chances were the mech wouldn't stay in one piece once I was done fixing it. Not for long, anyway. One or two sorties against the Antithesis and it would be battered and broken again.

The chill eventually convinced me to get to work. There was no way I'd be able to keep warm unless I started to move. The repair drone came out, and soon enough I was back in the guts of the machine.

This was a much, much better way to spend the day than chasing assholes.

ut how many samurai were dealing in prosthetics outside of personal
n New Montreal, right now?

ac only knew one, and Cat *was* the lazy type. She'd definitely pay off
mercs to do her work for her. "S-so, this mission, we're taking it?"

Definitely," Garter said. "Grapevine says that only a few of the bigger
companies are moving in, and most of the solos are still damned clue-
They don't have a Jerusalem to help them figure things out."

pider: Compliments won't save you.

You want in too?" Rac asked Jerusalem. The Meshrunner shrugged his
er-clad shoulders.

pider: I don't care too much about the pay on this one.

pider: The rep, though.

pider: It'd be good for us.

Plus, we'd be getting on the good side of a samurai," Garter said. "I
d a rumor it might be the same chick that blew the mayor's head off."

Yeah," Rac said to fill the air while her mind raced. They'd met
already, but they hadn't put two and two together yet. That might
ge with this mission. She'd have to do damage control at some point,
dn't she?

ac supposed that the reputation boost was worth it, though, and it
d be doing a favor for Cat. She was already sleeping in Lucy's house—
had set aside a little room for her, same as the orphans they kept, and
had never felt safer than when she slept there. She wanted that to con-
, because a rent of nothing, plus free food and ammo and electricity,
something no smart person would pass up.

You in?" Garter asked.

I'm in," Rac said. Garter cheered and patted her on the back, and she
another bite of her burger to hide her expression. She felt the touch
after it was gone.

Coco was in too, of course. The big woman was wondering aloud about
kinds of stuff she could get for the reward the job was offering. Rac
d them out a little. This was . . . good.

Yeah, it was good. She'd have Cat owing her a tiny favor, and that'd make
ss likely that she'd get kicked out the moment she wasn't needed any-
e. That was good.

erusalem might have been trying to hide it, but he was just as excited
arter as the two started to strategize. There was nothing for Rac to
yet, not for a while. She might be sent ahead to scout, but that would
e later.

She looked over her team, and hoped that they wouldn't freak out too
h if they learned that she knew a samurai, and that she'd even intro-
ed them already.

A ROAMING RACCOON'S
REASONABLE RELATIONSHIPS
[PART TWO]

Rac was growing to really love the Barber Shop. The little club was . . . nice.
The music was weird and old, but it was still catchy. She wasn't sure what to
think of all the people dressed as animals—that wasn't her thing—but they
were mostly nice, and she . . . fit in?

Yeah, that's how she decided to put it. She fit in.

"Hey! You're here," Garter said. He was smiling, and Rac found herself
suddenly a little nervous, at least until she shoved the feeling down.

The others from her crew were in the same booth as Garter. Jerusalem
was splayed out across the table, eyes on an old-school tablet, and Coco was
sitting half in and half out of the booth. It was a little too small for her to fit
into normally.

"Hey," Rac said. She slipped in next to Garter, very aware of when her
hip bumped into his. "We have a job?"

"We do," Garter said.

Rac got a ping in her aug, and she connected to the team's chat. It let her
see that there had been some discussion going on that she'd missed. Most of
the speaking was Jerusalem, though.

Spider: Hello, Rac.

Spider: We have a job.

"What's the job?" Rac asked.

"Hey, calm down," Coco said. "Let's get something in you first. You look
like you haven't eaten anything in a week." Coco raised a hand, gesturing to
one of the servicers. She got a wave back, and soon enough a small wheeled
robot with a touch-screen to order on rolled over. "I'm starving," Coco said
as she started to punch an order in.

"While Coco gets us snacks," Garter said with a laugh, "did you hear the
news? About the samurai contract?"

"No?" Rac said. She'd been a little busy today. That morning she'd run into Lucy, and the rather intense girl had asked Rac if she could help them print out some more prosthetics. Rac didn't mind. She'd needed to print out some more ammo for her gun anyway, and the printer could do multiple things at once if it was loaded right.

Garter grinned. "Right, right, so it's big news in the merc circuit, at least here. Story goes that someone stole from a samurai. One of the mid-listers, you know?"

"Okay," Rac said. That happened sometimes. It was like people didn't know any better. It wasn't smart to punch upward, but people did it anyway.

Garter nodded along. "So, samurai tracks them down, but the trail goes cold. So they give up, right?"

"That's weird," Rac said.

"Yeah, a samurai's like a dog with a bone," Coco said.

"Anyway," Garter continued, "Instead of going after the stuff themselves, they put out a contract. And that's where it gets interesting. See, they didn't put money on the line, they put *points*."

Spider: Not enough of them.

"Any amount is a lot," Garter said. "That's like paying in . . . gold, or something even more valuable. Anyway, it took a while for people to decide if it was worth it, but now every merc worth their salt's jumping on the contract. Mostly the solos."

"Why the solos?" Rac asked.

"Can't split the pay well," Coco said. "It's twenty points. That's like . . . a few top-end guns? Depends on what you're wanting to get. But yeah, if your crew's big, how do you split that?"

"Oh," Rac said.

"Ah, but our crew has four members," Garter pointed out. "Hey, Spider, twenty divided by four?"

Spider: Are you fucking kidding me?

Spider: It's five.

Garter laughed. "Five more than any of us would ever get to play with."

Spider: I've seen what you can buy for five points.

Spider: It's not much.

"Then I'll take your five, if you don't want them," Garter said. "Give you five hundred credits for them?"

Spider: Fuck off.

"So, we're taking this job?" Rac asked. She wasn't sure if it was worth it for her. What could she get for that kind of reward? Her gun was probably worth a few dozen points, maybe? She wasn't sure how that kind of stuff worked out.

"We're *definitely* taking the job," Garter said. He ing bot came back with a tray and slid it on the tal burgers on it, fries, and some drinks. Coco rubbed h pushed one of the burgers toward Rac.

"Eat," she ordered.

"Jerusalem, privacy?" Garter asked.

Spider: I'll do what I can.

There was a faint whine, and Rac tried not to w ered. Spider was doing some hacker stuff to disable c It was a pretty typical move on his part. He said i would be enough to stop low-level spying.

"So, Spider and I have been on the case since dropped," Garter muttered conspiratorially.

His words surprised Rac, but she was too enrap front of her to respond right away. Rac picked it up started eating. It was good. Hot and meaty and filled secret sauce, which was really sweet. "Mm-hmm?"

"Yep. And we've discovered something."

Spider: I discovered something.

"Right, right," Garter said. "We think we know Sunrise Technologies is this low-level corp. Place is ov owned by nobody, who's owned by a numbers corp. place. Just like our last job. Well, this one's *really* big in samurai tech."

"They're the ones that stole from the samurai? way?" Rac asked.

"Prosthetics," Garter said.

Rac choked on her bite.

"Whoa, you okay?" Coco asked. She pushed a s popped the tab open, then put an all-plastic straw th let it out, girl."

"I'm fine," Rac said with a few more coughs. "Wror

"Don't do that on a mission," Garter said. "I rem Coco swallowed a mosquito. Nearly died."

"Not from the choking, it was from every damned all at once. It's why you should wear a mask on ops. I ID, you know?"

Rac nodded along while her mind raced. Prosth samurai had artificial limbs. There were some *weird* she'd heard Cat mention that Deus Ex, who looked nor sending clones out, so there was stuff like that too.

"I hope we get to meet them!" Coco said. "I've always wanted a samurai to sign my tits."

Rac sighed. No, no, she was screwed.

Rac woke up with a start to a buzz in her head. No, not her head. Her augs' alarm was ringing, which could only mean one thing. She sat up, one leg dropping off the side of her bed to swing there while she stifled a yawn and fumbled through the menu on her augs.

The alarm wasn't one she'd set, but it was one she'd given permission for. Specifically to Jerusalem, who had better, in Rac's humble and currently violent opinion, have a good explanation for why he'd set it off.

The moment she shut the alarm off, she saw the team chat blinking. A twitch of her eyes and it opened up.

Spider: Wakey wakey

Spider: Got a lead.

Spider: Need you all at the coffee place.

PrettyBoy: I'll be there in 30.

TheGorilla: I hate you.

TheGorilla: See you in 45. Anyone need a ride?

Rac groaned. She needed to reply, and then get ready and going. She didn't believe in pajamas, but she'd rather not have her friends smell her, so she at least needed to change out of her crusty old shirt.

GutterBaby: I'd like a ride. Can you pick me up on the rooftop?

Coco would know which rooftop Rac was talking about. Rac just needed to be there in time. She jumped out of bed, flung off her shirt, then grabbed a new one from the pile next to the door. It was one of those shirts that Lucy made—this one had Cat's logo on it, but there were long, electrified wires sticking out of it and the words "Wired to Whisker" above it and then a line of bottom text that read "Ten Million Wands Recharged: Time for Hysteria."

Rac had no idea what that meant, but assumed it was some obscure sexual thing that Lucy was into. That woman was, in Rac's opinion, a deviant.

She found some pants she'd only worn twice without washing, then slithered into her favorite jacket. It didn't have many holes in it yet. She was, of course, also wearing armor.

Specifically the under-armored suits that Cat had gotten a catalog for. They were pretty expensive, material-wise, but Rac had been quick to get one, and slow to remove it. It wicked sweat away as if she was standing in front of an industrial fan and yet was warm and cozy. She hadn't tested being shot yet, and wasn't planning on it, but it was supposed to be resistant to small-arms fire.

The last thing she did was pick up her gun before tossing it onto her back. Then she was out of her room and trying to sneak her way out of the house unnoticed.

She didn't make it.

"Rac!" Lucy said. The woman was all smiles as she took Rac in. "Going to work?"

"Yeah," Rac said.

"That's nice. Did you get enough sleep?"

"Uh? Probably, yeah," Rac said.

Lucy shook her head. "Give me a second, I have something for you," she demanded, and Rac paused, not really daring to deny Lucy to her face. In the meantime, though, she opened up an auto-taxi app on her augs. It would cost her a few thousand credits for a two-minute ride, but it was much faster than taking the elevator down, then walking to the nearest transit point.

She didn't have to wait long before Lucy returned. "Here," Lucy said as she shoved a grocery bag into Rac's hands. "You need to eat more. You'll never grow big if you're malnourished." Lucy crossed her arms.

"I don't need food," Rac said.

Lucy snorted. "More men have died from hunger than from bullets, Rac," she said, then gave her a wink. "Have fun, alright?"

"Yeah, alright," Rac said before she left.

She scrunched the bag up to her side, then darted out of the front, ignoring the kittens as she went. Rac didn't dislike the kittens, but . . . well, they didn't feel mature? Some were her age, yet all they really did was lounge around and waste the day away. They'd had rough lives too, but now that they had everything they were just . . . enjoying it.

It kind of disturbed Rac. They weren't planning ahead. They weren't assuming that the worst would happen. They had a safe home, for now, so why not use it to get better, make contacts, get rich independently, or at least earn a fair chunk of credits for themselves if shit went down?

She slipped outside, then wished that she'd brought a hat. Actually, a helmet would be nice. There were a few skintight helmets in that catalog Cat had gotten, but when she'd worn one to meet her friends, they'd laughed at her.

Well, Garter had. That was enough.

Rac glanced to the side and discovered Cat staring at the leg of her mech in incomprehension. The samurai's eyes darted to Rac, back, then returned to pin Rac on the spot. "Oh, hey," she said. "You got a minute?"

"Um, sure?" Rac said. She really didn't have much time to waste, but the taxi wasn't here yet.

"Cool, hold this thing." Cat gestured with a small part as Rac came over. "It goes in here, like this, see? And then you're supposed to click this bit and that bit, and that one there in all at the same time. It's like, a press-fit? But it's bullshit, because you need at least four hands to do it . . . No,

Myalis, I'm not getting more limbs. Cats only have the four, and I thought you wanted to stay on theme. What? The fuck would I care about alien cats?"

Rac just awkwardly followed the instructions, holding the piece steady and feeling like she was pressed in way too close to Cat as they finagled the piece into place. It clicked, eventually, and Cat let go with a pleased noise.

"There! Fucking perfect."

"Is it going to stay?" Rac asked. "It felt a little loose."

"Yeah, trust me, I know what I'm doing," Cat said.

"Alright," Rac said, very much *not* trusting Cat.

A car pulled up next to the landing pad, and Cat looked up. "A taxi? You heading out? Be careful out there, alright? And if you need a hand, gimme a call. I've still got the one!"

"Sure," Rac said noncommittally. Things would have to go really bad for her to call on an actual samurai to help. "See you, and, uh, good luck with your repairs?"

"I'm almost done!" Cat said.

Rac nodded, then ran over to the auto-taxi. She wasn't sure how almost-done Cat was. The mech looked in worse shape now than it had when Cat brought it back with holes gouged out of it. About halfway to her ride, Rac heard something drop and clink a few times, and then Cat started swearing a lot.

She slipped into the taxi, which already knew where to go and which was already running up the clock, and buckled up as quickly as she could so that it would get moving.

As it drove off, she emptied the bag Lucy had given her onto the seat next to her. There were two bright pink cakes in little plastic-wrap covers, like those from vending machines, and an energy drink.

Shrugging, Rac got to eating. It was a better breakfast than a lot of previous ones she'd had. She ate while the auto-taxi shot through the city, lights blurring past until, inevitably, they got caught in traffic.

Rac groaned, but there was nothing to do about it. Complaining would only have the taxi mark her as a "troublesome" rider, and then she'd lose whatever fidelity points she'd earned, along with the micro-discounts that came with them. She took another bite of her cake and let the colorful crumbs go everywhere in revenge.

A few minutes later the auto-taxi landed on a rooftop that was surprisingly barren. It was the top of one of those massive agricultural towers in the middle of the city, and the roof had large panels of glass that were stained by decades of rain.

Coco's van was parked on the far end, and the woman herself was bobbing her head to something within.

Rac ducked out of the cab, made sure she had her gun on her, then darted across to Coco's van. The side door opened as she came close, and she jumped in. "Hey, sorry I'm late," she said.

"All good," Coco said.

Rac nodded, then clambered over the armrest to sit up front next to Coco. She rarely got to call shotgun. "So, what's the news?"

"Didn't get much yet. I think Jerusalem's playing this one close to the chest. Strap in, I'm taking off now."

Rac frowned, but she secured herself. The van's engine grumbled to life, and they took off, joining the traffic above. It, of course, started to rain again.

"Jerusalem's not usually secretive with us," Rac said.

"Eh, no offense, but you haven't been there for some of our biggest gigs. This is the normal MO for big deals. And I think this is one. At least when it comes to clout, you know?"

"Right," Rac said. It was important, at least to Garter and the others. This would secure their little group as real mercs in the eyes of some, or at least make them stand out, which would mean better gigs in the future. "I dunno, it just feels like a lot of work for nothing," Rac said.

"Sometimes, that's just how it is," Coco said. "Sometimes that's just how it is."

CHAPTER THIRTY-SEVEN

THE CALL

I think the idea of a work-life balance is a myth. There's no such thing.
Not for a samurai, at least.

—Deus Ex, while still wearing pajamas, 2055

It took me an hour to fish out that one part that had fallen into the mech's leg. I almost gave up, but then Myalis told me that if I didn't get it out, the mech would make a constant rattling noise each time it moved that leg, and I couldn't live with the idea that my failure would be broadcast out there like an all-metal maraca.

That would go counter to the whole stealth thing I was aiming for.

Anyway, that frustration aside, I was actually getting things done pretty well. All I had to do was close up a few dozen things and I'd be good to go with the leg. Then it was back to work on the gun mount above. That was going to take . . . about twenty hours, give or take. It depended on how easily things fell through tiny cracks and had to be fetched.

"So, she's pretty much functional at this point, huh?" I asked.

Yes, it is. Have you decided that the mech is female now?

"Is that bad?" I asked.

No. It's very human to decide that an object needs to be personified to the point where it has its own gender.

"We can't be the only ones that do that," I defended.

Of course not. There are literally tens of thousands of species with their own cultures. Nothing humanity has done is unique to humanity.

"Wow," I said. "Way to make a girl feel special, Myalis."

You're very *special.*

I snorted. Myalis usually spoke in a pretty even tone, but right there she'd really pushed the condescension to the max. "Thanks, I appreciate it."

I was about to go on with the work, starting on the next part, when I heard the door open. A glance toward the entrance showed a familiar face walking out. Delilah, without her full samurai getup. Instead she was in a knit pullover and one of those long, modest skirts that stopped near mid-calf.

"Yo, Delilah!" I said. "What are you doing up here?"

"I live here now, as you may or may not have noticed," she said as she came over. "Or I will eventually. Turns out massive renovations are more trouble than I'd expected."

"Yeah, it might take a while. I know you have your stuff moved in, but did you need help with any of the rest?" My repair drone was up here helping me, but I could send it down to Delilah's place. It could do . . . renovation stuff, probably.

"We're fine," Delilah said. "If it takes a couple of weeks, then that's what it takes. We're working on things bit by bit right now. The plumbing's almost done, and then it'll be the kitchen, bathrooms, and the bedroom. I'll get the rest done as I go."

That was probably fair. "How are you on points and such?" I asked.

"Good. Really good. Those fire tests I ran the other day helped a lot. There's a pretty big shortage of samurai right now, so if you're ever looking for easy work, there's a lot to be had."

I groaned. "Yeah, I should. Kinda enjoying the vacation life right now, though."

"Really? I heard that you've been hard at work fixing the sewers and shooting the mayor."

I shook my head with a snort. She wasn't entirely wrong. "Yeah, sure, but it's mostly about bullying others into doing the work. I'll pop over to the Family tomorrow, do a quick spot-check to see if they're getting any work done or if they're just messing around. Thing is, the problem's kinda way too big for me to handle, so I need to rely on these guys instead."

"That's how it is," Delilah agreed. "Well, I appreciate you doing all of the boring work. I'm . . . not so fit for that kind of stuff."

"Really?" I leaned up against the leg of my mech. "You're a nun, I figured that charity was right up your alley."

"Oh, I've done my share, but it's not something I necessarily enjoy. It always feels like we're just patching over a problem instead of fixing it at the root. You can give food to people who can't afford it, and that'll feed them for a day or two, but it doesn't change the fact that there's not enough good work, or that food is priced too high. It feels like a waste of time."

"Hmm, you're basically giving the corps more time to rip people off instead of just blowing up their headquarters and shooting their shareholders until the problem's fixed," I said with a nod.

"See, that kind of thinking was always very frowned upon at the convent."

That was silly. The solution seemed pretty obvious to me. "Hey, Myalis, can we have some drinks? Just soda or something."

Two cans appeared on the workbench next to me, one covered in neon cats and the other with sick flames on it. No points for guessing which can was meant for whom.

"Thanks," Delilah said.

"Point-bought food tastes best." The tab popped with a carbonated hiss, and I took a big gulp while the drink was still at its fizziest. "Ah. Yeah, that hits the spot. So, you said something about a kitchen? Does that mean you know how to cook?"

"If you're trying to convince me to cook for you like Lucy has been, you'll be severely disappointed," Delilah said. "I can manage. We all took turns at the convent, but it's not something I'm overly fond of."

"Aww, but what if you cook Franny a nice romantic meal? Like, steak and potatoes or whatever."

Delilah flushed a little, but she quickly turned that into a confused glare. "Steak and potatoes? That's your idea of a romantic dinner?"

"I mean, I guess?"

"Wow. How did you ever end up with someone as good as Lucy when your idea of romance is steak and potatoes?"

"Mostly blind luck, and the fact that I was the only gay girl within arm's reach for long enough I eventually convinced Lucy she should give me a chance," I said.

Delilah chuckled. "Yeah, that sounds about right. Things are . . . interesting, right now."

"With Franny?"

"Yeah," she said. "Just . . . I don't know exactly where we stand, but it's going in a . . . nice direction, I think?"

"Still tiptoeing around each other and blushing like innocent little maidens?" I asked.

She glared some more. "Yes, essentially. But I don't think it's all bad. At least, I hope it's not."

"Is she moving in with you?" I asked with a vague gesture down toward her new place.

"I think so. I got her a room. Well, a guest bedroom. If she wants it."

"Build it last," I said. "And make sure your room has a big enough bed for two."

Delilah shook her head. "I'm not going to try to trick her into my bed or whatever. I don't want that. Even if it might work with you and Lucy."

That was probably fair. Lucy and I liked coming up with stupid excuses to spend time together. We'd definitely have jumped on the "Oh no, there's only one bed" scenario, but Delilah was uptight, and Franny was . . . also uptight, but she tried not to show it. They'd probably spend a lot of time talking about their feelings and slowly pushing boundaries before anything serious happened.

A waste of time, as far as I was concerned, but if it worked for them, then that was their thing.

"Do what works for you," I said. "But if you need a bit of advice, well, there's this thing I do with my ton—" I paused as my augs went off. I raised a hand in a "one second" gesture and looked at the incoming call.

"What's wrong?" Delilah asked. "It's not like you to stop mid-perversion."

"Got a call coming in from Rac," I said. "You know, the girl we picked up a while ago. Gimme a second." Delilah nodded once, and I picked up. "Yo?"

The line was quiet for a while, then Rac spoke. "Cat?"

"Yes?"

"I, ah, might be in a bit of trouble."

"Okay. How much is a bit?"

"Well, we're pinned down right now. Spider hacked one of the bots, but it's only distracting them. Coco's shot, and Garter's saying that we're going to have to try and save our ammo. And I'm out of grenades."

"A bit," I said dryly. Then I set my can down and started to fret. "Where are you, exactly, and what the hell are you up to?"

"It's complicated," Rac said.

"Uh-huh," I replied. "Can you not die for like, a few minutes?"

"I'll try?"

I pinched the bridge of my nose, then turned to Delilah. "Sorry, something's come up. I need to get geared up. Rac? Hey, can you still hear me? Yeah, so . . . this trouble, is it 'show up with a pistol' trouble or is it more than that?"

"More? Definitely more."

At least Rac had called! That was about the best thing I could see in all of this.

A ROAMING RACCOON'S REASONABLE RELATIONSHIPS [PART THREE]

Everything that could go wrong had gone wrong, and all at once too.

The info that Jerusalem had picked up pointed to a part of the city that was way, way off on the edges of New Montreal.

It was still within the walls that had been put up last week, but only barely. A fully industrial sector that was impossible to fly over. There were literally thousands of smokestacks and chimneys all squeezed in together over large brown and black buildings that were all function and no form.

En route, Coco said that no one sane lived in this part of the city, and Rac believed her. She'd spent most of her life living in the undercity of New Montreal, where a lot of smaller factories and assembly plants were tucked away. She'd met some workers, usually maintenance people for the droids that worked the lines, so she'd picked a few things up, if only by osmosis.

The factories under the city didn't make things from nothing. Instead, they received refined, already-processed materials, and turned those into stuff.

A factory making toys would receive blocks of plastic, metal ingots, and stacks of processed and recycled rubbers from elsewhere, then turn that into an end product.

Those materials came from here. The chemical heart of New Montreal.

The things brought into this part of the city were all precursor chemicals. Petrochems, monomers, polymers, plant extracts, unprocessed minerals and metal, heaps of auto-sorted recyclable goods. They were trucked in by the metric shitload, then synthesized or broken apart, boxed, and shipped out to some other dreary, dank place.

The stolen gear was hiding in a warehouse smack in the middle of this industrial sector.

As it turned out, the "ground" level was actually about four levels off the actual ground. There wasn't an undercity here. The entire industrial landscape was above a thick, multi-leveled platform, with interior roads, warehouses, factories, and plants all over. Only the plants that needed more vertical room poked out above the rest.

They started by looking at a few incomprehensible maps that Jerusalem drew up. The underground here was a maze of passages and corridors and interconnected spaces. The 3D-mapping software didn't have the guts to lay it all out, but Rac got the broad strokes. She'd lived in a place just like this, so it wasn't hard to orient herself. Navigating the undercity was a basic skill to anyone who lived there.

The plan, once they'd figured out where to hit, was simple enough.

The stolen goods would have to be moved eventually, and they happened to be stored in a large warehouse with only one exit. Attacking the warehouse was . . . not a good idea. There were PMCs hired to protect it.

So, they'd hit whatever transport left the place.

That meant parking a floor below the target warehouse, then breaking into another warehouse next to the parking lot. They cut into the ceiling of that warehouse and hoisted themselves up through the floor.

In the end, Rac, Garter, Spider, and Coco were all hiding in the warehouse right across the road from the one with the prosthetics.

The plan was nice and simple, and of course, it went to shit about two hours after they arrived at their location.

"Fuck, fuck, fuck," Garter swore under his breath. He'd stuck his head out from cover for just a split second and three rounds had zipped by.

Rac had just discovered, a few minutes prior, that when she heard a bullet hiss, it was close, and when it made a snap, that meant she'd almost lost her head.

Garter leaned against their cover, which was a large cement barricade that was absorbing a fair bit of damage at the moment, and started to reload his gun. "We can't stick around here," he said.

"Can't exactly leave, now can we?" Coco shot back. She was cradling her leg, which was pissing hydraulic fluid blood all over.

She was grounded, just like the rest of them. The only one with a good idea of what was happening on the other side of the barrier was Spider, and he didn't look ready to move either.

About two hours into their wait, six trucks had rocked up out of nowhere and mercs started rushing their target. The news, it seemed, had gotten out.

Garter had Spider open the door to their warehouse, which predictably had led to the mercs opening fire at Rac and her team.

Then the PMCs guarding the prosthetics joined in on the fun.

This wasn't some low-budget rent-a-cop outfit. These were professionals. Of the "oh shit, oh fuck" variety.

The guard APCs had torn into the merc's technicals.

The firefight was almost entirely one-sided. For about ten long minutes.

Then, more mercenaries showed up. These ones better equipped, with armored vehicles of their own, deployable cover, remote-firing guns, and all sorts of gadgets.

The whole thing had devolved from there.

Now there was a three-way fight, sorta. Some mercs had started opening up on other mercs, but mostly they were all fighting the PMCs.

Spider: Fuck.

Rac blinked. That was the first thing Jerusalem had said in a while. At first, he'd mostly been keeping them apprised while they kept their heads down. The mission had gone tits up, and Rac for one wanted nothing more than to leave, but their path out was blocked. They had empty space to their left and right, and were across the street from the PMCs. Any fire shot at the mercs flew in their direction.

"What's wrong?" Garter asked.

Spider: PMC mecha.

"What?"

There was a loud explosion, and Rac winced as a wash of hot air and dust burst past them.

She blinked, then did something she knew, consciously, was stupid. She glanced over the top of the barricade.

There wasn't *a* mecha, there were three of them. Big things, standing on four articulated legs that ended with treads like a tank's. Their top halves were boxy and armored, and covered in guns.

"Where the fuck did those come from?" Coco asked.

The mechs started firing on the mercs, answering that question.

The mercs returned fire with some haste, and the mechas flowed to one side, taking cover behind the burning wrecks of a few vans and an old six-wheeled APC.

"We are so fucking fucked," Garter swore.

Rac didn't like that one bit. He was usually so cool and composed. Now it almost looked like he wanted to cry.

Spider: Dear Mom,

Spider: I know I wasn't always the best son.

Spider: But a lot of the time you were a shit mom.

Spider: My will leaves all of my money to Aunt Katia. I know you hate her.

Spider: Fuck you.

Spider: P.S. I'm dead.

"Is that your fucking obituary?!" Rac shouted.

Jerusalem raised his arms in a sort of "what do you expect me to do" gesture.

Rac grit her teeth. She was dead. Was going to die. Caught in the crossfire of a street war she was totally unequipped for.

And here she'd thought she was hot shit with her cool bulletproof skinsuit and big-ass shotgun.

She didn't need a shotgun, she needed . . . the kind of shit samurai had. Giant railguns, huge flamethrowers, weird alien weapons. Which meant . . . she only really had one option if she wanted to survive this.

"Damnit," Rac swore.

She dialed. Somehow, the call connected through what was probably six layers of ECM. "Yo?" It was Cat's uncaring, casual voice on the line.

Rac still called out her name. "Cat?" Coco looked her way, but quickly returned her attention to the bullets whizzing by.

"Yes?"

"I, ah, might be in a bit of trouble."

Spider: Got one!

"Got it how?" Garter asked.

One of the mecha stomped out of cover and turned. Its side-mounted guns opened fire, spraying explosive rounds against the far wall of the street.

"Okay. How much is a bit?" Cat asked.

Rac shrugged back down into cover and tried to tune out the explosions, the swearing, and the renewed fire. She was pretty sure a *new* group of mercs had just arrived. Or PMC reinforcements. In either case, it had just gotten worse. "Well, we're pinned down right now. Spider hacked one of the bots, but it's only distracting them. Coco's shot, and Garter's saying that we're going to have to try and save our ammo. And I'm out of grenades."

"A bit. Where are you, exactly, and what the hell are you up to?" Cat asked.

"It's complicated," Rac said. She didn't want to sound like she was on the verge of panicking. But she kind of was.

"Uh-huh. Can you not die for like, a few minutes?"

"I'll try?" Rac said. She didn't sound so certain, even to herself.

"Sorry, something's come up. I need to get geared up," Cat said. She wasn't talking to Rac. "Rac? Hey, can you still hear me? Yeah, so . . . this trouble, is it 'show up with a pistol' trouble or is it more than that?"

There was another explosion, someone shouting "He's got an RPG!"

"More? Definitely more," Rac confirmed.

"Hmm, alright! See you in a bit!"

Coco shook her shoulder. "Rac? Stay with me, sweetie."

A ROAMING RACCOON'S REASONABLE RELATIONSHIPS [PART TWO]

Rac was growing to really love the Barber Shop. The little club was . . . nice. The music was weird and old, but it was still catchy. She wasn't sure what to think of all the people dressed as animals—that wasn't her thing—but they were mostly nice, and she . . . fit in?

Yeah, that's how she decided to put it. She fit in.

"Hey! You're here," Garter said. He was smiling, and Rac found herself suddenly a little nervous, at least until she shoved the feeling down.

The others from her crew were in the same booth as Garter. Jerusalem was splayed out across the table, eyes on an old-school tablet, and Coco was sitting half in and half out of the booth. It was a little too small for her to fit into normally.

"Hey," Rac said. She slipped in next to Garter, very aware of when her hip bumped into his. "We have a job?"

"We do," Garter said.

Rac got a ping in her aug, and she connected to the team's chat. It let her see that there had been some discussion going on that she'd missed. Most of the speaking was Jerusalem, though.

Spider: Hello, Rac.

Spider: We have a job.

"What's the job?" Rac asked.

"Hey, calm down," Coco said. "Let's get something in you first. You look like you haven't eaten anything in a week." Coco raised a hand, gesturing to one of the servicers. She got a wave back, and soon enough a small wheeled robot with a touch-screen to order on rolled over. "I'm starving," Coco said as she started to punch an order in.

"While Coco gets us snacks," Garter said with a laugh, "did you hear the news? About the samurai contract?"

"No?" Rac said. She'd been a little busy today. That morning she'd run into Lucy, and the rather intense girl had asked Rac if she could help them print out some more prosthetics. Rac didn't mind. She'd needed to print out some more ammo for her gun anyway, and the printer could do multiple things at once if it was loaded right.

Garter grinned. "Right, right, so it's big news in the merc circuit, at least here. Story goes that someone stole from a samurai. One of the mid-listers, you know?"

"Okay," Rac said. That happened sometimes. It was like people didn't know any better. It wasn't smart to punch upward, but people did it anyway.

Garter nodded along. "So, samurai tracks them down, but the trail goes cold. So they give up, right?"

"That's weird," Rac said.

"Yeah, a samurai's like a dog with a bone," Coco said.

"Anyway," Garter continued, "Instead of going after the stuff themselves, they put out a contract. And that's where it gets interesting. See, they didn't put money on the line, they put *points*."

Spider: Not enough of them.

"Any amount is a lot," Garter said. "That's like paying in . . . gold, or something even more valuable. Anyway, it took a while for people to decide if it was worth it, but now every merc worth their salt's jumping on the contract. Mostly the solos."

"Why the solos?" Rac asked.

"Can't split the pay well," Coco said. "It's twenty points. That's like . . . a few top-end guns? Depends on what you're wanting to get. But yeah, if your crew's big, how do you split that?"

"Oh," Rac said.

"Ah, but our crew has four members," Garter pointed out. "Hey, Spider, twenty divided by four?"

Spider: Are you fucking kidding me?

Spider: It's five.

Garter laughed. "Five more than any of us would ever get to play with."

Spider: I've seen what you can buy for five points.

Spider: It's not much.

"Then I'll take your five, if you don't want them," Garter said. "Give you five hundred credits for them?"

Spider: Fuck off.

"So, we're taking this job?" Rac asked. She wasn't sure if it was worth it for her. What could she get for that kind of reward? Her gun was probably worth a few dozen points, maybe? She wasn't sure how that kind of stuff worked out.

"We're *definitely* taking the job," Garter said. He glanced up as the serving bot came back with a tray and slid it on the table. There were several burgers on it, fries, and some drinks. Coco rubbed her hands together, then pushed one of the burgers toward Rac.

"Eat," she ordered.

"Jerusalem, privacy?" Garter asked.

Spider: I'll do what I can.

There was a faint whine, and Rac tried not to wince as her augs flickered. Spider was doing some hacker stuff to disable comms and recordings. It was a pretty typical move on his part. He said it wasn't perfect, but it would be enough to stop low-level spying.

"So, Spider and I have been on the case since the moment the news dropped," Garter muttered conspiratorially.

His words surprised Rac, but she was too enraptured by the burger in front of her to respond right away. Rac picked it up with both hands and started eating. It was good. Hot and meaty and filled with the Barber Shop's secret sauce, which was really sweet. "Mm-hmm?"

"Yep. And we've discovered something."

Spider: I discovered something.

"Right, right," Garter said. "We think we know where the goods are. Sunrise Technologies is this low-level corp. Place is owned by nobody, who's owned by nobody, who's owned by a numbers corp. You know the kind of place. Just like our last job. Well, this one's *really* big into grabbing discarded samurai tech."

"They're the ones that stole from the samurai? What was taken anyway?" Rac asked.

"Prosthetics," Garter said.

Rac choked on her bite.

"Whoa, you okay?" Coco asked. She pushed a soda across the table, popped the tab open, then put an all-plastic straw through it. "Drink this, let it out, girl."

"I'm fine," Rac said with a few more coughs. "Wrong pipe."

"Don't do that on a mission," Garter said. "I remember once, I think Coco swallowed a mosquito. Nearly died."

"Not from the choking, it was from every damned guard turning on me all at once. It's why you should wear a mask on ops. Not just to hide your ID, you know?"

Rac nodded along while her mind raced. Prosthetics? Sure, a lot of samurai had artificial limbs. There were some *weird* ones out there. And she'd heard Cat mention that Deus Ex, who looked normal, was actually just sending clones out, so there was stuff like that too.

But how many samurai were dealing in prosthetics outside of personal use, in New Montreal, right now?

Rac only knew one, and Cat *was* the lazy type. She'd definitely pay off some mercs to do her work for her. "S-so, this mission, we're taking it?"

"Definitely," Garter said. "Grapevine says that only a few of the bigger merc companies are moving in, and most of the solos are still damned clueless. They don't have a Jerusalem to help them figure things out."

Spider: Compliments won't save you.

"You want in too?" Rac asked Jerusalem. The Meshrunner shrugged his leather-clad shoulders.

Spider: I don't care too much about the pay on this one.

Spider: The rep, though.

Spider: It'd be good for us.

"Plus, we'd be getting on the good side of a samurai," Garter said. "I heard a rumor it might be the same chick that blew the mayor's head off."

"Yeah," Rac said to fill the air while her mind raced. They'd met Cat already, but they hadn't put two and two together yet. That might change with this mission. She'd have to do damage control at some point, wouldn't she?

Rac supposed that the reputation boost was worth it, though, and it would be doing a favor for Cat. She was already sleeping in Lucy's house—Cat had set aside a little room for her, same as the orphans they kept, and Rac had never felt safer than when she slept there. She wanted that to continue, because a rent of nothing, plus free food and ammo and electricity, was something no smart person would pass up.

"You in?" Garter asked.

"I'm in," Rac said. Garter cheered and patted her on the back, and she took another bite of her burger to hide her expression. She felt the touch long after it was gone.

Coco was in too, of course. The big woman was wondering aloud about the kinds of stuff she could get for the reward the job was offering. Rac tuned them out a little. This was . . . good.

Yeah, it was good. She'd have Cat owing her a tiny favor, and that'd make it less likely that she'd get kicked out the moment she wasn't needed anymore. That was good.

Jerusalem might have been trying to hide it, but he was just as excited as Garter as the two started to strategize. There was nothing for Rac to do yet, not for a while. She might be sent ahead to scout, but that would come later.

She looked over her team, and hoped that they wouldn't freak out too much if they learned that she knew a samurai, and that she'd even introduced them already.

"I just called someone," Rac said.

"What, did Spider give you ideas?" Coco asked. She squeezed Rac's shoulder. "We'll make it, we'll make it." It didn't sound as certain as Rac would have liked, but she appreciated the attempt to reassure her all the same.

"We're so fucked," Garter contradicted Coco.

The firefight actually cooled off a moment later. Rac peeked out, then hid again when something like a security bot spun around and snapped a shot in her direction. The PMCs had gotten even more reinforcements: a half-dozen androids and war drones.

The mercenaries had taken the entire right side of the street while the PMCs had set up barricades and defenses on their side. It was a stalemate, but Rac had a feeling that wasn't going to last long.

There were more mercs on this job than PMCs. It didn't matter that one side had mecha. They'd be overwhelmed, especially if someone like Spider could get through their protections, even for a moment.

Rac clutched her gun close and waited, hoping that Cat didn't take her time getting over here, because she really couldn't afford that right now. Also, now that the adrenaline was wearing off, she realized a few things. Her hands hurt from gripping her gun so hard, her teeth hurt from clenching so much, and she really had to pee.

Spider: Oh.

Spider: Well, it was nice working with you.

"Spider?" Rac asked as she read the message on her augs.

Then she heard it, the crunch of treads moving over concrete. The shadow of something large swept over them, and she looked up as the top of one of the warmechs became visible over the makeshift barrier.

It was over.

The mech was large, with a gun on its right side, and a large shield on its left that was already marked and blemished by bullet scores and burns.

Coco rose up on one leg, screaming incoherently. She fired her gun right up at the mecha.

Rac, deciding that she would go out fighting too, jumped to her feet, and fired as well.

It wasn't doing anything. Their crew's guns were made to take out people, not heavily armored war machines. There was laughter crackling out of a loudspeaker, and Rac realized it was coming from the machine. Whoever was controlling it thought that they were funny. Garter was on the ground, crying, Spider was . . . doing something hacker-like.

Rac wasn't sure if these were the people she'd planned on dying with, but it looked like she didn't have much of a choice in the matter.

Then she ran out of ammo. She dropped her gun, going for the next thing she had, a little handgun strapped to her back that would do even less.

The mecha swung its gun around to aim at Rac and her friends, but before it could lock on its target, something *wavered* in the air.

"Sorry I'm late," a very familiar voice said. Rac felt her heart lurch at the sound as something weird and unfamiliar hit her. Hope.

A moment later, the mech that had been about to kill her was sent flying backward.

A shadowy, warped vision filled the air. A huge cat, larger than any real feline had any right to be, was there and then not, its form a slight shimmer only visible because of the moment of contact with the other mech.

It pounced away just as the mech crashed back-first onto the street, sparks flying all over as it skid across the road.

The second mech in the group turned, raising its large gun and opening fire.

Something blurred to the side, then there was an unholy *brrrrt* and a stream of lead came out of nowhere and splattered across the front of the mech. It raised its shield, and Rac jumped into cover as what felt like thousands of rounds ricocheted all over the place.

The *brrrrt* eventually slowed down to a stop. "Well, shit, these really do lack penetrating power," Cat's voice said.

It seemed like Cat was done hiding. Her mech melted out of thin air, and Rac had never been happier to see the strange robotic cat.

Rac had seen the machine sitting out at Lucy's place. It was impressive, sure, but . . . well, it had always been a large, immobile, cat-shaped thing. The entire house was topped by a giant metal cat. She'd kind of grown dismissive of it.

Now it was bounding to the side, weaving out of the way of shots from the warmech like something *alive*. It moved like nothing mechanical should. "Alright, what about these, then?"

The sides of the warmech opened up and two massive guns folded out of it. They were each large enough for Rac to fit a fist into their barrels. Almost as soon as they clunked out of hiding, they both opened fire, leaving two thin trails of vapor in their wake and a pair of twin bangs that made the floor jump.

The mech that Cat had fired at exploded in the middle, scrap chunks of metal flying all over.

The third decided not to stay still and charged forward, shield raised in front of it at an angle to deflect the next shots.

The cat mech raised its head. Its chest opened up. Energy collected in its frame. The entire cat lit up, as if there were hundreds of LEDs hidden along every angular edge of its all-black armor. Rac felt the hair on her head and arms rising.

Then there was a flash.

The third mech was vaporized from the hips up.

So was the wall behind it, and the one behind that.

A few of the little security bots opened up on Cat's mech, but their bullets pinged uselessly off of its armor, and its single shoulder-mounted Gatling gun swept all the way around, wiping them out with ease. The mech casually walked up to one of the larger drones, placed its paw on its head, then activated four claws that were so dark they sucked in the light around them and swiped through armor and plastic as if it was nothing.

"Alright," Cat announced. "We're done here. Next fuckwit that raises a gun gets dead. Got it?"

The mercs seemed to agree with the general sentiment, and the PMCs didn't seem to have much of a fight left in them anymore.

Spider: Dear Mom,

Spider: Sorry about earlier.

Spider: We still on for brunch Saturday?

The battle seemed like it was over.

The mech leaned forward, and its front half unfolded to reveal Cat, in her samurai gear, standing up from a tiny, cramped cockpit.

Rac almost started to step forward when she saw the first mech, the one Cat had thrown back, turning its gun toward Cat. "Watch ou—"

The world became *heat.*

A wash of fire and light and stinging warmth filled the corridor for just a split second, then receded.

What remained in its wake was a large hole in the ground where the PMC mech had been. The concrete road had melted in a large circle, the edges of which, still with some pieces of the mech melted in, were still on fire.

A woman all in black was standing nearby, casually holding a little flamethrower. "Cat. *Please* pay more attention," she said.

Rac swallowed while Cat laughed it off.

She was, she realized, never going to have that casual ability to do violence and shrug it off that a samurai had.

And now she had to *talk* to two of them and say thank you.

She almost wished she was hiding behind a crumbling barricade again.

CHAPTER THIRTY-EIGHT

BOO-BOOS AND BODY BAGS

It's easy for the average person to forget that the idea of a dedicated emergency-response force is actually relatively new.

Firefighters have been around for millennia. Policing forces for almost as long. But paramedics and emergency services were only fully modernized with the 1966 White Papers to push them along.

Current EMT training is less than a hundred years old. It's a developing system that's far from perfect, and still has much room to improve.

Which is why the Toronto Paramedic Services is now instituting obligatory firearms training into its basic paramedic training courses.

—TPS Newsletter, 2028

The first thing I noticed was that my mech now had a scattering of scuffs all across its armor.

The small-arms fire hadn't penetrated anything. At least, I didn't think it had. There were some parts, especially on the side that I hadn't yet finished repairing, that lacked the sensors that would let me know if anything was damaged.

That entire side read as a stream of errors and unresolved issues. A few more holes poked into it would get lost among all of the other warnings.

I ran my metal hand over the surface of the mech's ribs. A few bits of melted bullet clinked off the surface. That was going to need some looking at. I was pretty sure the stealth stuff would be mostly unaffected, but this might also mean a few tiny black spots that weren't camouflaged when I moved.

"For fuck's sake, I *just* fixed this thing," I muttered.

Add about twenty-six hours to the repair time.

"Just for these scuffs?" I asked.

And because of the damage to the not-fully-repaired leg. Some of the warnings you chose to ignore were highlighting issues within. Misaligned actuators don't need much effort to break, and those hydraulic lines that were poorly sealed have ruptured.

I cursed under my breath, but . . . yeah, that was par for the course. In an ideal world I would have finished everything, then run the mech through some light testing before going back in and fixing anything that needed touch-ups. Then I'd be able to call it properly done. This was . . . not entirely ideal. Worth it, though. Even below its full capability, the mech was a ton of fun to pilot, and this was for a good cause.

I turned away from the mech and took in the scene on the street. It was, in a word, bad.

When I arrived, I'd initially been more focused on finding Rac and making sure she was alive. I discovered her firing blindly at a warmech designed for heavy riot-protection duties. It had a cannon that would turn her into a smear.

So I'd taken it out, and the other two light mecha. Ripping apart the gun emplacements on the APCs and technicals parked around here had been quick and easy too, and that left nothing but some security drones and guys with small arms.

I'd made a bit of a mess cleaning up the mechs, but the place was already far past being just messy. There were bodies. More injured.

A few mercs had crawled out of cover and were helping their pals. I had a lot of them giving me looks, but as long as I wasn't aggressive, I was pretty sure they wouldn't run just yet. Rac and her friends were still near that warehouse, looking alright for the most part.

"Myalis, why aren't emergency services here yet?" I asked.

Because there was a battle that took place which featured several large mechanized assault vehicles?

That . . . probably made sense, yeah. The average paramedic probably didn't want to fuck with this entire situation, and I really couldn't blame them. "Send them the all-clear. Let them know that there are two samurai on the scene keeping things clean."

Sent.

"Hey!" I called out, and more than one head rose to look my way. It helped that Myalis had caught on to what I was doing and was projecting my voice from the mech. "I called in the paramedics. Try to keep the injured alive until they arrive. Someone check on the dead, line them up over to the side there. And someone start clearing out the middle of the damned road. We don't need to slow down the ambulances when they do arrive."

There was a pause. None of the mercs were moving quite yet.

"Well, get to it!" I snapped.

That actually had them jumping into action. It looked like there were maybe half a dozen merc outfits here, maybe more. Some looked like one-car teams. Just buddies that loaded up into a single van and rushed over. A few others looked like more professional outfits.

What the hell were they all here for? Fights broke out all the time. This was New Montreal, the police didn't give a shit, and neither did anyone else. But usually that was between gangs, not mercs. And Rac . . . she was supposed to be on easy, safe jobs. Not jobs with a two-digit death toll.

I turned toward the other side. The PMC guys were doing the same as the mercs, moving their injured to one side. It looked like they had at least one medic in their bunch, and he was probably earning his pay right now with the number of injuries to tend to.

"This is a bit of a mess," Gomorrah said as she came up behind me. I could feel her approaching.

My gear was fireproof, on account of how often I worked with her, but I still had a bit of exposed skin in this loadout, and I could feel the heat wafting off of Gomorrah's gun. The end was glowing, and there was a faint waver in the air above it.

"Yeah," I agreed. "Think you can do me a favor?"

"That would depend," she said evenly.

"Keep an eye on this whole bunch for me? I'm going to go check on Rac. Myalis, can you set the mech to autopilot and, uh, patch Atyacus into it?"

I'm certain he'll appreciate the permission.

I wasn't sure what she meant by that, but I figured that Gomorrah's AI wasn't likely to try and fuck me over. Worst case, I'd come back to find the thagomizer on my tail replaced by a flamethrower or something.

Or there would be religious iconography all over the mech. "Don't give my mech one of those gold rapper chains with the crosses," I said before I took off.

"Huh?" Gomorrah said after a moment's pause.

I was already heading over to Rac, though. The girl was standing off to the side with her friends. Coco, the big woman with the cyber arms, was leaning onto that Garter guy. She was also grinning creepily.

Rac looked like shit. All of her friends did, actually, and I didn't miss how Coco was injured. The wound didn't look all that bad, considering, but it probably still hurt.

"Hey," I said as I came over.

"You're Rac's friend!" Coco said. "From last time. You're a *samurai*!"

"Uh, yes, and yeah," I agreed.

"Coco . . . likes samurai," Rac explained.

"Hell yeah, I do," Coco said. "Sign my tits!"

I blinked. "Do you have a pen?"

Coco brightened, then her face fell. I don't think I'd ever seen someone look so sad so quickly before.

"Ah, I'm sure we can find a marker," I said. Coco's grin came back, a little more reserved, and a little more pained. "Myalis, got something cheap for . . . little boo-boo wounds?"

Yes, I have boo-boo treatments, Catherine.

I caught a small box out of the air, then read the package before rolling my eyes. *Boo-Boo Treatment: 1x Dose.* It looked like it was mostly just a bandage and maybe some antiseptic powder. My point total ticked back by one. I tossed it to Coco. "Put that on your leg before you bleed out," I said. "The paramedics will be too busy once they get here to look at you."

"Thank you," Coco said with a huge grin. "So, last time . . . why didn't you tell us you were a samurai? Rac, why didn't you tell us you knew a samurai?"

"I have my reasons," Rac said. She sounded perfectly petulant about it and wasn't meeting her team's gazes.

I noticed that Rac was looking a little pale, and her hands were shaking, just a little. Still, she looked like she was trying hard to at least seem as if she had her shit together. I wouldn't trust her with a gun right now, though. She was probably crashing from the adrenaline. I sent Myalis a quick text, and felt something settle in the pocket of my coat. I pulled it out, and handed the can to Rac bottom-first. "Drink," I said. "You need some sugar in you, and something cool."

Rac hesitated, but took the can. It didn't take a genius to know that it wasn't normal-grade shit, not with the anime-style cats on the can, but she took it anyway and drank up.

Food would do her good. At least, that's what I'd do for a kitten if they were distressed. Food was a good way to remember that things weren't that desperate. "So, I never really expected to get a call from you. Happy you did, because this looks like a clusterfuck and a half, but, uh, what happened here?"

"We were on a job," Garter said. He was standing a lot taller now, trying to look more professional despite the dust and grime.

"A job?" I asked.

"We were getting your prosthetics," Rac said.

Everyone looked at her.

I slowly turned and took in the carnage. "What? All this shit for some prosthetics?" The goal had been to help people, to give some messed-up folk a new lease on life. Not spark a fucking war in the industrial district.

"And your pay," Rac said. There was a bit of accusation there. I wasn't sure if that was deserved, but I rolled with it.

How was I supposed to know that a bunch of people would go nuts over twenty points? "Man, people are stupid," I said.

CHAPTER THIRTY-NINE

SHOTS, SPOTS, STRETCHERS

I'm not paid enough for this.
—Jacob "Redundant" Smith, Private PMC Contractor, 2057

The ambulances arrived soon enough and parked themselves along one side of the road. It looked pretty organized, with the vans spinning around right away so that they were back-first to the mercs and PMCs that needed them.

Paramedics jumped out, followed by hovering drones that carried cameras for legal documentation, some remote-controlled guns, and small toolkits with medical supplies and whatever equipment the paramedics needed.

The vans were the bigger sort, with bunked gurneys so that each one could carry half a dozen patients at the same time.

I imagined that they'd all be filled up soon enough.

The mercs had stood down already, but now some of them were tossing guns and gear away as the medics arrived and started unfolding their gurneys to load up the worst and richest of the injured first.

I nodded along, happy to see that things were operating smoothly. It meant that I could refocus on Rac and her friends. "So," I said.

Rac and her little gang of weirdos were still focused on me. Especially Coco. I'd thought she was pretty cool before, but now I wasn't so sure. The woman definitely had that fangirl vibe going on, and while that was fine, it was less fine when it was pointed my way. Rac, at least, looked better. Color was returning to her cheeks and her eyes were sharp. It didn't look like she was going to pass out anymore.

Her friends looked better too. They'd been tense right after the conclusion of the fight, ready to jump back into it. Now that there were paramedics all over and most of the mercs and PMCs had been kind enough to lower their arms, the situation was definitely taking on a less . . . dangerous feel. Garter and Jerusalem were still eyeing the other mercs, but they didn't seem to be on as much of a hair trigger.

"Uh, I guess we should see about those prosthetics?" I said. This whole mess started because of that. Might as well put an end to it. "Oh, and you can meet Gomorrah. You remember her, right Rac?"

"Yeah," Rac said. "She's moving into your building."

I nodded slowly, then decided to clarify the statement for the audience. "Yeah, she's taking over some of the floors in the building under my, uh, house."

It looked like Coco was vibrating a little as she turned toward Rac. "You know where she *lives*?" she asked.

Rac looked supremely uncomfortable, but also reluctant to answer. "I, uh, live with Lucy. That's Ca—Stray Cat's wife."

"Girlfriend," I pointed out. I didn't point out that living with Lucy meant living with me. There wasn't much of a difference, but if Rac wanted to keep that bit of separation going, I didn't mind. "At least until I propose."

"You're going to propose?" Rac asked.

"Really, Cat?" Gomorrah asked as she came up behind me.

"What? No, I mean, I will. Eventually. I guess. If Lucy wants."

Gomorrah gave me a very unimpressed look, which was impressive considering the full-face mask that was permanently stuck in glare. She did sigh after a moment. "Actually, that makes perfect sense. She would be the one to propose first."

"What's that mean?" I asked.

"Never mind," Gomorrah said. "I'm keeping my stones uncast here."

"Changing the topic for a moment." I turned toward Rac and her friends. "How did you learn where the prosthetics were? Or did you just keep up with the others swarming the place?"

Garter spoke up at last. "We were here first," he said. "Jerusalem was the one to track things down. It took tracking the goods moving around the city, then backtracking to local private military companies, which led us here."

"Why backtrack to PMCs?" I asked.

"Because the trail was really well covered. It had to be professional work. We know what mid-level mercenaries can do, and his was better. So that left either full-on corpo black-ops, or well-paid PMCs. Or, I guess samurai, but the gig's client was ah, you, so that wouldn't make sense."

"I'm following you so far," I said.

"So, yeah, Jerusalem and I got a short-list of active PMCs in the region, then worked our way back from there. Checked on the media feeds of some members. Mostly tedious shit, but we got a few suspicious hits that led us to this place." He gestured across the street to the warehouse the PMCs had been guarding. "After that, it was just a matter of checking the cameras until we saw some sketchy-looking vans pull in and unload the goods."

I turned and stared at the warehouse across the street. The front of it was . . . kinda fucked, really. The amount of gunfire that had been let loose around here had done a number on the thin concrete walls, leaving them chipped and cracked all over. "So, they brought my shit here, huh?"

"Yeah," Garter said. "Although with you coming to help, uh, do we still get the payment from the contr—" He cut off with a cough, and when I glanced back Rac was rubbing her elbow and Garter his lower ribs.

"We'll see about that," I said noncommittally. It was one thing to pay up for a finished job, but it was another to pay up after I had to fly over and wreck shit with my mech. Plus, now I was down a bunch of ammo and up a few scratches. The whole point of the contract was for me to *not* have to do anything.

Something didn't add up, though.

"Hey, Gom," I said.

"Yes?" Gomorrah asked.

"Okay, so these punks stole some of the prosthetics I was going to basically give away. They passed themselves off as another gang to muddy things, then handed them off to someone else, who traded them to someone *else*, and at some point the things ended up here."

"I'm following you so far," Gomorrah said.

"Right, so there's a level of . . . uh, I guess, organization there, right?"

"Yes."

"But like . . . ." I gestured to the road-turned-battlefield. "This is a bit much. Those are mecha. Those are APCs with fuck-you guns on them. Those PMCs are all wearing professional gear. They're probably not working for cheap."

"Ah, I see," Gomorrah said. "How much were the prosthetics worth?"

I let out a breath. "I don't know. Couple hundred points if you were to buy all of them outright." I pretended not to hear Garter choking behind me. "But like, Rac printed them for me at home. They're basically free. Right?" I asked Rac.

"I mean, I had to gather scrap for the printer," Rac muttered.

I grinned and ruffled her hair for a split second before she ducked away. "Right. Sorry. So not free. They cost a few Rac-hours of work each . . . ."

"Rac, you *work* for a samurai?" Coco hissed.

"I get free rent," Rac muttered back.

I went on pretending that I couldn't hear them. It was too much fun, embarrassing Rac, though I didn't want to push it too far. Fun was fun, but I didn't want to actually piss her off. Even if her pouting was cute.

"So, these fucks spent . . . what, a few million credits just to steal shit that was not worth a tenth of that? It doesn't add up."

"We haven't looked into the warehouse yet," Gomorrah said. She hefted her flamethrower. "Do you think they're hiding more stolen samurai tech?"

I hadn't thought about that. It would make some sense, but it wasn't a very comforting thought. "Well, now I'm worried about it, yeah," I said. "Rac!"

Rac jumped. "Yeah?"

"You and your buddies okay to play babysitters for a bit? We're gonna line up the PMCs that aren't bleeding out and have them stay in one place while you watch."

"Uh, okay. But if it's just us, they might not listen."

"You'll have the mech," I said.

"Can I ride it?" Rac asked.

I laughed. "No."

Rac pouted some more. Really, if she knew the face she made when she was disappointed, I was pretty sure she'd never express herself ever again. I was determined not to let her find out from me, though. She'd probably grow out of it soon enough.

"Right, let's see what the PMCs have to say, then . . . well, I'm breaking in there whether they want me to or not," I said.

"That seems reasonable to me," Gomorrah said. "Atyacus is pulling up some concerning results. The credit trail is extremely suspect."

Yeah, that only made sense. I sauntered over to the PMCs, who didn't seem all that happy when they noticed me and Gomorrah walking over. Though they also didn't seem ready to try anything.

Honestly, if they did, I might have been in a bit of trouble. I was only bulletproof at the moment. If enough of them piled on quick enough, I'd have to buy a grenade or two.

Gomorrah, on the other hand, could fuck them all up no problem. She was still wearing nun-stuff, but her head was clearly helmeted and her boots looked like they were made of the kind of steel used on tanks. The rest of her was hidden, but there was a lot of . . . thickness there that suggested she was well covered.

Also, she had a big fuck-off flamethrower. Those were really handy in negotiations, because not only could she kill you, but it would hurt the entire time, and there wouldn't be anything left to bury.

"Hello, boys and girls," I said. "I have a *lot* of questions, and I think I deserve some answers. But I'm not in an interrogative mood, so how about you all sit tight and be polite little PMC boys and PMC girls while my friends here keep an eye on you? Then I have a few easy questions!"

It didn't take long to reorganize the PMCs. The lightly injured were set aside, the officers and ranked members were brought to one spot, and the rest got to sit pretty under the watchful eyes of Rac, her friends, and my very large warmech that frequently went invisible and reappeared elsewhere.

I think that last bit was just Myalis fucking with them, but I wasn't going to stop her.

CHAPTER FORTY

CREATIVE KLEPTOMANIA

Samurai technology might very well be the most valuable thing in the world right now. But humanity is catching up. It's not fast, but it's consistent, and the more time we spend breaking down their alien tech, the faster we'll learn basic principles that will allow humanity to catch up to, and eventually surpass, the Protectors.

Just give us a few years, a decade at most, and we will turn this world into a utopia!

—Professor Henry, MIT, 2031

Predictably, the PMCs knew nothing.

In fact, they seemed willfully ignorant. They were "not remembering" a lot of things, and that was probably my fault for questioning the group together. Once one of them insisted he couldn't even remember how long he'd been working at this location for, or what his hours were like, or how much he was being paid, or even what day of the week it was, the others decided to join in on the rapid forgetfulness, especially when it became clear that I wasn't going to shoot them for not giving me the answers I wanted.

It was frustrating, but at the same time, more or less understandable.

They were *very* insistent that they didn't know what they were defending, and I was even inclined to believe them. Myalis tapped into their augs and was able to confirm that none of them had been any deeper into the warehouse than the first dozen meters past the entrance.

That left me one option.

Of course, I obviously assumed that the place was booby-trapped out the ass. If whoever had set this up could afford private contractors this well-equipped, then they could afford a few grenades and some string, or probably some more complex options.

"I don't want to go in there," I admitted to Gomorrah.

She eyed the interior of the warehouse. "I'm not picking up any obvious traps. But I also don't have anything designed for picking out traps in the first place, and I don't think traps would set off my thermals."

"So, options?" I asked.

"Get trap-disarming equipment?" Gomorrah proposed.

I took a deep breath, then shook my head. "Expensive, I bet. And I don't want to sink all of my points into this. The electronics for my augs to see traps might be fairly cheap, but then again, they might not cover everything."

"So we send in some of these PMCs one at a time? We have . . . a decent number of them."

"Wow," I said. "That's . . . really fucking cold."

Gomorrah paused, then nodded. "You're right. That is a rather uncharitable way to treat people. And a war crime."

"That's never stopped us, but I'd rather keep the war crimes aimed at the aliens, not . . . well, these chumps aren't innocent, but they're not exactly *evil*. If they'd shot Rac up for real, then sure, but they didn't hurt me or mine."

"So we leave this to the police?"

I flinched back. "No way," I said. "They'll take forever, and we might never learn what's actually going on. Though . . . Alright, I'm gonna send a cat drone in. It's small, so it might not trigger every trap, and even if it does, then it's only a dozen points gone, not a huge deal."

I can get you something simple and disposable for about twenty points. Any lower and its utility would be highly questionable. It's already not going to be very impressive, armed, or capable of long-term operations.

I nodded along. Another point sink. But I could live with twenty points less. A box appeared next to me, and I popped the top off, aware that Rac's friends and some of the PMCs had frozen up at the sight of the box.

A fat cat ambled out of the box. It was . . . exactly that. A large, chonky boy of a cat drone. "Myalis, why does this drone look like it needs to go on a diet?"

Cheaper parts are often larger and heavier. This is the price of compromise.

"Huh?" I . . . decided not to question it. Instead, I lifted the cat drone up while making sure that the fact that it was damned heavy wasn't obvious. I should have lifted with my knees. Bringing it over to the entrance of the warehouse, I set it down, then gestured within. "Go ahead."

Certainly.

The cat strutted in, tail swaying from side to side while its head scanned left and right. At the same time, a small screen opened up on my augs' display, showing me what the chonker could see. I made sure that the screen was shared with Gomorrah.

The outer parts of the warehouse weren't anything too special. There were a few bays to the side where APCs and a few more ordinary vans were parked. Farther in was a small maintenance-hangar-like thing. I guessed that that's where the mecha were parked when they weren't terrorizing local mercs.

There was a small set of rooms to the right, and the cat drone sauntered on over there first. It was a bit of a dead end, though. The rooms had a small office at the front and a decently large break room. There was an air hockey table, a small kitchen, and a couple of couches around a small TV. At the back was a locker room with a shower space and some washrooms, and to one side a small room with three bunk beds crammed into it.

So, this was where the PMCs slept and waited when they weren't on duty. The computers in the office had scrubbed themselves already, but Myalis and Atyacus were able to tell that they were mostly duty rosters and emails from the PMC's headquarters. Everything was encrypted in both directions, but even after poking through, it was all mundane shit.

The most interesting part wasn't in that room. The drone continued to scout around until it reached the rear-center of the warehouse. There was a building set atop a large platform of scaffolds. A few weak lights underneath let us see all the way through, and the rear didn't touch the back wall, nor did the top of this building-in-a-building touch the ceiling.

"That's weird, right?" I asked.

"You mean a decently large building hidden within another so that none of the exterior walls, floors, or ceiling touches anything solid?" Gomorrah asked. "Yes, Cat, that's weird."

I could kind of guess why it was done this way. Rac had mentioned coming up through the floor. This would prevent that entirely, and Myalis said that the outer scaffolds and the metallic netting around them were electrified. Weakly, but enough to create some sort of big signal-fuckering thing.

The only way in was at the front, at the end of a metal ramp that led up to a large, bulkhead-style door.

I'm going to break through the door's lock now.

I nodded along, then started moving people back and away from the warehouse. I didn't think that it was actually a danger, but . . . well, better safe than sorry.

Myalis had the cat stare at the keypad for a good long while before it went green, and then the big door slid open.

Inside was . . . an airlock. The cat stepped in, then waited while it cycled.

I suspect that the gas the room is filled with is lethal to humans. Though it might not be on purpose.

"How's that?" I asked.

I suspect that it's pure argon. But I don't have proper analysis systems on the drone.

"Then what makes you think it's argon?" I asked.

The drone pointedly stared at a large pipe with the word ARGON painted on its side.

"Oh." I scratched at my neck. "Why argon?"

"Argon doesn't react to very much," Gomorrah said. "It's non-flammable, and non-explosive. Probably relatively cheap as well. If you're going to preserve things, then it's maybe not the *best* choice, but it's not far from it. And it makes the air lethal to breathe, but if it leaks, it won't be that big of a problem as long as there's good ventilation in the space around it."

Well, this operation was looking more and more expensive by the minute.

The inner airlock door opened, and the cat drone walked into a large room that seemed to take up most of the space of this inner building. The cat stopped a few steps in and scanned its head around.

I stared at the video feed.

The room had a wall covered in cubbies with glass doors. I could see all sorts of random trash in there. The rest of the room was a sort of factory space, with large robotic arms suspended from the ceiling and multiple workstations with more remote-controlled systems. Lots of hanging cameras.

"Myalis, what the hell am I looking at?"

Surprisingly, Gomorrah answered first. "It's a deconstruction space. They're taking things apart."

"Why?" I asked.

I noticed one table had a rather familiar-looking prosthetic leg on it, held in place between two vices. Small robotic arms were frozen in the act of removing one of the plastic-like coverings.

It seems as if we've discovered a reverse engineering lab.

CHAPTER FORTY-ONE

RECREATIONAL URBAN WARFARE

Anon: Sunrise Technologies . . . The Future, Today!
Anon: No, that's too cheesy.
Anon: Our in-house AI came up with it. I think it's a perfect slogan.
Anon: Our in-house AI is a fucking moron.
—Discussion Chat, Sunrise Technologies, 2055

"What the fuck are we supposed to do about this?" I asked.

Chonker the remote-controlled cat had managed to spring up and onto one of the workbenches. Its head scanned left to right, so I got a nice panoramic picture of the entire space. There was a lot of tech here. Nothing too big. Mostly it looked like discarded guns, some small containers, lots of medical stuff, I noted, as well as gun mags, loose ammo, healing inhalers, and filtration devices.

Basically a lot of small, quickly discarded crap. I had left some of that kind of crap laying around over the past couple of weeks, and I guessed that I wouldn't mind someone picking it up and trying to figure out how it worked.

The table next to one of my prosthetics had what looked like a quadrupedal turret drone. It was a big bulky thing, with armored legs and a twin-barreled gun in its center. The entire thing was partially melted from the front, and it looked like it had lost a fight with one of the freakier sorts of Antithesis.

There's another of your drones here. And Atyacus recognized a flying scout drone that belonged to Gomorrah as well.

Myalis highlighted a couple of the cubicles at the back in red. It looked like they were filled to the brim with scrap.

"It looks like a lot of junk," Gomorrah said. With her mask on, it was impossible to tell if she was looking at me or at what Chonker was capturing for us, but I assumed we were looking at the same thing.

"Yeah, but it's *samurai* junk," I said. "Probably worth a small fortune to the right collector. I don't know if I should be angry about them reverse engineering some of this stuff or not," I said.

It wasn't all bad, obviously. Lots of modern tech was based on shit that samurai had bought and distributed. Tech had to improve, and being able to steal from other, more advanced civilizations was probably the cheapest, easiest way to improve things.

The concerning part was the weird secrecy of this place. And the fact that they'd stolen *my* shit to disassemble. "Myalis, is samurai gear tagged? Like, can you tell who bought what?"

Yes, of course. There are serial sequences encoded onto most items.

"Like a serial number?" I asked.

Somewhat more complex, but for the purposes of keeping things simple, yes.

"Alright, so can you look at that junk and tell what belongs to who?"

Certainly. Though my awareness doesn't necessarily allow me to communicate that information to you.

Right, our AI had a sort of agreement not to share private information about their Vanguard between each other. When it came to the privacy of anyone who wasn't a samurai, though, Myalis didn't seem to do more than pass lip-service.

I can confirm the presence of four items that are yours. Three from Gomorrah. That is, not counting the prosthetics.

"Looks like one surveillance drone I used . . . well before we met, and two tanks of fuel for my flamethrowers," Gomorrah said. Was she patched in with Myalis, or was that Atyacus letting her know? "Some of these things I used a while ago. I don't know what I'd even do with them now."

"If it was just samurai trash, I don't think I'd have any sort of problem with this whole operation," I said. "Can you figure out who is running this op?"

Sunrise Technologies.

I blinked. That name was eerily familiar. "Wait . . . aren't those the fucks who tried to kidnap Katallina?"

"They did kidnap her," Gomorrah said. "And then we un-kidnapped her. Isn't she still staying at your place?"

"Yeah," I said. "What the fuck, I thought I'd ruined that company like, a week and a half ago?"

You emptied their accounts. It seems as if that didn't really do much. It was clear that they were a company designed to take the fall for others already, and it seems that purpose continues here.

"And I bet that figuring out who actually owns them is going to be a nightmare," I said. I rubbed at my face. "Right. I'm calling the Family about this. Some of the shit in there is theirs, right?"

I can't confirm that definitively. However, it's statistically improbable that, out of several thousand Vanguard-quality items seemingly gathered from around this city, not a single one belongs to a member of the Family.

I groaned. "Alright. Gom, can you keep an eye on things? I need to call . . . fuck, what was the name of that weaselly secretary guy from the Family? The one I keep bullying?"

"You're bullying a secretary?" Gomorrah asked. Her voice was flat, more so than usual, even.

"He's a bureaucrat," I defended, which judging by her indifferent shrug, was enough of an excuse to pass. I searched through my contacts list, which was much longer than I remembered it being. It used to only have Lucy, a few of the kittens, and some of the kittens that had "graduated" from the orphanage and whose numbers I'd grabbed.

I . . . probably should check up on some of them, even if they were older than I was and probably doing alright for themselves. Or so I hoped.

My contact list now had a few samurai, some people I'd met, and others that I couldn't remember. "Myalis, is this your doing?"

I included notes. The man you're looking for is Eric Withersmith.

I found an Eric on the list and opened the contact. There were, in fact, notes. A small, head-on image of Eric that looked like it was from some paperwork, and a short profile beneath that. Nothing extensive, but enough to remind me who he was. "Huh. Thanks," I said before I tapped "call."

You're welcome. I'm not overly fond of secretarial work, but it's hardly an imposition.

"Still, appreciate you doing it," I said.

Oh. I'm not. I offloaded that to a smaller AI I designed decades ago to take care of it for me. I have better things to do with my uptime.

The call connected before I really had time to figure that out.

One screen had an image of Eric's face. It looked like he was parked in some cubicle, staring at a webcam. The lower screen was of myself, as seen from above and at an angle. I turned that way, then noticed my warmech staring at me with its camera-equipped eyes. Neat. "Hey," I said.

Eric perked up, quickly adjusting his tie to make himself a little more presentable. "Hello, Miss Stray Cat? How can I help you? Did you want an update on the sewer situation?"

Oh, shit, I'd almost forgotten about that. "Not just yet," I said, trying to keep my cool. "So, you know how I'm on vacation?"

"Yes?" he asked. There was a lot of trepidation in that one word.

"Well, one thing led to another, and it started a gang war, of sorts? If PMCs and mercenary teams count as gangs."

"Your . . . vacation started that?"

"Yeah," I said. "Anyway, I ran into a sort of . . . samurai-tech cache? It's a big building, lots of remote-controlled shit, chock-full of stolen samurai gear. Mostly disposables, but there're guns, ammo, explosives, medical tech. Probably a few thousand points' worth of random stuff."

"A few . . . okay," Eric said. He wiped his brow. "Okay. Yes, that is something we'd like to look into. Is it a storage unit?"

"Nah. Here, Myalis, can your secretary AI send Eric some of the pics Chonkers took?"

"Chonkers?" Before he could ask further, his eyes widened—he'd received the packet from Myalis. Then he stared off into space for a few long moments. "Is that a fully automated site?"

"Looks like it," I said. "Deconstruction and disassembly and maybe some reverse engineering shit. They stole from me, and I, uh, kinda hired some mercs to track my stuff for me. The company is called Sunrise Technologies. They've fucked around in the past. Obviously didn't find out hard enough."

Eric was nodding along.

He was probably thinking of all the ways this could be good publicity, or good for his career. Or maybe how this was making me forget about the sewers, which it admittedly had. But he didn't need to know about that last part.

I cleared my throat and Eric jumped. "So, do you want the Family to secure the site?"

"That'd be nice," I said.

"We'll have a team there within an hour," he promised. "And did you want a portion of the profits?"

I almost repeated that last part aloud, but I caught myself. "That'd be . . . more than nice. Also, Gomorrah is here. She helped."

"Yes, of course. We can make sure she gets a fair share as well. Thank you for calling, Stray Cat. Is there, ah, anything else I can help you with?"

"Uh . . . no?" I tried. I noticed that Rac and her team had started arguing nearby, which meant they weren't watching the PMCs as much as they should have been. I was going to have to step in. "I'll be waiting for your team. Tell them to make it snappy, and maybe come loaded for trouble."

CHAPTER FORTY-TWO

TRASH PANDA FEELINGS

As we modernize, it's becoming increasingly obvious that the youngest generations are lacking crucial real-world communication skills. Small talk is becoming harder. Connections are more difficult to establish.

More notably, the time and opportunity to improve on these skills, meet new people, and create bonds is shrinking. More work is remote. Open gathering spaces are less common. Our new society isn't designed to encourage community.

And this will have a powerful impact on any new society's ability to rebel.

A counterculture needs to start from the roots, from people who are tired and want to see change, and who are willing to work together to achieve it. This new world we're developing is stomping on the very foundations needed for rebellion to function.

—*A Study of Sociology and Rebellion*, 2028

The first thing I did was send Rac and her friends off to wait by one of the APC wrecks. If they were going to squabble, they could do it out of sight of the PMCs they were supposed to be guarding.

I had to keep an eye on the mercs and paramedics. I think they sensed that there was a whole lot of loot around, and their fingers were starting to feel sticky.

Things finally calmed down around the same time as the Family arrived. When they arrived, they *really* made a show of it. Seven heavy vans, escorted by a trio of light combat vehicles. Enough spotlights to turn the dreary tunnel street into a bright-as-day space.

The Family settled off to one side, and then the doors to their vans opened up and the teams within dispersed. It was all orderly and careful, soldiers with clear training moving in a predetermined, practiced way.

I decided to stand aside. Eventually one of them would come over to brown-nose, but for now, I could leave them to it.

Which meant that I had nothing better to do than annoy Rac and her friends. It looked like Rac was being raked across the coals by Garter.

"Hey, Gom," I said before heading over. "I'll be back in a minute or two. Just gonna check on Rac."

"Sure," Gomorrah said. "I'll direct the Family. I don't want them stumbling into a trap."

I nodded my thanks, then started walking toward Rac and . . . her team. Did they have a team name? I couldn't remember them mentioning one, and I was afraid that if I asked about it, it might come off as corny.

My ears twitched as I got closer. Garter was clearly not happy about something. "If we'd known, it would have changed everything," he said.

Rac crossed her arms, but she wasn't meeting his eyes. I knew that look. She wanted to stand up to him, knew he was wrong, but was afraid of pushing back too hard. "It shouldn't change anything," she said.

"Of course it does," Garter said. He swiped a hand through his hair. "You know a samurai. Two of them! Maybe more? That's huge! Do you know the kind of rep that comes with that? The kind of doors it opens up?"

"Garter, chill a little," Coco said. "It's cool that Rac has friends in high places, but they're her friends, not ours. You know I'd love to work with a samurai, but even I know better than to push it."

"Cat's not like that," Rac said. "She'd figure out that you're trying to scam her right away."

"Scam her?" Garter asked. "No, I just want to be her friend too. There is so much to gain from just knowing a samurai. After tonight, our rep is going to be damned solid. We can lean into that, grow the crew, get Millennium to give us a few more jobs that pay better. We can take more careful risks if we have a samurai to fall back on like tonight."

"Cat won't rescue us that often," Rac said. "She's on vacation right now. I think it's the only reason she came."

"Wait, *this* is vacation?" Coco asked with a gesture to the street and the carnage laid out across it. The motion was why she was glancing my way and saw me coming.

She wasn't the first. Jerusalem was staring already, but it looked like he'd elected not to let his team know.

"I *am* on vacation," I said. "At least until I don't feel like it anymore, or I run out of points to spend, which at this rate is gonna happen sooner than I'd like," I said as I came up behind the group.

Garter jumped and spun around. "Ah, Miss Stray Cat."

"Just Stray Cat," I said. "Or Cat, if you're a friend."

"Cat, then," he said.

"You're not a friend," I pointed out.

Garter's jaw worked, but he wisely chose to keep his mouth shut as I turned my attention to Rac.

I nodded to the side. "Can we chat?"

Rac nodded, then practically scampered after me as I moved on. We left her friends behind and relocated closer to one of the walls alongside the road. There was an actual bike and pedestrian path, which was kind of weird to find in an underground street. Maybe it was for the few people working down here to get from one location to another without the overhead of having a car? I hadn't seen all that many non-hoverbikes in my lifetime, so it was a little strange.

In any case, it was a space separated from the rest by a wall of hip-high plastic bars, and it served to keep us apart from the rest well enough.

"Hey," I said as I turned to her. "I overheard Garter a little."

Rac pouted. "Yeah," she said. Then she sighed, and it was at once wistful and . . . very disappointed. "You know, I kinda liked Garter?"

"Liked?" I asked.

"Yeah," she said.

"Ah," I replied.

To be entirely honest, I'd kind of missed out on the whole "crush" phase of my life. I mean, I could vaguely recall a younger me thinking that some characters on shows that I liked were hot, and I might maybe have had a crush on a fast-food mascot—she had big tits—but that was passing. My first real crush was Lucy, and Lucy caught on . . . pretty much instantly.

Then Lucy abused the shit out of that crush until one thing led to another and we were mostly all over each other.

Anyway, I didn't have much experience with failed romance. I wasn't going to lie to myself and say that I wasn't pleased to see that this thing between Rac and Garter wasn't working out. Mostly because Garter had been pinging my "piece-of-shit-dar" for a while.

"So," I began.

"Yeah?" Rac asked. She stared at me, expecting something.

I resisted the urge to let out a sigh. "You did alright," I said. "Tracking the prosthetics, getting here on time. Shit went to shit, but that's hardly your fault, you know?"

"I know," Rac said. "I'm . . . I'm not the sort to blame myself for things going wrong. Things have been going wrong forever. Shit flows down, and I've always been at the bottom, but I'm not the one making the shit."

I squinted. "That's a roundabout way of saying you're not an asshole."

She pouted harder. "Maybe I should be."

"Aww, don't be that way," I said as I reached over to pat her head. She ducked away from it, but I thought it was the thought that mattered. Lucy was better at this kind of stuff than I was. "Look, I'm sorry things didn't go as you planned. Still, I'm happy you called. I'd rather have you annoyed at me or whatever, than have you not show back up at home for a while and us find out you're dead."

Rac glanced up, then nodded. "Alright," she said. "So, you're not angry? With me? What about with Garter?"

"Eh, I'm ambivalent about Garter right now. He seems like a bit of a dick. Don't let him schmooze you just to get to me, alright? Coco seems cool, and Spider . . . well, he at least isn't pretending to not be a dick."

"Spider's pretty cool," Rac agreed. "And Coco's . . . nice. She doesn't treat me like she's my mom. More like a cool older sister."

There was a pointed look there. Did . . . did she think I was *mothering* her?

That couldn't be any further from the truth.

If anything, I was more of a deadbeat dad. I got her food and a place to stay, then left her with chores for days on end without checking in.

Was that bad parenting?

It was better than what my parents had done for me, which was mostly just dying.

I did sigh this time, then placed a hand on her shoulder. Rac didn't seem to mind the contact. "I'm sorry," I said. "For not being around as much. I guess I kinda just . . . lumped you in with the kittens, then left you to do your own thing. You're kind of in a weird spot. One of mine, but without all of the background, you know?"

Rac squirmed a little, but nodded. I wasn't actually sure if we were on the same wavelength, but it didn't feel like we were entirely on opposite ends of things either.

"We can talk more later . . . actually, no, *Lucy* and you can talk more later. She's the good one to talk to about this kind of stuff," I said.

Rac nodded, and I wasn't sure how to feel about her instant agreement there.

"I'm gonna go check up on Gomorrah. Will you be able to make it back home alright, or do you need a ride?"

"In the mech?"

"Nah, there's barely room for two in there," I said. "And, uh, no offense, but we're not close enough for you to lay down on top of me while in a tight confined space. I was thinking more that I'd pay for your cab."

"Oh," Rac said. "No, I can manage."

"Alright," I said. This time I did make it to her head, and her pout was accompanied by a glare, one that was severely diminished by how ruffled her hair was.

CHAPTER FORTY-THREE

FINDERS, NOT KEEPERS

Note to self: Don't fuck with Rac's weird catgirl friend.

—Jerusalem "Spider" Smith,
personal notes, 2057

I found Gomorrah chatting with not one, but three Family people. One of them was in a simple set of armor and was wielding a clipboard. The other two looked like they were a step ahead of the average PMC. Good gear, very sleek armor, slightly rounded in that smooth, modern sci-fi way, and pitch black. It looked like they were custom fits too, or damned near to that. The kind of stuff that no real army would buy because they'd need a million different sizes to outfit a battalion.

Their helmeted heads turned my way as I came over, and I made a conscious effort not to be intimidated even a little.

There was definitely a samurai providing their gear, and I wasn't sure where my own gear sat in terms of quality.

Then again, I had a large mech standing nearby, so fuck them and their little armored suits. "Hey," I said as I came up. "So tell me, good news, no news, news that's not so good?"

Gomorrah let out a breath. "Something like that," she said. "This is Officer Kennedy." She gestured to the lightly-armored guy with the clipboard.

"Ma'am," he replied with a nod. "We were just going over the assessment with Samurai Gomorrah. Do you want us to start over?"

"Just give me the quick version," I said.

He nodded, then glanced at the tablet he held. "We've secured the area around the disassembly factory. No explosives found. No traps. The area within is still filled with unbreathable air, but that is an incidental matter and only a complication, not a method to prevent ingress."

"Uh-huh," I said. "Did you find a way to clear it out?"

"We're opting not to," he said. "We have a team coming in with PPE suitable for the task."

Gomorrah nodded along. "The plan right now is to check what they have and catalog everything."

"And then what?" I asked.

She shrugged. "Leave it to the Family?"

I frowned. They couldn't see my expression, but I think everyone caught on to the fact that I was hesitating. It was the plan from the start, sure, but I didn't trust the Family all that much.

This whole situation was a new sort of fucky. The gear in there was stolen, yeah, and now we'd taken it out of the hands of the people who'd stolen it, but I only had the Family's word that it would be returned to its owners.

If someone jacked something that belonged to me, and then I discovered that the cops had caught them, I'd be pretty pleased about it. But if I didn't get my shit back, then I was basically no better off than if they hadn't caught the thief.

"What are you guys going to do with all the stuff in there?" I asked.

"We're going to move it to a more secure facility, for starters," Kennedy said. "I don't know what will happen to the materials beyond that."

"Mm-hmm," I said. I raised a finger in a "one moment" gesture, then popped open a text chat for Myalis. *What will they do with it?*

Historically, the Family has made most of its fortune from the selling of blueprints and Vanguard equipment onto the open and gray market.

Right, figured. "So, priority number one right now is figuring out which samurai all those things belong to," I said. "Then we call them up."

Kennedy froze for a moment. "Our orders are to move the items to a secure location first, for cataloguing and safety."

I shook my head. "There's got to be a record, right? Something that'll let you know where everything is from?"

"There is a small server here. Its only connection is to a private network, the same one used to operate the machinery within the facility," Kennedy said. He tapped his tablet a few times. "It has dates and times, item descriptions, but nothing on which samurai each item belongs to."

"It can't be that hard to backtrack," I said. "Myalis said that everything she makes has a sort of serial thing on it. Does Atyacus do the same?"

Gomorrah paused, as if listening to something, then nodded. "He says so, yes."

"Great. So everything is tagged. We'll be able to know who it belongs to."

I think I see where you're going with this. You won't be making many friends in the Family, but I do find it incredibly entertaining. Do go on.

"I'm sure if you can't find the tags, Gom or I can give you something to check them out. Like a fancy barcode scanner or something?" I nodded, liking the idea. "Then we just need to contact each samurai and tell them that their shit's right here for pickup."

"I . . . see," Kennedy said. By his facial expression, I could tell he'd realized that giving this stuff right back to its owners would mean that the Family wouldn't be profiting from it.

Well, not profiting *as much* from it. Most of the things in there looked like discarded junk to me. If someone called me up to tell me they'd found a magazine I dropped a week ago, I'd tell them to keep it. It was the big-ticket items that were more interesting.

"I'm sure we can arrange that," Kennedy said. It didn't sound like he *wanted* to, but I was pretty sure he would.

"Hey, don't worry. Some of those samurai will be dead, and maybe their next-of-kin or whatever will let you keep the shit in there. Or you could break a deal with them for hard cash or something." They'd still make their profit, so I wasn't entirely going back on the vague outline of a deal I'd made with Eric. I was just . . . making it less fun for the Family.

"I'll let HQ know," he said.

In all likelihood, most of the items here were discarded weeks ago. The Vanguard to whom they belong will have moved on. And yes, there's also the possibility that they've perished, or that some of the items belong to Vanguard who are off-world at the moment. The Family will still profit from this venture.

Yeah, figured. I'd cut into their bottom line a little, but I hadn't cut it apart. They'd still make their credits here.

I let the conversation stretch into silence as I watched the Family's soldiers move.

I didn't think the Family was bad. They had their own best interests as their first priority, but they *were* working to make things better, to help. I couldn't exactly dislike that. But at the same time, that didn't mean I wouldn't be at least a little suspicious of them.

"Right," I said at last, cutting into the silence. "I think that's it for me here. I'm going to need to get my mech back home, which isn't going to be the easiest thing to do. I'll leave you guys to your work?"

"We'd appreciate that, ma'am," Kennedy said with a serious nod. "We'll keep you informed. HQ should be sending a link to an updatable file structure. If you want, we can have any goods that are marked as yours shipped to your residence?"

"That would actually be nice, yeah. Those prosthetics they stole were supposed to go to people that needed them. I guess if they're disassembled . . . well, maybe we can use them for parts?"

I had no idea, but maybe See-Three would know better. I expected that having a heap of spare parts for the prosthetics we were making wouldn't hurt.

Speaking of spare parts . . . I glanced at my mech and sighed. Yeah, I was gonna need to get back to work. There were a lot of repairs left. The leg I'd been tinkering on for a few days was leaking hydraulic fluid. There was a small puddle around it.

"I think I'll be heading back as well," Gomorrah said. "Keep me informed. Atyacus can take your messages. Cat, do you need help moving your mech again?"

"I'd appreciate it," I said.

Getting the mech here had been . . . tricky. It was fast on the ground, but this was halfway across the damned city. So to get the mech here, I'd ridden it on top of the *Fury* while Gomorrah drove. The articulated paws were able to get a good grip, and Gomorrah flew her car well enough to keep it stable throughout.

Still, it had been . . . harrowing.

I'd only been pretty sure that I'd survive a fall.

"This was . . . interesting," Gomorrah said as she walked up next to me. She glanced around the tunnel. "Is this the kind of stuff you've been up to lately? Shooting politicians and getting into trouble with the Family?"

"More or less, yeah," I said. "Is it weird that I almost miss fighting the aliens that want to eat me?"

"No, not at all. They don't have politics. Unless 'eating you' is political?"

"In some places," I said with a laugh. "Maybe. But yeah. It's simpler. See the alien, shoot the alien. Easy. This shit is all about competing interests and figuring out who wants to screw with me the most. It's a pain in the ass to deal with."

"I don't know. You've been handling it well enough. And the aliens are always out there waiting to be killed if you want to end your vacation early."

I hummed. "I'll think about it. I do think that this vacation of mine is coming to a middle."

CHAPTER FORTY-FOUR

JAMS AND DRAINS

. . . Samurai Stray Cat was exceptionally dismissive of protocols. I do not know if she was unaware or uncaring about them. Samurai Stray Cat assumed that the troops on site would act in the best, most professional manner, while carrying out whatever plan she had in place prior. Information sharing was not complete.

Samurai Gomorrah seemed more careful and precise before the arrival of Samurai Stray Cat. It might be worth noting that Samurai Gomorrah initially seemed willing to work with Family personnel, but her real feelings are hidden by a layer of polite obfuscation which Samurai Stray Cat lacks . . .

—Excerpt from field-investigation report of Officer Kennedy, 2057

I woke up early the next morning.

Then I promptly started to snuggle with Lucy, which turned into more than cuddling, which turned into a pillow fight, which then turned into a more physical, less dressed version of "more than cuddling," and then that ended with me falling right back asleep.

So really, my day only started at the crack of eleven-thirty.

"What's on the docket for today?" I asked Myalis as I lifted a shirt from the floor and gave it an experimental sniff. Eh, it was good enough.

You have a few things to address. First, your point count has been slowly dropping, even with your daily allocations. Some points have come in from Burlington overnight, from the equipment you left there.

"Not bad," I said. "How many points?"

Thirty-two.

I shrugged. Well, it was something. "Enough to buy a dozen or so Fox-teeth and send them over to be used. I can see that generating some point-income over time."

The price of Foxtooth-type handguns has been revised.

I paused, pants halfway up. "What?" I asked. "Wait, what do you mean by that?"

Foxteeth were like, the cheapest shitty handguns I could remember buying. They were a whole five points, and just enough to take out the lower-tiered Antithesis. They were an alright civilian-grade gun otherwise.

They were worth five points. As far as I was aware, they'd always been worth five points.

The point value was reduced to four per unit. You seem confused about the change in price?

"Yeah, no shit," I said as I tugged my pants on fully and started with the button. "I didn't know things *could* change prices. Since when?"

It's always been the case. Though the market for Vanguard equipment is far more stable than any other market on Earth, mostly because it's fed and influenced by outside sources. The value of an item is calculated from several factors: its potency and level of danger, its material cost, the cost of transporting it, its technological level, and its perceived value. The Foxteeth's technological edge was reduced by several recent initiatives pumping the civilian market with similar quality human-made guns. Therefore, the value was lowered.

"And that's normal?"

If you had been alive in 2030 and were a Vanguard at the time, for example, the Foxteeth would be worth twice as much as it was when you first purchased one.

My mind was a little blown at the moment. I hadn't known that things could change that way at all. But I supposed that in hindsight it kind of made sense. What would happen in a hundred years when there was a new samurai and the only things they could afford were handguns that were a century out of date?

"Okay . . . well, alright. That'll be something to wrap my head around later. So, uh, where were we? And where's my belt?"

Under the bed. And we were discussing today's agenda.

I got on all fours, then gestured for Myalis to continue while I searched.

There are three matters you wished to look into today. The state of your mech was the first. You also wanted to get into contact with See-Three regarding your prosthetics clinic. She has placed a notice on the clinic's media feeds delaying the first operations. Finally, you wanted to observe the state of the repairs on the sewage system.

"Ah, that," I said. "Alright, so . . . any idea of what I should do first?" I couldn't find the belt, at least until Mr. Tentacles slithered it over to me, the belt held at the end of a long tentacle. "Thanks."

I would suggest looking into the matter of the sewer system first. That is the project with the greatest impact and likelihood of causing lasting harm.

I fitted my belt on, then nodded. "Yeah, that makes sense. Let me grab breakfast before anything else. Or lunch? Whatever. Can you ping the Family, let Eric know that I'll be driving over this afternoon?"

Message sent.

"Thank you," I said as I slipped out of the bedroom with just one final glance back. We . . . needed a cleaning person. Lucy was picking up as we went, and the place *was* brand-new, so it wasn't like there had been much time for grime and messiness to build up, but still, things were getting a little dirty. Heck, I wouldn't trust the water in the pool in the corner. This many kids in one big home, most of them not the cleanest, meant a lot of small messes all over.

I found Lucy in the kitchen, leaning over the counter with a plate with toast in front of her and a pair of steaming mugs next to that. "Hey," she said.

"Hey," I replied before swiping a piece of toast and making my way to the fridge. I opened it and stared at all the food within. I was probably fine with just one piece of toast, but it was nice seeing a full fridge anyway. "You okay?" I asked.

"Sore," she said.

I flashed her a smug grin. Yeah, she would be. "You'll be alright?"

"Mm-hmm," she said. "Better if someone stopped stealing my toast."

"Who did that? I'll catch the fiend and dangle them upside down by their toes off the side of the building," I declared while waving my toast around.

Lucy rolled her eyes. "What are you doing today, toast-thief?"

"I need to check up on the sewer thing. So that means visiting the Family first thing, then maybe checking up on things myself right after, to make sure they're still afraid of fucking with me."

Lucy nodded. "Anything I can help with?"

"Hmm, I don't think so? But if you want, could you check up on Burlington? I don't know if there's much we can do from here, but I think they murdered a few aliens overnight, so either they're clearing some pockets out, or things have gone wrong."

"I'll see what I can do," Lucy said. "I was supposed to call some of my contacts over there this morning, but someone kept me from them."

"I'll hang them next to the person stealing your toast," I promised.

I gave Lucy's cheek a quick peck, then swiped her other piece of toast.

She screamed, so out of the great mercy in my heart, I only took a huge bite from it before putting it back on her plate. "Gotta go!" I said through a full mouth.

Lucy laughed and I slipped out of the kitchen and started through the house. It was surprisingly busy considering it wasn't even noon yet. Some of the kittens were gathered together in the living room, sitting around a low table. "Hey Cat," Junior said as she looked up from a tablet. "You're heading out?"

"Yeah," I said. "What are you all doing?"

"Grasshopper's homework," she said. Then she frowned. "Did you do yours?"

"Uh . . . I'm too busy for that," I said. Grasshopper had left me with a dozen pages of work. Mostly math, but some history and long-form essay questions. It was a lot!

"She's going to be disappointed," Junior said. It was accusatory.

"Come on, it's not a big deal," I said.

"She'll be disappointed *in you*," she said before dropping it entirely. She sounded almost like she was pitying me.

I slipped out before I could let that get to me. The homework was all stuff like math anyway. As if I'd ever need help with that. I had more than just a calculator jammed into my head.

I won't help you with the homework.

Grumbling to myself, I found my coat by the entrance, and my helmet, which I slipped on. I made my way over to my bike, then sighed at the bench, which was covered in a drizzling of water from the constant rain. I swept it off with my sleeve as best I could, then hopped onto the bike.

Before taking off, I sent a quick text to Gomorrah, just letting her know that I was heading out to meet with the Family.

It wasn't that I didn't trust the Family, it was just that I trusted them a lot more if a fire-nun was on standby as backup. Gomorrah was probably well-versed in the biblical sort of vengeance that I figured would keep even corpos in line.

I got a thumbs-up emote back as I took off.

The trip over to the Family HQ wasn't all that far, though it was raining hard enough you could drink your fill just by craning your neck back. It was a decent amount of time to catch up on reports, specifically what Myalis could gather about the whole sewer situation.

It seems like repairs started in earnest yesterday morning, though most of those repairs meant cutting off the water supply of areas adjoining the worst-hit parts of the city.

"That'll leave lots of pissed-off people behind," I said.

It's necessary.

Maybe so, but unless people were convinced that things were getting better fast, it might just be a way to piss off the average New Montrealer even more than they already were.

"Let's just get on top of things," I said. It was time to put on a brave face and do some politicking.

CHAPTER FORTY-FIVE

CORPO SHIT SHOW

Never assume that corporate incompetence is corporate maliciousness.
Corporations don't care about you or yours. They don't aim to hurt you.
The reason you were hurt was because not hurting you would require a
sacrifice of effort or money or both that's too big to be excused.

—Anonymous PR specialist, 2028

I parked my bike on the rooftop parking lot, slipping into a free space that
was "reserved for visiting samurai" according to a small sign hanging above
it. It was right next to the handicapped parking section.

I silently appreciated that it was on the far side of the reserved handicapped parking spots. There was a small space in my heart for cripples, and
I appreciated that they didn't block the spot off just for some up-jumped
samurai or whatever.

Interestingly enough, it wasn't Eric who walked out to greet me, but
some woman who I didn't recognize. She was in corpo chic, a tight skirt
and a weird top with large openings on the sides that showed off the curve
of her hips.

I didn't let my eye linger. Who knew if Lucy had convinced Myalis to
tattle on me for any wayward gaze. "Hey," I said as I pushed the thought
aside. Instead, I wondered what Lucy would look like in that kind of outfit.

"Hello, Stray Cat," she said. There wasn't nearly as much formality there
as I'd come to expect from Eric.

"You're a new face," I said. "Is Eric busy?"

"Ah, Eric was promoted," she said. "Though he will still be available as
your liaison. Did you come here to speak with him specifically?"

"Hmm? Nah, it's fine. I called ahead. Well, my AI called ahead. I'm here to
see how shit's going." Eric got promoted? I had to wonder how much of that
was how he'd handled me and how much was just him climbing the ladder.

She nodded, then gestured to the entrance and elevators a little ways
behind her. "I'm prepared to give you a summary of events, if you wish?

Eric and a few of the others working this case are making time to meet you in Boardroom 17-G."

"I'll take that summary, sure," I said. "Also, what's your name?"

The woman smiled. "Piper, ma'am. I've been working here for almost a year now. If my inexperience is an issue, I'm certain Eric can fill you in better."

"It's fine," I said. "So, summarize away?"

Piper nodded and I followed as she started toward the elevator. "The majority of the projects only really started yesterday morning. Prior to that we completed a partial sweep of the entire sewer system. Four locations were discovered with hidden Antithesis threats, though only at a yellow danger level. Cleanup teams were dispatched in the afternoon, and they've reported successes on all fronts."

That part about the Antithesis was . . . concerning. Probably not all that surprising, though. Antithesis needed biomass. Shit had plenty. "Is there anything in place to alert us of hives like that before they turn into a cluster-fuck beneath our feet?"

"There are systems for monitoring the sewers. Or there should be. They were mostly offline, malfunctioning, or missing," Piper said.

"Of course," I grumbled.

"In any case, the surveys should be complete by this time tomorrow."

"Slower than I thought it would be," I said.

"Yes. We're having a difficult time with the hiring process. And the payment structure is complicated by the discovery of those nests."

"How's that?" I asked.

Piper shrugged, then held the door open for me. "Antithesis presence means that the survey work is now high-risk. That means better pay, but it also limits us to only hiring workers that are certified for danger pay to begin with. We've decided to have the surveyors who were originally tasked with exploratory work focus instead on double-checking previous areas to ensure a more thorough layout."

I nodded along. "Thanks. So survey work is all well and good. What about the actual work?"

"That's coming along. But we're running into more complications. Most of them were expected. Some of the infrastructure around the sewage facilities is crumbling and will need repairs. Some of the equipment is sub-par. Some of it is ancient. Then there are some areas that are owned by specific corporate entities."

"Wait, the sewer system is corpo-owned?" I asked.

"Only some segments. But yes."

I shook my head. There was no way having that kind of stuff be the property of a corp was a good thing.

"We ran into some issues there. Here, if I may?" Piper asked.

My augs pinged as I received a file a moment later. Myalis vetted it in a fraction of a second. Opening it, I discovered a rather dry report, some sixty pages long, about one specific two-hundred-meter-long segment of the sewers.

Fortunately, there was a summary at the end of it . . .

Unfortunately, it read like the summary of some unfunny comedy.

The section was run by a numbers company called D-UCK Corp, Ltd.

Yesterday, at around 10 a.m., they were contacted by the Family and told that there was an Antithesis nest in their section of the sewers.

At 11 a.m., D-UCK denied that.

At 11:30, the Family double-checked, and confirmed it. Then the survey team was chased out by corpo security who'd been informed that "something" was happening in their underground section.

At 11:45, the Family got in touch with the D-UCK CEO, who lives in Calgary. He said he'd look into it.

At 12:03, a security member was eaten.

At 12:09, the corp-wide security level went from green to orange.

At 12:34, the corp released a notice that they were going to begin maintenance on the lower sewer levels . . . in three weeks.

At 1:32, the head of security demanded to know what was going on.

At 2:12, he was informed that nothing was going on.

At 2:13, he said he had the corpse of a member that said otherwise. The HQ said that that wasn't confirmation.

It took until 2:31 for confirmation to arrive from accounting, because the dead employee's time charts didn't add up—on account of him being dead—and dead people don't get overtime pay. This was enough confirmation that HQ raised the warning to red, which finally prompted security to allow the Family's waiting team to step in.

It was, basically, a hot mess of conflicting procedures, misinformation, people shoving their hands over their ears and screaming, and probably more that I couldn't be bothered to read into.

"Is this kind of shit common?" I asked.

"Yes," was Piper's reply. She pursed her lips. "It's mostly factored into our estimates on repair times and cost, but it's difficult to predict. This kind of event can sometimes be solved in minutes, or sometimes it'll drag on for days."

Right. I'd never been happier to foist off some work onto someone else. If I had to deal with all of this, a lot more people would be dead. Which would probably be bad for the economy, or something.

"Next time you run into something like this corp down there, let them know that unless they want me to give the mayoral treatment to their board of directors, they'd better have a damned good reason for preventing us from fixing the city."

Piper blinked, then flushed. "J-just to be clear, you want us to threaten to kill the board of any corporation that interferes with our proceedings?"

"No, I want you to threaten to *tell* me about it. Let me do the actual, direct threatening," I said. I didn't need the Family using me as a whip to get the corps to move. It was another thing if they politely informed me, and then I went in and started whipping of my own volition.

"Noted," Piper said.

"Cool, cool," I said. "Now, anything else? You didn't go into the actual repairs."

"The start was a little slow, and we expect to run out of essential materials before the day is over, but we have two teams on supply-acquisition already. We're starting with the areas that are least damaged."

"Not the worst-off parts?" I asked.

"Repairs require that we divert sewage flows. It would be a disaster to divert from an area in grade B—that is, in need of maintenance but not urgently—to an area that's grade F—that is, uh . . ."

"Fucked?"

"Essentially. Usually it's best to have some areas that are fully functional to divert into. We're fixing those first since the other areas are already in need of nearly full replacements. Mostly this is relying on the suggestions of experts."

I nodded along. "Myalis, can you make sure these experts aren't just fixing stuff for their own benefit first?" I asked.

It seems like everything is actually running according to procedures. I can't find any purposeful malfeasance or diversions of labor for personally-motivated reasons.

That was good enough, I supposed. I couldn't expect perfection here. Just having things underway was a big comfort. We were definitely going to run into more trouble, but it was a start, and if people knew things were going to get better, then it would calm down the likelihood of them rioting.

Piper and I paused before the glass door of a boardroom. Eric was inside, as well as a few others. "This is it, Stray Cat," Piper said. "I'm glad I could be of service."

"Yeah. Thanks, Piper," I said. "Now, let's get to the boring part."

CHAPTER FORTY-SIX

GETTING DOWN
TO YOUR BUSINESS

Why do cats push things off of high places?
I don't know, you'll have to ask a cat.

—Miss Kitty K@, Dog whisperer, 2031

I noped out of the meeting about twenty minutes after it started.

Honestly, I'm impressed you made it that long.

"Me too," I muttered exhaustedly. It felt like I'd spent hours in there. I knew it was only twenty minutes though, because there was a wall clock that tick-tick-ticked menacingly in the corner, and I'd practically counted the seconds go by. That had lasted until I remembered that I was a samurai and I wasn't no one's bitch. I could up and leave, and that's exactly what I'd done.

Was the meeting important? Yes. Was it important that I be there? Probably. But my goal was to show up and ensure that work was getting done. I didn't need to know about the allocation of every credit.

"Stray Cat?" Piper asked as I started through the corridors. She ran after me, an impressive feat given the heels she was wearing. Then again, it looked like she might have cybernetic ankles.

"Yo," I said, then paused before asking her a question. "Are you single?"

Piper blinked. She'd obviously been coming over to ask me something, and my question had derailed that. "Yes?" she said before her cheeks started to redden. "Are you, uh, asking me out?"

"Huh? No, I have a girlfriend, sorry. Just asking to make sure," I said.

"Make sure of what? Uh, if you don't mind me asking."

I shrugged. "Look, sometimes I run into wayward and lost souls . . . It's good to keep a running tally of potential people for them to meet, you know?"

"I . . . don't think I do."

"Huh. Well, whatever. Anyway, I'm heading out. I want to check on the sewers in person. Honestly, I don't know how corpo-types do it. I'd rather wade in shit than sit in on a meeting like that for another hour."

"I . . . see," Piper said. I think I'd set her off balance there. "That's fine. Let us know if you notice any issues that the Family needs to address."

"Yup," I said before I started walking off.

Right, it was time to check out the sewers themselves. Though I wasn't entirely sure how to do that. The system spanned, literally, the entire city, and I had no idea where to start. Still, I had been thinking during that meeting. Everything I knew about the project had been filtered by the Family. They were probably being honest, but having me be on-site to check things would make sure that they were *real* honest. I'd have to find a good place to enter the sewers; I wasn't going to just dive into the first manhole I found.

My brain hiccupped as I reprocessed that last bit.

I shook it off and rephrased what I was about to ask Myalis. "I need to hover around and make it clear there's a samurai overseeing things," I said. "It'll keep people honest."

I left Piper behind and made my way outside, where it was, predictably, raining again. I started toward my bike, then stopped. There was a car parked in one of the handicapped spots. Actually, parked at an angle across the handicapped spot, so that it literally took up three spaces.

It was a nice car, one of those extremely sexy models that seemed like it was expensive just to look at. The kind of car that people bought posters of.

"Myalis, whose car is that?" I asked.

One moment . . . Ah, it's the car of one of the CEOs of Sunrise Technologies. They have an appointment with the Family at the moment.

"Wait, the fucks who stole from me?"

Yes.

"Hey, Myalis, is there anything . . . that way?" I gestured to the side, where the parking lot ended and the building dropped off.

Below? Nothing in that exact location, no. Though there is an—

"Mm-hmm," I said. I walked past the car, got on my bike, then started to push the bike around. It was tricky, but I eventually had the front of my bike pressed right up against the sidedoor of the car. Then I turned the bike on and gave it some gas.

It wanted to twist to the side, but I kept it level with the car, and soon my torque overcame the weight of the car, and it started to move . . . sideways. The wheels made a disturbing chuffing sound as they scraped along the tarmac, at least until we got to the end of the roof.

The car tipped up onto its side, then disappeared over the edge.

"Oops," I said. "My bad."

Very funny.

"Thank you," I said before taking off in earnest. "I'm glad you appreciate my humor." I caught a faint and distant *boom* as the car hit the ground far below. I just hoped that I didn't block traffic or something down there.

Oh well, the car was probably insured.

After giving it some thought, I decided that my first destination would be the City of New Montreal Sewage and Maintenance Headquarters. I couldn't remember the name of anyone who worked there, but I figured I'd remember their faces well enough, and I'd definitely recognize that big room with the giant screen.

I parked somewhere nice, then got off my bike and headed in. It didn't take long to reach the headquarters. Surprisingly, there were about ten times as many people waiting in the lobby as last time, all of them looking about ready to murder the poor guy behind the counter.

I waltzed past them, earning more than one curious look. I was aware of pictures being taken, and I didn't really care.

I wasn't deep in when someone came running out to greet me. "Oh hey, it's you!" I said as I pointed to the guy. It was . . . Button-up, the guy with the button-up shirt, an accountant or something who I'd first met here a few days ago.

"Miss Samurai. Hello, what are you, ah, doing here?" he asked as he fell in next to me. Button-up looked like he hadn't changed shirts in a while. Had I ever asked him what his name was? Did it matter? He wasn't cute enough for it to matter, I decided.

"Here to make sure things are moving in a forwardly direction. Did any of the C-suite come back?"

"No . . . ah, I even heard that one of them . . . walked off a building."

"Really? Wow, small world."

"Pardon?"

"Never mind," I said. "So, Button-up, how's things? Is shit starting to flow downstream at last, or are things still messed up in a bad way?"

"Ah, I think things are better? It's a lot busier," he said. "We're hiring and onboarding people as quickly as we can. There's basically no training. Everyone already here was promoted, then promoted again, which is nice, but it doesn't change how much work there is to do."

"That's a shame," I said. "But the work is getting done?"

He nodded quickly. "We're working nonstop. I haven't been home in two days. I think some of us won't be seeing our families again until this whole thing is done, but it's . . . it's a lot?"

"Huh," I said. When I set off to make people fix the city's problems for me, I'd never considered that there would actually be consequences for normal folk.

Actually, I was generally pretty bad at thinking about consequences in general. "I'm . . . actually sorry to hear that," I said. "I'd be pretty pissed if I couldn't see my family for that long. Or if I couldn't go back home. You must be very pent up."

"Huh?"

"Yeah. But hey, you're doing good work. So tell me, *are* things coming along?" We'd reached the command room by then, and I was met at the entrance by . . . that guy who was the head of maintenance. He was wearing a tag, fortunately. Ethan Brown.

"They're moving," Brown chimed in. "Not as quick as I'd like, but much faster than I'd hoped." He nodded to me. "I don't know what kind of fire you lit under the asses of the Family and their sort, but they've been hustling to get work done. I think almost every plumber in the city has work now, and plenty of other types of contractors too."

"That's good," I said. "It'll keep people busy." It was probably good for the economy or something too. I gave myself a pat on the back for that one.

"It's costing the city billions," Brown said. "But it was going to cost the city that much anyway. It would be a lot less if things hadn't become so under-maintained to begin with, but there's not much we can do about that now."

I followed him into the command room and then paused to take in the big sewer map on the far wall.

There was still red. Lots of red, and now some of it was flashing purple, which seemed somehow even more urgent. But, at the same time, there was a lot more orange than there had been the last time I was here, and the number of pins showing where workers were located had increased exponentially.

"Looks like you guys are actually getting shit done," I said.

Brown grunted. "We're *trying*, ma'am, and I hope that it'll count for something in the end."

"I think it will," I said. My entire life, I'd been left to fend for me and mine because no one was trying much of anything to help. On the rare occasion when someone would try . . . well, it counted for a lot, even if it didn't amount to much. "Is there anything you need me to look at? People you need me to threaten for things to get done faster?"

Button-up stared at me for a moment, coming to terms with that. "You want to threaten people?" he asked.

"Want to? Yes, actually. And also, it's a great way to get things done, I've discovered."

CHAPTER FORTY-SEVEN

FELINE FRINGE

I know it was very hard for you not to accept those bribes. That was very big of you, and I'm proud. Here, you can have this.

Yes, it is a gold star! Good job!

—Grasshopper, to the CEO of GeneriCorp, 2056

I trudged home about three hours after dark, stinking of shit and probably sweat, and far more exhausted than I should have been.

I was on vacation, for fuck's sake.

Groaning, I kicked off my boots by the entrance. I'd bully one of the kittens into rinsing them off later. Then another one to do it again, because those little shits half-assed everything. My coat went onto a rack by the entrance (when had Lucy gotten that?) and then I slipped further into my place on socked feet. I only started to suspect that something was weird when I was nearing the living room.

It was quiet.

My place was many things, but quiet wasn't one of them. The kittens had sleep schedules scattered all around the clock at random, and none of them had been discreet or quiet for a single day in their lives.

I tugged my Trench Maker out from its holster. "Myalis, should I be worried?" I asked.

No. At least, not to the extent that you need to be armed.

I lowered the gun, then slid it away as I entered the living room.

Everyone was here, and sitting on the floor.

The couches had been pushed back so that the center of the room was cleared out. Cushions were piled onto the floor. I had no idea where they'd come from, because they didn't look like anything we had.

The kittens were laid out across the room, with . . . paper notepads, either in hand or on their laps, and pencils. Old-school graphite pencils, with the yellow sides and little pink eraser on the top, like something out of a museum.

"Cat!" Lucy said. She waved to me from a spot on the far end of the room, then patted the edge of the cushion she was on. "There's room for you here."

"Hello, Stray Catherine," said the only person who could have orchestrated this.

Grasshopper was at the front of the room, a proper blackboard behind her. She was wearing a summer dress, deep blue, with crooked stars across it. She was waving with her two right hands while her left was on her hip, and her other left arm was writing on the board behind her. What jumped out to me more than the extra arms were her glasses. A pair of thick things, like the bottoms of old glass bottles, but cut so that they had hundreds of tiny facets that were filled with reflections of her glowing eyes.

"Uh, hey, Grasshopper," I said. "What's all this?"

"We're learning about statistics," Grasshopper said. She clapped her lower hands together. I squinted. I couldn't tell which pair were her original arms. "You should join us!"

"I think I'm good," I said. "Are you really doing classtime at . . . ten p.m.?"

"Statistics are exceptionally useful to know," she said. "They might be nothing but lies, but they're lies that approximate truth. For example, everyone, what's the statistical likelihood that Catherine has done her homework?"

Every hand raised, even Lucy's.

"Hey," I said.

"Miss, what's the statistical likelihood that Cat's the one who brought in that fart smell?" Junior asked.

"I was *saving the city*," I snapped.

Grasshopper clapped her hands. She smiled, but it was so serene and nice that I really couldn't tell if she was mocking me or not. "That's good. I'm very proud of you. Even during your time off, you're trying to help people, and I'm sure you're making a difference."

I felt my cheeks warming up and I glanced away. I couldn't meet her weird bug eyes, not when she was praising me like that.

I glanced over at Lucy, and she was looking at me like she had *ideas*, which really wasn't better. "Yeah well, whatever. I'm gonna go take a shower and get changed. You guys have fun."

"Miss Hopper, do you mind if I go help her?" Lucy asked.

"Of course, Lucy," Grasshopper said.

I slipped into our bedroom, with Lucy coming up behind me. "Did you want casual stuff or PJs?" she asked. "You can jump in the shower, if you want. I'll find something."

"Pajamas would be nice," I said. "It'd be nicer if you joined me yourself."

Lucy came closer. "Oh?" she asked before climbing onto the tip of her toes to give me a kiss. "Maybe later."

"Later?" I asked.

"Grasshopper's here," she said. "And you really do smell like fart. It's not exactly a turn-on. Go on, hero, get yourself cleaned up, then you can complain to me about your day."

I grumbled, but she had a point. I really did smell like fart. I cast off my gear, peeled out of my skinsuit, then jumped in the shower. Just for good measure, I tossed my gear into the corner of the shower stall and used the telescoping showerhead to wash it down.

Lucy came in with some fresh clothes, which she set to one side of the sink, then she jumped onto the other. I wondered if she just planned on watching, and was thinking of putting on a show when I got a call on my augs.

From Lucy.

"Yes?" I answered.

"Hey," Lucy said. "Did you want to talk?"

"I . . . sure, but why the call? I can hear you just fine," I said.

"Yeah, but I can't. The water's too loud. You're the one with the good ears. Also, don't forget to wash the backs of your knees."

I shook my head and continued my very unfun shower. "So, when did Grasshopper arrive?"

"Just after lunch. She brought food. Well, no, she brought ingredients, then *made* the food. It was weird, to be honest. Tasty though, that chick knows how to cook. Too bad she's into men."

"Really?" I asked.

"Mm-hmm. Only took her like, half an hour, and she made this stir-fry with real chicken and everything," Lucy said.

I started to rub some shampoo into my hair, an entire handful, because I didn't need any stink lingering. I still hadn't recolored my bangs. I'd have to look into that soon, the color was fading. "Sounds like I missed out," I said as I dug my nails into my scalp. "Today turned into a long day."

"Sewer stuff?" Lucy asked.

"Yeah. I didn't even get to the clinic stuff. That'll have to wait for tomorrow. And I promised See-Three I'd look into it, but . . . yeah."

"Oh! I got ahead of you there. At least until Grasshopper arrived. I invited See-Three and some of her friends to check out the floor below. They were properly spooked when they learned they'd be squished between two samurais' homes."

"Did they come?" I asked.

Lucy shrugged. "They said they'd be here tomorrow. Also, I think once she thought about it, then got used to the idea. It's not a bad spot to be in."

"Do you think the clinic will need the whole floor?"

"Weren't they originally going to just use a little storefront?" Lucy asked. "If that was enough, then I don't see why they'd need that much more room. Maybe some more, but not a whole floor."

I agreed. And it would be so much easier and cheaper to only have to fix up one corner of the floor below for the prosthetics clinic. The rest of the space . . . meh. It could stay empty for now. We'd figure out something to do with it later. "Think we could fit more shops downstairs?" The floor between our house and Gomorrah's was pretty large, and just above a parking garage level too.

"What, like a merch store?" Lucy asked.

"No, not that," I said as I rinsed off. I gestured after shutting the water, and Lucy grabbed a towel and tossed it into the shower so I could dry off while still warm.

"I think I could use some space for Kitten stuff," Lucy said.

It took me a split second to catch on to what she meant. Capital-K Kittens, as in the group we'd left in Burlington. Which . . . we'd kind of left in the hands of a sex android and some dozen volunteers. It had worked out well enough at the time. "You want to make something of that?"

"You know, I always dreamed of running my own gang," Lucy said. "This is basically the same idea, isn't it?"

"If you're going to make it a whole gang, you'll need a better name than Kittens," I said. I pinched a corner of the towel and used it to wipe the inside of my cat ears. Water always got caught in there.

"The Killer Kittens?" Lucy tried.

I laughed. "Still too cute."

"Well, whatever. There aren't any rules against having a cute gang."

"I feel like there might be," I said. "Like, unspoken rules, but still rules."

"You try then," Lucy goaded.

"Hmm, the Cat-astrophes?"

Lucy threw my underwear at my face. "Veto!" she said. "Now get dressed, because Grasshopper has to dress you down for not doing your homework!"

CHAPTER FORTY-EIGHT

RECREATIONAL RESPIRATORY DETERIORATION

Do you suffer from agoraphobia?

Fear of open spaces is entirely natural. Most mammalian creatures live in tight, secure dens, and exploring the wider world is a dangerous thing! There's no shame in being afraid of stepping outside of the comfort of your megabuilding, but it can be a little awkward.

PsyOPs is here to help! Our three-month all-VR training course will slowly push you past your agoraphobia. In no time at all, you'll be walking under the sun and stars with a bright smile on your face!

Contact us today for pricing plans!

—PsyOPs Agoraphobia Treatment Center advertisement, 2047

The next day was a vacation day.

I wasn't heading out to snoop around the sewers. I wasn't saving the city. I *was* going to work on my hobbies until sometime in the afternoon when See-Three and her pals were going to show up.

Yes, helping her settle in and check things out would be work, but I wasn't leaving the building so I didn't count it as such. I'd change into something nicer and less stained for the occasion, then say hello and walk them around. I wasn't worried about it.

What I was worried about was getting some sensation back into my hands. "Fuck, it's *cold*," I said.

The current temperature is four degrees Celsius, which is approaching cold, yes. The humidity is making it far worse, I suspect, as is the wind.

I cupped my hands before my mouth and blew some hot air between them. I was seriously considering a change of venue for my mechanical work. Up until now, doing it just outside the apartment had been mostly fun. If I needed a snack, I was only a hop away from the kitchen. Needed to shit? The bathroom was right there.

It was nice and convenient. But not when I was freezing so hard that I was having a tough time picking up the pieces on my workbench. Besides, I'd been dealing with wind and rain a lot lately. There was a reason people did things indoors. I should have worn my suit for this, but it felt wrong to put on armor to do mechanical work.

"Probably not good for my lungs, either," I muttered.

Are you speaking about being outdoors?

"Yeah," I said.

You're correct, the level of VOCs in this region is quite high. I suspect that the time you spend out here every day is leading to increased deterioration of your lungs.

I coughed, but it was mostly because we were talking about it. Imagining cancer-causing stuff going down my throat made it feel scratchy. "That's . . . not ideal," I said.

It's a slow deterioration. You'd need to spend a dozen hours exposed to outside air every week in order for the damage to start being noticeable in a short time frame.

"And you didn't feel like telling me?" I asked.

I'd be very impressed if you still have your organic lungs three months from now. The current damage is, therefore, meaningless. You also frequently use medicine that heals the damage to your lungs as an incidental side effect.

Ah, right, the nano-repair stuff. I did use a lot of that whenever I got smacked around. It was probably topping up my lung health. "Maybe I *should* get super lungs," I said.

Are you going to mention how they'll improve your sexual prowess?

I pouted. I'd been going to, but not anymore. "I'm not that predictable," I said.

If that's what you choose to believe.

Sighing, I shook my head, then gestured to the workbench. "Hey, Repair Boy, can you store all of this for me?" I asked the repair drone. It wasn't an organization drone, but it could handle this much. "I think I'm going to head downstairs early. Maybe Gomorrah wouldn't mind letting me have a corner of the parking garage."

A few walls, some outlets, better lighting, and I'd have a much warmer, less toxic place to do my hobby stuff in.

With the bot packing my equipment away, I gave myself a minute to stretch, then walked back inside. It was so much warmer in our house. I hadn't actually looked at what kind of temperature-control shit we had. If I just ignored it, then I wouldn't have to be anxious about changing filters or whatever.

I slipped into the elevator and made my way down, then stepped out into the parking garage and tested the air with a sniff. It stank of hydrocarbons, but it was warmer than outside, though not by all that much. It was also still pretty humid. Probably all the exposed concrete walls and the big openings to let cars in. Unsurprisingly, the space was cleared out of most cars, except for a couple parked in one corner.

The rest of the room was being taken up by several containers and a couple of large construction drones slowly moving supplies around.

That's where I found Franny. She was frowning at a tablet next to the drone when I came up behind her. "Hey!" I said.

She started, spinning around to face me. "Oh," she said. "Hi, Cat. What's up?"

"Nothing much," I said. "How's the building coming along?"

"Slower than I'd expected," she said. "Which is still much faster than normal. These machines aren't quick, but they're efficient, and they don't need to stop. Did you need help with something?"

"Ah, maybe? I'm tired of working outside. It's getting cold as tits out there. I was thinking I could get a corner of the garage to park my mech in and work on it."

Franny blinked, then shrugged. "Can't see why not. You're not going to rip into the ceiling or anything?"

"No? I was thinking of getting some walls built around my corner. Maybe I'll take a spot with a door leading out?" It would give me a space to park my mech into, and one for my bike. It was a bit farther of a walk than having it outside, but not by that much.

"Yeah, I think that would be fine," Franny said. "You might want to wait until the construction work is done, though. We'll be finishing that up in a day or two, I think. Then it's all furnishing and finishing stuff, but that's not as big a deal."

"Right," I said. "Do you still only have one bedroom?"

Franny flushed, then leveled a glare at me. "If-if you must know, we haven't been sleeping in the same room . . . but I intend to change that tonight," she said.

"Oh-hoh!" I said. Gomorrah was my best samurai friend at this point, so poking at her private life was definitely not something I should be doing . . . but it was definitely something I'd be doing anyway, because I was a bitch like that.

"Nothing like that's happened," Franny said.

"Really?" I asked. "You're sleeping in the same room, but not . . . you know."

Franny sniffed. "We're saving that kind of thing for after marriage."

I . . . didn't know what to say about that. Maybe "poor Gomorrah," or maybe it was more "poor Franny," but that was on them.

"Okay," I said. "I won't dig if you don't want. Can't say the same for Lucy though, but if you lay down the law with her, she'll probably leave you alone."

Franny let out a long breath. "Thanks," she said. "This whole thing is . . . new for Delilah and me. We're both kind of feeling our way through this."

I nodded along. I had no idea what that was like, but I could imagine it. "So, things going well enough otherwise?"

"Yes. Slower than I'd like, but faster than we'd have any right to expect. I think by this time next week we'll be settled in," she said. "It'll be nice to have a place to crash that isn't the convent. What about you?"

"Eh, still on vacation," I said with a shrug. "Probably not for very long."

I wasn't paying too much attention to the news, because I never liked that kind of reality entertainment stuff, but I was still vaguely aware that things weren't all rainbows and puppies past the new walls of New Montreal. There were plenty of cities in rough shape, and Antithesis hives growing all over the damned place. New Montreal had taken a beating, but the city still stood, bruised nose and all.

I'd have to move out to help sooner rather than later, do my part and all that. But that could wait another day or two. I had maybe been pushing myself too hard before. Nonstop action with no breaks and mounting stress and responsibility. It was getting to me. The pace of the last couple of days was much more relaxed than the all-day killing marathons I'd been on before.

It felt . . . off, to only have free time like this. I was almost looking forward to being back on the front lines.

Weird how that worked out.

"Hey, you lemme know what Gom has to say about me using the corner of the garage. And if you need anything, just . . . I don't know, come knock at our door."

"Like to ask for milk?" Franny asked.

"I don't know if we have any, but hey, if you need cookies or something, I think we have, like, six brands," I said with a grin. I gestured to the floor above. "I need to head back up. I'll get my mech down . . . later today, somehow, and then we'll see about walling off a corner."

I had that meeting with See-Three, then it was a full day of rest for me. Perfect!

Delilah was somewhere approaching exhausted when she arrived at . . . home?

She wasn't sure if the place was home yet.

She flew the *Fury* around the building a couple of times, idly watching the fading sunlight play across the silvery cat sitting atop the skyscraper. It was . . . extremely gaudy. Cheesy, even. But also very *Cat*, and very samurai.

Most corps shied away from anything this overt. That was asking for trouble. Cat never seemed to think about how her actions made her look to others, not until she was done acting. Which was one of the big reasons why Delilah . . . *Gomorrah*, chose to make this place her home.

It was an overt declaration. "A samurai lives here. Don't mess with it." And Gomorrah liked that.

She slid the *Fury* into the parking garage and into her slot. Soon she'd have a parking spot for the *Fury* in her part of the building, but for now this place was private and secure enough.

She wasn't impressed with Cat's security so far. It was lackadaisical. Especially for a place that so overtly claimed to be a samurai's residence. Some turrets were tucked away on the outside of the building, none of them hard enough to break through the armor of a flying APC. It was enough to deter civilians, maybe, but that was it.

She was working on upgrades, which started with the suite of flame-throwers tucked into the ceilings of the elevators. Anyone riding it with ill intent would reach their destined floor as char.

She'd be adding more, of course. Scanners, and security drones on patrol routes. Some flamer turrets here and there. Maybe some missile pods hidden in the walls able to fire out of the building?

She didn't plan on turning it into a fortress. Just a place that would be so costly to attack that it wasn't worth it.

Her home, when it became home, would be safe. For her, and for . . .

For Franny.

Delilah swallowed. She'd gone a whole ten minutes without thinking of Franny. Almost a record.

She had no idea what Franny was to her at the moment. A girlfriend? Maybe? She hoped so.

They certainly kissed like girlfriends did.

They were getting better at it. No more clicking teeth together, no more bruised noses. Though . . . the fumbling early stuff had been nice too, in a way. Inexperience and awkwardness all led to something that was as funny as it was . . . hot.

Delilah found herself licking her lips. She wanted that taste again.

Franny liked a particular brand of lip balm. It was minty.

Delilah had never been a big fan of mint anything. From cookies to toothpaste, she found the taste too strong.

Although she loved it on Franny's lips.

The elevator opened so suddenly that Delilah jumped a little. Atyacus sent her augs a silent report from the house. There wasn't much to report, really. Everything was still under construction.

She stepped out and took it all in. More walls had been added, but they were unpainted and rough still. The construction drones were deeper in, moving at a snail's pace as they lifted a precut piece of metal and then bolted it into place on some framing.

Her home wouldn't have anything flammable in it. That meant metal walls and tile floors. It would be tricky to decorate, but that would come in time.

A soft "Oh," came from behind her.

Delilah turned, then paused to take in Franny. She was standing there, out of her habit. Instead, Franny was in tattered, very tight jeans, with a belt that looked like it had little bullet casings all around it. Her shirt was a size too small. Maybe two, judging by the amount of stomach it left exposed, and the way it clung around her chest.

"Hi," Delilah said as her brain engaged. She blinked as she finally noticed Franny's hair. Or one lock of it, in any case. It was a bright, almost neon blue. It clashed hard with Franny's natural, orange-y hair.

"Welcome home," Franny said with a grin. She was blushing a little. It was always very obvious with her. Her skin was too pale to hide it, and her freckles stood out whenever that line of red blossomed across her cheeks and the bridge of her nose.

"Yeah," Delilah said. "It's nice to be back. Did . . . did you need a ride back to the convent, or something?"

It was getting kind of late. Delilah wouldn't mind driving Franny back though.

"I thought I'd stay the night," Franny said.

"Oh," Delilah replied. She could feel the blood rushing up to her face, but she willed it away. "Is the guest bedroom done?"

"No," Franny said matter-of-factly.

Delilah started jumping to conclusions. "Oh," she repeated a second time. Then she cleared her throat and pushed on. This wasn't the first time she'd been tongue-tied, but it used to be a rare occurrence. She'd always prided herself on having a good demeanor, on being stable and level-headed. Recently, that had been harder, and not because she was frequently facing off against hordes of ravenous aliens.

It was her ravenous maybe-probably-girlfriend that was a bigger threat in Delilah's mind.

"I'm starving," Delilah said. "Do you want to order something?"

"Yeah, sure!" Franny said. "The kitchen's not ready, but there's an island to eat at, and I found a couple of stools we can use."

"Alright," Delilah said.

So they ambled over to the kitchen while Franny talked about food. Delilah only glanced down at Franny's rear once. A quick peek which still made her feel impossibly guilty. It was wrong. She needed to have better control over herself.

They ordered from a place nearby, just one building over, in fact, and Delilah abused her control over the few drones she had on security duty to have one waiting in the parking garage, ready to bring the food down to them.

They started talking about furniture while they waited in the barren kitchen. "We'll have to decide what you want to buy for points, and what we'll buy for credits," Franny said.

"It feels almost sacrilegious to spend points on something like a couch," Delilah said, and she was happy to see Franny nodding.

"Yeah. Probably ninety-nine percent of our stuff we should buy the old-fashioned way. We need a fridge, some cabinets, couches, seats." Franny patted the stool between her legs. She always sat inappropriately, knees apart. It was distracting.

"I think we can manage that," Delilah said.

"But some things we should get Protector-made," Franny said.

"The doors," Delilah replied instantly. "I want them to be safe."

"And the bed."

Delilah felt her mind hitch, but she didn't let it show.

The bed.

Singular.

As in, only one.

"Ah, yeah," Delilah said. So far she'd been sleeping on a small blow-up mattress she'd grabbed from the convent. It was easy to set up, and durable. She didn't need luxury. "The bed," she said.

I have several beds I could supply. Based on the dimensions of your room, I think I could easily find one that you and Franny would find comfortable. Sleep is important.

She swallowed again. "Maybe later," she subvocalized to Atyacus.

Franny gave her a look. Delilah chose not to read into it.

The food arrived, and Delilah delighted in being distracted by some extremely fatty poutine with smoked meat while Franny chewed through a salad and occasionally stole a forkful of Delilah's meal.

They talked, about not much at all, and soon Delilah realized that she didn't own a trash can either.

"Want to see about the bed while I get freshened up?" Franny asked. She was trying to sound casual. Delilah had lived most of her life near Franny— she could tell when her friend was nervous about something.

"Yeah," Delilah said.

Franny came closer, leaning in toward Delilah. Delilah leaned in too, and they kissed. It was surprisingly chaste.

She watched Franny go, and participated in a little bit of sin as her eyes wandered down before she could snap them up.

They had . . . rules.

Delilah, in a fit of what was possibly divine inspiration or insanity, had told Franny that she, Franny, was in charge. She'd dropped the reins of whatever power they had in their relationship by Franny's feet, and decided that that was . . . that.

The memory of what she'd done, in their old classroom, no less, was seared into her mind to this day, and would likely stay there until she died as either one of the most arousing or embarrassing moments of her life. Maybe both.

Franny had decided to use that right that Delilah had given her. It happened in Burlington, a few awkward days later. After some kissing, Franny had *demanded* to know what Delilah's limits were.

The idea didn't seem like one that came from Franny. Delilah suspected Lucy was to blame, but . . . she wasn't all that disappointed by it.

Franny had Delilah's permission to do whatever she wanted with Delilah, and the first thing she did with that was ask Delilah what *her* limits were.

It was extremely sweet.

Delilah had to think on it, but she'd eventually drawn a line, and it was a hard one to follow.

She didn't want sex.

Actually, no, that was an awful lie. Delilah wanted sex a lot, with Franny, at a frequency that was likely unhealthy. What she meant was she didn't want . . . intercourse? Penetration? She didn't want to spoil herself, not before marriage.

It was stupid, and antiquated, and even a little haughty. Delilah was terrified that Franny would laugh at her, or push past that line (and Delilah would fold, because she'd given Franny that right, and she wanted it as much as she didn't), but Franny had been beautiful.

They hadn't pushed things since.

Oh, there was lots of kissing.

Very nice kissing.

Some hugging. A few . . . many moments where hands wandered. Franny seemed to really enjoy Delilah's breasts, which Delilah enjoyed the enjoying of.

Delilah snapped out of her state of wasteful pining and followed after Franny, who was already far ahead. She found the redhead in the bedroom, folding the blow-up mattress up into its little box. The main floor space was clear and empty. "I made room for the bed," Franny said. "Well, more room, since there's only a chair, really."

Delilah nodded, then paused. There *was* a chair. A nice, plush one that she didn't recognize at all. "Where did you get that?"

"It was in the building already," Franny said. "I think it was in some C-suite office? It's kinda heavy, but nice. I washed it off, so it's fine."

It was a nice chair, a bit modern, all leather. She didn't know if it fit the decor style she was going for, but she didn't complain, not when it accounted for almost one hundred percent of her furniture at the moment.

"Right, a bed," Delilah said.

She started to subvocalize with Atyacus. A bed wouldn't come in a box, she hoped. The AI was usually good at pointing her toward what she needed, but he also tried to upsell her often. In this case, she wasn't sure she needed a self-heating and cooling bed . . . until she started to think about it.

A warming bed would mean that she couldn't naturally gravitate toward the nearest source of warmth, who might also be occupying the bed. A clever way to avoid sin . . . she hoped.

That would be nice, actually. And blankets. Two sets.

It didn't take long before the order was up, and she asked Franny to step aside to make room.

With a thump, a bed appeared. It was done up with blankets already. Black and white, with a faint flame pattern embroidered into them. A bit . . . on the nose, but not too badly so. It was large too. King-sized, or something close to that. Its footprint was almost as large as her car's.

"Nice!" Franny said. She hopped up, knees first onto the bed, then bounced onto it, rolling onto her back with a laugh. "Oh, it's sinky."

"It can harden," Delilah said. "Or . . . change consistencies, I suppose. So you don't move as much as you sleep. And it stays warm or cool."

"That's interesting," Franny said. "I'd never really thought about . . . bed technology, before." She reached toward the pillows, grabbing one and hugging it even as she sat up. There were two small thuds as she kicked her shoes off over the side.

Franny eyed Delilah.

Delilah stared back.

Then Franny smiled. "Sit," she said.

Her voice had that same laughter in it, but also an edge. It was a Command.

Delilah swallowed, then moved to the chair. It was facing the side of the bed that Franny was on. She sat. Properly, at that, with her knees together and her skirt adjusted just so. She waited for Franny to say something.

Instead, Franny shifted on the bed, then fell back. Just for a moment. She arched her hips up, then undid her belt with a clinking noise that sounded louder than most of the gunshots Delilah had heard. The belt came loose, then Franny started to remove her pants. Slowly.

Delilah felt like some sort of perverted voyeur as she just sat there and watched as Franny squeezed out of her pants. "Oh, you have no idea how tight these are," Franny said as she finally pushed the jeans down her legs.

Delilah had an idea.

Franny let the pants fall to the floor. It was slovenly, sinful, but they were sinning in much more interesting ways at the moment.

Delilah didn't know where to look, but she had the impression that it was part of the game here. So she stared.

Franny was wearing black panties. Not the kind of underthings they had at the convent, which were all beige and kind of square and about as modest as such things could be. These were shapely, sporty. They covered all of Franny's . . . derriere, but little else. There was text on the back, and it took her a moment to parse it.

"God's Chosen." In large, white all-caps.

She found her mouth incredibly dry at the moment.

Franny sat up, then reached down, crossed her arms, and tugged her T-shirt off in one move. Her breasts jiggled and Delilah discovered that she didn't know where she wanted to stare more, because Franny wasn't wearing a bra.

A little "Oh," escaped Delilah's lips. She was saying that a lot today.

She noticed Franny grinning at her and realized that she felt very warm. "You haven't seen these in a while, huh?" Franny asked. She wasn't as endowed as Delilah, though Delilah didn't really care.

"Not since . . . we went to that park, with the water slides," Delilah said. "Two . . . three years ago?"

"Huh, oh yeah, with those awful bathing suits," Franny said. She casually reached up and squeezed a breast. "I remember those. They were itchy."

And they'd covered everything from mid-arm all the way down to their knees. Delilah hadn't cared for them either. Though she still vividly remembered the changing room where . . . anyway.

"What are we doing?" Delilah asked.

"You're sitting there," Franny said. A leg came up, bending in half until Franny leaned back onto one elbow. Her free hand carefully slid across her torso, then down to the underwear. There was a cross on the front of them. White against the black cotton.

Franny's fingers pressed against the material, pushing over the cross and outlining exactly what was just beneath that thin layer of cloth. They went down, then slowly moved back up, then back down again.

Delilah's eyes almost boggled as she realized what was happening. She adjusted the way she was sitting, just a little, still keeping her legs together, but making damned sure that her thighs weren't rubbing as she watched . . . as she watched Franny casually masturbate in front of her.

And Franny was watching, half-lidded eyes, a small knowing smile, fingers still stroking across her very lewd panties. Franny's breathing stayed careful and even, and Delilah continued to watch.

A minute passed, then another. There was silence except for Franny's breathing, which was coming in quicker. So were her strokes across her panties.

Delilah wondered if she was imagining the stain on the front of the panties or if the wetness was just a trick of the light.

Franny leaned back, her arm which had been holding her up moving to squish her breast and pinch her nipples. There was a gasp, a faint moan, and Delilah stopped her legs from rubbing against each other with a force of will.

Franny's movements grew faster. Delilah grew more desperate to do . . . something. She didn't know what. She was ordered to sit. So she sat, and watched, and sweated.

She wasn't sure what she'd do if she hadn't been ordered to sit.

Delilah perked up as Franny's breathing started to hitch. She wasn't imagining the warmth in the air. Then Franny jerked upward to a sitting position, and Delilah started in her seat, startled at the sudden motion.

Franny swept a hand through her hair, then locked eyes with Delilah. She reached under the pillow next to her, then scooted to the edge of the bed and stood. Delilah leaned back as Franny walked over to her. She could definitely smell the arousal in the air, the faint scent of Franny's shampoo, the taste of mint.

Then Franny sat on Delilah's lap.

It was only possible because the chair had no arms. Franny sat with her legs wide apart, her weight on Delilah's thighs and her butt resting on Delilah's knees. Franny leaned in for a kiss, which Delilah very gladly reciprocated.

The kiss ended all too soon. It had done nothing to help Delilah calm down.

She had no idea what to do with her hands. Grabbing was . . . out of the question. So she sat with both arms loose by her side, awkwardly.

Franny moved a hand up, the same one that had been . . . rubbing a moment before. "Open," she murmured. Delilah opened her mouth, then almost gasped as Franny's fingertips traced along her bottom lip. "Don't swallow," Franny ordered.

Delilah blinked at the command, but endeavored to obey as Franny carefully moved her fingers *into* Delilah's mouth.

In a way, this was pushing the "no penetration" rules, but Delilah's brain was far too fuzzy in that moment to start rules lawyering. Her mouth was filled with saliva, and she hyperfocused on Franny's fingers as they touched her tongue.

Was . . . was she *tasting* Franny?

Delilah squirmed a little, which made Franny grin. "Let's try something new," Franny whispered.

Delilah nodded, then something unexpected happened. Franny pulled her hand back and raised the other which held . . . a small black object. It looked shiny, like plastic, and was all curved and soft edges.

"Kiss it," Franny said as she held the thing close to Delilah's mouth.

She complied, kissing the little thing.

Franny grinned. "Open," she said. When Delilah did as she was told, Franny slipped the little thing into her mouth. It was about as long as Delilah's middle finger, with space for a sort of curved handle on the end. It was thick, and soft, and warm. It slipped into her mouth, where she still hadn't swallowed. "Lick it," Franny said. "Make it wet for me."

Delilah had no idea what this was about, but she didn't fail to obey. She worked her tongue under the thing, then around it.

"I said all wet, Delilah," Franny ordered. "As wet as you can make it."

Delilah worked her tongue some more, even as Franny started to push and pull the thing almost all the way out of her mouth, then all the way back in until it was nearing the back of her throat. It was almost enough to make her forget Franny's weight, Franny's presence so *close* to her.

Franny reached up and touched Delilah's breast with her other hand, squeezing it through the material of her sweater. It wasn't skin-to-skin contact, but it was contact all the same. Franny kneaded it, and Delilah found her breathing speeding up as Franny toyed with her and the thing in her mouth.

"I think," Franny said, "that's enough."

She stood, and instantly Delilah missed her warmth even as the thing in her mouth "popped" past her lips.

Franny raised it, and Delilah had her first good look. It was a small, black, very phallic *thing*. She'd had no idea while it was in her mouth.

She gulped, swallowing even as she felt a line of drool running down the corner of her lip. There was a gossamer-faint line of her spittle going from her mouth to the . . . to the dildo.

Where had Franny even gotten that?

The thought soon left as Franny turned and swayed to the bed. She climbed back on, then knelt and leaned forward, her rear toward Delilah, raised in the air, her weight on one shoulder as she twisted a little so that she could look back.

Franny shifted her hips, spreading her legs wider apart.

She moved the hand with the dildo back, then reached over with her other hand.

Carefully, she tugged at her panties, pulling them slightly to the side. There was wetness there. So much that the fabric *clung*. But Delilah was only passively aware as she stared, in the dim lighting of the room, at Franny's . . . most intimate parts.

There were lips, puffy and wet, and shadows that Delilah could almost not make out. She swallowed again, not even bothering to hide the way she was squirming in her seat.

Franny moved the dildo back, to her entrance, and Delilah gasped as she watched, her face aflame. Delilah had never . . . never pushed anything into herself before. Rubbing, sure, but only when she was *desperate*. Penetration felt taboo, it felt wrong to do in a way that she could barely articulate. And yet here Franny was, a piece of silicone sin poised by her entrance, covered in Delilah's drool.

It slipped in, knuckle-deep, and Franny moaned softly. The drool leaking off the dildo pooled by the entrance, then started to slowly leak down.

"Franny," Delilah gasped.

"I love you," Franny replied quickly.

It was enough to muddle any words and thoughts Delilah might have had.

Then Franny pushed the dildo in, and Delilah was transfixed as she watched it slip in. It moved in deeper, disappearing within Franny, who moaned at the penetration.

Then Franny was there, gasping, panties still only pulled aside a little, "God's Chosen" in brazen defiance above an act that was certainly unrepentant. She flicked something, and the little device started to *hum* as it vibrated.

"Oh," Franny gasped weakly. She started to move, mostly her wrist, pushing and pulling, pushing and pulling. It was slick and dark and wrong and very, very hot. Delilah almost felt faint as she watched Franny defile herself. She couldn't think of another word for it.

Delilah wanted to . . . to do something. Touch her. Kiss her. Lick that little thing some more for another taste of Franny.

Instead, she sat, as she was ordered to, and watched. Her hands were on her lap, kneading. Then she noticed Franny looking back at her through half-lidded eyes. Yes, there was a lot of lust there, but also a hint of worry. Delilah's mind might have been foggy, but not to the level where she didn't catch on.

Slowly, Delilah spread her knees apart, then started to push against the fabric at the front of her skirt. She could barely feel the press through the material of her skirt and her underthings, but it was there, and she made a show of rubbing herself.

The worry she saw in Franny faded, and Franny's moans took on a new, more frantic pace even as she continued to move her wrist faster and faster. "Oh, Delilah," Franny said, and it was almost a complaint.

Her head turned, and Delilah saw her bite into their brand-new blankets.

Then Franny's entire body shuddered. Her thighs wiggled, and she let out a moaning little squeak that almost made Delilah laugh before she let go of her panties and fell to her side, panting.

They were both quiet for a good, long minute while Franny caught her breath. Then she scooted to the side, reached down, and carefully extricated the dildo that had continued humming away inside of her. She turned it off and let it lay on the bed next to her.

Franny looked over to Delilah, and Delilah could barely read her expression. Worry, shame, lust, fear, more lust.

"That was . . ." Delilah began. She swallowed, adjusted her skirt so that it was more natural, then fixed her hair. "S-so, is that, uh, your side of the bed?" she asked.

Franny giggled, then laughed.

Delilah joined her a moment later, feeling a lot of relief.

And a whole lot *more* pent up than she'd been just an hour ago.

If things continued this way, Delilah was afraid that she would be the one breaking her own rules first.

CHAPTER FORTY-NINE

I SPY WITH MY MEATY EYE

Physical space is a commodity that few people recognize until they're stuffed into a room the size of a closet and told that this is their home.
—Jim Moom, Warden of CNW Indebted Credit Repayment Facility #147, 2036

I got back into the elevator, and rode down a level to the floor above the garage. That was where See-Three and I were supposed to be meeting.

Of course, she wasn't there yet. I'd know if she was, because I'd been in the nearest parking garage all of a minute ago, and I didn't see her show up.

So, I was going to be unfashionably early, but that was alright. I kind of wanted an idea of the lay of the floor first. "Lemme know when See-Three arrives," I said.

Can do.

With that set up, I started to look around the floor. It was actually pretty large, once I looked past all the shit in the way. Unlike two floors below, where Franny and Delilah had ripped down all of the walls and made space for things, this one was still largely occupied by stuff.

Notably, there were still old offices here.

The floor being as big as it was meant that there was room for several firms in here. There was a law firm, an accounting place, some online retailer's physical location, and then a few rent-a-day offices. The sorts of places with okay-enough internet (with free spyware, probably), little cubicles, free coffee of the undrinkable kind, and some secondhand furniture.

They were places that someone could rent by the day, or have the company that hired them for remote work rent for a day. Probably for way too much money, too.

The place had a small lobby space at the front, with seats and a desk with bulletproof glass for a secretary, and then offices behind that, in a series of cubicles, some of which were still standing.

That . . . might not be the worst spot for that clinic, actually. It had space for a waiting room at the front, and as I explored the back, turning on any still-working lights as I went, I discovered a couple of generic meeting rooms, probably also rentable, and a corner office at the very back with a view.

A shitty view, delivered through two narrow windows, but still, a view. And that back room had plugs and lights and an office chair that was missing one of its rollers at the bottom.

It was better than nothing, I figured.

See-Three has arrived, along with two companions.

"Good timing," I said. "Is she on this floor yet?"

She's moving toward the elevator.

I nodded along, then started that way myself. I timed it just right, the door to the elevator opening and See-Three and her pals slipping out at the same time I was coming down the corridor.

"Hey!" I called out.

See-Three's eyes scanned the area, then landed on me. I figured she might actually be seeing more than I could with those three eyes of hers.

Actually, that made me think . . .

"Myalis, remind me to upgrade my still-meaty eye." My right eye was full-on cybernetic, and pretty badass, but my left was organic version 1.0 still.

I'll do that. Repeatedly.

"Stray Cat," See-Three said. She reached out a hand and we shook. "So, this is where you live?"

"Here? Nah, the floor above. It was a museum before we took it over and turned it into our place. I can show you around one day." After whipping the kittens into cleaning the place. "Anyway, the rest of this building's being spruced up a little too. Bit by bit. The floor below us belongs to Gomorrah now."

"The flamethrower nun?" one of See-Three's friends said. It was one of the guys from the other night. I couldn't remember his name, and was too lazy to look it up.

"That's her," I said. "She's turning it into a private house-slash-armory-slash-church thing. With a large garage. She likes muscle cars. Almost as much as she likes fire and sexy nuns called Franny."

"Specifically called Franny?" See-Three asked, clearly confused.

I nodded. "Yup. So if you know any Frannys who are religious, you tell them to keep an eye open."

"Uh . . . will do," she said a little awkwardly. "Is this the place for the clinic?"

"It will be," I said. "We're going to need to put up some cordons or something, and I might have to buy a couple more cat drones and maybe something big and scary to act as security. But yeah, the clinic would be right over here."

The rent-a-day offices were a corridor and a turn away from the elevator, past a couple of emptied-out spaces. "There's a lot of unused room here," See-Three said.

She wasn't wrong. And it was probably worth commenting on because of the sheer value of space, especially in a city as packed as New Montreal. Right now, with everyone from the suburbs being pulled in, there was probably a huge lack of living spaces in the city. And here I was, sitting on an entire floor of a large building which was completely empty.

"It'll be used," I said. "My girlfriend, Lucy—you'll meet her eventually, too—runs this organization of volunteer mercs and like, rescue personnel called the Kittens. We'll probably be moving their HQ into one of these offices. Might move the big material printer from upstairs here too. I'm probably going to buy a second printer soon, and that'll mean more storage space."

"Ah, so all of this will be filled up?" See-Three asked.

"Hmm, maybe not all of it. Two of the offices that are here, at least." Which would mean about a third of the space that was available, give or take? That still left a lot of empty room. "The rest . . . we'll probably wall up, then reopen them as needed. I'm sure we'll find some use for everything here. If this floor starts getting enough traffic, we might want to look into getting a place set up for a coffee shop or something, and maybe some space for janitorial stuff."

The coffee shop was a fresh idea, but one I liked the sound of. Maybe I could get the kittens upstairs to work as baristas. They'd finally earn their keep, and it could serve as a way for them to earn some change.

I didn't have illusions about housing them forever. One day they'd want to move on, and having both work experience and credits on hand would help a lot with that.

Lucy would probably just find more orphans to fill the void.

"This is it," I said with a gesture at the place. It was better to move on before my thoughts spiraled and I eventually decided that we all needed therapy or something.

See-Three eyed the office front. The corridor lights were down, but I suspected that all of us here had enough cyberware to see in the low light. At least the lights within the office were on, and they painted the lobby as . . . well, a sterile, very inoffensive lobby, minus a few chairs and potted plants.

"It's larger than the space we had before," she said.

"There's a lobby to get people to sit down and shut up in, then offices at the back," I said as I opened the door and let everyone in. Then I moved ahead, feeling a bit like a realtor as I showed the space off. "There's a heavy door between the lobby and the back. Not sure how tough it actually is, but it's something."

"I see," See-Three said.

"And then we have the cubicle farm," I said as I gestured grandly. "It's . . . not much to look at, but it's better than nothing. We can toss all of this shit out, or shove it into the printing machine to break it down. Then we'll have plenty of room."

"Can we renovate this?" See-Three asked.

"It's basically my building, so . . . consider yourself permitted. I'd lend you the construction or repair drone to help, but it's a bit busy. Still, I think we can get something temporary set up quickly enough."

See-Three nodded quickly. "It's a lot of space. We'll use it well."

"There's the back here too," I said as I led them in deeper. "There are two meeting rooms. Honestly, it might be worthwhile to turn at least one of them into something else. Like a place for patients or something?"

"A convalescence room," See-Three suggested. "Post-op, a lot of people need a few hours, sometimes a day or two, on their back. Especially for more complex operations. Most places will shove you in a taxi and you have to hope you can make it to your bed."

"Mm-hmm. There's also a small break room, and some bathrooms. Honestly, I think you might want to look into hiring a full-time nurse or something while you're at it."

See-Three took a deep breath. "Yes. I think we might have to do just that. This is . . . growing to be bigger than I expected. We were expecting to do a few operations a day, out of a small nonprofit clinic. This is starting to look like a whole career that just popped out of nowhere."

"Ah, it's not so bad, is it? Look! Free corner office. With a view!"

CHAPTER FIFTY

A DATE AMONG GHOSTS

The nice thing about VR dating is that it's a lot less about how you look and who you are physically than it is about your personality and the way you present yourself.

It's not fair, sometimes, that some people are born ugly, or end up unattractive, but in the Mesh, you don't judge people based on the circumstances of their birth.

You judge them based on the fandom they picked their avatar from.

—Meshizen Interview, 2039

The meeting with See-Three continued for another half hour. That was a little long for my taste, since other than exploring the space, there wasn't *that* much to do. See-Three took some notes on what they'd need, but most of those things were still at the first clinic location. It would just be a question of moving things from one place to another, which anyone with a car could manage.

"If it's acceptable to start things without fully renovating the space," See-Three said, "then I think we can open the clinic within a day or two . . . definitely leaning more toward two. It'll mean shutting down the first clinic, but I feel like we'll make up for it with this one."

Two days was very acceptable.

See-Three and I shook hands over it all, and I told her that if she needed anything specific, she just had to let me know. She bowed at me at the waist after, then quietly thanked me. It felt genuine, and was genuinely weirding me out.

It would take a good long while to renovate the clinic properly, but with the amount the clinic would be charging for its services (basically fuck-all), I expected that some more-well-off people might also donate to the cause or be willing to pitch in to help a little.

We'd need chairs, benches, and a secretary. Further down the line, we'd need proper renovations too. Walling off some parts, fixing up the floors and ceiling lights. Normal maintenance shit too. Maybe a sign out front?

In any case, I expected that to kind of just happen organically.

The people we were serving were exactly the kind of people that wouldn't want to be in a full-on corpo-chic place. Having the clinic look a little scuffed up would probably reassure them a lot.

With that all taken care of, I decided to head back upstairs. I was starving, and I wanted to get back to work on the mech now that my fingers weren't threatening to freeze off.

I arrived upstairs via the elevator (man, this was unsafe—I needed to install an HMG or something by the entrance) and then almost ran into Lucy. "You're back!" she said.

"I never even left the building," I replied. On a whim, I wrapped my arms around Lucy's shoulders. "Did you miss me so much?"

"Mm-hmm," she said. "I'm always worried. What if you decide you need a girlfriend on every floor, huh? What'll I do then?"

"Well, you'd still be the top . . . unless I get a food girlfri—ow!" Lucy had pinched the skin on my side, and I let go of her to rub it. "That hurt," I whined.

"You deserved it," Lucy said. She tilted her head back, pretty little nose pointing haughtily at the ceiling. "We're going on a date," she said.

"A date?"

"Yeah. I need to get my evil hooks into you before any other scheming, wandering lesbian comes along," Lucy said.

I couldn't help the giggle that escaped. "Sure, because there are so many of those throwing themselves at me. I'd be more worried about you. Desperate, lonely housewife, all alone at home—besides her seventeen kids—with nothing to do. The neighbors are heavily repressed nuns, open to her evil predations . . ."

Lucy snorted, then climbed onto her tiptoes to give me a quick peck. "Date," she said. "I'm gonna get dressed, and you should do the same."

"Wait, really?" I asked.

"I ordered a taxi already," Lucy said as she ran off across the house with me heading after her. Of course, she almost tripped, and then she wasn't running so much as walking fast.

I caught up with her changing in our rooms. It seemed as if she was taking this date thing seriously, so I decided to do the same. A glance at what she was picking out to wear suggested that this wasn't anything too formal.

Not that we had anything to wear for formal-type stuff.

I hopped into the shower, then dressed in new cargo pants and a loose T-shirt. Lucy was dressed similarly, though with my old coat tossed on. Her shirt was just small enough to expose a bit of belly. "God, you're hot," I said.

Lucy smiled. It was hard to tell with the color of her skin, but I noticed she was a little flushed. "We'll see if you still think that once you pay for the date," she said.

"Hey, I have to pay? You invited me," I complained as I walked next to her. She bumped me with her hip, and I laughed.

We made it outside—I grabbed a coat too, because I liked my skin unexposed to whatever the fuck was in the New Montreal rain—just as an autotaxi pulled up to the rooftop ramp. I opened the door for Lucy, then ran around to the other side before we took off. "You still haven't told me where we're going," I said.

"You'll see in a minute," Lucy teased. "Ah, but I don't know if you'll actually care for it."

"I'm sure it'll be fun," I said. I was with Lucy, after all.

The taxi flew us across a good tenth of the city. It wasn't a fast flight, especially not after it slipped into the low-priority aerial traffic. But it wasn't all that bad. Lucy and I talked, then kissed, then talked some more. That had a tendency of making time pass a lot faster.

My first clue about where we were going was the taxi dipping out of traffic, then starting a holding pattern around a squat skyscraper. It had a large dome above it, all glass filled with greenery and several glowing blue forms. I'd maybe flown past this place once or twice before, but never really gotten a good look at it.

Banner ads hovered around the building, calling it the Hologardens of New Montreal.

The taxi pulled into a drop-off zone a few floors below the top, then the doors locked while my augs got a ping from the taxi demanding that I pay up.

I rolled my eyes and allowed the transaction. There was a faint hitch as Myalis noticed some fucky surcharges, then insisted on contacting support to have them removed. Since it was all automated, I imagined that her "contacting" support was the equivalent of driving a tank through the wall of an office and then waving the receipt around.

It was fixed in a second or two, and I leapt out of the taxi and ran around to help Lucy out of her side.

"Is this the place?" I asked. There were more ads here for the Hologardens, and I was faintly aware of more intrusive ads trying to get through my augs and bouncing like flies off of steel plating.

"Mm-hmm!" Lucy said as she leaned against my side. "It's not much, really. I heard that it didn't pull in nearly as many people as they wanted to make the place profitable. Bad timing and everything, but it has a nice walkabout, and there's a zoo!"

"A zoo?" I asked with a laugh. Actually, yeah, that tracked. Lucy had several terabytes of animal gifs with her at all times. It didn't surprise me that she'd want to see the cute animals up close, and I really didn't mind being with her while she cooed and awwed.

We walked in, then passed an automated gate that asked us to pay to enter. I almost winced at the price before remembering that I wasn't actually poor anymore. The entry cost was a pittance compared to the amount of credits I had.

Lucy picked up the pace, tugging me along after her and onto an escalator that brought us up and into the gardens proper.

The gardens were relatively large. Big trees flowing up, the ground around them covered in greenery, with wider, more open spots here and there. The plants even looked real. The crowd, as sparse as it was, was guided through the gardens via some walkways suspended a little bit over the ground.

"Look!" Lucy said as she pointed to a holographic animal. It was . . . a gorilla? My augs pinged on it, and I got a prepackaged dataset courtesy of the holozoo. It said that the last silverback had died in captivity some ten years ago, but the wild ones died out earlier on, when the Congo rainforest was burned down to wipe out some Antithesis hives hidden within. "They're so big!" Lucy said.

"Yeah," I agreed. I pointed further ahead. "There're some seals over there . . . Seals don't live in jungles, do they?"

"I mean, maybe some of them?"

"I'm pretty sure none of them," I said as we walked past the seal enclosure. There was a sort of pond that the holograms would dive into. The effects with the water left a lot to be desired.

"There's a place to eat, up ahead," Lucy said. "It's a classic restaurant, with menus and everything."

"Huh, alright," I said. "I could eat."

Lucy beamed, and I grinned right back. This was a lot more fun than the dates we'd had before. Less stealing shit and running away, or "dating" while hiding in a closet somewhere.

Our date quickly turned into the highlight of this vacation of mine.

CHAPTER FIFTY-ONE

LIVE, LAUGH, LOBSTERS

Some traditions, rooted in various cultural hang-ups that we find distasteful, still survive to this day.

A large part of that can be attributed to the prevalence of those traditional actions in the media we consume and the history and stories of our previous generations.

—Excerpt from *The Ongoing Tradition*, 2035

Lucy gasped. "Cat!" she said. We were sitting across from each other in a restaurant, and Lucy was hogging the menu. She leaned forward and spun the booklet she was holding around.

The restaurant was a pretty fancy place. It was set a floor above the zoo, along one of the walls. There were big glass panels between us and the zoo itself, angled so that the seats closest to the wall could look down into the jungle-y gardens below, or up and through the large dome just above.

There were actual flesh-and-blood waitresses coming to the tables and paper menus to order from, like in an old-timey movie. The prices, unfortunately, were not so old-timey. Not that I really minded too much.

"What is it?" I asked as I squinted at the menu. Lucy was too excited to hold it level, so the words were bouncing around and hard to read. The pictures helped a little. "Is it the seafood dish?"

"There's *lobster*," she said. "It says it's real lobster too."

"Okay?" I said. "Can't be that hard to grow some of those in captivity, right?"

There was no way it had actually been fished. If the weather over land was wild most of the time, then I couldn't imagine how nasty it was over the ocean. And the ocean housed a lot of horrific alien bastards too. There was a constant operation to cull them, but they'd come up to nibble on a fishing ship, I was sure.

Besides, I was pretty positive that wild lobster was extinct.

"This is rich people food," Lucy said.

At rich people prices too. "Order some," I said. "There're two claws, right? We can share one. Or is it the tail?"

Lucy turned the menu around. "I don't know. The picture is just a red thing. Oh, and it comes with brussels sprouts and a sauce and a salad!"

I grinned. It was impossible not to when Lucy was this excited—especially over something like food. For my part, I stuck to something that looked a little more down to earth. They didn't have what I'd usually order at a restaurant, but that was probably for the best. Chicken nuggets and burgers didn't seem very fancy. So I stuck to the pasta section and hoped that I wouldn't make too much of a mess of my face while eating.

Our waitress came over, a twenty-something girl with a few piercings that clashed with her uniform. She took our orders and was very patient when Lucy asked about how to eat lobster.

"You do need to crack the shell. We serve the meal with some special cutlery to help."

"Oh," Lucy said. "That's cool! Cat, you're stronger than me, can you help if it's too hard?"

"Uh, sure," I said.

The waitress smiled, then left, and I found myself reaching a hand to the middle of the table. Lucy did the same, and our fingers entwined next to a very unnecessary scentless candle. "This is nice," Lucy said.

"It's better than some of the dining experiences I've had lately," I said.

Lucy nodded, then paused. "Do you mean the food I've been cooking?"

"What? No, never. Your cooking is perfect," I backpedaled like someone discovering they'd accidentally tripped into a minefield.

Lucy's grin turned teasing for a moment before she dropped it. "Have you eaten during an incursion? I mean, when you're out murdering things?"

"Huh, uh, yeah, once or twice? I mean, Myalis will let me order food. Snack bars and stuff to drink. Gomorrah actually has a minifridge in her car, so whenever I ride it around I make a point of stealing a drink."

"No!" Lucy said with a grin. "That's awful."

"Eh, she probably orders them by the dozen. Besides, they're tasty."

"Steal me one next time," Lucy said, and I laughed at the switch from condemning it to wanting to be in on the theft. "I wanna taste it!"

"I will," I promised. "You know. You could probably steal one yourself. Gom and Franny are basically our neighbors now."

"That's super weird," Lucy said.

"Them living nearby?" I asked.

"No, having neighbors. I mean, we've always had them, I guess. But usually it's . . . I don't know. People that we'll never meet or interact with. It's strange knowing that there's someone you know living two floors down.

Makes it feel like one day the whole building might be full of people that it wouldn't suck to meet."

"Wasn't that always the case?" I asked. The orphanage was on the lower floors of a pretty old megabuilding, one of those early ones that went up in the '30s or so. "We never lived in a place that didn't have others in the same building."

"This is different," Lucy said.

"How?" I asked.

She shrugged. "I don't know. But it *feels* different, so it's gotta be. Are you going to be inviting more samurai friends to live on the other floors?"

"Are they all empty? As far as I can tell, there's still stuff going on in the lower floors." One of the lower floors had those bridges connecting to the other buildings around ours, so there was definitely still foot traffic crossing through every day.

"Meh. If you asked nicely, I bet the businesses would scamper away to someplace else. It would be cool to have a whole building that's nothing but samurai. Oh! I could become a . . . what do you call those people that specifically take care of one place?"

"A custodian?"

"No, no . . . a butler!"

I laughed. "You want to be a butler?"

"You don't like the idea?" Lucy asked with a pout.

"Well, you would look cute in a suit," I said. An all-black suit, with a white undershirt and . . . "Oh, maybe a little mustache? And you'd have to speak in a posh British accent, of course."

Lucy chuckled. "I don't think anyone wants to see me with a mustache. Maybe a goatee?"

"Oh no," I said. "At that point, why not a full beard?"

"Have you seen what my hair is like? I don't think I could have a beard that tangly."

"Is this one of those 'would you love me if I were a worm' things, but it's about facial hair?" I asked.

Lucy cackled, leaning back so far that her hand almost let go of mine. "No, sorry, it's not that. Uh, I don't know how we got onto the subject."

"It's okay," I said. "Looks like the food's coming."

The waitress came around with a tray, this one covered with our drinks and appetizers. We'd both ordered something a little alcoholic. I went for something simple, and Lucy went for the cocktail with the fanciest name and which looked prettiest in its picture. It came in a weird cup with several umbrellas and slices from six different fruits.

We, of course, sipped from each other's drinks. Hers, for all of its overly fancy presentation, did taste quite a bit better.

I wasn't even sure what brandy was before I ordered it, but it had sounded cool and I only had to work a little not to make a face as I sipped at it.

"Have you gotten any news from . . . what's her name?" Lucy asked.

"You'll have to be a bit more detailed than that," I said.

"Short, lasers, you said she had clones all over?"

"Oh, Deus Ex? No, I haven't heard back in a while. I don't know if I *can* hear back from her. It's not like there's internet between here and Mars. Why did you want to know?"

"Mild concern about the bigger picture stuff," Lucy said. "It's all way, way out of my control, but I'd rather see shit coming than not."

"Yeah, that's fair, I guess," I said.

The main course arrived just as we were finishing off our apps, but I kept my focus on Lucy throughout. "So, no news from here. Honestly, no news from the Martian front at all. I don't know if that's a bad thing or not."

"I think it's probably good," Lucy said. "Wouldn't the Family let you know to prepare if things were going really badly?"

"I hope so, yeah," I said. "Or things are going *so* badly that they won't tell us anything because that'll just make the last few days we have left all the more depressing."

"Hmm, so nothing new there," Lucy agreed.

"Nothing new," I repeated.

Lucy did end up having trouble with her lobster. Or maybe she just wanted to let me feel good by cracking it open for her. I, of course, stole a bite. It was . . . alright. Not as good as a fresh vat-meat burger, but alright.

"You know, if we're all going to die horrible deaths, then at least we'll get to die together," Lucy said.

"Hmm . . . yeah, I'd like that. There's no one I'd rather die with."

"Love you too," Lucy said. She waited for me to be halfway through a sip before asking her next question: "So, when are you going to propose?"

I, of course, inhaled a mouthful of brandy and proceeded to almost die.

CHAPTER FIFTY-TWO

CAT NAP WRAP

If you can't uwu with sincerity, then don't owo with infidelity!
—Hyper Cutie Zoom Ranger Sparkle Girl Bubble-chan!, 2048

After dinner, and after my heart stopped trying to beat its way out of my chest, Lucy and I took a walk through the little park again, visiting the petting zoo off to one side of the gardens.

They had real animals here as well. Or animatronics realistic enough to stink and poop. Lucy made all of the appropriate cooing noises as a little goat hopped its way over to her and accepted some loose goat mix from Lucy's hand.

"This place is nice," she said as she tried to scratch the goat's head. It bobbed away, then hopped off when it saw that she had no food left. "There're a lot of nice places in New Montreal that we haven't gotten to visit yet."

"Yeah," I said as I kept my attention solely on Lucy. "There're some beautiful things here."

Lucy glanced up, then tugged a stray lock away from her face. "You're silly," she declared.

"No, you're silly," I retorted with all due consideration.

Lucy smiled and pressed herself into my side as we continued our walk. I wrapped an arm around her waist, my hand naturally finding its place on her hip. Lucy used that to press in even closer. It was a little chilly at this end of the zoo, but we kept each other warm, even if we were only walking at the kind of pace that would make the geriatric think that we were going too slow.

Lucy had brushed off her marriage joke earlier, and it was all forgotten by the time we got to dessert. Well, maybe she'd forgotten it. It was still at the forefront of my mind, even if I was trying to push the thought away.

It . . . it would happen, eventually. Probably.

I was better at facing hordes of enemies than that kind of problem.

"Should we go home?" Lucy asked as we started to come full circle around the zoo. We weren't too far from the entrance, and I wasn't feeling nearly as bloated now as I had felt just after eating.

"Yeah, I guess so," I said.

"Worried?" Lucy asked.

"Hmm? About what?"

"I don't know. You've been taking some time off, even if your vacation was rather busy. I think it was good for you," Lucy said. "You don't seem as stressed, which is good. But you do still seem a little worried."

"I don't feel as stressed," I admitted. "But it also feels like there's a ton of stuff that's going to happen soon. The more I try to get things fixed, and the deeper I get involved, the more I realize that the problems that caused the problems that caused the problems I want to fix are more complicated than I imagined."

Lucy nodded. "It's not your fault. Or even any one person's fault."

"No, I think a lot of my problems are generational. People were allowed to get away with shit fifty years ago, and now that's hurting us here, today. It's all very . . . messy. I'm surprised that no one's tried to fix it by wiping the slate clean. And people are still pulling that kind of crap."

"I don't know. Sounds like you'd need to really start over from scratch for that," Lucy said.

"Bit of a depressing end to the evening," I said while suppressing a yawn. "Sorry."

Lucy pressed herself into me. "No, it's okay. I guess your vacation will be ending soon?"

"I guess so," I said.

There was a small lobby space before entering or exiting the zoo. It held a few kiosks, the booth to buy tickets, some vending machines, and the elevators leading to the parking space below. There were also a couple of televisions mounted to the walls. Some were playing loud ads on loop, but one was turned into a 24/7 news channel.

It was showing some PMCs from above, firing into a small horde of weaker models rushing toward their emplacement.

The banner at the bottom said that it was live, and taking place just outside of New Montreal.

It was strange how unaffected the people here were. I could imagine myself there. Hell, a small part of me felt like I should have been there instead of here.

There were other couples. A few workers. Some people who looked like they'd just finished their shifts and were moving by. They'd glance at the screen with the news and pay it as much attention as the ads playing next to it.

The world was ending, and it was as noteworthy as the newest hard-on pill or the freshest toothpaste recommended by eleven out of ten dentists.

I couldn't even be angry. Not so long ago I would have been a lot more concerned with keeping me and mine fed than I would have been about the impending tide of hungry aliens. One was an issue I needed to address now. The other was something terrible that, if it happened, there was nothing I could do about.

These people had their own shit going on. The people displaced by the aliens, those that had lost family, they'd be really concerned. Same with those fighting on the front lines. But the rest of us? Life went on.

The vacation I'd taken had been a nice way of stepping back from the bigger picture to fix the little-picture stuff that bothered me.

But that didn't mean that I could sit back forever. I hadn't set a time limit for it, but . . .

There was a weight of responsibility that came with being a samurai, and it was one that was pressing on me now. "I think I'm gonna be working normally again tomorrow," I said.

"In the morning?" Lucy asked.

"Well, whenever I happen to wake up. It looks like things around the city are getting spicy. Besides, I think I could use a few more points, right?"

Lucy locked eyes with me for a good long while, almost as if she was seeing if I was serious. Then she nodded. "Okay. As long as you stay as safe as you can manage, then I think it's okay that you head out. Will you be doing another thing like Burlington?"

"Hmm, no, I think I'll be staying closer to home," I said. "There's something nice about sleeping in my own bed, you know?"

"Oh, I think I do," Lucy purred.

I grinned, then leaned into the side to press a kiss onto the top of her head. I wasn't sure she felt it through her bushy hair, but that didn't matter.

We took a taxi back home, and maybe got a little handsy on the way back, at least until the taxi's rudimentary AI warned us that by taking this taxi, we waived any rights to footage taken of us in the back. Then it tried to sell us on a subscription to Feisty Taxi, which . . . no.

The moment the car landed, we stumbled out of it and into the pouring evening rain. It was cold, and some of it immediately found its way past the collar of my coat. Still, it was kind of refreshing, and we both laughed as I tried to shield Lucy from the rain while running toward the front door.

"So," Lucy said as she pressed a rain-wet kiss against my lips. "Ready for second dessert?"

Someone cleared their throat, and I looked up to find Junior standing outside by the entrance, arms crossed and looking unimpressed. "Hey," I said.

"Hey," she replied. "Before you two start your little rabbits-in-heat thing, you have a visitor."

"Oh . . . shit. Wait, who is it?" I asked.

"Delilah, from downstairs," Junior said, her posture relaxing, though she was looking at me with suspicion. "Is she *actually* your friend?"

"Uh, yeah? Why wouldn't she be?"

"Because Delilah speaks and acts like someone who has their shit together," Junior said. "I kinda figured that people like that would have a natural aversion to our sort."

Lucy laughed. "Delilah's good people, yeah. But Cat's not all that bad either," she said before pulling away from me and adjusting her outfit. "I'll grab some drinks. You go chat with your friend."

I watched her leave, then smacked my cheeks to help myself refocus. Delilah wasn't the sort to interrupt things just because.

I found her in the living room, sitting on the edge of a couch and listening to Nose prattle on about . . . something that he'd hyperfixated on. "Oi, brat, leave Delilah alone for a bit," I said as I patted him on the head.

He gave me the finger, then ran off, leaving us more or less alone in the busiest room of the house. "Hello," she said.

"Hey. So, what's up?"

"The wall was breached," she said in a way that sent a shiver running down my spine. "We've sealed it, killed the Antithesis that made it through, but with so many PMCs moving to other cities where things are worse, we're going to see more trouble. That, and the Antithesis are starting to act smarter."

"Ah," I said. "Well, fuck, I guess vacation time really is over."

CHAPTER FIFTY-THREE

WHO LET THE WORMS OUT?

The common nomenclature for Antithesis names follows a simple pattern, one which was determined by the first responders in the Ohio incursion and then adopted globally and refined.

A model's general type will be given a number. Sub-types are given an alphabetical marker.

The common model three has sub-types A, B, and C, which are all relatively common and also distinguishably still model threes.

This system is fantastic on paper and for reporting.

It is, unfortunately, less useful when it comes to memorization, as numbers are harder to retain for most than names.

Still, the plethora of nicknames for the various Antithesis models does lead to more confusion than the official nomenclature, and their use is therefore discouraged.

—Mrs. January, licensed educator for teenagers, Jan 2033

"So, what's the sitch?" I asked as Gomorrah and I both stepped into the kitchen. The moment we walked out of the living room, some kittens had reclaimed it, and none of them wanted to be in the kitchen in case they were bullied into dish-cleaning duty. It made for as quiet a place to talk as any.

Plus, I was a little thirsty, so I pulled a can of something from the fridge and offered one to Gomorrah, who nodded and took off her mask. "The . . . situation is turning a little rough on the outskirts of the city."

"Really? Damn, I thought we were doing alright."

"In comparison, we are. New Montreal is one of the safest cities in the world right now," she said. "We were lucky that there was an incursion before this global one. Ironically. And we did a decent job pushing the aliens back and reclaiming territory around the city. The problem is the north."

"The north?"

"To our south is the old USA. There's plenty of force down there. Burlington might have been in bad shape, but other cities handled themselves better, and were cleared out over the last week. Territory's being reclaimed and hives are being burned. The issue is that north of New Montreal is a lot of nothing, which also means there's a lot of room for hives to grow."

"Right," I said. That made some sense. Even with the winters mellowing out and the northern parts of what was Canada becoming prime real estate, there still wasn't much in that direction. "So we're gonna get fucked from that way?"

"I wouldn't put it in those terms, exactly," she said. "But we can expect resistance and some assaults from that direction, yes. And some samurai, once freed up, might be coming here as a staging ground for the East Coast assault on the far-north."

"More samurai in the city, huh?" I asked. "That's not so bad. Could use a few more."

"There are plenty we haven't met. But getting samurai to work together can be like—no pun intended—herding cats," Gomorrah said, and I replied with a snort. "There's Battlepoet, who's relatively new. She's been around the city for a while, but not in it until recently. This samurai from Calgary, Teddy, sent some mechanized war-bears to help once we start the push north. There's more, too."

"It'll be nice to have lots of samurai around all at once," I said. Less work for me.

"Yes, but they're not all willing or able to work right away, and the problems with the infiltrations are problems right now. Especially with this round of Antithesis acting strangely."

"Acting strangely how?" I asked.

"Atyacus suspects that it's a network of model seventeens."

I shrugged. I had no idea what those were. Also, the normal naming convention for Antithesis was not doing me any favors. I was bad enough at math as it was without having them all be called numbers all the time. Why couldn't we give the Antithesis names that were easy to remember?

"They're the models that make the model sevens," Gomorrah said. At my continued incomprehension, she went on. "The zombie worms?"

"Oh," I said. I knew *those*. "Nasty fucks."

"Seventeens are hard-shelled models, small. They lay worms that can control people, but also worms that can control other Antithesis. And they can lay out long strings of organic wires that can let a hive communicate over long distances. Atyacus thinks that the way the hive is moving now, tactically, means that we have a few model seventeens playing games just outside of our defenses."

"Great," I said as I rubbed my face. "And this is right up against the walls, huh?"

"PMCs can't keep up with shifting battlelines. Not when they're changing approaches and testing different areas this quickly," Gomorrah said.

"And the wall?"

Gomorrah leaned back. Two of the legs of the stool she'd taken over tipped backward for a moment, then clunked back down. "It was a good idea, I suppose. And it is working, for the most part . . ."

"When do they need us there?" I asked.

"Ideally, right now?" Gomorrah said. "I think the PMCs in charge want to do a counteroffensive."

"Really? That's ballsy."

"It makes sense."

I frowned at that. Did it? Then again . . . yeah, I supposed it did; giving the Antithesis time to attack meant giving them time to scrounge up more biomass and make more combat models. Time was not on our side.

A big push, a big move to wipe some of the planty fuckers out? That would certainly buy us more time than just sitting on our thumbs and waiting.

I sighed. "Alright. I'll come."

"Thank you," Gomorrah said. She stood up, clearly ready to take off right then, but I waved her down.

"I need to get my gear. Get dressed. Hell, I'd appreciate taking a quick shower." I needed to cool off. And maybe I could convince Lucy to join. "I won't be heading out for another hour, at least. Unless the aliens are literally climbing up the walls right now?"

"I think we can spare an hour or two," Gomorrah said. "Did you want me to wait, or . . ."

"Eh, no, go ahead of me. You can deal with all of the boring logistical shit that I don't want to mess with."

Gomorrah looked unimpressed by that admission, but we both knew I wasn't wrong—she was way better at dealing with that kind of thing than I was. "Fine. I'll fly over with the *Fury*. I imagine you'll be leaving the mech behind?"

It was probably too banged up to take out still, so I nodded. "For this? Yeah. Are they going to launch that big push overnight?"

She shook her head. "Tomorrow afternoon. Fifteen hundred hours. They want the sun above and well-rested soldiers. And they're bringing in people from elsewhere too. Tanks, special vehicles."

"Ah, alright . . . so why are we going there tonight?"

"Because someone needs to act as Vanguard, and that's literally our job," Gomorrah said. "I'll send your AI my location. See you in about . . . call it an hour and a half?"

"Damn. Alright," I said.

Gomorrah nodded, then left. I stood there, finishing my drink on my own while thinking for a bit. "Myalis. Get the repair drone on the mech." I really wanted to get more hobby-time practice, but I wouldn't be getting anything done in so short a time. "Sucks to suck, but I might need it tomorrow."

That's understandable. Will you be doing any self-upgrades?

"I'm due, aren't I?" I asked. "Yeah, but not tonight. Let's see what I need overnight, then I can do them tomorrow, when we head out with the army. Or before bed? Whatever. Just . . . not right now."

I was always reluctant to go through any self-modding. Needs must and whatever, but I could put it off for a couple more hours.

First, I'd see about that shower.

"Did it go well?" Lucy asked as I found her in our bedroom.

"Well enough," I said. "Gom . . . and the entire city, actually, kinda needs me. Tonight and probably tomorrow too. I'll be heading out in about an hour."

Lucy nodded. She didn't look surprised. "I've been catching up on the news. Did you know that they're making a big push on Mars tonight? It's a huge attack, with like dozens of samurai working together. I think I saw Deus Ex there."

"The Mars stuff is public?" I asked.

"Someone had to let people know where all the samurai have gone," Lucy said. "It leaked a while ago, but now it's more official. Anyway, the big push is right now. Things should be heating up soon."

"Damn," I said. "I've been more out of touch than I expected."

"You've been busy . . . for a vacation," Lucy said.

"I guess so," I said. I started to look for my things. Then Lucy shook her head and started to *find* my things. They were exactly where I'd been looking, but somehow she was pulling them out as if I'd missed them, which wasn't possible. I was sure I'd searched.

Frowning at Lucy's magical ability to find stuff, I started to gather all of my things in one place. I'd need to bring my Trench Maker, a Laser Pointer, and ammo for both. My undersuit, of course. And if we were venturing out of the city, my good armor.

I had a few loose grenades in our little armory/Lucy's walk-in closet. Those could come as well.

"Are you gearing up now?" Lucy asked.

"Shower first," I said. "Maybe a cold one."

"Cold?" she repeated.

"*Someone* couldn't keep her hands to herself on the drive over, and now I'm afraid that I'm not in the right state of mind to be shooting aliens."

"Oh," Lucy said. She grinned. "You know, we do have a pretty big shower, and you did say you had an hour, didn't you?"

CHAPTER FIFTY-FOUR

IT'S FUN TO PLAY WITH THE PMC, EH?

As a soldier, you need to be aware that you are NOT a mercenary. You are a part of a greater fighting force whose goals are to defend the people and integrity of your nation. You are a fighter for justice, not mere credits.

—US3 army propaganda, 2042

I hugged my bike close, the rumble of its engine sending a bassy vibration through me, which was nice. I was still feeling fresh and tingly from my shared shower, but the flight was giving me time to recenter myself.

What was coming up was probably not going to be fun and games.

I got a warning from the city's automated traffic systems as I shot past the exterior wall of the city. Myalis calmed them down for me, and probably told whatever automated AA they had to chill out as well.

Flying past the security of the wall wasn't exactly safe, but I figured it wasn't all that dangerous either. Not as long as I was moving quickly and staying far off the ground. Anything that could attack me would have to come from the air, and this close to the city it would get gunned down in a blink.

I just wanted to see things with my own eye, and I figured it was worth the risk.

The northern wall stretched across the city. There was a river here, trailing from a lake in the west and leaving out of the east. The main part of the river was buried under the megastructure of the city proper, but some parts of the source lake were visible from my altitude.

The wall circled around the entire northern part of the city. A flat gray of concrete and metal, with evenly spaced towers along its length.

It would have been impossibly imposing from the ground, but from up here, it wasn't quite that impressive.

For one thing, the wall wasn't straight. It didn't just curve out to encompass the swell of the city, but it had small, randomly placed sections that pushed further out, or that were uneven to account for crooked terrain.

The suburbs around this part of New Montreal were still lived in, even those beyond the wall. Probably because the wall wasn't the only wall in the area.

There was a second, much less impressive set of fortifications some ways out from the main wall. "How far is that second wall from the big one?" I asked.

The spacing isn't even, but the farthest section is four kilometers away.

That was a fair bit of space "Why was this section left here?" I asked with a gesture to the space.

I believe because some four million people live here. There are several small cities growing out from New Montreal. To the west is Deux Montagnes, then Saint Coke of Cola, Nimbleland, and Rosemere. You're currently above Nimbleland. The secondary wall meets the main wall not too far from where we are. But there's a tertiary wall installation around Mascouche and the city of Amazon Prime. There are an additional twelve million living in those suburbs.

"And these walls keep them safe enough?" I asked.

That's unlikely. The quality of the walls varies significantly from city to city. From what I can find with a cursory look, the walls are paid for by either corporate entities, or the cities themselves.

Which meant lowest bidder shit all the way, at a time when no one wanted to spend anything. "Right, I can see how this'll go already," I said.

Gomorrah had sent me a ping with a location to meet. It was just outside of the main wall, next to one of the big openings designed to let traffic in. I noticed the spot, but flew on anyways, making a quick circuit along the outer wall. There were some defensive installations out here, and a few of them looked like gated camps and muster grounds on the outer edge of the suburbs.

At a guess, the local PMCs had discovered that buying lots of high-risk land was suddenly worth it for them. Or they were being given the right to use the land. Or . . . well, it didn't matter. The *outer*-outer walls were mostly mesh and barbed wire, with the occasional cement wall that wasn't much more than three meters tall and already crooked.

Some sections of the walls were new. Others had probably been around for a few decades. It was easy to tell the old apart from the new. The new didn't have graffiti covering their every surface.

I turned back toward the big city and flew over to where Gomorrah's signal called for me. I found her *Fury* parked in the middle of a wide open exterior parking lot in front of what looked like a recently converted grocery store.

There were two rows of thirty main battle tanks. Then four land fortresses parked nearby. Men and women were swarming around, though it didn't look like they were moving with any real hurry.

I noticed a couple of squads of three-legged mechs parked nearby too, along with some APCs and smaller wheeled tanks.

I couldn't see Gomorrah, but I imagined she wouldn't be too far from her car, so I came down and parked nearby, then slipped off my bike and tried not to make it obvious that I was stretching the kinks out of my back. There was something of a crowd here, after all.

A row of cheap mobile homes and trailers was parked to one side, all of them so close together that there was no way they could open their doors fully. Each had a sign painted on the front, and it looked like they were serving as barracks for the soldiers.

And there were soldiers.

I was used to working with PMCs. Well, moderately used to it. There were a few styles that they tended to fall into. The gruff, tacticool ones with a big budget; the ones that sold safety for cheap and kept things cheap by being cheap; and then the *really* low-end PMC outfits that were little more than gangs with some administrators. Burlington's militia had stood out to me as a sort of middle ground between the super cheap mall-cop PMCs and the high-end corpo outfits.

This wasn't any of that. This was the army.

Men and women in fatigues, with minimal cybernetics. Lots of very standardized gear, but not so cheap that it was worthless.

That, and the kind of armored force that even a corp might have a hard time justifying.

Tanks were expensive. I knew this because while Lucy liked watching cute videos of baby animals, the algorithm tended to push pseudo-military content my way. Stuff about tanks and cool army tech shit. The content wavered, and it would only come up every so often . . . but I still had a soft spot in my heart for large lumbering vehicles of war.

So I knew that they were expensive as fuck, not just to buy, but also to maintain. My mech was really driving that point home too. And my mech wasn't a fifty-ton tank built by humans. It was probably a lot easier to repair and maintain than any of the tanks parked out here.

A soldier ran up to me and saluted. "Samurai Stray Cat. Samurai Gomorrah is waiting in the command unit. Follow me, please."

No nonsense there. And no groveling either.

Then again, it was late, and things looked like they were winding down for everyone here. I didn't comment as I followed the soldier toward a mobile base near the center of the lot.

It was one of those typical eight-wheeled behemoths, with multiple gun emplacements bristling out of every corner and more turrets on the roof, along with a ramp that jutted out of the front a little.

I found Gomorrah within, leaning over a table with a digital screen for a surface, along with two officers. "Hello," she said. "You're twenty minutes past our meeting time."

"Huh . . . more punctual than I'd have guessed," I said. "So, what's going on?"

"Long version or short?" she asked.

I could tell from the glance the officers shared that they were caught a little flatfooted at the moment. "Short?"

"Short version it is. Maybe that'll make up for you being late." She tapped the screen, which was currently displaying a map of the area I'd just flown over, though zoomed out and in daylight colors. "The convoy tomorrow will be heading northbound along this road, until they reach here." She tapped a point some fifteen kilometers past the shitty wall.

"Alright," I said.

"The problem tonight is this." She pointed to a red circle a bit to the west. "There's a hive somewhere in this area, and it'll be the perfect spot to ambush the convoy. Since the Antithesis have been smarter than usual, there's a good chance this hive will be trouble. Our mission is to burn it down."

"Easy enough," I said.

Maybe this wouldn't take all night after all.

CHAPTER FIFTY-FIVE

I MEANT TO DO THAT

After the first incursion, the people of the world turned to the scientific community for answers. Samples of the first aliens to make verifiable landfall on Earth were brought to labs across the country, footage was shared, and speculation and hypothesis began.

On the same day as the Antithesis arrived, a whole new branch of scientific study was born.

—MIT pamphlet on Xenology, 2026

Gomorrah and I hitched a ride in the back of a troop transport.

Not one of those big armored ones. This was basically a four-wheel-drive truck, with a low bed filled with twin rows of seats facing each other and an optional tarp roof—currently down.

It wasn't fancy, but it was pretty fast. Or the driver was pretty fast in any case, cutting through red lights like it was nothing, and the escort of light-armored vehicles probably helped. People tended to slow down when half a dozen cars with turrets on their roofs came rushing down the road, police-lights flashing and sirens wailing the entire time.

I had expected our plan to be simple. Gomorrah and I would rock up to the hive, burn and-slash-or explode it up, then head back home for a quick nap.

Instead, we were heading to the hive with an escort. A full platoon of force recon.

I glanced at the row of men and a few women next to me. They were serious-faced, probably because their sergeant had immediately chewed out the guy who'd dared to whistle when we came in. The lot of them were dressed for war. Thick gambesons to stop bites, armored collars around their heads, and helmets that covered everything but their mouths and noses.

They had a very standardized kit. Some sort of bullpup assault rifle, a few magazines strapped to their chest, a sidearm at their hip, and the same pale-green armor all around, with a few highlighter-green bands around their rather ugly helmets.

The only good thing I could say about their gear, at least as far as looks went, was that it would make Gomorrah and I stand out.

I got a ping from Gomorrah, and glanced across at her a moment before we were connected for a call. "Stop staring. You'll make them nervous," I heard inside my helmet. Notably, I couldn't hear her saying it aloud.

"I'm not usually this close to the soldiers while sitting in a car with nothing better to do," I said, after making sure my voice wouldn't escape my helmet. "Are these guys good?"

"Seventy-Seventh recon," Gomorrah said. "They're pretty much the best. At least as far as normal soldiers go. They've cleared out hives without any samurai support before. Even if we weren't here, they'd still be rushing over to the hive right now."

"Huh. Brave of them," I said.

"Someone has to do it," Gomorrah said. "I think a lot of them have family in New Montreal. They have a reason to fight. So stop staring."

I raised my hands a little, a small gesture of surrender before I leaned back into my seat. It wasn't a very comfortable seat. "We'll see if we can't impress them, then," I said.

"I think shooting straight and not tripping over your own feet would impress them a lot," Gomorrah said.

I laughed. "Right, right. I'll try to be halfway competent for once. Are we expecting a lot of resistance?"

"Not really. The hives here aren't exactly dormant at night, but they seem less busy than usual. Atyacus explained it to me once. Something about the sun being down, the temperature dropping, and also there being less human activity and aggression. The Antithesis are very good at noticing patterns like that. So night is when they do a lot of digesting and expanding the hive."

I nodded along. I hadn't made a point of studying the aliens, but that sounded about right, at least from what I'd picked up from movies and TV. There were probably people out there with entire degrees about Antithesis behavior. In comparison, I was working from personal experience and a few tidbits I'd caught along the way. I'd trust Atyacus on this one.

We reached the secondary wall, and I noted that some of the buildings nearest the wall had been collapsed. I hadn't actually noticed that from above. It looked like someone was smart enough to create a killing field on the inside of the wall as well as the exterior.

The gate leading out of the city was manned, but they were quick to let us through.

Almost the instant we were past the gate, the sirens and lights were shut off. I hadn't realized it in the city, but the cars were practically silent. No engine rumbles, and their suspensions were good enough that they barely made any noise as we rode ahead.

I leaned back, glancing over the side of the truck. The cars ahead were turning off their lights, and soon the transport we were in did the same. The entire convoy was running dark on a road I could only see because of my better eye and my helmet's optics.

"Hope the driver can see," I muttered.

"Don't worry about it," Gomorrah said. "I vetted every one of the convoy drivers before we left. Otherwise we would have met them with the *Fury*."

"Still don't know why we couldn't go ahead," I said.

"Because we want the nice soldiers to want to protect us," Gomorrah said. "And they can help carry things too. It doesn't hurt to be kind."

I shrugged. Couldn't say I cared too much either way, but maybe she was right.

In any case, with the speed we were going at—probably twice the speed limit—it only took a few minutes to reach our spot.

The convoy slowed down, decelerating until we were all moving at a slow crawl. Then the car at the front went off the road and into a field, using a small dirt bridge to cross over a wide ditch. The moment we were off-road, I pulled back into the seat and sat properly. The suspension might have been good, but we were crossing an open field. It had probably been . . . corn or something, once. Now it was nothing but bumps for as far as I could see.

The off-roading continued for a good long while. We couldn't move as fast out here, and when we crossed from one field to another, it had to be done across more small dirt bridges over deep ditches. Once, the entire convoy stopped so that a truck just like the one we were in—but with gear in the back instead of soldiers and samurai—could slip ahead. A few guys jumped out, then literally installed an unfolding bridge for us to cross in about three minutes flat.

It took another ten minutes before the entire group came to a stop, this time for real.

The soldiers stood up, the sergeant in the group making a few quick gestures accompanied by a few clicking noises. Everyone disembarked, and they were going slow, moving so that they didn't make much noise.

Some noise was unavoidable, but they were doing what they could to be quiet. "Silent bunch," I muttered.

"You might learn something from observing them," Gomorrah commented.

I blinked, then glanced her way. "You okay? You're testier than usual."

"Sorry," she replied instantly. "Just . . . a lot on my mind. But you're right, I shouldn't take it out on you."

"It's fine. If I couldn't handle some amount of snark, I wouldn't be able to survive." I patted her on the back. "Would burning some xenos brighten up your mood?" I asked.

"It would."

"Alright, then let's go set some aliens on fire."

We clambered out of the back of the truck and were met by three sergeants and a guy that had lieutenant stripes. "Samurai Gomorrah, Samurai Stray Cat. We're ready to begin the operation."

"Any details we should know?" Gomorrah asked.

"Our latest satellite scan paints the hive as being within a two kilometer-wide radius of this forest. Mostly on the surface. We'd like to go in quiet, if at all possible," he said.

The more aliens that died without the others realizing, the easier it would be for the soldiers, I figured. "I can do quiet," I said. "At least until it's time for the bombs to go off. I'm not sure how stealthy fire is."

"It's bright, but fire doesn't need to be loud," Gomorrah said. "We can manage. Set your IFFs on. Let's get to the center of the hive, then burn it out from within."

That sounded like a plan to me. A fun one, even. I shouldered my gun, then started off for the forest. "I'll do a bit of scouting ahead," I said before going invisible.

It was just in time, too, because I tripped on my next step.

Fucking muddy fields.

CHAPTER FIFTY-SIX

COUNTRY CAT, CITY CAT

Keep the chatter to a minimum, we don't need to embarrass ourselves in front of the samurai. You don't see them goofing around, do you?

—Lieutenant Moreau, 2057

I reached the edge of the forest before realizing that I hadn't connected to the team comms. Fortunately, while I was an absent-minded moron at times, Myalis was on the ball.

Yes, I did grab a connection to the intra-team communication network. It's hard not to. The encryption is extremely basic. I suspect that they want to make it easy for other organizations to tap into their lines.

Why would they . . . actually, that kind of made sense. You wouldn't want a creative civilian with the right augs to pop onto your lines, but letting the local PMCs know your plans wasn't a bad move, especially not for a team that specialized in taking out aliens. It was probably easy to listen in because they wanted others to know they were around.

Or something like that. Maybe they'd just cheaped out on encryption stuff. I hadn't noticed a Meshrunner on the team, which made sense if they were mostly fighting aliens.

Linking you now.

I heard a faint staticky hiss that was easy to ignore. Then a few sniffles and light coughs that weren't so easy to miss. It seemed as if the entire group was on one shared channel. The soldiers were keeping to themselves, not speaking up, and their mics seemed like they were at least designed not to pick up breathing, but still, every cleared throat was loud and clear.

I opened a tab on my augs and fiddled with the volume. I didn't want to miss an alien sneaking up on me because I was distracted by Jenkins with the sore throat.

"This is Stray Cat, I'm on the edge of the forest. Uh, over," I said, trying to sound at least a little professional.

"Read you, Stray Cat," someone replied. A small text box at the edge of my vision identified the voice as Lieutenant Moreau. "We're catching up now. Anything to report?"

I looked around me. The forest was real . . . forest-y; more so than that zoo Lucy and I had visited. There were bushes all over, fallen branches blocking off otherwise passable parts of the woods, and the terrain went from flat-ish agricultural land to a hilly mess.

"Looks like shit, but no aliens, over."

There were a few restrained chuckles on the line, some that turned into coughs. I had the impression that this bunch wasn't used to joking around. They were all very serious about their work. Or were they laughing at me? That was probably fair. I imagined that those that didn't take it seriously became a pension check for their family rather quickly.

"We're moving in. If you want to press ahead and scout, we'd appreciate it," Moreau said.

"Pressing ahead," I said. I shouldered my gun and slipped into the brush. My invisibility would be useful here, of course, but I quickly discovered that being unseen didn't mean that I wouldn't be noticed. The ground was covered in a layer of broken branches and piles of leaves. Every step came with a crack and shuffle that my boots could only do so much to muffle. Worse, there were bushes all over, and they kept brushing against my coat with a faint rustle.

The wind coming in from the flatter fields around the forest helped a little. It made trees sway faintly and created a fair bit of noise to camouflage my own motions, but that would only go so far.

It was actually frustrating how out of place I felt here. I was a city girl; I wasn't made for woods and shit.

I at least tried not to make too much noise as I skulked through the forest. I had to move in a zigzag, avoiding trees and bushes, and sometimes I had to stumble over fallen branches. After a dozen meters, I realized that I'd gotten turned around. Not entirely—I could still see the edge of the woods, and I could make out the shadowy forms of the soldiers and Gomorrah coming up toward the edge of the forest—but I was no longer traveling in the direction I'd intended.

"Myalis, I need a small map up on my HUD. And a compass," I muttered.

Adding that now.

I got both. A small, semi-transparent map in the corner of my vision, as well as a compass running as a band across the top. I turned my head left and right, and the compass followed. We'd entered from almost due south, so I had to go north to get deeper in. Nice and easy.

I continued on my way in, realigning myself as I went. The map had a few dots where the soldiers were, so I was able to keep track.

"Hey, Lieutenant Moreau, I'm not seeing any xenos yet," I said. "Lots of plant life still."

"Our satellite images suggest that they haven't hit this part of the woods yet," the lieutenant said.

"Just keep moving," Gomorrah's voice came over the comms. "We'll see where they reached."

I shrugged and kept moving, and some three dozen meters later, I discovered that she was right.

There were fewer bushes and large plants here, not because the trees blocked the sun, or because the ground was rockier, but because they'd all been ripped out.

Trails of shredded plants and loose dirt flowed back and away from where I stood, marking the places where the bushes had passed, and I could easily make out the holes in the ground where the bushes had been.

"Shit," I said as I knelt down next to one hole and touched it.

"Stray Cat? Anything to report?" the lieutenant asked. He'd overheard that.

"Found a spot some . . . twenty-five meters ahead of your group. Bunch of bushes were ripped out of the ground and dragged away, heading more or less north. A bit east."

"Noted. That'll be the Antithesis grabbing biological matter for the hive."

"Right," I said. I'd never really seen an area like this before, but it made some sense. The aliens ate pretty much anything organic in their hives. Dragging things back only made sense, then. Given enough time, I was sure they'd come back for the roots and grass and all of the smaller plant life that they missed.

Maybe it was a good thing that most grasses and bushes and such were going extinct. It meant fewer things for the aliens to feed on.

I stood back up and continued, but only for a little bit before I stopped again.

There was something that my vision caught, a faint glimmer in the air.

If my augs and eyes were normal, I'd have dismissed it as a glitch, but I had good shit—Myalis didn't *have* glitchy gear. I narrowed my eyes and scanned the forest ahead, then I moved up and down a little. If anyone could see me, I'd probably look stupid, doing half-squats in a forest, but it worked.

I caught that glimmer again, and now that I was looking for it, it was easier to find. It was a wire. A thin thread that cut across the space between two trees. I noticed a few more above me, and some at ground level. Hell, I noticed one snapped around my lower leg.

"What am I looking at, Myalis?"

Without closer inspection, it's impossible to say, however, I predict with over 80 percent certainty that these are the webs left by model sevens. Communication strands. They can also serve as tripwires.

"LT, hold," I said.

"Holding," the lieutenant said. I noticed the dots on the map freeze and I imagined the soldiers tensing up behind me.

"Found some wires. Look like spiderwebs, hard as fuck to spot."

"Prep for ambush!" the lieutenant snapped in a low hiss, and I saw the dots regrouping into a rough circle in a hurry. I heard them too. So far, they'd been moving so quietly that I could only barely make out the occasional snap of a branch. Now they were hustling to get into formation. I wasn't expecting them to move so suddenly or get so loud.

I raised my gun too and waited with bated breath.

Nothing showed up, though.

"Huh . . . maybe that was a dud?" I asked.

"That's possible, if there isn't a mo—"

I stopped listening to what the lieutenant was saying as I jumped aside.

Something huge and spiky crashed through the branches above and then came rushing down. I think it would have missed me if I stayed still, but I jumped aside anyway.

The large ball of spikes thumped into the ground, then burst apart, scattering dozens of long spines across the forest.

I covered my head and felt a few pinpricks stabbing into my suit and the less armored joints between. "Fuck," I said as I looked up.

It was an artillery ball, flung by a model fifteen with surprising accuracy.

"I think we've been spotted," I said unnecessarily.

"Good," Gomorrah said. I heard a *whoosh*, and when I looked back to where the soldiers were, I could finally see the orange glow of a light in their midst. The pilot light on Gomorrah's flamethrower. "I'm not one for all of this stealth business," she said.

CHAPTER FIFTY-SEVEN

HIT EVERYTHING, EVERYWHERE, ALL AT ONCE

Mortar fire isn't great against heavily wooded areas. Not for the first round.

Once the forest is burned down, it's a perfectly viable tool.

—Sergeant O'Mally, 1978

The moment after the Antithesis' artillery strike landed, the lieutenant called for his guys to spread out, watch for enemies, and open fire on anything shooting our way.

"Mortar teams need coordinates for the enemy artillery," Moreau said over the line. He was surprisingly calm, all things considered.

"We have mortar teams?" I asked.

"Two of the trucks have roof-mounted mortars," Gomorrah explained. "If you spot something, let us know."

"Got it," I said as I climbed back to my feet. The forest was lighting up as the soldiers behind me gave up on going full infrared and switched on their helmet-mounted lights and little flashlights clipped onto their rifles.

The light, motion, and sudden sound didn't go unnoticed. I started to see movement through the forest in the opposite direction. It wasn't time for me to be laying my ass down on the ground and waiting, so I rose up, brought my rifle to bear, and started to move sideways.

I trusted that the soldiers behind us were pretty decent, but I didn't want to be in the crossfire anyway. My armor was good, but I wasn't sure if it was "point blank armor-piercing rifle round" good. Hell, even if it was, that shit probably hurt.

I was still moving to the side when I noticed some aliens skulking through the underbrush. Small forms, their bodies a deep brown, with a darker green carapace that was molted and patterned not too differently from some of the pine trees and spikier bushes around.

If they had been standing stock-still, I might have missed them, but their movement gave them away.

I squinted, then raised my gun and took a few quick shots.

Silenced rounds, delivered from an invisible person, with the slight flash hidden by the trees meant the aliens had no idea what hit them. A few missed shots kicked up dirt, or dug into some of the trees, but most of them . . . well, some of them, at least, found their way into alien flesh and they went down.

"Just model threes here so far," I said over our shared comms.

"Likely the early warning models they have on the periphery of the hive," Gomorrah said. "We can expect a lot more resistance if we move inward."

"Yeah, sounds about right. I'm seeing a few more threads hanging around too," I said. They were damned hard to notice, with how thin and semi-transparent they were. It was only when the light from the soldiers caught them just right that I spotted the lines.

"Try not to walk into them," Moreau said as he waved some of his guys back. "They'll alert the model seventeen of your location. We don't need more biobombs hitting our location."

"Right," I said. "Can I use the lines to trace back where the seventeen is hiding? I'd like to put an end to it if it's going to be coordinating things for the bastards."

There is a relatively inexpensive non-cataloged item that should allow you to do just that. You'll need to find a piece of the biological wiring that's properly connected to the network and then touch it with the device.

"LT, can I have two minutes before you move up?" I asked. "Just hold your spot, I'll be trying something."

"Affirmative, Stray Cat."

I nodded at that, then ran into cover. "What's the thing you're talking about?" I asked Myalis. "And how's it work?"

It's a disposable frequency-tapping device. It connects to a model seventeen's network, copies the current signal going through it, then relays it once again. Most of the time the Antithesis ignores the additional signal. I won't go into the math involved, but the oscillation allows the device to pinpoint the location of the model of origin. The device costs ten points.

About as much as a single grenade? Hell, I'd made three times that just now gunning down a few randoms. "Yeah, I'll take one," I said.

The device was a small black thing, about the size of one of those old TV remotes, with a pair of metallic pincer-shaped arms sticking out of the top. There was only one button on it, and my curious press made the pinches snip closed then open again. Kind of idiot-proof.

I knelt down behind a bush, then found one of the wires on the ground. There was noise coming from deeper in the forest. The hive was waking up fully, and it didn't sound happy about our intrusion. I had to be quick.

Pinching one of those thin wires with the device, I waited for just a second before Myalis updated my HUD.

It seems as if there's more than one model linked to the network and in control of it. There are also several hundred models connected by these wires across the hive. I can pinpoint the location of several of the leads.

"Give their coords to the mortar team. Uh . . . unless it's really close to me or the soldiers. Don't wanna see us getting bombed by our own side," I told Myalis.

Noted. And sent. I'll add the coordinates to your map as well.

A few red dots appeared on my map. One of them was surprisingly close by.

"Stray Cat, we received the coordinates. Mortar team is adjusting to fire now," Lieutenant Moreau said a few seconds later. "Keep your head low. We want to start our advance right after the first strikes land."

"Copy that," I said. Then I hesitated. Was "copy" the one that meant that I understood?

I didn't have time to ask before I heard a strange, echoing whistle overhead. Three of them, all at once.

Then the mortars came rushing down some two dozen meters deeper in the woods and I ducked down by instinct just as they struck the treeline. Explosions ripped branches apart and sent wooden shrapnel flying all over.

A moment passed, as I raised my head up and looked ahead. The mortar hit had created a messy opening in the forest. Sorta. Trees had fallen over and now the path ahead was partially blocked by branches. "LT, looks like that did . . . jack shit. I think your mortar guys are striking trees and not much else. The, uh . . . canopy won't last forever, though."

"Noted. I think we only have HE shells with us, nothing penetrative. We don't have timed fuses."

"Try just shooting each target a few more times. Something will go through eventually."

"I don't know if they brought enough ammo for that," Gomorrah said. "But it should let us clear out this side, at least. You and I might have to take care of the rest ourselves."

That sucked, but whatever. I hadn't expected mortar support to begin with.

Another whistling rain of shells came down, and this time a pair of them made it through the canopy and thumped into the ground. It shook underfoot as the rounds exploded, sending up dirt and debris and flipping half of an alien carcass into the air with a spray of plant blood. "One down," I said.

"Mortar team will continue to soften up the farther targets. We're moving in," the lieutenant said.

The soldiers started to move forward behind me, and I decided to drop my invisibility and jog up to where they were waiting. I saw a few heads turn to track me with their lights before I found Gomorrah and the lieutenant in the center of the formation.

"The hive's not too far off," Gomorrah said. "Once we're on the edge, we'll move in while the soldiers keep our perimeter safe and keep the lane of retreat open."

"So we just dip in, plant a big old bomb, then run the hell away?" I asked.

"I'd couch it in more professional terms, but essentially yes," Gomorrah said.

"Alright! That's my kind of fun," I said. "Myalis, can I have a small box with a replenishing supply of resonators? Just like, six or so?"

Certainly. You're going to be handing them out to the soldiers?

"Like hotcakes," I said.

Once the box appeared, I tucked away a pair of grenades and watched two more appear in the case. There was a small dip in my points counter, but nothing bad. "LT, hand these out to the boys. They're shit at killing aliens, but they last a while and make for good . . . long-ish term deterrents."

He stared for a good long moment, then nodded his head firmly. "Thank you," he said. He sounded a little emotional about it.

"Have some of your guys plant them behind us, it'll keep a route open from here to our extract. I've got this feeling that we'll be running a lot in the next few minutes."

"Yes, ma'am," he replied.

I might have underestimated how enthusiastic they'd be, because the soldiers, as silent and professional as they were, were soon passing resonators off to each other. A few were activated and flung way out into the woods.

Well, whatever. It meant more dead aliens and more points for me, so I wasn't going to complain too much about it.

CHAPTER FIFTY-EIGHT

BURN SILENT INTO THAT GOOD NIGHT

There's no such thing as an unprepared samurai.
Only a samurai who isn't prepared at the moment . . .
What do you mean, that's an oxymoron?

—Longbow, to a new samurai, 2056

Walking toward mortar fire was . . . probably not the wisest thing I'd ever done, but so far the army had been professional, and I trusted them to hit more or less where we told them to, instead of bringing down shells right on my pretty head.

Gomorrah and I were at the front of the formation, which had stretched out to the sides with a pair of "wings." Some soldiers were running backward toward the trucks and the edge of the forest. They were the ones laying quick traps with resonators behind us, setting up a route that we could use to extract from when the time came to run the hell away.

I raised my Laser Pointer up and tapped a model four center-mass with a trio of shots, which sent it flopping down, very much dead. Gomorrah and I were in the middle of the formation and a bit ahead of all the soldiers. They were moving at a very slow, steady pace. Gom and I were moving at a less slow, less steady pace.

"They make walking in the woods look so easy," Gomorrah muttered.

I chuckled. "I know, right? These fucking roots, man."

"Burn the whole place down. See how these bushes and stuff handle being turned to ash. That'll be easier to cross."

"Hehe," I said. It wasn't my most convincing chuckle. "Just . . . hold off on that until we're through, yeah?"

"We'll see," Gomorrah said. She stomped ahead, and I jogged to catch up. I popped a few more rounds into some aliens that my augs highlighted for me. The light from the soldiers behind and from the pilot light on the end of Gomorrah's flamethrower was useful, but it wasn't exactly lighting up the whole world out here. Some aliens were sneaky enough that I only caught sight of them as they moved. They'd show up in flashes when the mortar team struck out far ahead of us, just quick glimpses that disappeared behind the falling canopy.

"You have any ideas for how to get rid of the hive?" I asked. Gomorrah took a moment to torch the upper half of a tree that had fallen into our path.

"I figured you'd want to bomb it," Gomorrah said. "But we don't want to alert all of the other local hives to anything going on here, so I'm afraid we'll have to be a bit more subtle with the bombing."

"Right," I agreed. Bombs could be subtle.

We crossed from the part of the forest that still had some vegetation into an area that had been completely cleared of plant life. Even the trees looked like they had been stripped of their bark, and a number of them had their branches pruned, with what looked suspiciously like little bite marks around the points where those branches met the trunks.

Gomorrah stopped, and I did the same a moment later. She raised her flamethrower, then fired a cyclonic blast of twisting flames into the branches above.

Usually, the Antithesis were deathly quiet. It was one of those things that made them so obviously un-Earthly. They never made a sound. No noise, no screaming, no growling.

These squealed as they burned, however. Faint cries that I suspected were more about their lungs boiling than actual screams of pain, but it was still a surreal noise to hear while burning carcasses fell from the trees.

I could almost, *almost* see what Gomorrah enjoyed in those flames.

I raised my own rifle and put a few out of their misery, then started scanning ahead. The fire wouldn't go unnoticed. Not with the dark of night to contrast against the glowing tornado of flames and the now-burning canopy above.

Just as I suspected, some aliens took umbrage at Gomorrah's actions, and the alert was sounded. Dozens of blurs started to rush out toward us. Some were covered in thin layers of fresh mud, camouflaging them against the ground as they slithered forward.

I took aim, then started firing. A moment later, the area filled with far more noise as the soldiers did the same. Their guns were equipped with large suppressors on the end, and those did a lot to quiet them down, but they were far from perfect. There was a constant cracking sound, like a thousand whips going off at once, as the first wave of the hive was annihilated.

"Hold!" the lieutenant called to his troops.

I put down a final dog-like model three, then glanced around. There were lots of dead aliens, most of them spread out ahead of us, and plenty of seriously fucked-up forestry, but not too much else. The guns mounted to my shoulders scanned along with me, and I switched to infrared, then to other forms of vision, just in case.

"Looks clear," I said.

"For now," Gomorrah said. "Let's keep moving. I want to get a little closer in." She stepped ahead, stomping through a fire without a care in the world before I jogged after her. I didn't step right through the flames, though. Fuck having fireproof gear on, I wasn't risking it.

I suspect that the main hive is just ahead. You should be within a hundred meters of it already.

"Noted," I muttered.

There were fewer trees as we moved in deeper. There were stumps, however, and it looked like they'd been assaulted by the mother of all beavers too. Whatever trucks might have fallen had been dragged away, and the ground was picked clean of detritus, bushes, and fallen branches.

We could all see the hive ahead, but I didn't know what to do about it.

I'd seen some hives before. They'd all been dug into the ground though, or tucked away into a building somewhere. This was . . . different. "What in the fuck is that?" I asked.

A normal above-ground hive.

The hive looked like an anthill, if ants slurped up their body mass in steroids every day. It was a massive brown bump, three times as tall as I was, and covered in thick, half-buried roots. The roots had small branches coming off of them, with deep, dark-green leaves covering them. From above it probably looked a little strange, but not unlike a weird tree surrounded by a clearing.

From here, it was clear that this wasn't normal, not natural.

"Stop gawking," Gomorrah said over a private channel. "This is what normal hives look like when they don't have an environment to hide in. Check the entrances."

I shot her a glare. I wasn't gawking. But she was making sense, I supposed. The dirt had clearly been pulled from all around, and then piled up over the hill. There were small entrances and holes all over. Some were small enough that my closed fist would barely fit. Others I could crawl into without difficulty. Most had roots around their entrance, acting as supports of sorts.

There was some actual engineering going on here. Weird, fucky alien engineering, but engineering all the same.

And I was looking forward to blowing it up.

"Down!" Gomorrah shouted.

I didn't question her before I leapt down, crouching on one knee almost too slowly to avoid something blurring past over my left shoulder. Gomorrah had dove aside, missing the blur altogether.

Some poor fuck behind us wasn't so lucky. I heard him screaming a moment before some spines rained down around me. Another Antithesis artillery ball? I noticed dirt raining down from one of the holes.

The damned hive could shoot outward? "Is that artillery inside the hive?" I asked.

It's likely that there's a model fifteen within, with enough space to maneuver. Notice the small wires leading out of the hive. A model seventeen is likely acting as a spotter for it.

I didn't know that was possible at all. Still, we had our own support like that. I sent the coordinates to the mortar team, then raised my gun and took some shots into and around the hole that the spiky ball had been fired from.

Aliens started to pour out of the ground around us. Mostly smaller models that popped out of hidden tunnels and scurried our way. Headless, monkey-like model tens scampered and tossed themselves toward us.

The model tens were expected. They lived around hives, tended to them. I'd seen some of these freaky little monkeys with no heads and knife-hands before. They went down easily when we shot at them.

Some . . . tentacled things that I didn't recognize got rounds punched through them as well.

I saw and heard a few resonators fly overhead while the night was lit up by muzzle flashes and swaying flashlights.

"Myalis!" I shouted as I reloaded in a hurry. "I need something that produces some light! And I need . . . fuck it, something that'll shake the earth a little. Let's collapse their little anthill right on their ugly heads."

"I like that idea!" Gomorrah shouted next to me before she opened up with her flamer and drew a line of fire across the clearing. "If you're gonna do that, please do so in a hurry."

"Hey, it wouldn't be so slow if I'd known what we were getting into," I snapped back.

This whole thing was a disorganized mess.

Still . . . kinda fun.

CHAPTER FIFTY-NINE

HOT HIVES IN YOUR AREA!

We don't like the term "trailer trash." We find it all sorts of offensive to our long heritage and ancestral culture. My great-great-grandfather bought that trailer with his own money.

If you need to call us something, then perhaps "trailer-privileged community," would be more respectable.

—Jim "All Teeth" Vincerella, 2038

"Myalis, 'nade. Preferably high explosive," I said as I brought my left arm back. Something small and weighty fell into my hand, and my thumb naturally touched upon a trigger. It started to beep a moment before I flung my arm forward.

The grenade sailed through the air, then smacked on the bottom lip of one of the holes in the hive. It bounced, then rolled in, disappearing from sight into the darkness within.

I brought my arm back around and continued to shoot.

Gomorrah was laying down a wall of fire that didn't seem to want to extinguish, even with nothing to burn. It looked like her gun had shifted from firing . . . well, fire, to launching large, swelling masses of some goopy material that formed a large barricade ahead of us.

That barricade was, of course, on fire, and any alien that tried to climb over it soon found themselves glued onto a surface that was literally burning. They'd tug and thrash and sink in deeper into the goop even as they burned alive.

It was a sight to see.

I put a few of the smaller ones out of their misery, but I had bigger, meaner targets to focus on just behind the line of fire.

Then the grenade in the hill went off. Myalis hadn't cheaped out on the "high" part of high explosive.

The mound exploded outward, man-sized chunks of dirt and roots flying away from the top while a rush of looser dirt was flung upward and out.

I ducked my head as small pebbles and clods came raining down all around me. Some of them landed atop Gomorrah's fire, as well as a few larger stones that could serve as stepping stones across the barricade, at least until she started hosing those down too. She wasn't about to leave a single square centimeter uncovered in fire.

"Did that do it?" I asked as I stood back up.

The tactical comms from the soldiers registered a few crackles. One guy was swearing up a storm after being smacked in the face by a jagged piece of rock. I felt a little bad for him, but that was the price for playing with high explosives.

"No notification," Gomorrah pointed out. "Atyacus thinks the hive's still alive."

"I can toss in a few more," I suggested.

That stunt had earned me plenty more points than the cost of a single grenade, after all.

"Let's move up instead. We don't know how deep it goes. Lieutenant, hold here, if you can. If it becomes too hot, then feel free to start pulling back," I said.

"Acknowledged, Samurai Stray Cat. We'll hold," the LT said.

That was simple enough, then. "So, we charge in?" I asked Gomorrah as I took a second to reload.

"We can at least get to the edge of the hive," Gomorrah said. "I have some new equipment that I haven't had the opportunity to field test yet. Your gear is heat-proof, right?"

"Uh, a little?"

"We might want to set my next purchase off from afar, then. Just in case. I'm looking into replacing my skin with something less flammable. You might want to do the same."

"I'll add it to the list," I said.

Once I got back home, I was probably going to give in and get a few upgrades. I didn't wanna go full cyborg, but maybe being faster and tougher wouldn't be so bad. I'd been planning on doing this for a while anyway.

Gomorrah moved up, and I trailed right behind her. She'd opened a gap in the wall of fire. It was still damned close to the flames, but there was enough space that we could cross without getting cooked.

The Antithesis had noticed too, and were crowding on the other side. At least, until Gomorrah switched the nozzle from "tight" to "spray" and lit the fuckers right up. I shot into the bunch as well, punching holes into the tougher models that hadn't seemed to mind being on fire.

Honestly though, this . . . wasn't that much of a challenge.

I had decent gear, better than what any soldier had. Gomorrah was burning everything down, and we still had a few mortar strikes coming in and blowing up the Antithesis on the other side of the hill long before they could get to us. The soldiers were staying behind, but that didn't mean they weren't working. They fired ahead, more often than not landing shots that had aliens flopping down before they could do anything.

We reached the hive, and I stepped up to the edge of it and aimed down into the hole. There were large roots squirming around inside, and a few smaller models trying to climb their way out of the crater we'd left. I put them down, taking my time while Gomorrah knelt down next to me. She tossed something small down the chute and it made a loud beeping noise before going quiet.

"The hive extends another five meters down, with some tendrils reaching the water table below," she said.

"That doesn't sound good."

"I doubt they'll have spread through the entire thing. They probably just tapped into it for fresh water. Even the Antithesis need water to operate. Well, they use it when they have it, at least."

"So, blow it all to hell?" I asked.

"More like burn it all," she suggested. Gomorrah summoned up a small box, opened it, then tugged out a cylinder with a pair of handholds on the sides. It reminded me a little of those rugged speakers some cool types carried around and set on the street corners they hung out on so that everyone could enjoy the shit noise they called music. Only this one had a bit more "bomb" in its DNA.

Gomorrah tossed it down into the hole, then sprayed the top of it with burning goop.

"Is that, uh, wise?" I asked.

"It's fireproof," she said. "At least, until I set it off. We *definitely* shouldn't be here when it goes off."

"Alrighty," I said as I started back. We beat a steady retreat. By the time we were back at Gomorrah's firewall, there was barely any Antithesis resistance left.

The soldiers were waiting for us still, and we all started back through the woods as a big unit. There was no stealth this time. We had lights on, and the resonators I'd given them were screeching along our entire path.

"We're far enough," Gomorrah said after a long silence.

I didn't have time to respond before she activated her bomb.

I felt the rush of warmth pressing against my back, as if I was standing next to a bum fire. The forest lit up in reds and oranges, and when I looked back and squinted, I saw that the sky was painted in the same colors.

"Wow. Lots of fire. But uh, is that it? I expected the big boom to be bigger?"

"Eh, it's medium-sized," she said. "It'll boil the water table a little, but that's probably for the best. Most Antithesis don't survive boiling like that.

We're going to need to comb through the unburnt parts of the forest for remnants."

Lieutenant Moreau shielded his eyes while looking around. "We'll have a team come in and do just that," he said. "That's one of our specialties."

"Let them know how that goes, then. I don't see much fun in rooting around in the dirt for a few last aliens," I said. It was important work, but it sounded tedious as hell.

"Do you . . . want us to start right now, ma'am?" the lieutenant asked.

I blinked, then checked my wording there. "No, I meant . . . just make sure it's done. I'm sure your guys want some time off as much as I do. Not that tonight was very hard. This was pretty easy, actually." Well, maybe not for that one guy who had a battle buddy pressing a bandage to what looked like a broken nose at the back.

"A couple thousand points, but relatively low-risk," Gomorrah said. "I'm starting to understand and appreciate those samurai who specialize specifically in hive removal like this. It might be tedious, but it's not nearly as dangerous as being on the front line of a large surge, or tripping over first responders during an active incursion."

"Yeah," I said. It probably took a special kind of nut job to want to be out there when an incursion was just starting up. On the edges it probably wasn't so bad, but I was pretty sure the center of a new incursion had all sorts of nasties.

Then again, that's why people like Deus Ex showed up.

"Hey, any news from Mars?" I asked Gomorrah after switching to a private channel.

"I haven't looked into it in a few hours, but they were launching a big offensive last I checked. If it goes well, I think they'll be on their way back."

"Huh," I said. So, no new news. Still, I wasn't expecting that they'd have too difficult of a time. "So we'll be able to chill while the big boys do all the hard work?"

"I hope so," Gomorrah said. "But their return might be a while off. Travel from Earth to Mars isn't instantaneous, you know?"

"Right, right," I said before I sighed and dropped the subject. "So . . . think I can bum a ride back home? We do live in the same building and all."

Gomorrah just sighed.

CHAPTER SIXTY

HOW TO SKIN A CAT

Hair loss is such a 2010s problem. Beautiful, full, healthy hair! Hair so strong you can strangle a man with it. Hair in such a wide array of colors and styles that you'll want to replace it every week, just so that you can try something new and dazzle your friends with how incredibly unique you are!
—Because We're Worth It campaign, 2035

As much as I would have loved to sleep in as long as I wanted, I had shit to do, and time was pressing ever onward. The night's job might have been quick, but that was only one checked thing off an ever-growing to-do list.

Myalis woke me up with increasingly hard nudges at around five in the morning.

I stumbled out of bed and into the shower. Fortunately, the water did help to wake me up some, which was more than necessary. With only a few hours of sleep in me, I wasn't feeling very useful.

Some sleep was better than none, but it didn't feel like it just then.

"Alright," I said as I stepped out and smacked my cheeks before the mirror. I let out a sigh, then looked at my reflection.

I had some bags under my eyes. Nothing too alarming, but it wasn't pretty. My hair was matted down, and I could only barely make out the once-vibrant blue of one of my bangs. Still hadn't gotten around to fixing that.

Are you well?

"I'm fine," I said. "What's my point-total looking like?"

Current Points: 34,771

Not bad. I'd spent a few here and there, on consumables and also on crap that I probably didn't need, but last night's run had buffed things back up a little. "I've been putting a few things off," I said.

Are you preparing yourself mentally for some upgrades?

"You don't need to spell it out like that," I said. "But, yeah, pretty much. I think I'm starting to get to the point where I should be a lot better than I am. I don't think I ever want to go full-borg, though."

Your current augmentations include one self-healing system in your chest, a pair of prosthetic ears, a cybernetic eye, and your arm. You have spent relatively little on improving your physicality. You do have access to two relevant blueprints. One for the Feline Cat Reflex Augmentation suite, and one for some prosthetic ear implants.

"The blueprints are mostly if I want to make that shit myself, no?" I asked.

Yes, and if you had the time and surgical systems to install them, then that would be the less expensive option, though obviously time isn't something you have in great supply at the moment.

"Right," I agreed. Then I placed a hand on the counter. "Okay, this is what I want: Mostly, I need to move faster. I don't just mean like, physically, I mean . . . my reflexes. I want to act quicker and have more time to react to shit. It'll make up for me not being able to think as quickly."

Something could be arranged.

"And I need to be a little tougher. Like I said, I don't wanna be a borg, but I don't think it would hurt if I was harder to kill." I pinched the skin on my arm a little with my cybernetic arm. It was squishy. During the hive clean-out, I had been wearing my undersuit, and then some armor on top of that. I had a decent suit of power armor waiting for me in the bedroom. The Tiger's Mane. It was damned tough and pretty stealthy and had cost me a little chunk of change. But Gomorrah had been talking about new skin, and she wore just as much armor as I usually did.

I didn't need to replace my power armor just yet. Plus for any big engagements, I'd be in my mech.

So that was . . . several layers of safety. The mech, the power armor, the undersuit. But past that? I was still just flesh and bone.

Understood. Here are my suggestions: First, for the reflex adjustments, you'll likely want to avoid anything too sudden. I would advise three items, totaling nine hundred points.

That was on the steep side, but I was also a point-pincher, and the purchase was something that I knew would help in the long run. "Go on."

The first is a set of nerve replacements. The second is a system to actually introduce these to your body. The last is a mental-reflex enhancement system. The nerve replacements would change out your current nervous system for a bio-electrical system that runs via minute electrical discharges. The main sheath would run through your spine and out across your body.

"That's more or less what I was imagining. For the nervous system bit, how are we, uh, getting that installed? Am I gonna be flensed alive?"

That's what the second purchase is for. A small vat of medical nanites plugged into your bloodstream with access to the microfilaments of the nerve replacement. They'll travel through your body and replace your nerves. This will not be pleasurable, but it won't hurt, either. The transfer should take approximately two days.

"So . . . what, I swallow both?"

No, the system will hook into your back, along your spinal cord. It'll feel similar to a heating pad placed along the center of your back. The final item will be inserted along the base of your skull. It's an injection that will travel to your brain and reconstruct itself into a small computerized system linked between your meat brain and your new mechanical nervous system.

I took a deep breath and looked at myself in the mirror. "Will it be worth it?" I asked.

Your reflexes will slowly but steadily improve over the course of a week or less. You will be able to command your limbs to move faster.

"Command my limbs to move faster?" I asked. "Not actually make them *move* faster?"

They are still organic, and you don't seem interested or ready to replace all of your musculature or bones.

"Ah, no, yeah, okay." I shivered. This was already pushing it. I . . . didn't mind the cybernetic arm, much. Before becoming a samurai and having the arm replaced, I'd never really fucked with prosthetics. They felt like they were a shitty replacement for something I'd lost.

This one was fine. Better than a real arm, but it didn't feel entirely . . . me. I did appreciate the vibrating function, but it was not . . . eh, whatever.

I'd need a real good therapy AI someday to get over that hangup.

At the end of the day, I still wanted to be *me*. New nerves? That wasn't so bad. I'd get used to them. New muscles and bones and probably all the rest? Fuck, at that point I might as well tuck my brain in a jar and pilot a suit.

I knew there were some samurai who did just that.

"Okay, what about being tougher?" I asked.

Would you be partial to skin replacement?

"That sounds horrific," I said. "But . . . yeah."

It's less invasive than you'd think, all things considered. I can have the skin replacement take a similar approach to the nerves. A suite of nanomachines that would slowly replace all of your skin with fresh, new skin laced with materials to improve it. Your skin would flake off, as it does already, though at an accelerated rate. The replacement skin will be indistinguishable to human sight, but it will be less conductive, slightly thicker, and capable of resisting minor cuts and abrasions. It would also have a series of capillaries beneath the surface to better allow regenerative materials to travel through your skin. You would, essentially, heal faster and bleed less.

"Would it be bulletproof?"

No, but the average Earth dog would find you exceptionally hard to bite through. Sensation-wise, you'll retain your sense of touch, though it may even be slightly improved. Your skin would also be much smoother to the touch, and should you manage to live that long, will wrinkle far less with age.

"Okay, okay," I said. "Any downsides?"

You'll need new hair.

"Uh."

Yes, all over, or wherever you wish new hair to be. Your current hair will fall out, though it won't be immediate. You'll have a day or two before it starts to come off. You might want to consider shaving your head before that happens, then picking a suitable hair replacement.

Right, that wasn't that bad. There were lots of fake hair replacement things available. Neon-colored hair was pretty common, as was RGB hair, and there were wilder things out there. Self-styling hair, and hair that could move itself and shit.

"Yeah, I'd be alright with that. How much is this skin stuff?" I asked.

Five hundred and fifty points. This one will require that you drink a rather large bottle of a liquid substance. You will find that it has no taste.

"It tastes like water?"

No. The actual *taste is horrific. Your sense of taste will be deactivated almost as soon as you first smell it, and it will return to normal within the hour.*

"Oh, great," I said. "Well, let me get started with one of those super-coffees of yours first. I think I need one if I'm going to be doing all of this shit."

Of course! I'll make it extra-strong. Maybe the taste will linger a little.

CHAPTER SIXTY-ONE

WITH GREAT CATS COME GREAT RESPONSIBILITY

Not all samurai are capable of command. It's a common myth, and something seen in plenty of media, but whatever selection process exists for samurai, it doesn't select them based on their ability to lead.

Still, every so often one of them will step up and do a good enough job of it that it's worth noting.

—Excerpt from "On Samurai and the Role of the Leader,"
The Family Internal Press, 2049

I exited the bathroom half an hour or so later to discover that Lucy wasn't alone in bed. She had company.

Company in the form of a large robotic cat, the one I'd bought for her in Burlington. It was laying like a sphynx on the bed, head turned toward the doorway and eyes slowly scanning the room.

"Isn't that thing cold?" I asked, keeping my voice low so that I wouldn't wake Lucy up.

It's capable of regulating its temperature for stealth purposes. At the moment, the unit is overheating itself to give off a comforting amount of warmth. It's part of its bodyguarding routine.

That explained why Lucy had one leg over the cat's back and her face pressed into its flank.

I walked over to the bed, tugged the blankets free a little, then covered Lucy properly. She didn't even stop her quiet snoring as I tucked her in and pressed a quick kiss to her forehead. "Keep her warm," I advised the cat mech, and it nodded its big head.

I had to get over to that forward base where Gomorrah was probably waiting, which meant putting on my undersuit, something which immediately proved somewhat difficult.

The two processes I'd just started left me feeling . . . tingly. It wasn't super noticeable if I wasn't looking for it, but my skin was itchy in a few random spots, as if I had the start of an allergic reaction. That, and my nerves were already being rewired, but it wasn't entirely even.

I closed a hand, only to feel like some fingers responded slightly faster than others. It was *off*, but just in a small way. I didn't even know if I was just imagining it.

The nervous system upgrade will settle soon enough. Given six or so hours, the upgrade will have spread across your entire nervous system. The remaining time will be spent on the installation of reinforcements and adjustments. Until then, you might feel slightly uncalibrated in your actions.

"Good to know," I muttered as I scratched my side. Yeah, there was definitely an itch. I slipped the skinsuit on anyway, pulling it on tight and bouncing on the spot to make sure the leg portion was tugged all the way up.

Next was my power armor. That was far easier to get on, all I had to do was step into it, and the armor folded itself around me and locked into place.

I tilted my head left and right, making sure my neck was loose, then shifted the arms a little before I twisted my waist around back and forth. Everything felt alright. If anything, that slight delay in motion with the suit might normalize any of the weirdness from the nerve upgrades.

"Okay," I muttered. "I think I'm ready."

I slipped out of the room, popped into my armory to pick up my Laser Pointer, Trench Maker, and a handful of grenades, then made my way to the elevator. But not before pausing to scratch Catkiller on the head and to nod to Chonkers, the cat spy drone who was loafing in the middle of the corridor, right where someone might trip over it.

I rode the elevator down to the garage level, then stepped up to my mech.

I'd wanted to repair it on my own, but needs must, so I'd left the repair drone to the task. It looked decent, at least from the outside.

The experience wasn't lost, because at least now I knew enough to tell that it looked decent as I climbed into the mech's cockpit and closed it up behind me.

I linked up to the mecha's system, then checked the diagnostics. It all came back green, which was . . . better than I could realistically have managed on my own.

"Alright. Let's get moving," I said.

I stepped out into the main part of the garage, and found two construction drones waiting for me with a hastily assembled system of scaffolds. I stepped the mech into the scaffolds, then felt a moment of squished guts as the construction drones rose up and pulled the mech up along with them.

It was a bit kludged, but it would do for the moment. I'd look into buying a dedicated transportation . . . thing, later. Maybe a small moving-van-sized car that was decently fast and roomy? But then I'd never be able to get a really big mech.

That was something to consider. Maybe a flatbed, then?

The construction drones weren't smart-smart, but with Myalis at the helm they turned and pulled out of the garage. I felt a faint twinge of vertigo as the mech's very good sensor suite—fed directly into my brain—told me exactly how high up I was at the moment.

The drones flew onward, making a straight path out of the city.

I had very little to actually do, in that moment, so I pulled up my private chatroom with Gomorrah and pinged her. "Hey, are you up?" I asked.

"I have been for an hour," Gomorrah said. "I'm at the forward base. The same one we met at earlier. We're waiting on you."

"Right, I'm on my way. ETA, uh, call it twenty minutes?"

"The operation's launching at six a.m.," Gomorrah said.

"And it's . . . not six a.m. yet," I pointed out.

"Cat, it's five fifty-nine."

I refused to acknowledge that. I wasn't late, I was . . . just a little unearly. "I'll be there soon enough," I said.

And I was. Flying over the scene a few minutes later, I could make out a long convoy headed by some tanks and APCs, with a couple of mobile bases in the middle and middle-rear. The back of the convoy had more tanks, but also a few dozen large supply trucks and a lot of pretty normal-looking vans and all-black city buses.

I noticed a familiar car following one of the mobile bases. The *Fury* looked entirely misplaced in the middle of an assembly of tanks and army vehicles, but I knew it probably packed more of a punch than the entire front line of tanks.

My construction drones scooted ahead, and then I was unceremoniously dropped from a few meters up way ahead of the formation.

I walked the mech out of the scaffolding, then watched the drones pick it up and fly off.

With a mental touch, I opened the canopy of the mech, then pushed myself up to standing. It was less about being able to see things for myself than it was for morale.

I wasn't a genius when it came to that kind of thing, but I figured . . . well, if I was some poor fuck in army greens at the moment, seeing a massive cat-shaped warmech with a samurai standing casually atop it would give me a serious boost when it came to morale.

The front row of tanks squeezed to my side as they passed, and a few of their crew stuck their heads out of opened hatches to wave my way.

I waved back, then hopped down from my mech and walked across the road in time to jump into one of the slow-moving mobile bases. The mech closed up behind me, then leapt into the formation to saunter along next to the *Fury*.

I found Gomorrah in the mobile base's main room, arms crossed and impassive mask turned down to stare at one of those needlessly fancy holographic maps that command-types probably had wet dreams about.

"Yo," I said.

"Good to see you joining us," Gomorrah said. "I hope you got some rest. It's going to be a long campaign."

"Campaign?" I asked. "I thought this was a day-long thing?"

"*Days* long, more like," she replied before looking up at me. My comms crackled for a second before she spoke directly into my ear, the others in the room kept out of the loop. "We're waiting for news from Mars. But I heard some hints that it's not all good."

"Ah, fuck. What does that mean for us? End of the world?"

"Not that bad, I don't think. Just that we might have to clear out the still-active hives without the help of big names and high-tier samurai. It's not going to be a walk in the park."

"We'll manage, right?" I asked.

"We'll either manage, or it really will be an end-of-the-world situation. Better to act and do something about it than wallow and sit around until we're all alien food, though. Did you have a good time at home?"

"I barely had any time at home," I said. She should have known, she dropped me off late last night.

Gomorrah nodded. "Sorry about that. So . . . do you want to take over here?" She gestured to the map and the room, with its many commanders watching us have a conversation they weren't part of.

"What? This is your gig, no?"

"I hate every minute of it. You're better at this."

"Fuck no," I said.

By the blank look on her masked face, I had this sinking feeling that my "fuck no" sounded a bit like a "yeah, sure" to Gomorrah.

CHAPTER SIXTY-TWO

MINIATURE WARGAMING

The main difference between a corporate army force and a national army force comes mostly from the ideology behind both.

One is designed to protect and promote profit.

The other is designed to protect civilians and national interests.

In this essay, I will show how legislating for a shift from national to privatized armies is a net positive for the people who matter.

—"A Study on Profitable Militarization," The Kissinger Foundation, 2027

It was hard, dealing with Gomorrah's crap while also feeling extremely twitchy and irritated all over.

The reflex package was definitely kicking in at the moment. I could *feel* it working across my entire body, especially my fingers and toes, which I couldn't stop from spasming slightly. Unfortunately, with the power armor I was in, that slight twitching turned into far more noticeable motions of my hands.

"Are you okay?" Gomorrah asked midway through the briefing she was giving me. She was mostly listing out the forces at *her* disposal. Not mine. I didn't want to be in charge of jack or shit, and no amount of Gomorrah shoving the responsibility my way was gonna change that.

"I'm fine," I said. "I got a nerve replacement thing going."

"Oh," she replied with a nod. "That's an annoying one."

"Wait, you did the same?" I asked.

The nun shrugged. "Recently, yes. Nerves, some changes to my musculature. I have sheathing over my bones too. I've started the skin replacement as well."

"Really?" I asked. I remembered her mentioning something to that effect yesterday, but we didn't go into it. Something about fireproofing her skin.

"Cat, do you have any idea how much time I spend next to fire?"

"I've got a decent idea," I said. "More than the average person." And a lot more than anyone sane.

She nodded. "Good. Now, do you have any idea how flammable skin is? Not to mention hair."

"No, no I don't think I know that, and to be perfectly honest I'm not sure I want to know."

If it's any reassurance, your new skin will be significantly harder to burn, though you won't be flame- or heat-proof. I suspect Atyacus will have offered his Vanguard a type of skin far more suitable to resisting that kind of threat than what I suggested to you.

I filed that away for never. "Well, whatever. Did you get used to it yet?"

"I've worn scratchier clothes. I can endure. My new skin's nice, I think. You get to decide where hair grows back, which is useful as well," Gomorrah said.

"Oh, yeah. Myalis mentioned that when I got my own skin stuff going. No more shaving your legs and armpits. That's huge."

Someone cleared their throat, and both Gomorrah and I stared across the holoprojector at a man in fatigues with a few extra markings on his shoulders. The general in charge of this operation.

Fortunately, Gomorrah and I had been chatting over a private channel. "Sorry, General," she said. "Stray Cat asked for clarification on something and I informed her privately. Anyway, as I was saying. Our current force disposition includes two battalions and an additional attached company."

I raised a hand. "Sorry, dumb question, but you're tossing terms around that I'm not familiar with. What's an attached company?"

Gomorrah glanced my way, then the projector shifted from a map to a collection of teeny-tiny models of soldiers and tanks and bigger vehicles. These split into three distinct groups. "The smaller semi-independent group is the recon company under Lieutenant Moreau," she said.

One group flashed, and I recognized them easily enough. A dozen vehicles, mostly on the lighter side, and some fifty or so soldiers divided into smaller squads.

"Our second group is the Fifth Battalion, under Lieutenant Colonel Juno," Gomorrah said.

One of the men across from me at the table nodded, and I noticed that the little tag on his chest read "Juno." I still had no idea how to read the chevrons on their shoulders. They were just fancy triangles to me, but the boys seemed to like it when they had more than anyone else. "Puck's Battalion is ready to serve," he said.

A bunch of vehicles and soldiers lit up under the label of the Fifth Battalion. There were two groups bigger than platoons, with maybe some two hundred-odd soldiers in each, and a number of APCs and a few wheeled tanks.

"Alright," I said. "And the last group?"

"The Twenty-Second Battalion," Gomorrah said. "They call themselves the Maple Battalion. They're heavy armor."

This time what lit up were mostly tanks and what I imagined were the drivers and pilots for said vehicles. "Isn't there support staff?" I asked as I gestured to the projector.

"I'm not including them here," Gomorrah said. "Support crews will be staying on the safe side of the wall for the foreseeable future. We'll have some long-ranged artillery as well, missile batteries mostly, and we have the air force on standby for strafing runs, aerial recon, and if it comes to it, aerial superiority, but looking at similar events, history suggests that we'll probably not need it."

"Alright," I said. "Thanks. And the general here's in charge of everything?"

"I'm Brigadier General Thibodeau," he said with a grunt. I got the impression that he was being very tolerant of me at the moment. To be fair, I wasn't giving off the best impression.

"Thanks," I replied. "Sorry, look, I've been in a few shitshows before, but usually it's with like, militias at best, or a few PMC companies that need to be threatened into working together, or just civilians with guns. Never really got to work with people who have . . . you know, order."

"Hmm," he replied, and that was all I got from him. Actually, it felt like I'd earned some points there, but I had no idea how or why.

Should I paint some triangles on my shoulders? Would they take me more seriously then?

"Okay, so the plan's to head north. Are we setting up there or just sweeping in, fucking everything alien up, and then heading back home for some R&R?" I was hoping that it wouldn't take too much time, even if Gomorrah seemed to think otherwise.

The general grunted something and the company list disappeared, replaced by a map of everything north of New Montreal for some distance. "Our first stopping point will be Saint-Janvier. We'll be reaching that today. Tomorrow, we're continuing to Saint-Jérome. There's a walled settlement there which has held up so far. It'll be our final staging ground before we continue our move north."

"The idea is to wipe out every hive within fifty kilometers of New Montreal," Gomorrah said. "That sounds like a deceptively small area, but it's actually fairly large." The map lit up, a great big section now highlighted. "It would take weeks to scout it all manually, but we have some support tools from the Family that will pinpoint hives. The army group will be assaulting those in force."

"Huh," I said as I leaned forward.

Overall, it seemed pretty reasonable. If we wanted to keep the city safe, it made sense to take out any nearby hives. Sure, the aliens would just group up farther out, but then they'd have to *travel* to New Montreal, and that would mean time to spot them and rain artillery down onto their ugly heads, or move out to intercept them in the field.

"Okay, okay, so, where do you want Gomorrah and me?" I asked.

"On the front," the general said. "We've worked with samurai before. You're likely to kill a lot more xenos without losses than our forces in a short engagement. We're here to mop up and hold a line. You'll be the primary strike force."

"Alright," I said. "Yeah, that recon group was pretty useful last time. We should make sure mortars are supporting us again."

The general frowned, then nodded. "I'll make note of that. Some samurai don't like indirect fire installations. It 'steals their points.'"

"Oh, trust me, I don't mind," I said. If this was going to be as busy as I expected, then there'd be no lack of opportunities to make bank. "As long as I can get back home every night, I think this whole operation is going to be a cakewalk."

"You'd rather make the trip back home every night than stay with the army? You're really just asking for trouble, aren't you?" Gomorrah asked.

"Hey, trouble's done good by me so far, and I like my bed," I said. "So, what's next?"

"You won't enjoy this part," Gomorrah said. "But we need to go over it anyway: force disposition, material acquisitions, logistical trains, and everything we need to do to make sure that we can keep this army group fed and stocked up on enough bullets and explosives so that everyone comes home alive."

She was spot-on when she said that I wasn't going to enjoy it. The mobile base rumbled on while I at least made an effort to keep up. Gomorrah might claim that she wasn't good at this sort of thing, but damn did she seem to love making sure deliveries were on time.

A faint alarm sounded as we finally crossed the outer wall and were out of the city. From this point onward, it was possible, even expected, that we'd be running into aliens that wanted to do nothing more than chow down on us.

Despite everything, I was getting pretty excited for this. It was gonna be fun.

Now, if only it could distract me from how my everything was itchy. Fucking power armor. It needed some holes cut out so that I could scratch myself.

CHAPTER SIXTY-THREE

MEALS REFUSING EXIT

Are you certain about these two? They don't strike me as being as competent as their files suggest.

—Brigadier General Thibodeau, internal memo, 2057

I was expecting some action.

Unfortunately, we could only move as fast as the slowest vehicle in the convoy, which meant we were moving as fast as the tanks with more interior volume than most three-bedroom apartments.

Sure, I knew we'd talk for a bit, do some planning, and point troops in the direction they needed to go in, but I expected to fight *something*.

The entire day passed without a shot fired, and the mounting tension made me feel like I was slowly losing my mind.

A month or so ago, not shooting at anything, and especially not having anything trying to eat me (Lucy excepted), would have meant that it was a good day.

Now the only thing I could think of was that if the aliens at least tried, then I'd have an excuse to not be in the increasingly stuffy command room of the mobile base with some of the stuffiest people who had ever stuffed.

Our progress was tracked in the slow rumble of the mammoth vehicle as it moved forward at a pace that I could outwalk. It was so slow and steady that I could barely feel the motion, but we were moving—I knew because we were tracked on the large holographic map. Tiny pinpricks, moving ahead one pixel at a time.

The worst thing was the itching.

Actually, no, that wasn't true. The itching was a close second. The *actual* worst thing was the shitter. The mobile base had a tiny little bathroom, like something in an old-time airplane. So small that you needed to enter from the side and duck your head not to bash it against the ceiling.

Navigating that in power armor was not possible, so I'd had to ditch the armor in the corridor, then squeeze my way in there. It was clean, at least.

Some poor low-ranked fuck probably had the glorious task of scrubbing the whole thing out with a toothbrush every day, but "clean" was the only positive modifier I had for the washroom.

I knew it was a bad day when I was honestly considering the pros and cons of wearing a diaper under my power armor.

The convoy came to a stop at around eighteen hundred hours, a bit before sundown, which would give them time to set up a proper camp before dark. The spot was, until recently, a little layover town with a big gas station for automated trucks and a small row of old last-century homes. There was a supermarket with a big parking lot, all abandoned, but it was a wide open space with solid asphalt below.

A perimeter was formed, tanks were lined up in neat, orderly rows, and a corps of engineers started unfolding fences around the entire lot while others set up a series of "mobile bunkers" (because the army was too fancy to call them mobile homes) for the soldiers to rest in.

"That was a good day's work," Gomorrah said as she stepped out of the mobile base. She placed her hands on her hips and stretched her back out.

"Are you serious?" I asked as I slunk out after her. I was exhausted in a whole new way, and I hated it. "That was *awful*. Damned waste of time." I had a million new facts rattling around in the back of my head, and I couldn't wait for them to leak out.

Why had it been so important that we have a forty-minute discussion about the type, quantity, and quality of rations?

The soldiers carried little MRE packs. Not the old shitty ones from back in the day, but these little flat-packed boxes that came with everything they needed and apparently tasted okay enough while still being full of nutrients and calories.

That was the marketing pitch, at least. The few actual soldiers in the room with us that had eaten them looked like they'd rather eat the no-ply toilet paper they had in their godawful washroom.

As it turned out, the army had *options*, because whoever ended up supplying them the absolute fuckload of MREs they'd need to keep this operation going was going to make a tidy profit, and that meant that there was more than one corp willing to secure that deal.

Hence, a too-long discussion about which corporation to go with for supplying the grunts for this trip. Some corps offered discounts, others came with subscription plans for each soldier, and still others were just offloading old shit for relatively cheap.

I hated every second of it, even as I learned how it was all actually kind of important. Yes, figuring out how to supply the troops with food sucked, but it would suck a lot more if they all started to go hungry. I *got* that. I wasn't moronic. I just didn't want to be the one in charge.

"I'm having Lucy join the army," I said.

Gomorrah turned to look my way. I couldn't see her face, but something in her body language let me read her confusion. "Is this a uniform kink?"

"Yes. But also she's just better at this kind of thing than me. The uniforms *are* kind of hot. Why aren't the guys in the command room all dressed up?"

"Because you don't wear a dress uniform while out in the field. It's not made for running around and shooting things in," Gomorrah said.

"That makes a startling amount of sense," I said. The brigadier general and lieutenant colonel had been in fatigues that weren't different from any soldier's, minus the rank insignias. They didn't wear as much armor over them, though.

Just about every soldier I saw had padded leg armor strapped on, as well as a chest rig over a breastplate and some vambraces over their forearms. The kind of shit you'd want—at a minimum—when fighting enemies that like to jump up and bite your extremities. It was probably pretty subpar for fighting armed humans, but that wasn't the goal here.

"You're heading home, I imagine?" Gomorrah asked.

"Yeah. I need it."

"If you want, you can leave your mech here. I'll give you a ride back," she said.

I smiled. "Thanks. Are you sure? I can always call my bike over if you want to ride alone. It'll only take a few minutes to get here."

"It's fine," Gomorrah said.

We walked over to the *Fury*, which was parked right behind the mobile base it had been following this entire time. Gomorrah tsked, then started to circle the car, looking for something. "What is it?" I asked.

"Look at all this dust," she complained. "Would it kill them to put some mudflaps on their base? I swear, they'll flick rocks all over my hood and windshield."

"Did it scratch any of the paint?" I asked. The *Fury* was a cool, very matte black. I couldn't see any scratches, just a lot of road dust and dirt caked on.

"No, the paint's rated for the inside of a sun. It'll take more than a tossed rock to scratch it, but it's the principle that counts. You can't just . . . not respect someone's car."

"Uh-huh," I agreed.

She sighed and the car's doors opened for us. I made a show of tapping my boots on the ground before getting in. If she was this pissed about the outside, I didn't want to carry mud inside, especially if I ever wanted her to give me a ride again.

"Tomorrow should be better," Gomorrah said as she took off vertically, spun us around, then accelerated toward New Montreal in the distance.

"Really? Are we going to go over acquisitions for every kind of bullet again?"

She laughed. "No, but we might do peripherals! But more seriously, we'll be in higher-danger areas. The road between New Montreal and Saint-Jérome has been patrolled a few times, so we know it's mostly safe. There are more antithesis further out. That, and we'll be getting some more samurai on board tomorrow."

"Anyone I know?" I asked.

"I don't know exactly who's coming," she admitted. "Jolly Monarch just let me know that we'd be getting support from some other, newer samurai."

"Huh, alright," I said. There were a few newbies around. Cause Player was local, and so was Crackshot Cowboy. I knew firsthand that Emoscythe and Grasshopper were around, but they felt . . . not *new*. They both had some years under their belts and were probably able to handle bigger problems than Gomorrah and I could.

Maybe I'd get to meet a few other new faces. With the global incursion going on, I didn't doubt that there were plenty of opportunities for new samurai to pop up.

Home came up ahead soon enough, and Gomorrah slipped into the parking garage at a speed that had me subtly grabbing onto my seat. "Home!" she declared.

"Yeah!" I said. It was nice to be back.

Now I just had the oh-so-enviable task of explaining to Lucy that I'd be gone for most of the day for the next . . . while and a bit.

Damn, how did people with jobs do relationships if they couldn't be home all the time?

CHAPTER SIXTY-FOUR

NEW HAIR DAY

Once is happenstance, twice is coincidence, three times is enemy action [. . .]

—Ian Fleming, *Goldfinger,* 1959

"Can I come?"

I think Myalis might have been impressed by just how quickly I came to a conclusion on that question. No need for improved reflexes to make that choice.

"Fuck no," I said.

Lucy pouted at me, which was downright lethal. She was in bed, wearing a blanket and nothing else. She tugged it up around her neck a little, so that the only part of her I could see was her chubby-cheeked pout. "Why not?" she asked.

"Because it's dangerous?" I stated the obvious. I sensed that it was something of a trap, though. "And no, that doesn't mean that *I* can't go. Or that I could just give you stuff to keep you safe."

Lucy's pout deepened, and then she flopped backward onto the bed with a bounce and kicked her legs from under the blankets. It almost looked like she was a brat throwing a tantrum. "Fine! But I want to help."

"Ah, well, that's different," I said. "You could, uh . . . "

I quickly wrote a message on my augs directed to Myalis, basically begging for assistance.

Perhaps you could suggest that Lucy uses the spare time that she has, and which you lack, to look into some of your current projects?

"Oh, I know!" I said with a snap of my organic fingers. "Can you check up on my shit for me?" I sent a "thank you" to Myalis and an apology for stealing her ideas.

You can have some of my ideas. I'll consider it charity to the impoverished.

Lucy perked up at that, her tantrum ending. It was probably for the best, because she looked out of breath. "What shit do you need checking up on?" she asked.

"Well, there's the prosthetics clinic downstairs. I didn't look into it at all yesterday. We need to make sure they're up and running. Then there's the whole sewer thing. I don't think you should go check on the sewer itself, but the Family is doing some work and I need to keep an eye on them. Maybe pop over to their HQ and remind them that I'm paying attention. Oh, and look in on Rac. Heck, hire her to come with you all armed up. It'll keep her busy and her nose out of trouble."

Lucy hummed, then jumped out of bed. "Alright!" I said as she spread her arms and legs wide and stretched. "Yeah, that actually does sound kind of useful."

"As long as you're safe about it," I added.

She turned a *look* my way. "Really? Since when are you so focused on being safe?"

"Hey, I always want you to be safe and warm and have everything you ever wanted," I said. It had the advantage of being true. Lucy smiled, but it was one of her softer smiles, not her usual quirked smirk. "It's just that I didn't think I could give you all of that until now. If you *really* want to come, I'm sure we can work something out?"

She shook her head. "No, you're right. Thanks, Cat." Lucy ambled over. "Hugs? Or are you not leaving right now?"

"Not just yet," I replied as I very easily accepted a hug. "I need to get ready."

"Alright. You can use the washroom first, I don't have as far to go. Actually, I'm gonna check on the people in the clinic downstairs first."

"Not naked I hope? Oh, wear that jacket," I said. "And the emergency necklace. And bring at least two of the cat drones with you."

"Really?"

"They're intimidating," I said.

"And I'm not?" Lucy frowned.

"You're *terrifying*," I replied, which earned me a swat.

Lucy laughed. "Go get ready. You'll be late, and then Delilah's gonna complain to Franny, who'll complain to me."

"Urgh, maybe having them as neighbors was a mistake," I groaned as I finally let go of Lucy and wandered over to the washroom. I paused inside as I saw myself in the mirror again. It was still me, obviously, but I came closer and then reached a hand up to my right side.

My stump meshed well with the prosthetic arm there, going from flesh to machine almost seamlessly. What was strange was the scarring. I'd been burned pretty fucking horrifically. I couldn't remember most of it. Actually, it might have been more of an explosion?

Fuck if I knew. But it took an eye, messed with my hearing for a long time, and cost me my arm. The whole of my right side was scarred. It wasn't as bad in some places. There was only some permanently-wrinkly skin on my cheek and neck. The scarring was worse around my arm and upper chest on the right.

Now it was . . . not entirely gone, but almost.

In just a day and a bit, the wrinkled red mess had been reduced to a few faint patches of rough-looking skin. It looked more like I had a slight rash than old burns. That was the whole skin treatment at work, I supposed.

For some reason it hadn't crossed my mind that replacing all of my skin would take the scars with it.

Well, fuck it, not like I cared overly much, and I knew Lucy still found me plenty attractive.

I raked a hand through my hair, then grimaced as it came away with clumps of it. "Okay, the hair is annoying though," I said.

Do you want to fix that?

"Honestly? Yeah. Got like, a tech-wig or something like that?"

It didn't take too long, surprisingly, to find something suitable. It wasn't too much, either. Under a hundred points and ten minutes later, I stepped out of the washroom, the toilet flushing away a disgustingly large clump of hair while I tied my new hair up in a quick and sloppy ponytail.

It was some semi-fancy tech-hair. Rooted into my scalp and able to grow more or less naturally if I really wanted it to, but for now it would stay as long as it was. It was also tougher than real hair, and the blue highlight on the front actually glowed faintly.

I noticed that Lucy was missing, but I could hear her rummaging around in the armory. I'd save the surprise for later, I decided, as I got dressed and ready to go.

"See you after work!" I called out.

"Bye! Love you!" Lucy called back. "I'm stealing one of your guns by the way. Ohh! And a grenade!"

"Uh . . . okay, don't kill yourself!" I called back.

"Hey!" Lucy shouted.

I paused, already halfway through the living room. A few of the kittens were out and they paused to stare. "What?" I asked before slipping my helmet on.

"You didn't say it back," Lucy accused. She poked her head out of the armory. She was at least wearing an oversized T-shirt now. I was pretty sure most armories required a dress code that was more than "just a shirt," but I didn't really care.

I sighed. "Love you too," I said with a wry smile. Then I pointedly ignored the snickers from the kittens before I beat a hasty retreat.

I got in the garage and noted that the *Fury* was gone already, which meant Gomorrah was ahead of me, and probably waiting impatiently for me to arrive. I sighed and hoped she wouldn't be all judgmental about it as I hopped onto my bike and took off.

It felt like it took forever to reach the little walled-off mini-city where the army was planted. It looked like there had been some action overnight too. Not at the army's camp in front of the old supermarket, but to the north of the city. Some smoke was rising out of fresh craters, and I suspected that there were a few homes burning out in the mini suburbia.

I came down and parked next to the *Fury*, which happened to be where Gomorrah was hanging out.

"You're finally here," she said. "We did agree on oh-eight-hundred, right?"

"I think so," I said. I didn't look at my internal clock. If I did, I might start feeling guilty. "Sorry, I had to buy my hair."

"You could have done—*buy* your hair?" she asked, cutting off her complaints with her own confusion.

"Yup. So, what's the situation?" I asked before she could get her footing. It looked like the entire camp was doing its best kicked-hornets-nest impression, but I wasn't sure if that was because trouble was here or if that was just the army preparing to get a move on again.

Gomorrah sighed. "Everything was fine until about three hours ago. A group of Antithesis pushed in from the north just as the sun was coming up. It's very likely a coincidence, but they arrived as the guard was rotating, and they got a lot closer than they should have."

"How sure are we that it's a coincidence?" I asked, immediately on guard.

"Ninety-nine plus percent, and a few decimals besides," she replied. "It's likely that they attacked as the sun came up because it offered them more visibility. We just happened to time our guard rotation around sunup."

"Ah," I said. "Well, it's nice to see that things are already exciting! Yesterday was a slog. And, we're meeting new samurai today, right?" I couldn't wait. More people meant less work for me. Maybe they'd even be halfway competent?

CHAPTER SIXTY-FIVE

YOUR AVERAGE ROLEPLAYING GROUP

The average samurai isn't so different from the average person, I don't think. But . . . you know how there's perhaps one person in a thousand who's spectacular? They're a genius, peerless, insane in a way that leads to greatness? Within the ranks of the samurai, these geniuses make up something like a quarter of their number. Sure, the average is still average, just people tossed into tough situations and given great power. They're above average in all respects, but they're not so special.

—Excerpt from Deus Ex's Sleepy Time Blog, 2056

"So, what are we looking at here?" I asked.

Gomorrah was leading me through the crowd of soldiers and support personnel around the temporary base. "That surprise attack this morning is delaying things a little. We need to move up some road-clearing machines from the city."

"Road clearing?" I asked.

"Snow plows," she explained. "To ram through all the alien corpses."

I nodded along. "That makes sense, yeah. Surprised we don't have anything fixed to the front of a tank or something."

"I think that exists, but we don't have it on hand. Snow plows though? Those are readily available. There's some coming up the road at full speed. We'll have them here within the hour and then start moving out." Gomorrah turned her head my way. "Which happens to leave us with just enough time to meet the new samurai."

"Oh boy," I muttered. "How many newbies are we talking about here? That was plural, so at least two?"

"Four," Gomorrah said. "We know one of them already. Crackshot Cowboy."

"Oh!" I said, cheering up a little at the familiar name. Crackshot was actually a pretty cool guy. He had helped on the wall when defending New

Montreal a while ago. Had a huge—understandable—crush on Emoscythe. "His whole thing was being super accurate with that old gun of his, right?" I asked.

"Correct, and I think that's still his specialization," Gomorrah said. "Long-ranged single-target attacks. He'll fit in nicely with the two of us if it comes to a fight."

"And the other three?" I asked.

"I haven't met them," Gomorrah said. She sent a file my way, and I poked it open. It had some information on the people we were heading out to meet. Not much, but it was there.

"Princess, Knight, Hedgehog, and Tankette?" I asked as I read the names. "Gomorrah, that's four, and with Crackshot . . . four plus one is five, right?"

"Yes, Catherine, four and one make five," Gomorrah agreed. "Those lessons with Grasshopper are paying dividends. Knight isn't a samurai," she explained.

I frowned, but decided not to question it. We were heading out to meet them anyway.

The first I saw of the new samurai was a middle-aged woman who looked like she was very much in the wrong place.

She was kind of cute, in that pudgy motherly way. A woman maybe in her early forties or so, with brown hair cut into a bob and the kind of simple blouse-and-jeans outfit that was more suitable for sitting at home than being out on the edge of a battlefield.

If we weren't here, with a whole-ass army around, I might have dismissed her entirely.

But here she was, standing out because she was so normal in a place where she shouldn't be, so I checked her out a little more. She had some augs that looked decent, and a few ports on the side of her neck. Her hands were all silver on the inside. Smart palms? She had a ring, too.

This had to be Tankette, because that's what she was sitting on. The tank was minuscule, about three-quarters the size of a luxury hovercar, with four tracks on each corner that looked like they could all turn independently. There was a turret in the center of the tankette, with a stubby box of a barrel sticking out of it and pointing ahead. A panel was open on the side, and I caught a glimpse of the interior.

Tankette had to be a tiny woman, because anyone taller than four-foot-six wouldn't be able to fit in that tiny cockpit. Still, the interior looked high-tech. It reminded me a lot of my mech's cockpit, with screens all over and a yoke for controls.

I nodded to Tankette, then glanced around, looking for the others.

Crackshot was sitting on one of my mech's feet, his long rifle leaning up against his shoulder. He was still in jeans and a redneck-chic kind of shirt, but the quality had taken a leap upward since the last time I'd seen him, and I suspected that his getup was tougher than it looked. Otherwise, he looked much the same as usual, a crooked-toothed guy with a friendly smile and sharp eyes.

"Heya, Cat," he said with a tip of his hat.

"Hey," I said with a return nod.

I glanced to the right, where I found the two that could only be Princess and Knight. Those names *had* to be taken.

Princess was probably the teen girl in the poofy pink dress with some armor slapped on. It was like someone took a Disney princess and forced her into some modern body armor. She waved excitedly my way, but didn't step out from behind the one that I guessed was Knight.

Knight was wearing armor. All metal, all shiny, all very dated. But they . . . she? Yeah, that was a chick. Anyway, she had a rig on, with a radio and some 'nades tucked away. There was a longsword hooked on her belt across from a knife while a hammer sat on the ground next to her, its haft pointed skyward.

"Where's the last one?" I asked. Then I spotted a ripple and glanced over to what I'd dismissed as some trash. The trash stood up, warped a little, and came to reveal a man in black fatigues with some pretty fancy armor on.

His front was covered by only the basics. An armored vest with some rigging over it, some crap over his knees and elbows. The kind of gear that a mid-tier PMC would have. Where he stood out was the helmet and, most of all, his . . . was it a cloak? He had a few thousand spiky strands pouring down from the top of his head all the way down to his ankles. The cloak-thing shimmered a little, copying the color of the ground beneath.

So, that's where he earned the name Hedgehog, then.

Hedgehog was armed with a pretty standard bullpup rifle, and looked like he could have been just another soldier. A well-equipped one, but nothing too outstanding.

"Show's yours," Gomorrah said.

I scoffed. "Yay," I said before I spoke up so that everyone could hear me. "Alright. My name's Stray Cat, this is Gomorrah. We're not the boss of anybody, so feel free to tell us to piss the fuck off. But somehow we're the ones in the know, so for now, listen up a bit. If we're gonna work together, then we might as well not accidentally blow each other up. I'm not big on show-and-tell, but I think we can all give each other the basics. Gom, you can start, since you're in charge."

Gomorrah shook her head, but she did speak up. "I'm Gomorrah. I'm the second-in-command of the samurai side of this operation, behind Stray Cat. I'm a fire specialist. I burn things. When I'm not burning things, I watch over our logistics."

I rolled my eyes, then gestured to the lady on the mini-tank. She pointed to herself, then smiled.

"Oh, hello everyone. My name is Heather, but people have taken to calling me Tankette. I, ah, am not much of a fighter. This is Baby Girl, my tank." She patted the armored vehicle she was sitting on. "We've gotten up to a bit of trouble together. Oh! And the AI in my head's called Tynker!"

"Pleasure," I said.

"I'm Princess!" the girl in the dress said. "And this is my big sister, Knight."

"Sup," Knight said.

"We're going to be the best samurai you've ever seen," Princess said.

Crackshot chuckled. "Well, she's enthusiastic, at least," he said. "I'm Crackshot Cowboy. Howdy. I shoot things good. Gimme a target and I'll poke a hole in it like a ripe melon."

Hedgehog was the last, and we all turned his way. He started to salute, then paused halfway in the act. "I'm Hedgehog," he replied. "I work for a certain group as a private military contractor. I happened to become a samurai over the course of my duties. I'm here to grow and improve my skills."

"Cool," I said. "So that gun's not just for show?"

"I've been in active service for six years," he said.

I nodded. "Great. Can we depend on you for all the army-related shit? I'm god-awful at that kind of stuff, even if Gomorrah keeps throwing me at it."

One of his eyebrows rose, but he nodded anyway. "I'll do what I can to help," he replied.

"Thanks. Anyway, like I said, I'm Stray Cat. My job is to be loud here, and sneaky out there. I blow things up. Pleased to meet you all. Now, who wants to murderize some aliens, eh?"

CHAPTER SIXTY-SIX

PEANUT BUTTER AND LESBIAN TIME

Channel 69 Nice News Now will be running a mini-doc series on the style and function of the modern-day samurai. From the most common gear choices to the strange and bizarre ways the Vanguard of humanity chose to fight the good fight!

Available now to all subscribers!

—Channel 69 Nice News Now, 2046

I clapped my hands together, and they made a strange cracking sound as my armored palms met each other. It kind of surprised me, though to be honest, it had been a few years since I'd had the ability to clap.

"Alright!" I said. "Gomorrah here has the plan for our deployment. Feel free to follow it, or not. Right Gom?"

Gomorrah glanced my way, then back to the samurai. "I do," she said. "Hedgehog, Crackshot Cowboy. Would you mind riding above the main mobile base? There's a platform at the top that should afford you some decent visibility."

"Can do," Hedgehog replied.

"No prob," Crackshot said. He grunted as he stood up, then stretched his back out before grabbing his rifle. "We can make a game of it, huh?"

"That wouldn't be very professional," Hedgehog said. Somehow, he managed to stand even straighter.

"Oh, we don't need to wager on it, just a friendly one-up. I don't like gambling. My uncle lost it all to the slots, you know?"

"Right," Hedgehog said dispassionately.

Gomorrah glanced between the two, then refocused on the others. "Tankette, we have some light armor at the front of the formation already. Do you think you could join them?"

"I think so," Tankette replied with a nod.

"I'll send my mech with you," I replied. "It won't steal your kills, but it'll be around if you need the added oomph."

"Oh, I'd appreciate that," she said with a kind smile.

"What about Knight and I?" Princess asked me. "Can we work with you?"

I glanced at Gomorrah, then shrugged. "Sure. If someone wants to do the logistics shit for me, I'm very much more than willing to give it all up."

"As long as we get to work with you," Princess said with a dainty little clap. She seemed . . . a little fangirl-ish. At least Knight, next to her, didn't start jumping around and squeeing.

"Um," Tankette said. It was a slight thing, but it still caught everyone's attention. She noticed that we were all looking her way and straightened herself, then tidied her blouse. "I brought lunch boxes for everyone," she said with a perfectly straight face.

"Lunch . . . boxes, ma'am?" Hedgehog asked.

"Ah, hell yeah," Crackshot replied. "Man, I haven't had lunchboxes since my grandmamma passed."

Tankette seemed encouraged by Crackshot's enthusiasm. She turned to her mini-tank and opened a case on the side. I thought it would be for ammo stowage, but instead it was filled with a half-dozen little tin boxes with thermos containers stuck to the sides. "It's nothing too special. I don't know what everyone likes. If there are allergies, then please let me know. Ah, the boxes aren't labeled. They're all the same."

She pulled out the little lunchboxes, then started passing them around. "Uh, thanks," I said when I got mine. Then I blinked and lifted it up. The box was actually shaped in the rough outline of a tank, instead of being a normal rectangle.

"Thank you," Gomorrah said. "This wasn't necessary."

"Oh, I know," Tankette said with a grin. "But I woke up at five, as usual, realized that I had nothing to do until I got here, and I'd be driven crazy if I just sat back and did nothing all morning."

"Holy shit, is this PB and J?" Crackshot asked, his box was already cracked open. "Ma'am, are you married?"

Tankette tittered. "Yes, I'm happily married. Sorry." She wiggled her hand, flashing a little band around a finger.

"Damn," Crackshot said. Then he stuffed half a sandwich into his mouth.

Hedgehog slipped his box into a small satchel by his hip, and the others put theirs away too. I was left holding my lunchbox kind of awkwardly before I tucked it under my right arm. "Anyway, I think that's it for now. The convoy will be moving out in . . ."

"Ten minutes," Gomorrah filled in.

"Which gives us plenty of time to get to our places! The army was attacked this morning already, so keep an eye open for trouble and aliens. Gomorrah, the samurai have a private channel for chatting, yeah?"

"I'll have Atyacus send everyone an invite," she replied.

A fraction of a second later, I got a small ping on my augs for just that. There was now a little chatroom, with all of the samurai listed to the left with their status below. Interestingly, Knight was missing from the group. Gomorrah *had* said she wasn't a samurai. I wondered what the deal was there. I blinked the chatroom away for the moment. It would probably flash or something when there was a new message to read.

"Okay. Any questions?" I asked.

Hedgehog raised a hand. "Where are we heading to today, and what are our rules of engagement?"

"I think . . . Saint-Jérome. Rules are, uh, if you see an alien, kill it. We'll probably split the points we make between the lot of us, as long as everyone's participating at least a little. Otherwise, don't die. This is an escort mission. Honestly, if it's boring, then that's probably for the best. We don't have to listen to the army, but they generally know what they're doing, so maybe pay attention, at least," I said. Hedgehog nodded at that last bit. Figured he'd appreciate that kind of thing. I was all for more excitement than yesterday, but I didn't want to end up with dead newbies either.

With all that said and done, we kind of just . . . split off. Tankette packed up her things, then squeezed herself into her mini-tank. I was surprised that she wasn't wearing anything more armored in there. Hedgehog and Crackshot went ahead a little, the two boys already deep in conversation about guns, which left Princess and Knight to walk alongside Gomorrah and me.

"So, uh, Knight," I started.

"Yeah?" she asked. Her helmeted head turned my way, and I could just make out an eye through her visor.

"You're not a samurai, right?"

"Is that a problem?" she snapped.

"No?" I tried. "Just wondering. Sorry if I stepped on a landmine or something."

She stared for a moment more, then looked away. "It's fine."

"Aww, Knight, don't be that way!" Princess said before she skirted around Knight and came to stand next to me. "I saw you shoot the mayor! And that big fight with your mecha against those PMCs! That was so cool!"

"Oh, uh, thanks," I said.

"And Gomorrah too! You got to fly in her car, the *God's Righteous Fury!* That car is so sexy! What was that like?"

"You're asking me what it was like to ride in Gomorrah's car?" I asked.

Gomorrah was literally standing right there with us. She could probably go on about the car for an hour or two. It might not be safe for anyone underage to hear, because that kind of passion should really be reserved for the bedroom, but still.

"Uh, it's nice? Seats are comfortable enough, and there's a minifridge. Uh, the viewscreen is pretty nice? It flies fast. Gomorrah's a pretty sick pilot, though her car did complain about aubergines the last time we flew together."

"What?" Gomorrah asked.

"Aubergines? They're like . . . a fruit? Vegetables? The purple ones," I explained.

"Cat, I have literally no idea what you're talking about," Gomorrah said.

"You remember, you did those twisty flying maneuvers, and then the *Fury* was like 'Aubergines, Aubergines!'"

Gomorrah's expressionless mask stared at me some more before she looked away. "It was saying 'Over-G,'" she replied. "You're a moron."

"Is that what it was saying?" I asked. "Actually, yeah, that makes a lot more sense."

You have ears that are significantly better than any baseline human's. But I suppose that hearing and comprehending aren't the same thing.

Princess laughed and tapped my arm with her hand. "You're so funny, Miss Stray Cat," she said. "Funny *and* cool."

"Uh, yeah, thanks," I replied. I was getting the uncomfortable feeling that Princess thought we were a lot closer than we were. Emotionally, that was. She was pretty much in my personal-space bubble already. I couldn't think of a nice way to shove her back though, not short of saying "I have a girlfriend" and possibly embarrassing the shit out of her in front of our new samurai crew.

This wasn't the kind of problem I came here expecting to have to manage.

"Anyway, you'll be staying with us on the command rig?"

"If that's allowed," Princess said.

"Yeah, sure. You know what, I'll ask the general to explain our logistical chain. That should be real useful for you to know. It should only take a few days."

"Huh?" Princess asked with a blink.

"It's good for you," I insisted.

Anything that would get me out of an awkward situation was definitely good, as far as I was concerned.

CHAPTER SIXTY-SEVEN

TANK YOU (FOR THE SANDWICHES)

> When it comes to at-home self-defense, the popular option, for years, has been a handgun in a safe. We think that's slow, and unlikely to scare off the prepared bandit.
>
> Our solution?
>
> The self-defense pillow frag!
>
> —Failed advertising campaign for at-home high explosives, 2045

I wasn't sure if I should have been disappointed or not, but the first attack against the convoy happened so quickly and was dealt with so rapidly that I hadn't even needed to get out of the mobile base before it was dealt with.

The attack hit our right flank, just as we were nearing one of the many little rivers cutting across the landscape. There was an old cement bridge crossing the river, maybe forty meters long. Not even a proper suspension bridge or anything, just a plain old boring thing.

The aliens came out from the side of the bridge, launching themselves out of the brush and rushing at our front flank.

The computer on the mobile base quickly made a headcount and marked out something like half-a-hundred model threes and twice as many model ones. There was a sprinkling of bigger models too, tankier ones, and some of those tentacled fucks.

Our tanks came to a stop, then started to rotate their guns to the right.

Then Tankette got involved, circling around and ahead of the formation so that she could aim back at the swarm. She opened up on the lot of them and turned the enemy into so much Swiss cheese.

I was left chewing on my sandwich (Tankette had cut them at an angle, then flipped one half around so that the sandwich looked like a little heart in the box. She'd also placed some baby carrots in the spaces left over.) while I watched aliens die in droves.

The boys on the roof were chatting over the comms while taking shots at the aliens in the lead. Once the tanks and support vehicles right behind had the aliens in sight, it was all over. Multiple crisscrossing lines of machine-gun fire was a pretty textbook counter to a charge.

The thing that surprised me the most was the reaction to the flying models. I watched through a dozen screens as the army opened up on them with a repeating net launcher. The shots would go out for a few meters, then explode outward into a net some three or four meters wide. The model ones in the net's path would get smacked out of the air by the net as it came back down, and it looked like maybe the netting itself was sharpened.

Once the last gun went quiet, I waited a beat, then opened up the "all" comms. "Well done, everyone," I said. "But let's not party too soon. Keep your eyes open as we cross the bridge. Good reaction out there, Tankette."

"Thank you," came Tankette's rather shy reply.

"She's pretty good," I said to the roomful of officers as I cut off the comms. "What kind of gun is that tank of hers rocking?"

Gomorrah glanced to the side, head tilting slightly. "Looks like a 25mm main gun, and a 5.56 NATO-standard secondary gun. Basically a gun with the same caliber as a basic assault rifle and a miniature cannon."

"Huh," I said. That sounded like it was on the smaller side. Which was probably fine for the smaller aliens, in any case. "Well, I guess with a tank that small, you can't have a big gun mounted. I mean, still bigger than what you could carry on your own."

She could probably reload just by buying more ammo from her AI, so that'd save her a lot of trouble.

"I'm sure we can do better!" Princess said. "Just wait, Knight and I will prove ourselves!" She pumped a fist into the air. Knight just shifted slightly from side to side next to her, clearly feeling about as awkward as someone wearing full plate could feel.

"You'll have your chance soon enough," I said. I hoped that I was right, because Princess kept edging her way around the central hologram tank in the middle of the command room. I was edging my way away from her, and so far we'd gone around the entire table twice. I'd tried to get the brigadier general to keep her pinned with talk of logistics, but she played dumb and continued to skirt around toward me.

I didn't know what this chick had going on for me, but I was pretty sure I didn't want any of it.

"Hey, maybe we could stick you and Knight with Gomorrah? She's a fantastic samurai. I bet she could show you all sorts of tricks."

Gomorrah's head snapped up and she looked my way, then toward Princess. "Princess, is that suit of yours flame-retardant and fireproof?"

"Uh, no?" Princess said, sounding pretty damned uncertain.

"Then it would be a bad idea, Cat. She should stick with you," Gomorrah said. The clever bitch. Did they teach girls to be this sneaky in nun school or something?

"We'll figure it out once we're in Saint-Jérome. We're going to have to do patrols around the city for a while anyway, right?"

The brigadier general, Thibodeau, glanced up from a tablet that he was looking at. "About that," he said. It had been a minute since he'd last engaged with us. I think he didn't like the presence of Princess and Knight. Sure, Princess was a samurai, and Knight was . . . well, she might as well factor in as one, but I think that Princess didn't feel as professional to him. Strange, I think he had been feeling the same way about me, but was now reconsidering it.

Fuck, did that mean that he now thought that I was professional?

What the hell was wrong with me?

"Yes?" I asked as I tried not to have a minor freakout. I couldn't be professional, could I? I was cool, damn it. Not some pencil-pusher, no matter how much Gomorrah might wish otherwise.

"We have new satellite imagery for the area around Saint-Jérome," the general said. He tapped the tablet a couple of times, and the image in the holotank switched from a drone's-eye-view of the convoy to a map of the city we were heading toward and its surroundings.

Saint-Jérome wasn't anything impressive. Actually, it was kind of the opposite. Bit of a shithole, really. It was only worth noticing because it was within an hour's drive of a megacity. Red splotches started to appear all around the city, locations of Antithesis movement and such.

"We know there's a hive in this area," the general said as he gestured to one of the bigger red splotches. "And we've narrowed it down to within an old water filtration plant along the North River."

"The North River?" I asked.

"Yes? That's what it's called," he said.

"Wow. Someone was feeling daring that day," I said. "Sorry, go on."

"In any case, we've identified one hive to the north of the city. It's been pushing into the city for some time. The defenses held until last night."

Gomorrah's head snapped up. "They fell?"

"The city guard, which is really just a militia, some local volunteers, and a small PMC contracted to keep the city safe, were unable to stop the hive at the northern wall. They've begun pulling back and into the city itself. Citizens were evacuated to the southern end of the city. There are a number of shops and chain stores there, with automated anti-theft systems and their own security staff. The city was able to convince the owning corporations to allow the citizens to use the stores as a temporary gathering point."

The general zoomed into the map, and I leaned forward to see what he meant. There were some two dozen stores in the area, with a small wall running along the south. A lot of the stores had large parking lots, some over multiple floors, and most of them had fences around their lots.

It looked like the parking lots were filled to the brim, with dozens more cars sitting outside of the area creating a makeshift wall. Everyone that had evacuated did so by car, creating a small fuckload of congestion on the roads.

"How old is this data?" I asked.

"Four hours," the general said.

"We could have been informed earlier about the breach," Gomorrah said.

"I don't see how it would matter overly much. We'll be arriving in three hours," the general said. "We want to treat this in a careful, organized matter."

I hummed. "Knowing earlier wouldn't hurt all the same, but yeah, we still have time to prepare. Do you have a plan already, General?"

The general nodded, then gestured over his tablet again. The map pulled back, then switched from a satellite image to a 3D render. A red arrow pushed into the city from the south, then split down the center of the city. "The Twenty-Second Battalion will push into the north end of the city, plugging the gap. Meanwhile, the Fifth Battalion will form a line in the center of the city and march forward to meet the Twenty-Second."

The formation was something of a cross, a beam down the middle all the way to the north, then a cross-line that moved forward, sweeping through the city until it reached the end. "And the recon battalion?" I asked.

"The Seventy-Seventh will be reinforcing the walls of the parts of the city that are still under human control," he said. "They're not entirely equipped for wall duty, but more bodies can only help. Some of them will remain behind to help set up our new base camp, leaving room for our supplies to come in."

I nodded. "Okay. Princess, Knight, you'll be on foot with Crackshot and Hedgehog. Gomorrah, can you slip ahead with Tankette and the armored battalion? I'll be on the ground too, I guess. Once we've got our respective areas of the city secured, we'll see who's available to hit up that hive."

CHAPTER SIXTY-EIGHT

DO NOT THE PRINCESS

Saint-Jérôme is a suburban city located about forty-five kilometers north-west of Montreal on the Rivière du Nord. It is part of the North Shore sector of Greater Montreal. It is a gateway to the Laurentian Mountains and its resorts via the Autoroute des Laurentides.
—"Saint-Jérôme," Wikimedia Foundation, November 2023

Saint-Jérome is a suburban city located about sixty kilometers northwest of New Montreal on the Rivière du Nord. It is part of the North Shore Defense sector of the New Montreal Anti-Antithesis Pact. It is a gateway to the Laurentian Mountains and its resorts via the Pepsi-Cola Highway.
—"Saint-Jérome," Wikimedia Corporation, November 2043

Saint-Jérome received us with a lot more fanfare than I expected.

In my mind, we were about to cruise into a city that had been fucked up. Sure, we were playing the roles of big damn heroes, but it didn't mean I expected the locals to give much of a shit while they were too pinned down to think about anything but survival.

Instead, we rolled into the city only to be greeted by a crowd swarming on a bridge above the exterior wall of the city. Some thousand-odd people, waving banners and flags and cheering on the army's convoy as we rumbled in.

Crackshot waved at the people above as the mobile base rumbled past and was promptly nailed in the face by someone's panties.

"We're a lot more popular than I expected," I said as I watched it all from inside the base. We had access to all of the cameras on the armored vehicles, and some drones hovering above. It gave a good view of things.

"This city was almost certainly going to be condemned if we weren't able to approach," Brigadier General Thibodeau said. "The city itself doesn't have the pull or money to encourage a large enough PMC presence, not with New Montreal so close. There aren't enough large corporate interests in the region for them to want to make a difference either. This is just a peaceful little city, with no true corpo worth beyond being a place with a few hundred thousand consumers."

"What would have happened, then?" I asked.

"The city's citizens would be told to evacuate to New Montreal itself."

I blinked. "It took us two days to get here. I mean, we're moving at a snail's pace, so someone driving straight could probably make it in a few hours, but . . . wait, how far is New Montreal from here? Like, the outermost wall?"

"Sixty kilometers," the general said.

I stared. "You, uh, mean sixty . . . thousand? Or you forgot a zero?"

He frowned in turn. "No? It's sixty kilometers to the south of here."

I turned to the holotank, then took control of it and zoomed out. I could see the place where the army had stopped for the night, and the route back, and . . . yup, that was sixty whole kilometers. "How in the fuck did this take us two days?"

"The first day was mostly getting things organized," Gomorrah said. "I wouldn't count today as a second day. It's not even noon yet."

"What kind of speed are we moving at?" I asked.

"We average about five kilometers an hour," the general said.

"That's walking speed!" I said. "There can't have been *traffic*, we have tanks!"

The general shrugged. "We're moving at the same pace as our slowest units. Some of our heavy armored vehicles are quite slow."

I couldn't wrap my head around it. Gomorrah reached over and patted me on the back. "This is the speed at which armies work," she said.

"It's so slow," I said.

"Miss Stray Cat likes going fast, then?" Princess asked. She was standing right next to me, and I hadn't noticed her edging closer.

I felt my spine straightening. God, that girl was rubbing me the wrong way. She was smiling, all teeth, and it was creeping me right out. "Let's get ready to hop out," I said. "Slight change of plans. Gomorrah, want to take, ah, Princess and Hedgehog and take the west flank? I'll go out with Crackshot and Knight, we'll slip around the east. Tankette can stay with the armored division?"

The last was aimed at the general, who nodded. "Certainly. I'm positive the tankers will take a liking to her. Hopefully not too much of one."

I had no idea what he meant by that, and I wasn't sure I wanted to know. "Right," I said. We were crossing the commercial part of the city, and the drone above was picking out some of the parking-lots-turned-refugee-camps that the general had mentioned earlier.

Princess and Knight were in the middle of a deep, hushed discussion. From the looks of it, my plan to split them up wasn't going so well. It ended when Princess frowned, grabbed Knight by the gauntlet, and tugged her toward me. "Miss Stray Cat," she said, this time with none of the weirdness.

"Yeah?" I asked.

She took a deep breath. "I'll let you borrow my sister," she said. "But only if you promise to keep her safe."

"I'm the one supposed to keep *you* safe," Knight said to Princess.

"I'll be fine," Princess replied. "I'll be with Miss Gomorrah. She's scary-strong. And Mister Hedgehog seems like he knows what he's doing too."

I stared between the two, then nodded. "I can keep Knight safe," I said. "Do you fight at all, Knight?"

"I can manage," Knight said. She sounded rather petulant. "I'm good at keeping Tiff—Princess safe. It's my job."

"Alright," I said. "Look, if you two don't want to be separated, we can work something out. I don't want to be a bitch here. If you're used to being together, then that's fine."

"You usually work with Miss Gomorrah, and you're splitting up now," Princess pointed out. "It's fine. I think we *should* learn how to handle ourselves when we are apart."

I hesitated, but she did seem certain enough. "Alright," I said. The mobile base came to a slow, steady stop, and I noticed the general looking at his table out of the corner of my eye.

The general shifted toward us. "We're stopping here to unload troops. The base will be staying here, as part of the defensive cordon for the civilians and to act as a fallback. Good luck out there, samurai."

With that said, we filed out of the base. Gomorrah's *Fury* was waiting outside, which was handy for her, since she wasn't carrying all of her gear in the base. Those big flamethrowers of hers would have been cumbersome in there anyway. My stuff was a little more compact, so it wasn't as big of a deal.

Crackshot and Hedgehog climbed down the side of the base and landed next to us, then stretched. "What are our orders?" Hedgehog asked.

"You'll be going with Gom and Princess. Crackshot is with me and Knight. We'll be taking the east, you'll be going west. Our job is to clear out the aliens, fuck 'em up as you see them, and keep the soldiers safe if you can."

"Don't take any needless risks," Gomorrah said. "The cleaner this job is, the better. The soldiers should know what they're doing. They won't need that much help with weaker models, but they might rely on us for anything bigger, or else they'll have to call in a strike."

"Do we *have* strike capabilities?" Hedgehog asked.

"Mortars only," Gomorrah said. "They're relatively accurate, but I wouldn't want to rely on them in the city."

I glanced back. There were troops hopping out of APCs by the dozen, with sergeants shouting for order already. Young men and women were doing last-minute gear checks, switching out mags, praying. Doing the kind of shit you'd expect people to want to do a minute before getting into a fight.

"We don't have specific positions or anything," I said. "So we can wander a bit. Gom, are you bringing the *Fury*?"

"I am," Gomorrah said. "Princess, Hedgehog, feel free to ride with me."

"Your car is a two-seater," Princess pointed out.

Gomorrah looked at her. "The roof."

"I, uh, suddenly feel even less secure about Princess's safety," Knight said.

"Gomorrah, Princess looks clean enough. I'm sure she won't track mud into your car. You can at least let her sit in with you," I said.

"I suppose she can't be messier than you," Gomorrah said.

"Uh, what about me?" Hedgehog asked.

I stared at him. "Hang on?"

With that decided, I called over my mech. I didn't intend to ride in it, not when most of the fighting was probably going to be done on foot, but having big guns at our beck and call could only be a good thing. Plus the mech had a few spots that I could grab onto while it moved.

"Okay. Keep your comms open, and shout if anything goes wrong. The faster we know about trouble, the faster we can blow it up," I said.

With that, we split. I showed Knight where she could grab onto the front leg of the mech (which made for a surprisingly smooth ride, if one that left us exposed), and Crackshot was quick to scamper onto the mecha's back where he hung on while trying to get his gun pointed forward.

The soldiers started to spread out, and I received an update on the tactical map in the corner of my vision. We were going to spread out, west to east on this side, then start northward toward the other end of the city. The tanks and armored battalion were already pushing ahead.

"So," I asked as I popped a private channel open between myself and Knight. "What's up with your sister?"

"You know . . . I thought you'd at least wait a few hours before asking."

CHAPTER SIXTY-NINE

NICE?

No, there's no way, that'd be too much of a coincidence.
—Discerning Reader forum, 2024

I shrugged. "If you don't wanna talk about it, that's cool too. I'm not gonna put a gun to your head."

Knight turned to look my way, not that I could really make proper face-to-face contact with her, with the way we were both hanging onto opposite moving legs. "It's complicated," she said. "Or . . . maybe not. Look, can we talk once we're on stable ground?"

That was fair. Riding on the mech wasn't exactly a smooth ride. There was a small bit of armor that stuck out just over the mech's ankles, which was more than enough room for a foot. And there were a few armored panels at about shoulder height that anyone could hang on to for dear life. It helped that I was making the mech walk at a speed that wasn't much faster than a quick jog. It was a bit bumpy, but not all that bad.

"I think we're gettin' close to our spot," Crackshot said.

I glanced ahead and tried to match my augs' map of Saint-Jérome with what I was seeing before me. At some point we'd crossed over the North River. The entire thing was probably capped over in this part of the city, so that there was more flat land to build on. Above us was a highway, held up by frequent pillars. Route 117, if I wasn't mistaken. Which meant we were on the east end of the city, past the area that was staging all of the evacuated civilians.

A few temporary barricades had been thrown up across roadways to our right, with some APCs parked behind sandbags and movable spike walls. "Alright," I said as I pointed out ahead of us. "We'll stay under the highway. It'll make for an easy point of reference, and it more or less goes from the south to the north of the city." Which was our path anyway.

My mech turned off to the side of the road and came to a stop. I took that time to recheck my gear real quick, in case something had fallen off during the ride.

In the meantime, a few truckfuls of soldiers rumbled past and started to stop further down. More were coming up behind, but those were mostly jogging along on foot.

"Give me two minutes," I said to Knight and Crackshot before switching channels. I found the command channel, currently being shared by the leader of that battalion, Lieutenant Colonel Juno, as well as a few more lieutenants and a heap of sergeants.

I was able to pick up on their chatter the moment I flicked onto the channel. "Samurai Gomorrah, Princess, and Hedgehog have made it to the far-west of our starting position," one sergeant said. "We're catching up now. Damn, that girl *drives*."

"Samurai Stray Cat has stopped her mecha right under the Route 117," another said. "I'm deploying half my men ahead of her and the others. The other half before that."

"If you want," I said. "We can move up to the front."

There was a beat of silence before Juno spoke up. "That won't be necessary, ma'am. A central deployment might even be best."

"Nah," I said. We didn't need to be behind the army. "Let me and the newbies charge ahead a little. We'll be the wedge. We're gonna follow the highway above."

"I'll move more men on our east flank," a lieutenant said. "The highway's not a straight line north."

"Noted," Juno said.

"Ping me if you need anything," I said. "We're gonna start our leisurely walk. Ping me if *anything*'s up. Or at the first sighting of some alien fucks."

I got some pretty cheerful "yes ma'ams" at that. Well, as cheerful as a bunch of military types could be. They weren't exactly singing our praises, but I had the feeling they were pleased about every alien we murdered that they didn't have to handle themselves.

They weren't being paid by the alien like we were, and every xeno out there was a threat for each and every one of them.

They were a threat to me too, but they were a threat I could handle with infinite amounts of high explosives, which was basically no threat at all.

"Alright!" I cheered, aloud this time. "Let's get to killing?"

"I'm down for that!" Crackshot said. He stepped off my mech's head and landed with a slight bend of his knees.

"How did you not just break your ankles?" I asked. That was a two-meter fall.

He grinned then patted his pants. "Got some exo-skeletal bits and thingie-whatsits. They're pretty slim, though, so I can still wear my old wranglers over them."

"Huh, alright," I said. "You're really working to keep the look, huh?"

"Looks are important. That's what Miss Mordeath Noir told me."

I didn't comment. Crackshot shouldered his big old rifle and started forward, and I jogged to make sure I was a bit ahead of him. His job was aiming and hitting things. I could take the middle and be the one to spray bullets in the general direction of shit I wanted dead. It was a job I was well-suited for.

"Alright," I said, voice pitched lower. Knight had tailed after me, keeping a step behind and to my right. "We're on solid ground now. You wanted to talk?"

"Not really."

"We don't have to," I said.

She sighed. "But I ought to," she replied.

We still moved up a whole block, past newer apartment buildings and past an old tan-color hospital building that looked semi-abandoned before she decided to speak up again.

"Princess is my sister. Half-sister. We have different mothers."

"Alright," I said. "That's fine, I think?" Did she lose a parent only for the other to remarry? If she wanted to talk about the trauma of losing a parent, then . . . I was a surprisingly good person for that. Well, usually it was every parent that was lost, but I could probably manage with comforting someone who only lost the one.

But I was getting ahead of myself a little.

"I was our father's favorite," she said. "From his second marriage. His firstborn. He, uh, coddled me, a little, I guess. Ti—Princess was born out of wedlock. Dad never even married her mom. His third and fourth marriages were to other women."

"O-kay," I said. This guy was sounding like a bit of a cunt.

"Dad never cared much for Princess, or her mom, but I . . . well, I got to meet Princess when she was still really young. She's very quick to fall in love. In a non-romantic way. It's nice. So I took care of her where I could, and my dad didn't mind that so much. I think he was aiming for her to be like, my secretary or something, when I eventually got into politics."

"Uh-huh," I said. She was really dumping now.

"Then, a few days ago, you shot Dad in the head on TV, the exact same day that Tiffani became a samurai."

I choked on nothing at all. "I did *what*?"

Knight stared at me through the slits of her helmet. "My—our—family name is Dupont," she said.

"Oh. *Oh*."

I took a moment to process that. "Fuck."

"Yeah," Knight agreed.

I wished that I could see her face, because I was really not sure if I was about to get stabbed or not.

Which is probably why I *launched* into the air reflexively when someone spoke right into my ear. "Cat!"

"Jesus fuck, Gomorrah," I said. "What? Yes?"

Gomorrah paused on the line for a moment. "Are you in danger at the moment?"

"No? Probably not. Maybe?"

"Good enough. We need to talk, it's important."

"I *am* in the middle of something," I argued back. "Besides, aren't you busy?"

"This is more important, Cat. We might have to call off the entire push."

I blinked. "Gom, we haven't even killed a single alien yet. Are we about to be overrun or something?" That would be a decent enough reason to pull back and consolidate things.

"In a manner of speaking, yes," Gomorrah said. She sounded deeply serious. "Cat, I just got news from the Family, who in turn just received news from the Martian front. Things went . . . well enough. Mars's surface was cleansed. But a large detachment of Antithesis broke off from one of the moons around Mars and started moving Earth-ward."

"What's that mean?" I asked.

"It means that on top of the remnants of the global incursion, we're about to have a lot of very pissed off, very powerful aliens rain down on Earth."

"Ah," I said. "Well, do we have a few hours, at least? I've got some interpersonal business to take care of before I can handle that. Need at least a few minutes."

"Really, Cat? Is your interpersonal business really more important than the impending apocalypse?"

"I just found out that I killed Knight and Princess's dad," I hissed.

"Oh."

Daisy was lying back in bed, staring at a display fixed to the ceiling and repeated through the neural network in her skull, when a smattering of pebbles moving at speeds scientifically described as "very fucking fast" rammed into her station.

Fuck! she thought as she was thrown out of her bed and into a wall. Before she'd even struck it, she twisted her hips around, then her upper body, executing a roll that had her slamming into the wall heels first.

Then she raised her hands over her head, blocking loose pillows and cushions from hitting her in the face.

The station's artificial gravity gave out a moment before the lights flickered off. Now, the only light she could use to see was coming from the wall-length window on the far end of the room. Fortunately, the station was angled so that she had a nice view of the burning surface of Mars.

"Lynus! Status report!" she shouted aloud as she batted away her pillows.

One moment . . . Your station was struck in seventeen places by what seem to be particulate remains. A scan of the incoming projectiles suggests that they are all inorganic matter. Rocks.

"They went through my shields?" she asked. Her augs connected to the station, and she ran through a quick diagnostics check. It wasn't looking so good. There was a lot more red than green at the moment, but she did have tertiary power.

The lights came back on. The gravity did not.

The shields are only rated to take so much damage. Most of the stones were stopped.

Daisy grumbled, then pulled up a wireframe of the station. The entire bottom half was missing.

"Oh, come on!" she said. "Get the repair drones out, salvage what we can. I need the shields back online, and the main generator . . . was right there, okay, but secondary power, that was in the top section, it should still be functional."

The reactor was struck, though it should be repairable.

Daisy grunted an affirmative and pushed herself off the wall, then with another rolling twist, she flicked her arms out and caught two things out of the air. Her bunny slippers. She'd been keeping them next to her bed. Now she slipped them on just as someone knocked at the door to her room. "Come in," she said.

The door opened, and Daisy found herself looking at herself. A clone, to be precise. Unit 054, currently wearing her off-duty uniform of a loose fluffy plaid top and pants. "We're in trouble," the clone said.

Daisy reached up, touched the ceiling for a moment, then pulled herself toward the doorway. It was slightly awkward. For all the time she spent in space, she didn't enjoy zero-G. Unless she was sleeping, in which case it was actually kind of nice.

"What kind of trouble?" Daisy asked.

"Phobos exploded."

Daisy pinched the bridge of her nose. She remembered now. 054 was the quiet one.

Why her clones all had to diverge slightly in personality and behavior was a mystery to her, and one that was really annoying sometimes. All she'd wanted was an army of like-minded but subservient individuals to do all of her work for her so that she could stay at home, wear nothing but pajamas, and watch cartoons and read books.

But no. Her clones all needed to start diverging away from the perfect workforce they were meant to be, which only caused headaches on top of headaches.

"How did Phobos explode?" Daisy asked.

Unit 054 looked over her shoulder, then back to Daisy. She blinked slowly. "I don't know."

Explaining how an entire moon exploded probably required more than three words strung together, so if Daisy hoped to get a more complex answer, she'd need to look into things herself. With a sigh, she reached a hand toward Unit 054 and the clone grabbed onto it, anchoring herself to the doorframe while pulling Daisy out of the room.

Daisy and her clones were linked. Yes, the clones had their own brains, but in reality most of their brainpower was reserved for autonomic controls and to keep themselves going. They could think on their own, form their own memories, and had their own reflexes, but for the most part, their upper-level thinking was simply missing.

That was reserved for Daisy herself. Hence the very advanced and very complex neural system jammed into her head.

In a very real way, she *was* her clones. Most of the time, she let each one do its own thing, but when needs must, she could swoop in and take more direct control of the individual clones. Which was why the sudden void she noticed bothered her. Her senses were reaching out and finding spaces that were missing.

"Shit," Daisy said. Seven clones were missing from the network.

"Bad air ahead," Unit 054 said. She swung over to one wall where a small panel slid aside, revealing masks and small silvery tanks with chartreuse lines painted across them. She flung one to Daisy, who caught it and squeezed it on.

"Set the second priority for the drones as checking the life support systems. Then comms, and finally, plugging holes," she subvocalized to Lynus.

Noted.

She'd have to buy more oxygen in bulk after this. Actually, she'd have to buy a new bottom half for her station.

"This is going to be so expensive," she muttered. Millions of points, even. She had been hoping that the Mars extermination campaign would be very profitable. So far it had been, but this fresh new expense was going to cut into her margins.

Arriving in the central room of the station, Daisy floated over to the command throne in the room's center. A few clones were already at their stations, plugged into the station's network and doing what they could.

"Maneuvering jets are partially online," Unit 038 said. "The station's stabilizing. We're going to need to adjust our orbit."

"Detecting a lot of scattered remnants of Phobos out there. Too many for our scanners. Longbow's ship is sending compiled data. We're out of the main disaster area, but still on the fringes," Unit 067 said.

Daisy pulled herself down into her throne just as a clone came closer and took a seat on the arm. "How does this make you feel?" Unit 005 asked.

"Really?" Daisy asked.

Unit 005 leaned forward, then very carefully, she reached out and patted Daisy on the head. "There there."

Daisy sighed. She should *not* have lent this unit out to Grasshopper. "Stop that. We have things to deal with," Daisy said. "How's the situation on the surface?"

"There's a full-scale evacuation order in progress," Unit 067 said. "Geiger, Jolly Monarch's Queen Drone, and Lady Kingpin are moving their ships to intercept the largest fragments of Phobos."

Daisy frowned. "Did we have any signs that Phobos was going to blow?"

Unit 067 took a moment to reply. "Previous scans of the moon suggested minimal Antithesis activity. It was cleared with a few tactical strikes. The resulting radiation on the moon's surface might have interfered with further scans."

Daisy was frowning harder when she received a ping from the Family. She glimpsed it, reading through the multi-page report in an instant.

Phobos hadn't just exploded. It had exploded in a specific way. Something massive had flown out from the destroyed moon, gravity warping around it unnaturally as that large thing flung itself out and away from Martian orbit.

Even now, it was being pursued. The Albatross of Love, Shard, and Saint George were after it. All three had picked up signs that the *thing* was at least partially organic.

So an Antithesis trap, and one triggered just as they'd finished bathing the surface of Mars in fire.

The thing vented more reaction mass, and Saint George had pulled back to deal with what were likely space-capable Antithesis models hidden in that mass. The mass was now heading for a new destination. Daisy guessed it before she even reached the end of the report.

Earth.

She tapped into a channel in her mind and felt her awareness expand and grow. "This is Deus Ex. I want units to EVA and check on the station's wreckage. There might be survivors out there. The rest of you, on full alert. This is . . ." She swallowed. "This is a No Sunday level emergency."

There were a few gasps in the room, but Daisy ignored them.

Ever since she'd arrived on Mars, she felt like it had been too easy. Sure, they had lost a couple dozen samurai, but that was far too few for an operation of this size. The loss of A-Okay had stung, but . . . but she came here expecting things to be a lot worse.

She reminded herself that there was no situation so dire that it couldn't be made worse.

"Right, let's get our shit together. Earth is going to be on its own until we do."

ABOUT THE AUTHOR

RavensDagger is a Canadian writer who wants to make people smile. The best way to do that, he has found, is by pecking away at the keyboard and hoping for the best.

RESPAWN YOUR CURIOSITY

follow us on our socials

podiumentertainment.com

@podiumentertainment

/podiumentertainment

@podium_ent

@podiumentertainment